Murder on the Rocks

J.S. Strange

Panther Publishing

First Published in Great Britain in 2019.

Panther Publishing is a Welsh publishing company.

Panther Publishing

First published in Great Britain in 2019 with Panther Publishing.

Copyright © J.S. Strange 2019.

J.S. Strange has asserted his right under the Copyright, Designs and Patents Act 1988 to be identified as the author of this work.

All characters and events in this publication, other than those in the public domain, are fictitious and any resemblance to real persons, living or dead, is purely coincidental.

Front cover copyright to Rhianedd Sion and J.S. Strange. Photographs used on the front cover belong to Rhianedd Sion and J.S. Strange.

ISBN-13: 978-1-5272-3552-6

For my family.

ONE

The tumbler glass of whisky stood alone on the oak table. Patterns of fingerprints crisscrossed the glass where it had been clutched two hours previously.

The dregs still remained of what appeared to be whisky. Lip prints, most likely the victim's, were visible at the rim of the glass.

"I suspect he was poisoned," an unfamiliar officer said. "Almost instantly. He would have drunk the whisky and he collapsed."

Horrible way to go, Jordan thought to himself. He looked at the chair that was jutting out from the table, the imprint of bum cheeks still in the padded leather cushion. The body had been moved, but not before Jordan had seen him.

His eyes had been bulging, wide open and staring at something. His mouth hung agape, white spit dribbling down his chin and wetting his cheeks. His skin had turned a blotchy purple. The man had been unable to breathe.

"And do we know who was in attendance tonight?" Jordan asked.

The officer looked at a notepad that he held in his hand. "Most people arrived, although I was told two regulars didn't attend this week."

"Names of the regulars?"

"I don't know."

Jordan glared at the officer he had never met. "I would like names. Is there anybody I can speak to? Any witnesses?"

"With all due respect, Mr…"

"Mr Jenner," Jordan said. "But just call me Jordan."

"Mr Jenner, with all due respect, this isn't your case."

"Actually, Mark, I called him here." DCI Vanessa Carter walked into the room wearing a police uniform. The woman was imposing, taller than average, and slim. Her blonde hair was tied up, and she looked like she hadn't slept for a good few days.

1

The officer known as Mark blushed. Now that his boss was in the room, his manner of authority deflated, a pin taken to a balloon. "You did?"

"This is Jordan Jenner." Vanessa placed her hand on Jordan's shoulder. "He has just returned from compassionate leave and is one of the best freelance private investigators I know."

"Nice to meet you, Mark." Jordan smiled.

"Very well, but I still don't see…" Mark began.

"He's part of this case." Vanessa's tone was final.

Mark seemed to get redder. He avoided eye contact and made a quick excuse to leave. Jordan and Vanessa watched him go.

"Sorry about him." Vanessa rolled her eyes. "He's new."

"Figured." Jordan looked at the table, at the tumbler glass, which hadn't been moved. "Have forensics been?"

"Not yet. We're short staffed tonight. Coming up to the new year, everyone wants it off."

"Quite selfish that this man should drop dead on us at such an inconvenient time, isn't it?"

Vanessa smirked. "I was thinking the same thing. Murder doesn't celebrate New Year's, unfortunately. It's work as usual for us."

Jordan reached into his back pocket and took out a notepad, but he realised too late that he didn't have a pen. Sensing this, Vanessa took a biro out from her jacket pocket and handed it to him.

Jordan nodded his appreciation. "Can you tell me what happened?"

"He was poisoned." Vanessa began to walk slowly around the table. "The writing group meets at this house every month. This was their last session."

"This is a writers' group?"

"It is indeed." Vanessa stopped directly opposite the whisky glass. "Ten people attend every month, although this month they were two down."

"Yes, Mark did tell me."

Vanessa eyed the door where Mark disappeared. "Well, at least he can do something right."

"And who does this house belong to?"

"Joseph Gordon," Vanessa replied.

Jordan snapped to attention. "The bestselling author?"

"The same one."

"What's he doing with a writers' group? Surely he doesn't need the support…"

Vanessa shrugged. "Your guess is as good as mine. Set the group up just over a year ago and has been going ever since. He only lets in the select few. It's very prestigious, by all means."

2

With pen poised to write notes, Jordan looked at Vanessa. "You've dealt with this group before."

It was a statement, not a question.

"Once, yes," Vanessa replied. "We were called because of a disturbance. Apparently, some members argued five months ago. It was quite a big argument by the sound of things. Two women, one man. When we arrived, there were a few smashed glasses, but the main culprits had left. We didn't follow it up. We didn't need to. Seemed like a drunken argument."

Jordan wrote all of this down. "Why didn't you follow it up?"

"Please, if we followed up all drunken arguments we'd have no time for anything else."

Jordan agreed. "Where is Joseph Gordon?"

"At the station, in for questioning."

"Questioning? You don't think…"

"Everybody is a suspect until proven innocent Jord. You know that." Vanessa indicated the tumbler. "That glass, that whisky, came from this house. They both belonged to Joseph Gordon. It's very possible that the poison that laced that glass also belongs to him. Famous or not, he could be a killer."

Jordan scratched down more notes, flipped the page, and wrote a short sentence.

"Are there any witnesses here I can speak to?"

"Not right now."

Jordan looked around. An antique bookcase stood at one end of the room, housing volumes that were considered to be literature greats and drivel. He glanced over at the mantelpiece where there were no photographs of family members but instead of two golden retrievers. The curtains were drawn over a bay-seat windowsill, and the only light came from a tripod lamp nearby. The room had a faint smell of cigar smoke, of spirits and alcohol, and the faint waft of food, something with garlic. Jordan remembered that he hadn't eaten all day.

"Were they due to eat?"

"The food was halfway done when the murder happened," Vanessa replied. "The stoves are off now, if you're worried about a house fire."

Jordan allowed himself a smile, but it was humourless. It seemed to be his default mood these days. An empty fruit bowl sat in the middle of the table, notebooks next to it.

"Is that their notes?"

"We're assuming so, though we're waiting for forensics to come before we touch anything."

Jordan sighed. "How long will it take for forensics to arrive?"

"They're coming from Port Talbot."

Jordan nodded. They were probably about forty-five minutes away from where the crime scene was in Cardiff, yet with people travelling home for the new year, Jordan expected them to be late.

"Are you sure you're okay?"

Jordan was startled by the question. He wondered why Vanessa's tone had changed from brisk and professional to caring and friendly.

"I'm fine."

"Jordan, it's too early for you to be back at work."

"You called me."

"Yeah, only because I was told you had to be involved because you had let the team know you were fit to come back to work."

"I needed the money."

"You were on compassionate leave."

Jordan slipped his notepad back into his back pocket and handed the pen to Vanessa over the table. "Honestly, I'm fine."

"It's only been…"

"Vanessa."

Vanessa quit asking.

Mark came back into the room. He appeared a bit more composed, but still avoided Jordan's eye.

"The pathologist is here to take James Fairview's body to the morgue. Did you want me to tell them anything before they go?"

Vanessa walked around the table again and came to stand next to Jordan. "I just want them to do an autopsy. Find out what poison was used and how much. If we can find the name of the poison, then we can know what we're looking for. It's somewhere to start."

Vanessa had been in the police force for ten years, but had only taken up her role of crime investigator for two of those. Jordan had worked with her since going freelance three years ago and always trusted her instincts.

"By the way, did you manage to find out the name of those in attendance?" Jordan asked Mark.

Mark turned to Vanessa for guidance.

"I've got them. Come with me back to the van and we can go over them."

Mark, relieved, quickly excused himself, and Vanessa failed to hide a wry smile.

"What are you smirking at this time?" Jordan asked her.

"Nothing." Vanessa said. "It's just good to have you back."

TWO

Jordan found himself sat in the passenger side of the unmarked police van that Vanessa used. The inside smelt like bubble gum. He realised the aroma came from an air freshener on the rear-view mirror. He wrinkled his nose: blueberry wasn't the nicest.

A police radio had been installed beneath the car radio, and an operator paged through to another officer. Stored away beneath the dashboard were police files. Strictly, Vanessa shouldn't have left these lying around, but Jordan wouldn't care to tell.

It felt odd to be sat here, back at the scene of a crime. He had taken only three months off, after saying he would be taking half a year, but he had needed to get back out there.

Yet being surrounded by murder was not the most ideal situation to be in. He didn't know what it was, but the murder of James Fairview had unnerved him. Before his leave, he had developed a skin of iron, becoming desensitised to the stabbings, rapes, and murders he had needed to investigate.

He put it down to being off for three months and being preoccupied.

"I know I've got the names in here somewhere," Vanessa riffled through a case note of files. "Come on, where are they?"

Jordan stared out of the windscreen at the streets of Cardiff. The residential homes looked innocent here. They were misleading in size, reminding him of terraced houses in the South Wales valleys: outdated and old and dilapidating. But Jordan was familiar with the area of Roath, and knew it was wealthy. Just around the corner of this street was a barrier where a fob key and a key pass were installed to keep the riff-raff out. The houses were three stories high, with high-ceilinged rooms and thick walls blocking out the sounds of your neighbours.

It was the perfect place to commit a murder.

"Ah, yes, here we go."

Vanessa withdrew a sheet of paper and handed it to Jordan. There was a list of bold underlined names matched with photographs.

He spotted James Fairview beneath Joseph Gordon. Beneath James was an older woman known as Margaret. Then there was Graham Neat, who had receding hair, and Franchesca Vittori, who had heavily eye-shadowed eyes in the photograph. He spotted a groomed-looking Sally Waters, and a chubby woman named Sarah Dixon. Finally, there was a middle-aged woman called Kim Bennedict, and then there was Andy Morgan.

Jordan lingered on Andy Morgan's photograph. He wore glasses; his hair was white, yet he looked mid-forties. He realised he recognised him.

"Andy Morgan," Jordan said. His training had given him the ability to remember faces and place them, though he was sometimes slower than he liked to admit.

"Do you know him?"

Jordan lifted his head and tilted it from side to side. "Not really. I met him once when a student turned up dead at Cardiff Metropolitan University. He'd been a personal tutor, so I wanted to find out what the student was like in class, whether or not depression had anything to do with it."

"And what was he like?"

Jordan looked straight ahead. "An odd man. Kept changing the subject, laughing about the weather, the news, anything that seemed to pop into his head. He just seemed a little bit disjointed."

"I suppose you would be if your student had died."

"He just seemed like a weird man."

"What does he teach?"

"English."

"Makes sense, I suppose." Vanessa looked at the home of Joseph Gordon. "No wonder he's in the writing group. A lecturer and writer. I guess that's pretty serious."

"To someone like Joseph, yeah."

Jordan began to write down the names. Once he had finished, he handed the paper back to Vanessa.

"Thank you."

"Who wasn't there tonight?"

"Sally Waters and Margaret Duncible."

Jordan marked their names on the notepad. "Can you get me their contact details?"

Vanessa eyed Jordan. "Yes, I suppose I can."

"Thank you."

From the end of the street came a dark blue van. It drove slowly, and the driver eyed each house on either side of him. Eventually, he appeared to spot Vanessa's van, and came to a stop next to her.

Vanessa wound down the window. "Hiya, George. Yeah, that's the house."

The man in the van drove into a nearby parking space.

Vanessa closed the window. "That's forensics."

Jordan peered around Vanessa as George went into the boot of his van. "He's wearing a Christmas jumper."

"Well, it is Christmas Eve in two days."

Jordan rolled his eyes. "Just get on with it. I want information."

"Do you want to wait for me here? I thought we could go and get a drink together?"

Jordan looked at his notes, knowing he had work to do. His house was messy, and he had meant to clean it after work today. Yet responsibilities right now were not calling loud enough.

"Fine, you twisted my arm."

Vanessa exited the van with a smile and disappeared back into the house of Joseph Gordon, the famous author. Jordan remembered reading three of his books when he was a little younger. Now, at twenty-eight, he felt like the old him had died a long time ago.

He had seen some shit. Children slain, women beaten, and men decapitated. The hidden crime in the Welsh capital was shocking and successfully covered up. Most cases seemed to be drug related, murders out of anger because the dealer hadn't been paid, yet there were the more sinister stories, the ones not even the press would touch.

Looking at the house now, he wondered how long it would take for the press to discover what had happened. A man murdered by poison at a successful horror writer's house was a gold mine. It was like Joseph Gordon was now living one of his own novels, just a lot more mysterious.

Someone had killed James skilfully, and they had known him. He had drunk from the glass of whisky without a second thought. He had known his killer.

Jordan eyed the list of names, thinking, wondering who could be responsible. Was it somebody in the writers' group? Or had there been other guests in attendance tonight?

Jordan didn't know, but he made it a priority to find out.

THREE

It was ten in the evening when Jordan and Vanessa found themselves sat at the bar of a Cardiff pub. It was a Thursday night, and with people off work ready for the Christmas and New Year's holiday, the landlord was seeing a boom in business. Vanessa was sipping from a pint of beer, whilst Jordan had settled for a Kopparberg.

"Alcohol really awakens my taste buds," Vanessa said. "I just get a rush. Sometimes I think if I indulged enough, I would definitely be an alcoholic. But I saw my mum go there, and I don't want to end up that way."

"You won't. It's only one pint."

"Then it turns into ten."

"Just lighten up. Relax. You're alive."

Vanessa bit her lip. "Jordan…"

Jordan shook his head. "I didn't mean it like that."

"No, there's me talking about my mum, when yours…"

Jordan sighed. "It's been really tough, Vanessa."

"I know."

The barman walked by opposite them, whistling a tune from a year-old pop song that was on the jukebox. Young twenty-something men came tumbling in, jeering and laughing and heading straight for the bar. Jordan eyed them, taking in their skinny jeans, rolled up at the bottom to reveal ankles.

"I still sometimes can't believe she's gone, you know," Jordan said. "When my dad told me she had died…Ah, I don't know, I just wouldn't accept it. I thought I had, but sitting and dwelling at home just isn't right."

"It's your mum. You won't get over it that quickly. That's why I can't believe you're back at it."

"I had to. I was going crazy."

"Yeah, but Jord, seeing dead people lying there, investigating cases…are you sure that's what you wanted to be doing?"

Jordan drank from the bottle of cider. "I'm glad to be back at work. I can't stop thinking about James's death."

"Well, take a night off. Stop it."

"You don't have to worry about me."

"But I do, Jordan. We've known each other long enough now to consider one another friends." Vanessa signalled a barwoman at the end of the bar. "At least, I hope so anyway."

Jordan was genuinely touched. "Yes. Definitely."

"Can I get two Woo Woos please?" Vanessa said to the barwoman, then glanced at Jordan. "How did your dad find her?"

Jordan felt uncomfortable, but he knew Vanessa wasn't being horrible. He swallowed another gulp of cider before answering. "I've not been the closest to my mum over the past few years. She didn't exactly agree with my career choice, did she?"

"No, she did not." Vanessa laughed.

The barwoman returned with the pink Woo Woos and placed them down on the bar. Vanessa handed her the money.

"My dad hadn't heard from her for a few days. He went over to her house and there was no answer, yet the door was unlocked. He went in and she was sat in her rocking chair. He thought she was asleep at first. There was a glass of wine half drunk next to her, and she had the newspaper open, and it seemed like she had just fallen asleep."

"But she hadn't."

"She hadn't."

At the same time, the two investigators sipped from their Woo Woos, their other drinks left momentarily forgotten. Jordan pictured the scene.

"When was the last time you spoke to her?"

"Probably about a year ago." Jordan sighed.

Vanessa looked at her fingers clutching her drink. "Listen, she's gone. I know that's harsh, but she's gone. You can't dwell on it, and you can't beat yourself up about it. I just want to make sure you're okay. It's too soon. She only died in September. You're working again too soon in my opinion."

"How many times?"

"I know you're okay. So you say, anyway. I'm just saying."

"Well, don't."

Vanessa shrugged. "What did they say it was?"

"How she died?"

"Yeah."

"Heart attack, it was ruled as."

"How old was she?"

"Sixty-three."

"Young."

Jordan exhaled. "That's what I thought."

"Life is shit."

"Then you die."

Vanessa was halfway through her Woo Woo. "Yes, indeed."

Jordan watched the programme change on the TV above the bar, signalling it was half past ten. The men who had walked in disappeared to find a table, and the people behind the bar relished in having a quiet few moments.

Jordan picked up his bag and threw it over his shoulder. It contained his wallet, phone, and the notes he needed for his first case since coming back from his mother's death.

Vanessa eyed him. "You're going?"

"Unfortunately."

"But I gave you a lift here."

"I can find my own way home. A taxi."

Vanessa shook her head, drinking the last of the liquid inside her jar. "No, I won't have it. I'll take you home."

"Vanessa…"

"No, you're getting a lift home with me."

"Fine." Jordan got off the bar stool and stood up. "Just don't talk to me. I'm tired."

They exited the bar, saying goodbye to a doorman who stood at the entrance. He told them to have a good night and watched them go.

They walked up the street and turned down a flight of stairs, which led to a small underground car park. By day, it was pay and display, but at night, it was free.

The car lights flashed as Vanessa pressed a button on her key, and they walked over to the vehicle, then got inside. Vanessa started the car, turned on the heating, and they drove out into the night.

"Are you okay to drive?"

"Jordan, I'll be fine."

Flashing Christmas lights lit up shop windows. Trees were at windows in flats above. Cardiff had put their Christmas lights on in December, so they hung extravagantly between buildings and on lampposts, creating the atmosphere that everybody adored, whether they liked to admit it or not. People walking the street were huddled against the cold, their coats done up as far as they could go and scarfs hiding their faces.

It was hard to believe there had been a murder only tonight.

"I always love those deer statues," Vanessa commented as they drove past Cardiff Castle. A Christmas tree was decorated with lights, and there was a cluster of giant reindeer statues that lit up a golden yellow. Tourists and inhabitants alike stopped to take photographs for their Instagram content.

"They are sweet," Jordan replied, as they drove down Cathedral Road, where big houses had been turned into office spaces.

They passed a new block of flats being built, where the price tag on a single bedroom was extortionate. A few moments later, they found themselves outside a Home Bargains, on Cowbridge Road East. Vanessa turned on her police lights and pulled over on a double yellow. There was nobody on the street, but further up the road, two women smoking outside Wetherspoon's turned to look.

"Are you sure you're going to be okay tonight?"

"Vanessa, I've been living alone for years," Jordan replied. "I'll be fine."

He opened the door and exited the van, clutching his bag. The night air chipped at him, and he shivered.

"Okay." Vanessa eyed the flats above Home Bargains.

"Listen, give me a call tomorrow, okay? I want to be kept updated on this case. Don't forget about me, now."

"I called you for a reason. You're our best PI."

Jordan smiled his thanks and said his goodbye. Vanessa drove away, and he headed to his apartment block entrance, keyed in the code, and stepped into the hallway, deciding to take the lift to the second floor instead of climb the stairs.

When the lift doors opened, he walked to his apartment, number six, and turned the key.

His apartment was small. It only had one bedroom with a small kitchen that linked into a small living room, which overlooked the street below. He navigated through clothes on the floor to get to the window and peered outside. Two cars drove by, but otherwise, it was a quiet night.

"Meow."

Oscar, his Persian cat, ran down the hall towards him. Just under a year old and wide eyed, Oscar was Jordan's pride and joy.

Jordan bent down and stroked Oscar's head. "It's been a wild one."

"M'ow."

He headed into his living room with the intent of getting Oscar food, and noticed his house phone was flashing with a message. He pressed the button and let the message fill the apartment.

"Jordan, it's your dad. Just ringing because I haven't heard from you in a week. Listen, I don't want you to disappear. Just…just give me a ring back. Please."

The message clicked off and the silence of his dark apartment came rushing back. Jordan sat on the sofa that was left behind from the last tenant and kicked off his boots.

He wasn't keen to see his dad again, but he knew he had to. It was quarter to eleven, according to the digital clock on the coffee table. The television was on standby as it had been for two days. Was it too late to ring his father back?

He picked up the phone but thought better of it, so left it unhooked and went into his bedroom, where an unsteady slumber waited for him.

FOUR

He ran through a field over uneven ground. There were holes, and unrecognisable people in front of him were disappearing through the cracks, slipping to their deaths, never to be seen again. Yet Jordan floated over the holes. He seemed to glide, and when he hit the floor, he bounced back up again. He didn't know what he was running from, but it was shrill and loud and kept ringing in a rhythm.

Just as he was coming down to the ground, about to land on the biggest hole he had seen, his eyes opened. But the ringing didn't stop.

In his haze, he recognised the sound of his mobile. He reached for his phone on his bedside table, saw his battery was on eighteen per cent, and answered the call before checking who was on the other end.

He answered in a tired voice. "Hello?"

"Jordan. It's Mark."

Mark, the new PC? "Yes. What do you want?"

"Joseph Gordon would like to speak to you. He's asked for you."

Jordan sat up. He didn't know what time it was, but it still seemed to be dark outside. "Me?"

"Yes," Mark replied. "At the station. Can you make it in?"

"Why me?"

"I don't know. He's just asked for you."

Jordan tousled his messy hair. "Give me an hour."

"Yes, not a problem."

They said their goodbyes, and Jordan opened the curtains at his bedroom window. It was not yet dawn, but the colour of the sky was enough to tell him morning was close. Oscar groggily stretched out an arm, displeased with the light.

Jordan pulled himself out of bed, adjusting his pyjamas, and then walked out to his bathroom. The clock on the wall told him it was twenty past five.

He yawned, as if in protest, and drenched himself under the shower.

13

Forty minutes later, he was ready and heading to his own car parked around back of the apartment blocks. It was a 2007 Golf, which his dad had gifted him when it was a year old. He'd treasured it ever since.

Today, as he drove through the quiet streets of Cardiff, he thought of his father. It had only been a week, but he knew he needed him right now. He had been a wreck when Jordan's mother had died. They had separated, yes, but the fact Peter hadn't moved on to other people was enough to tell Jordan that he still loved his mother.

Jordan listened to Capital FM but had it on a low volume. The presenters sounded alert and awake, not even a hint of tiredness in their media-trained tones. The news of the murder had finally reached the press.

"Author Joseph Gordon has been arrested on suspicion of murder, it has been revealed, after writer James Fairview was found dead at his home. The case is on-going. A spokesperson for the author had this to tell us…"

The voice changed to that of a woman. "Joseph Gordon is innocent and is keen to clear his name. He has been taken in for questioning and, on his own requests asked to stay the night in jail, as he did not want to return home to the crime scene. Whilst I cannot confirm if the incident at my client's house was murder, I can confirm that Joseph Gordon is innocent and is looking forward to his book tour in the new year."

Before the presenter of the show could return, Jordan turned the radio off. What did Joseph Gordon want with him? If he really was innocent, then there was no need for Jordan to be involved with him.

Jordan was used to expecting the unexpected. He took this as a good opportunity to ask his own questions and enhance his own case. He had to remember he was freelance. He was working on the case to find answers, but he wasn't working for the police. Vanessa had hired him, yes, but Jordan had a job to do by himself.

He pulled up outside the police station and headed inside. A light rain was falling, enough to dampen his hair. Jordan reported to the young girl at reception.

"Can I help you?"

"I'm Jordan Jenner. I'm here to see Mark…" It occurred to him that he didn't know his last name.

"I'm afraid we don't have a Jordan Jenner booked in today. Can I ask what you are here for?"

"The new officer. I had a call from him. Mark…"

"Without a last name, I may not be able to let you in," the woman said, clearly enjoying her artificial power.

"Listen, I'm a private investigator, and I'm here for the Joseph Gordon case."

"I've been told to be wary of people asking for Joseph Gordon today, in case they are journalists. Can I see some ID please?"

"Fine." Jordan took out a wallet from his pocket, but he couldn't find the ID. He began to feel embarrassed.

"If you can't find it, sir, I will need to ask you to step aside."

Jordan eyed the empty whitewashed reception. He was beginning to get annoyed with the woman at the desk, who pushed her feigned authority to the limits. "There's nobody here. Look, I know I've got it here somewhere."

"No ID, no entry."

"I didn't realise the police station had turned into a nightclub," Jordan hissed. "Fine. I will wait here until Mark comes to see where I am."

"Be my guest."

Jordan stepped back, but not far enough to make the receptionist seem comfortable. She turned to her computer and momentarily seemed distracted, aware that Jordan was glaring at her.

The front door to the station opened, and the receptionist, glad of a distraction, sprung to action.

Jordan turned to see Mark. He was wet and looked hassled. He was slipping a packet of cigarettes into his pocket when he spotted Jordan.

"Ah, you're here. Sorry, I was outside. Habit, see." He shook the cigarette packet and put them back in his pocket. "I suppose that's why Rachel here hasn't let you in."

"Actually…"

"Yes, that's right." Rachel smiled sweetly. "You can both go through now."

"Thank you, Rachel."

Jordan gave Rachel one final glare before following Mark through the electronic door.

"Manage to get much sleep last night?" He let him walk through the electronic door first, and escorted Jordan down the hallway.

"After seeing the face of the poisoned man? Not really," Jordan lied. He had, of course, slept very well, but he didn't want to appear a psychopath. "Not the best thing to see just before Christmas."

"Bet you've seen worse."

"Yeah. Yeah, I have."

Mark opened the door to his office, a rather small box room with beige walls and fibre carpet that had seen better days. His desk in the middle of the room was clean. A PC sat on top, left in standby. Next to it was a notepad, one scribbled sentence on the lined pages. Mark walked around his desk and sat down, indicating for Jordan to sit opposite him.

"How long have you been working here in Cardiff, Mark?"

Mark thought for a moment. "Just under a year."

"How old are you?"

"Twenty-seven."

"A year younger than me."

"You look younger."

"Where did you work before?"

"In Surrey, as a police officer there," Mark said. "Only graduated just over a year ago."

"Wow. You're fresh."

"I am." Mark looked at him. "But that doesn't mean I can't do the job properly."

"I know." Jordan thought that Mark seemed to be wishing desperately to prove himself.

"And my job here is to question suspects. Now, I know you're here because you're investigating the case, but I'm not really sure why Vanessa asked you on..."

Jordan had come across his fair share of men who thought he was just a cling-on. He had to prove himself countless times. Yet with Mark, he didn't feel the need to. Mark was a rookie. Jordan didn't have to answer to anything he did.

"I'm just here because I've been asked to see Joseph Gordon. He requested me, and I believe he asked you."

"Yes."

"Then why aren't we going to see him?"

"I wanted to see what you hoped to get from this case," Mark replied.

"I want to find out who killed James Fairview."

"Well, surely we can do that."

"Vanessa wouldn't have called me in if she didn't need me, Mark. Vanessa does things efficiently. I've got a proven track record, and that will show on this case."

"Vanessa told me you've been off lately."

"I have."

"Why?"

"None of your business." Jordan crossed his arms. "Can we see Joseph Gordon, please?"

"Let me tell you this, Jenner. We're fairly certain he did it." The bossy nature from the crime scene before Vanessa had arrived was back in Mark's tone. It seemed when it was Mark alone, he had his own ground set out. Vanessa was the detonator that could ruin him by just walking into the room.

"And how are you fairly certain?"

"The man is odd."

"There are plenty of odd men around," Jordan replied. *Mark being one of them.* "It doesn't mean they're all murderers."

"He was in the house at the time of the murder."

"As were other people. Would you like me to name them?"

"I don't need names, thanks." Mark turned to his computer screen and moved the mouse. "Have you done research on Joseph Gordon?"

"I know he's an author. There's plenty of content out there."

"Did you see he was arrested two years ago for having sex outdoors?"

"I didn't."

"Well, he was."

"And that proves he poisoned a man, how?" Jordan questioned.

"He's broken the law before."

"Outdoor sex is unfortunate, but I'm guessing he got off pretty lightly." Jordan almost smirked at his own joke. "Now, I don't want to be rude, Mark, but I have more experience than you do. Besides, there has been no conclusive DNA evidence yet."

Mark pursed his lips. "True. But this man had a grudge against James Fairview."

"Tell me how."

Mark logged in to his PC, and as the screen loaded, he leaned back in his chair. "Did you know James Fairview had been in talk with publishers? There was no deal made, as far as I know, but he had interest, a sort of buzz."

"And why would Joseph Gordon have a grudge about that?"

"Joseph Gordon has been failing lately. Have you seen his books on the shelves lately?"

"Can't say I've been following his career all that much."

Mark smirked. "Well, his sale figures have been going down. I know this because there is plenty of research on the man. He set up the writers' group to nurture new Welsh talent, but he never expected them to make any success at it. The man saw another member about to do a whole lot better than him and wanted to stop it. Whether jealousy was the motive, well, we'll need to find that out during more questioning."

"But you said it yourself. No deal had been struck."

"No, but…"

"So there's no motive?"

"I'm just saying…"

Jordan yawned. "Can we just go and see him, please?"

"Do you think he did it?"

"A bit difficult to tell, Mark, without questioning the man myself."

Mark nodded. "Well, I suppose you have a point."

Jordan stood, pushing his chair as close to the table as it could get. He walked to the door and placed his hand on the handle. "If you won't take me to see this man, then I will find him myself."

FIVE

Joseph Gordon was sat in the middle of a grey table, dim lights shining down on him. He was locked in the square room, staring at the mirror that reflected him and hid Jordan and a host of police officers.

"He knows you're coming," Mark said. "Just take that door there and…"

"I know where to go, thank you."

Jordan opened the door and walked into the hallway. He waited for the door to shut behind him before he unlocked the door leading into the questioning room. Joseph Gordon, handcuffed to the table, didn't even make to move. He looked at him and smiled as if this was a meeting over coffee.

"Jordan Jenner?"

"That's me."

"Wonderful to meet you. I'd shake your hand, but…" Joseph indicated his handcuffed wrists.

"Not a worry, Joseph." Jordan walked to the chair opposite Joseph, glancing once at the mirror and where he thought Mark might be stood. He knew they'd be listening, but he'd done this so many times. "Not the best view, is it?"

"Well, staring at myself is never the best," Joseph replied. "I seem to get older every day. And this unnecessary hassle adds to my years. I suppose I have to convince you of my innocence?"

"Well, possibly," Jordan replied. "But as far as I'm concerned, they want you to go today. You've just prolonged it because you've requested to speak to me."

Joseph nodded.

"Why?"

Joseph's gaze flickered to the mirror before returning to Jordan again. "I know this was my house. I know it was my whisky and my tumbler glass.

I know how it looks. But I wasn't the only one there. And I'm not the only one with a motive."

Jordan took his phone out from his pocket and opened the voice-recording app. "Do you mind?"

"Not at all."

Jordan pressed the red record button and checked that it was recording before speaking again. "Jordan Jenner. I am at Cardiff police station, in questioning room C, currently speaking to Joseph Gordon. He has spent a night in jail after questioning amidst the murder of James Fairview. Joseph, what is it that you need to tell me?"

Joseph leaned forwards, his focus on the tape recorder. "I did not kill James Fairview."

"With all due respect, the police are willing to let you go on bail. Did they tell you this?"

"Yes."

"Yes. The police do not have enough evidence as of yet to determine that it was you who killed James Fairview."

"Yes, but…"

"Please, let me finish. Because they are willing to let you go, you have been able to leave since you woke up this morning. Yet you have prolonged your time here by requesting to see me. Am I led to believe it was because you just wanted to tell me, like you have the other officers, that you did not kill James Fairview?"

"I wanted to get that on the record," Joseph replied. "On your records. I was not the only person in attendance that night."

"Please, can you tell me who was in attendance?"

Joseph nodded. "Myself, James Fairview, Andy Morgan, Graham Neat, Franchesca Vittori, Kim Bennedict and Sarah Dixon. And there was someone else…"

Jordan wished desperately to see the expression of the police officers behind the glass. This had not been told to them. "Someone else?"

"Yes," Joseph replied. "Though I can't get your hopes up just yet. You see, we usually had ten writers in attendance. Two were missing this time, but I know one of them arrived just before the murder and left shortly afterwards."

"Can you tell me who was missing?"

"Sally Waters and Margaret Duncible."

"And can you tell me which one came by to your home just before the murder occurred?"

"I'm afraid I can't." Joseph sighed. "You see, I'm an author. I've been an author for years. I spend all day, every day, sat in front of a computer screen that is ten inches away, writing down my damn novels and hoping they get read by people. Because of that I've developed myopia or nearsightedness. Do I have to tell you what that is?"

"You can see things close up, but things far away from you seem blurred," Jordan stated.

"That's right. Now, I know one of the women arrived, you see. I was in the kitchen when I heard the back door open. I turned to see someone coming in. I was about to ask who it was, when I was called from the other room. I left the drinks unattended and went to see who called me. It was Graham, said he wanted a gin instead of a coffee. He's got a drinking problem, though he doesn't admit it to himself." Joseph smirked. "I digress. When I went back to the kitchen, the woman was leaving. I know it was a woman, you see. I could see the blurred shape of a woman in shawls, and her hair was a light grey, and she was short. I could also tell by the perfume. I believe it was Vivienne Westwood. My wife used to wear it all the time. But Margaret and Sarah look the same. They're roughly the same age, and they dress similar. It's been a joke running through our meets. I didn't think anything of it."

"You were not alarmed to see a stranger come into your home?"

"I'm used to people coming and going. I have a cleaner. I thought maybe she had come back, though she isn't the right build. I realised that after the murder."

"Do you wear glasses, Joseph?"

"Sometimes."

"And where were your glasses?"

"In the room where I was hosting my writers."

Jordan thought for a moment. "Why were they left there?"

"Because I didn't need them on in that room. I can see everyone clearly, and the notes we were making and what we were reading was fine. It's far away things I can't see. I don't always wear them. I certainly don't think I need them when I'm making beverages."

"Was anyone else in the kitchen with you?"

"They were not."

"Just you and the blurred woman?"

"Correct."

Jordan leaned back in his chair. "I find this difficult to understand. Your home is a private estate. How can someone just waltz in and come and go as they please?"

"Because it's a private estate," Joseph replied. "We have perfect security on site. It's the safest place to be. I always leave my doors unlocked. Like I said, I have people coming and going all the time. I'm getting old now, if you hadn't noticed, so cleaners come regularly to clean up because I can't do it. Plus, those books won't write themselves. All my writers have the access code to the gates, and they know they can drop by whenever they like. I trust them all dearly. At least, I did."

"Joseph, if it was Sally or Margaret, why would they kill James, and why did they not just turn up to the writing group?"

"Don't ask me the workings of a killer's mind," Joseph replied. "Maybe they thought it was a good alibi to go by. By not turning up and a death occurring, they would immediately be ruled out."

"Okay, but that doesn't give me a motive."

"There was plenty of motive to hurt James Fairview."

"Why?"

"The man was a monster."

Jordan double-checked his phone was still recording the conversation before speaking again. "There has to be a reason."

"James was complained about a lot, by all members. He got into arguments. He caused drama. According to Kim, he sexually harassed her too. I don't trust Kim, though. The woman flirted and played into his hands."

"That doesn't mean she was interested."

"Trust me, the pair slept together a few times. All consent. Kim just liked the drama."

"So, he argued, he caused trouble, and he sexually harassed a woman in attendance at the party? Motives for murder?"

"Who knows how far James Fairview went?" Joseph questioned. "But my request is that you find out whoever killed him, and as soon as possible. The man was a swine, but he did not deserve to die."

Jordan closed the interview and stood up. "Thank you, Joseph. Now, I believe you're free to go, but just one more question. Why did you ask for me in particular?"

"Because I've been following your career for a while now, Jordan, though I never expected to be questioned by you," Joseph replied. "And also because you are involved in this case more than you think you are."

SIX

Joseph's comments to Jordan rang in his head. How could he be more involved than he already was? He wondered if he meant the words like he thought he did; as a statement that would unnerve him and leave him pondering on the possibilities of what could be.

He couldn't do anything to get that information from him. The man had said what he needed to say. There had been someone else there that night, but who, he either didn't know or was instead covering for.

"I want records that Joseph does indeed have myopia," Jordan said to Mark when he got back into his office. "I want proof that he isn't lying and that what he said is at least semi-plausible."

"He didn't say anything of the sort to us, which makes me think he might be making it up."

"Maybe, but we need to pursue it," Jordan replied.

"What are your plans now?"

"Kim."

Mark sat at his desk. "Good luck trying to get hold of her."

"Meaning?"

"She's disappeared off the face of the earth. Her phone is going straight to voicemail, and she isn't answering her door, and her neighbours say they don't know who she is."

"So, is she missing?"

Mark glared at him. "No, she's not missing."

"Have you considered that she could have been killed next?"

"What?"

"You haven't considered the possibility that this could be a serial killer?"

Mark blushed red. "No, that hasn't entered my mind."

"Then you are failing at your job," Jordan said. "I'm going. I'll let you know if I get hold of Kim."

Jordan turned and left. He pressed the button on the wall to open the automatic security doors and headed out into reception. Rachel, the receptionist, avoided looking into his eyes as he walked past.

Jordan got back to his car to find a note tacked to the windshield. He didn't touch it, but he could read what was written on the page: *Stop involving yourself in something that doesn't concern you.*

Jordan turned to the police station and walked straight to reception. Rachel looked a little wary. "What is it this time?"

"Get a police officer out to my car immediately. Tell them to bring gloves and an evidence bag." Then he turned and faced the bitter cold instead of waiting at reception with Rachel from secondary school.

The air was chilly with a wind playing over his hair. He wished he had brought a hat. He pulled his coat around him tighter, but it offered very little warmth.

Vanessa walked out of the police station, police gloves on and an evidence bag in her hand. "Jordan, what's happened?"

"I found this note on my car." Jordan pointed. "It could be anything, but with the case, I just thought it would be best if you got it and examined it."

Vanessa agreed and took the note from Jordan's windshield. She read it and whistled. "Someone knows you're digging."

"The press are reporting on Joseph Gordon, and there's been a police briefing. It wouldn't take long for people to know I was involved again. Besides, if this murderer hopes not to be discovered, then they're going about it wrong."

Vanessa smirked. "Good interviewing today, Jordan. It was like the old you came back."

"You know, I feel like he's back. And I didn't realise you were there."

"I left before you finished. But I was updated. Did he upset you with what he said?"

"Why would he upset me?" Jordan asked. "His comments were weird, and I'm intending to find out what he meant by them, but I also think he might just be stoking a fire."

"Good," Vanessa replied. "Keep a cool head, and hopefully this case will be resolved soon."

"I will definitely keep a cool head, Vanessa. Trust me."

With the note gone, Jordan was free to go home. As he was driving by, the doors to the police station opened, and Joseph Gordon walked out. He didn't notice Jordan and didn't even acknowledge the car. He was wearing round glasses and seemed to be waiting for someone. Jordan drove a little further but waited just before the junction, so if anyone did want to leave he wouldn't be in the way. Safely hidden in his car, he watched in the rear-view mirror as an old Fiat Punto pulled up next to Joseph.

Inside, there was a woman driving. Her hair was tied up, and she looked to be in her mid-forties. She clutched the wheel and looked around her as if she didn't want to be seen. Joseph got in, not looking around, and pulled his seat belt on. Before he could buckle it, the driver headed off.

As the motorist drove by Jordan's car, Jordan slipped down in his seat. The person behind the wheel looked left and right at the junction, but not at Jordan, and disappeared towards Cardiff city centre.

Jordan rooted in his glove pocket for his notebook and jotted down the number plate and car make.

Kim Bennedict was alive, and Joseph knew where she was.

SEVEN

Jordan had been home for an hour and was halfway through cooking spaghetti Bolognese while trying to keep Oscar away when there was a knock at the door. Annoyed, he dropped the wooden spoon on his worktop counter. It was unusual for someone to knock directly on his door. People from the street needed to be buzzed in. But of course, the apartment block he lived in was not quite as high tech as the street Joseph Gordon came from, so sometimes people got in without following the rules.

Being in the career Jordan was in, he was trained to be wary of these things. He slipped off his shoes and walked over towards the door as quietly as possible. There was a knock again. Oscar sat at the top of the hallway, curious.

Jordan peered through the peephole and viewed his dad looking to the left.

"Dad? What are you doing here?"

Peter Jenner looked at the door as if he could see Jordan through the wood. "Let me in. Please? I thought I'd pop by to see you."

Jordan sighed. He pulled away the chain and then opened the door. His dad looked at him, shorter than him ever so slightly. He smiled, although it was that of someone who felt a little out of place. As usual, his mother hung over them even though she wasn't here.

"Come in."

He moved aside and his dad stepped in to his apartment. "You need a bigger place, Jordan. Surely you can afford one."

"You say this every time, dad, and I say the same thing back to you. I've been here since university and I like it. I'm in no rush to leave." He shut the door, locking it once again.

"Yeah, but Jord, you deserve better."

"Want a coffee?"

"Milk, no sugar."

Peter led the way into the living room, where the ironing board stood up in the middle. He moved it out of the way and sat down. Jordan went to the kitchen, but he was still in view of him.

"So, Dad, why are you here?"

"I haven't seen you in a while."

"I've been busy."

"I hear you've only just returned to work."

"How do you know?"

"I've seen the newspapers," Peter replied. "You're in them. Only briefly, but it says you've been hired to investigate Joseph Gordon."

"Technically, not true." Jordan took his dad's coffee to him and went back to make his own. "No, I've been hired on the case."

Peter sipped at his coffee. "If you're sure, then I know you're right." He stuck out his tongue. "Can I get a sugar?"

It was always the same. He took the sugar canister to him and placed it on the table in front of him, a spoon on top of the lid.

"I'm not sure who did it yet. It's very early days. I'm assuming you know what happened?"

"Poisoned by someone in the writing group."

"That's right. I spoke with Joseph today. He told me I'm more involved than I think I am."

"What do you think he meant by that?"

"I'm not sure."

Jordan came to sit down next to his dad. He placed his mug on the table, where the coffee spun around after he had stirred it. "Your mum liked to write."

"I wouldn't know if she did."

"She did it every now and again when we were together. Though I don't think she ever took it seriously. Shame, really. I remember reading a poem by her. Very good, it was too."

"Well, it looks like James Fairview was a bit of a dick."

"Why?"

"Sexual harassment allegations, amongst other things. I got the impression he wasn't a very pleasant man to be around."

"Are there suspects?"

"Yes, there are suspects."

"Care to say who? The newspapers didn't know the writers' names. Are they famous like Joseph?"

"No, they're not famous," Jordan said. "That's why the writing group was special. They're non-identities writing with a bestselling author, hoping to pick up tips and get published themselves. A small group, very select."

"So, who are the suspects?"

"They all are."

"Anyone in particular?"

"I can't really tell you that, Dad."

"Come on. You can tell me."

"Two women," Jordan replied. "That's all I'll say."

Peter leaned forward and picked up his white coffee mug. Before taking a drink, he seemed to think of something, as if it had come to him all of a sudden. Oscar jumped up next to him, rubbing his head against his knee. Outside, a driver held down their horn in a moment of rage.

Peter waited for it to stop before speaking. "Do you think you've returned too soon?"

"No, Dad, I don't think I have."

"Are you sure?"

"We weren't close."

"She's still your mother."

"And I have a brother in Australia I never speak to. Family doesn't necessarily mean close bonds. I barely speak to you, Dad."

"And whose fault is that?"

Jordan avoided his eyes. "I've been busy."

"Ever since she went, you've been MIA."

"My job requires my full attention."

Peter looked at the ironing half done, the DVD left on pause, the food left uncooked on the stove. "That isn't full attention, Jordan. Look, I only expect a phone call every now and then. A text, something like that. You're all I've got."

Jordan felt his stomach clench. He sighed. "I know. I'm sorry."

Peter drank from the mug. "Don't be."

"Is that why you're here? To tell me I need to see you more? Because truthfully, I'm glad you came around. It takes my mind off a case that I feel like is going to consume me. But I don't really want to talk about Mum. She's gone, and we need to move on. I know that sounds harsh. I tried many times to get hold of her, to go by her house. She never answered, even when I knew she was in."

Peter placed his coffee mug down again. He looked out the window, biting his lip. "I know, Jordan. I didn't come here just to remind you of me."

"I'm being harsh. I didn't mean it."

"Her house is still untouched. You know there's stuff we need to sort out? You might want to keep some of her things."

Jordan shook his head. "I'm not keen on having anything from that house."

"Ah."

"But is something bothering you?"

"Hm?" He looked at him. "Oh, something is always bothering me. But I'm not sure it's even worth mentioning."

"You can tell me."

"I'm not sure I should."

Jordan put down his own mug. "Dad?"

He looked at him, fresh tears brimming in his eyes. "I think your mum was murdered."

EIGHT

That night, Jordan stared into a wine glass, wondering what the hell he was supposed to do. He had to follow up on the Kim lead. He planned to trace the number plate and see where Kim lived and if she was home with Joseph Gordon.

But now his dad had dropped a bomb into his small apartment and completely destroyed the block. Had his mother been murdered? The thought was startling, yet it was a drastic claim that had no proof to it. The coroner had ruled her death as natural. There was no evidence that she had been killed.

Jordan thought it was his dad trying to hold on to running water. He couldn't accept that his ex-wife had gone and now he was alone with a son who tried to avoid him and another son halfway across the world.

"But her death was natural," Jordan had said. "Her heart stopped beating, Dad. She probably had a stroke or a heart attack."

Peter had just shaken his head. "That's what they say, yes."

"Then we have to believe that. We can't go clinging on to false hope. She's gone."

Peter had left shortly after that. He seemed to think being with his son was not where he needed to be right now. Jordan let him go, only slightly worried that it was the wrong thing to do.

Now, he relished being alone. He let the thoughts swill around his head, refusing to drain away because the filter was blocked. His head was pounding and the alcohol was doing nothing.

He picked up his phone and opened WhatsApp. He found his messages to his brother, Ashley. The last messages had been in September. They barely kept in touch. Ashley was living a perfect life with a perfect boyfriend in Australia, and Jordan didn't know what he did, but he knew it was arts related. It brought him a lot of money.

Dad's been around. He thinks Mum has been murdered, Jordan texted.

He didn't know what time it was in Australia, and he couldn't be bothered to check. He looked at the time on his phone, ten past midnight. It was Christmas Eve.

He wasn't excited. As a child, the week leading up to Christmas would be full of restless nights because he was worried Santa would put him on the naughty list. Christmas Eve would always replace his worried thoughts with excitement. He didn't care if he didn't get presents for being naughty. He was just excited to see his family together, to enjoy presents regardless of who they were for.

Christmas when he was a kid had been enjoyable. His mother always entertained on Christmas Eve by inviting over aunties and uncles, cousins and nieces and nephews. Jordan would always get money from his grandparents on both sides of the family, and their little home in Caerphilly would be packed full of warm bodies.

Jordan recalled his flushed cheeks of excitement at running around with his cousins. He remembered watching his brother in awe as he hung out with his cool teenager friends. He recollected seeing his mother kissing a man he knew as uncle Terry, though he wasn't his real uncle and hadn't been in the family until a year previously.

Terry's appearance was when it had started to go wrong. Jordan had been twelve, and as usual, the house had been full. His aunty, Theresa, had found herself a new boyfriend. It was boyfriend number six, his father had said. They had laughed, though Jordan hadn't quite understood why that was funny.

Looking back Theresa appeared to him as someone who was unlucky in love.

Jordan had run away from one of his cousins, who was a year older than him and was starting to experience feelings for boys. Apparently, kissing your cousin under mistletoe was fine, and she had pursued him in an attempt to kiss him. Jordan had run into a blacked-out bedroom and hidden behind curtains, perching on top of a windowsill that overlooked their back garden.

He had seen his mother first. She wore a dress that didn't protect her from Jack Frost's chill, and tinsel in her hair and on her wrists. Then Terry came into view without Theresa. Terry's hand was on his mother's waist. They were laughing, smiling, both holding glasses of alcoholic drinks.

Jordan's cousin shouted for him, but he remained transfixed on his beautiful mother.

He remembered his world falling apart when they kissed at the back door, the music of Wham playing loudly downstairs, people singing along. He remembered feeling upset, feeling rage, feeling angry and confused.

Terry was a relative. He couldn't kiss his mother. What about Theresa? Did she know?

Had he actually seen what he thought he did?

For years after that, Christmas had been a sordid affair. As Jordan entered puberty, he became angry, feelings of resentment to his mother and confusion over who he liked going head-to-head to cause a horrible anger. His mother blamed it on hormones, but his anger was directed solely at the woman who had carried him for nine months. Terry always appeared, until one year when Jordan was seventeen. Terry turned up at the house, drunk, and he had answered the door.

Jordan had told him his mother wasn't in. She was but upstairs asleep. It was quite late.

Terry had argued with Jordan, said Theresa was out of the picture and he needed to tell his mother that. Jordan had refused to let him in.

His father had been out in the pub. He came home ten minutes later, but Terry had scarpered.

When Jordan had finished university, he told his mother everything. He recounted seeing them kiss. He asked if his mother was still seeing Terry.

"Yes," his mother replied. "I'll be leaving your father soon."

With things out in the open between the pair, their rift healed, if only for a little while. Soon, Jordan got to grips with what his mother was like. She was a manipulative, evil, selfish woman who cared only for her own well-being and nobody else's. She never apologised for hurting Jordan. She didn't care that she had left his father with everything to deal with.

Confused and angry, Jordan left his father with bills to pay and a house he couldn't afford. He cut out his mother all together and was pleased when he found out Terry had left her for another woman.

By the time Jordan was twenty-two, he had become a stranger to his mother. They still spoke, but barely.

Peter still didn't know that Annabelle had cheated on him. He'd thought there was still hope there, that they would get back together and live how they used to, with Christmas spent with family members who had deserted them since their break-up.

Now, this was Jordan's first Christmas Eve without his mother. Truly without his mother.

His phone vibrated, and he looked at the message. It was from Ashley.

What do you think?

I think he's clinging on.

Yep. Me too. Merry Christmas.

Jordan didn't bother to reply.

Half-drunk, he opened up Safari and searched for Kim Bennedict. An article came up in the South Wales Argus about the "amateur writer" who had just been published in an anthology. The article was dated in 2008.

It seemed since then Kim Bennedict hadn't had much success with her writing. Jordan went back to the search results and found an outdated website which had last been used in 2014. Her Twitter account had been inactive since 2016.

She only had three hundred and fifty-eight followers.

Kim Bennedict was a lonely woman, if social media was anything to go on. The photos she uploaded were of her in her house. Some were captioned with "Date night alone." Others were just about how she was writing something big and couldn't wait for her fans to see it.

Then Jordan came across a Facebook page. It was a public page that people could like. She had 878 likes, and it was dedicated to her writing.

The last post had been May 2017.

Jordan eyed the photograph, taken in a pub, and couldn't believe what he was seeing. Kim stood in the middle of the frame, portly and clutching a glass of lager. She looked like she was playing happy, and her forced smile could be interpreted as someone that just wanted to be included.

She was stood next to James Fairview, looking healthy and happy, with no idea he would be dead in seven months. Her chubby arm was draped across a woman that Jordan recognised as Sarah Dixon. Jordan thought Kim was turned more towards Sarah. Her other arm wrapped around James, hugging him as if he were a friend.

And then, behind her was a table, piled high with empty plates and glasses of drinks. It seemed to be a celebration of sorts.

But it wasn't the empty plates that held his attention. It wasn't the social aspect of Kim's new life.

It was his mother, Annabelle Skelton, stood in the background with her hand on Joseph Gordon's shoulder and a deathly glare at the back of James Fairview's head.

NINE

"Any updates on Joseph Gordon?"

Jordan was sat in a coffee shop in the city centre with Vanessa, who was dressed out of police uniform but had her credentials still on her. She was always still on the clock.

Vanessa shrugged. "The press are ripping into him, but it's all speculation right now." Vanessa eyed the people in the coffee shop again before speaking. There were not many people here to eavesdrop, but they could never be too careful. "It's looking unlikely that it was him. He's the easiest one to blame, however. It was his house and he made the drinks."

"But he saw that person enter."

"That's what is stopping us pinning it on him. We're trying to ask him who it was, but he's not cooperating."

"That's because he doesn't know himself."

"So he claims." Vanessa ripped a sugar sachet and poured it into her latte. "He hasn't returned home."

"Would you if there were press gathered outside?"

"It's a private street. It would be the best place for him to escape it."

Jordan agreed. "Maybe there are too many ghosts there."

"Maybe," Vanessa replied. "Or maybe he's not ready to face what he did."

"Who do you think the woman was?"

"Could only be two people, if we're going on the writers' group."

"Sally Dixon or Margaret Duncible." Jordan held his coffee mug but didn't drink from it. "Are we ruling out Franchesca and Kim?"

"Franchesca will be questioned, but she seemed pretty distraught when we turned up. Kim is still missing."

"Except she isn't."

Vanessa cocked her head. "Meaning?"

"She picked up Joseph from the police station. Sorry, I thought someone would have told you. I did request a track on the number plate."

"Jesus, no one told me a thing," Vanessa cursed. "Mark."

"Yeah, it doesn't seem like he's doing much work."

"He gets distracted easily. This is his first murder case, and he seems like an excitable child."

"That will wear off in time." Jordan smirked. "I remember my first day on the job."

"Yeah. Accused someone of stealing straight away and then got into an argument with old DI Rhodes, wasn't it?"

Jordan sipped his drink. "That's not how I remember it."

Vanessa laughed. "So, Joseph left with Kim. Do we think that's odd?"

"It did seem a bit strange, though I suppose if you're sharing a writing group you do become friends. I want to find out where Kim is, and then I plan to interview her."

"Find out how good of friends the pair are."

"I will." The music changed from Amy Winehouse to Adele. Cardiff was busy at Christmas Eve. Shoppers hurried from shop to shop, desperately trying to buy last minute gifts. It was a surprise this coffee shop was so quiet. It was like a sanctuary from everything going on outside. "My dad came to visit me yesterday."

"How did that go?"

"He told me he thought my mum was murdered."

Vanessa winced. "Murdered?"

"Yeah."

"But she wasn't," Vanessa said. "We all know that. The coroner…"

"Think she had a heart attack or a stroke, yeah, I know."

"Sorry. You know that, though?"

"Of course I know that," Jordan said. "But my dad is just clinging on to loose ends. He can't accept she's gone."

"It must be tough for him."

"Well, my dad can't accept much. He could never accept that she left him."

"Have you accepted it?"

"I accepted it a long time ago," Jordan bitterly said. "The woman became a stranger to me. Which is why I was so surprised to see this."

Jordan slid an envelope across the table to Vanessa with her name on it. He had printed out the photo from Kim's Facebook page last night.

Vanessa opened the envelope, not bothering to ask what was inside. She looked at the photo, and a few seconds later, her mouth dropped. "Is that…?"

"That's my mum, yeah."

"She's with Joseph Gordon."

"She knew them."

"How?"

"I don't know yet."

Vanessa exhaled. "You don't think it's possible that Annabelle was murdered by the same person who killed James, do you?"

"I haven't thought that far ahead yet, but no, I don't think so."

"Then what *do* you think?"

"I believe it's very possible my mum just happened to be there," Jordan replied. "Isn't it possible that she's just meeting an author?"

"I suppose it is."

"Joseph said to me I'm involved in this case more than I know."

"I know."

"Maybe this has something to do with that."

"Do you think Joseph was seeing your mum?"

"Going out with her? It's possible. They're roughly the same age."

"Your mum was single, wasn't she?"

"Like I said, after Terry, I stopped caring."

Vanessa finished her latte. "Right. Well, you keep looking into this, Jordan. There's definitely something going on."

"I'm going to. I was wondering if you could request something for me? Just something to help what I need to know."

"I'm always able to do that," Vanessa said. "What do you need?"

"I need the coroner's report and my mother's death records."

Vanessa looked a little shocked but quickly regained her composure. "Of course."

"Thank you."

Jordan sipped at his drink, his attention on a nearby couple as they talked about what else they needed to get for Christmas.

"Jordan?"

"Yeah?"

"You don't think your mother was murdered, do you?"

Jordan shrugged. "No."

Vanessa didn't look convinced. She put the photograph back in the envelope and stood up, her fingers clutching the envelope still. "I'm going to go. I've only got a half day today, but I want to get on with some other cases. If I don't see you until after it, I hope you have a merry Christmas."

"I won't be doing much," Jordan said. "But the same for you."

"And when we get records of that number plate, we'll let you know."

"It's taking a while, Vanessa. I thought I would have had it by now."

Vanessa took out her phone and lifted it up. "I'm on it." Vanessa stood aside from the table. "By the way, that note left on your car? No fingerprints. We were unable to trace anyone."

"Typical."

He felt angry. Someone out there was trying to intimidate him, leaving notes that told him to back off. How had no one seen the sender? But there was nothing that could be done. Jordan could only hope another letter would be delivered.

Vanessa left. Jordan didn't want to go out into the streets, head back to St David's car park where he had left his car. It was too busy out and too chilly, and he ached all over. It was the pain of a hangover, but also the cold outside. His joints hurt. He wanted to lie down and not move.

But he couldn't. He had a case to solve. Whilst everyone was enjoying the festivities, getting ready for Christmas and then planning their New Year's, Jordan was cutting himself off, shutting down, and focussing solely on the murder of a writer that hadn't made it. Years of work had taught him how to successfully close down, keep the guard up, and leave everyone else behind.

His phone buzzed next to him on the table. He closed his eyes and then looked at the screen. It was his dad.

I'm sorry about yesterday. I was wrong.

Jordan wanted to reply, but not yet. He read the message again, wondering if there was anything he could say. Something niggled in the back of his mind. That photograph of Annabelle behind James seemed too coincidental.

Finally, he replied. *Maybe you weren't.*

TEN

"Ethylene glycol," Hutchings said. "A killer dose of it. Probably finished off what was already in his system."

"He had it in his system already?"

"Twelve hours previously he had a dosage. This was the final one."

Jordan was stood in the coroner's office at quarter to eight at night. He'd braved the Cardiff madness and walked through the streets, window-shopping but refusing to buy. He had nobody to buy for. He had arrived at the police station a little after seven.

"Ethylene glycol. Where's that used?"

"Used for antifreeze," Lloyd Hutchings said. "It's an odourless, colourless liquid. It tastes sweet as well, which is maybe why it wasn't registered in James Fairview's drink."

"How was it administered?"

"A high dosage like that? Added to the drink."

Jordan exhaled. "Someone put it in his drink?"

"That's right."

"Shit." Jordan shook his head. "Is it even possible to die from antifreeze?"

"It would take some doing. It suggests more than one dosage was administered."

If Joseph Gordon was telling the truth, whoever had come in had indeed poisoned James. It seems like they had come prepared and been planning his death for longer than a day. If he already had it in his system, it meant he was being poisoned slowly.

"I only thought people used it to kill cats."

"Maybe someone went a step further and decided to see if it would work on a man."

"Any word on fingerprints?"

Lloyd shook his head. "Unfortunately not. I spoke to George from forensics. The glass only had Joseph Gordon's prints on it, as well as

37

James's. Not unusual considering it was Joseph's house and it was James's glass. Whoever administered the poison was wearing gloves."

"Thank you for letting me know the results, Lloyd."

"Anytime." Lloyd closed the folder he had been reading from and took it to a filing cabinet. "Vanessa tells me you want the records on your mother."

He was stating it, not asking. Jordan felt a tinge of embarrassment. "That's right."

"Can I ask why?"

"I'm just curious."

"I can try and get hold of them for you, but I have to request them. It wasn't my case."

"That's fine."

"Are you sure you're okay?"

Jordan sighed. "Why does everybody keep asking me that?"

"Because you're getting over grief and you've returned to work too soon."

"I'm not grieving."

"Then why are you looking at your mother's death?"

"I just want to see if anything was missed," Jordan replied. "Trust me, Lloyd, it's important."

"Okay."

Lloyd ran his fingers over his stubble, which Jordan noted he always seemed to have, yet never grew. Lloyd kept himself fairly groomed without appearing to do so.

"Well, I'll probably see you now after the New Year's celebrations."

"You will indeed," Lloyd said. "Although, if you wanted to get that drink…?"

He had been asking Jordan for a drink since Lloyd started his job two years ago. Jordan had been eager, keen to meet new people. He also thought Lloyd was good looking. But they'd never got around to the drink, mainly because the two were always so busy.

Jordan deflated. "I can't. Not right now."

"I'm beginning to think you're avoiding me, Jordan."

"Trust me, I'm not," Jordan replied. "But I'm not in the mood for a drink right now. I've got work to do."

"Sure," Lloyd replied. "Finding out who killed James."

"That's right."

"Sorry I can't be of any more help."

"You've certainly helped enough. Merry Christmas, Lloyd."

"Merry Christmas to you too."

Jordan wrapped his scarf around his neck and pulled his coat up tight as he left the police station. He spotted Rachel getting into her car and looked away before they would have to awkwardly wave at one another. Jordan got in to his own car, annoyed that it was older than Rachel's, and drove away into the Cardiff rush hour.

"Joseph Gordon has announced his retirement from the writing profession, amidst the investigation over the killing of James Fairview at his writers' group at his home in Cardiff," a radio presenter was saying on Heart. "The author, who has released three books yearly since 2008, claims it is because he is getting too old to spend time writing."

The audio changed to Joseph Gordon's voice. It sounded like he was on the phone. "I've decided to retire from writing commercial novels because I am an old man now. I think it time to give a chance to those writers who are younger than me but are struggling to break through because publishers believe there cannot be two Joseph Gordons, which is a narrow way of looking at things, if you ask me, but I digress. I hope that with me out of the picture now, new writers can take control. I will continue to nurture my writers' group, and hopefully one day, you will be able to read some of their work."

As the radio host changed the subject to Kim Kardashian, Jordan switched off. When he pulled up outside his flat he checked his phone. There was a text from Vanessa.

Opening it, Jordan saw that the number plates for Kim had been traced. She was living in Trevethin, Pontypool. Jordan smirked. If Joseph Gordon was there, Jordan wondered how he was coping with houses that were very tired and dilapidated.

Jordan texted Vanessa his thanks and slipped his phone into his pocket. He headed towards his apartment, the night air chilling. He keyed the entrance code into the apartment block door and entered. As he walked upstairs, whistling came from above. He paid it no attention until he came face-to-face with Arthur Blake, a man he had broken up with four months ago.

"Jordan."

"Arthur? What are you doing here?" Jordan shifted his bag up onto his shoulder, his hands clutching his keys. He wanted to get home, shower, and then rest, not talk to a man he hadn't thought about since leaving him behind at a restaurant in the city centre.

"I just wanted to come by and see how you were. It's Christmas. I wanted to spend it with you."

Jordan cocked his head to the side. "No, thank you. Arthur, we broke up. Remember?"

"Of course I remember. But we were angry. We'd been through a lot. I thought now, maybe…"

And then it dawned on Jordan why he was here. "You've read the newspapers, haven't you?"

"What? No, of course I haven't…"

But Jordan could tell when he lied. He looked away, he drew himself in. "Yeah, you have. You just want to get a sound piece from me. Well, no, Arthur. That isn't going to work." Jordan moved past him, walking down his hallway to his flat.

Arthur followed. "Jordan, please. The magazine is really interested in this story, and because I know you, it's a really good opportunity to get a great exclusive. Wouldn't you want to help me?"

"Remember why we broke up?"

"Yes."

"Tell me."

"Jordan…"

"Come on. Tell me."

"Because I got information out of you regarding a burglary and wrote about it in the magazine."

"So I'm not exactly going to give you any more information now, am I? Especially when it revolves around someone so high profile."

"But that's why I *need* it Jordan. Come on. Your career isn't paying you enough. We can offer you a lot of money for this."

"I'm not interested." Jordan, affronted, slid his key into the lock and turned. The door clicked open and he stepped inside his apartment. He was thankful the lights were out, so Arthur couldn't see the extent of mess inside.

He did peer in, looking around at the flat where they had met many times. "Come on, Jord, please."

"Goodbye, Arthur."

He shut the door and locked it quickly so Arthur couldn't push it open from his end. Thankfully, he didn't knock or call out. He swore at the closed door, probably knowing Jordan was looking through the peephole at him, and disappeared.

Jordan dropped his bag and shed his coat. All he wanted was for Christmas Eve to end and this year to disappear.

As he went into the living room, he took out his mobile phone. Apart from the odd notification from dating websites, there was nothing of interest. But then he saw he had a missed a call from his brother. He didn't think much of it. It was odd for Ashley to call, being abroad, yet it was too late to call back now. Jordan ignored the notification and thought nothing more of it.

ELEVEN

Christmas Day. When everyone else was waking up to spend time with their families, Jordan was waking up to nobody but his Persian cat. He lay in his bed, staring up at the ceiling, hearing the near silence outside in the streets. It was as if the world had come to a standstill. That was what he liked about Christmas. It was almost the only thing he liked about it. He went to move his leg, but Oscar was in between them, purring contentedly.

He had switched his phone off. Whilst he wasn't necessarily excited for Christmas, he was keen to shut out the world and not get disturbed, if only for a day or two. He briefly wondered if Ashley had tried calling again but didn't bother to check. His mind was elsewhere.

Ethylene Glycol had been James's killer. Administered by being added to the whisky. But he had died soon after consumption, and with proof that the poison had been building up in his system, it told Jordan this killing had been planned methodically. How had the killer got the poison to Joseph Gordon's kitchen?

The writers' group met only monthly. It was a possibility that each time James drank at the writers' group, the poison had been administered. Yet Jordan thought that highly unlikely. The dosage had been lethal because of how much was used. That could have been done at any time. No, the killing had been attempted but failed. That's what explained the build-up of the poison in his system.

Jordan had seen a case similar to this before, though the woman being poisoned had stayed alive. She had gone to the doctor's, and it had been determined there that she had been consuming the poison unawares. It was her brother that had hoped for her to die, because he knew she had a fund of money that would have to go to him.

Was this the case in James's murder?

Jordan sighed. He needed information, but he knew he wouldn't get it over Christmas.

He sat up, rubbing his eyes, wondering what the hell he was going to do in this awkward lull of the year when there was a murder case he needed to work on. He eyed his turned-off phone, where he had the information for Kim's whereabouts. The woman would see him. She'd have no choice if he turned up today, uninvited.

Jordan got himself washed and dressed, and an hour later, he was leaving his apartment and driving from Cardiff towards the small town of Pontypool. When he exited the city, he felt a sense of release. It was like the weight of the world was melting like a polar icecap, and he was no longer tied to everything that held him in the growing city of Cardiff.

As he entered the valleys, mountains appearing alongside him, he felt a sense of freedom, despite the houses looking a tad tired and the people walking the streets looking fatigued and poor. There had been many reports published about the welfare of valley residents, most of them detailing how many were on antidepressants, but he had seen his fair share of sadness and depression in the city.

He got to Pontypool and climbed the mountain roads to Trevethin, the main area in Wales to be in poverty. Down one of the streets, the satnav told him he had finally arrived.

Once parked on the side of the road—another great thing about valley parking was no permit was needed—he locked his car and walked past the broken wooden fence towards a house that was half-painted and flecked with damp.

He knocked on the door. Eyeing the street around him, he spotted a nosy woman staring at him from her bedroom window opposite. Jordan didn't respond when the woman waved.

The door opened and he came face-to-face with Joseph Gordon. He was wearing a Christmas cracker hat, and he looked half-cut. He smiled at him as if he had known all along he would arrive.

"Merry Christmas, Jordan. Would you like to come in?"

"Joseph," Jordan breathed. The woman at the window was still staring, though she couldn't see who had opened the door. "Is Kim in?"

There was Christmas music playing from somewhere in the house. Pots and pans scraped in the kitchen, and he wondered if Kim had indeed invited her whole family here.

Joseph stepped aside. "Of course."

Jordan hadn't told anyone where he was going. Nobody knew he was at the house. It could have been a mistake walking in here today, but he did it anyway. He had connections that could find him in an instant if he truly disappeared.

"Who is it?" a voice called, and then Kim appeared in the kitchen doorway, holding a wooden spoon and wearing an apron. Her eyes narrowed and she looked at Joseph. "Is this…?"

The sentence didn't need to be finished. Jordan knew the pair had spoken about him.

Joseph grinned. "It is."

Kim deflated, looking pissed off. "Well, merry fucking Christmas."

"I hope you don't mind me dropping by, but I was hoping you might be able to answer some questions for me, Kim."

"At least let us have our Christmas dinner first."

"Christmas dinner is perfect," Jordan replied. "I can ask you over lunch."

Joseph chuckled. "Get this man his own plate. Looks like we've got another guest, today. It's compulsory you wear a Christmas hat, though."

Jordan looked at Kim's unwashed blonde hair with black roots. "She isn't wearing one."

"I will once dinner is done." Kim disappeared back into her kitchen, where the music was playing.

Joseph directed Jordan into a spacious living room, but only because there was a significant lack of furniture. There was an old table at one end, decorated for Christmas with a red tablecloth, wine glasses, and crackers. There was a TV, about forty inches. On it was the queen, who was giving her annual speech. She was halfway through discussing the residents of Grenfell tower when Joseph poured Jordan a glass of wine.

"I've driven here, so I can't drink too much."

"One glass won't hurt." Joseph held it out to him and he took it. "I knew you'd come."

"How?"

"Because you're not going to let this case drop."

"Obviously not."

"Why Kim?"

"Because I saw her pick you up, and I want to know why."

"I could tell you."

"I'd rather hear it from her."

Joseph shrugged and sat down at the dinner table. Jordan decided to do the same. He chose the chair at the end of the table, furthest away from Joseph. There was only one chair between them, but it was enough for Jordan to feel secluded.

"Why aren't you with people for Christmas?" Joseph asked him.

"I could ask the same for you," Jordan said, the bare room weighing on him now. How could people live like this, with no home comforts? There weren't even any photos on the walls.

"Please, you don't need to ask me those questions."

"Why not?"

"I'm an old man. I don't have a partner, and I'm afraid my parents died a long time ago. Besides, with current circumstances, I wanted to disappear for a little while."

"Great idea coming here, of all places. Though risky. The press truly have no idea you're here?"

"Why would they?" Joseph questioned. "Kim is a nobody. They wouldn't think I'd be staying in an ex-council house in one of the most deprived areas in Wales, would they? They'd expect me to be at home, or catching a flight to Dubai."

"And why didn't you catch a flight to Dubai?"

"Never fancied the country."

The queen's speech ended. Jordan drank from his glass, taking small sips, letting the silence drag out between them.

Eventually, Joseph spoke again. "I really am telling the truth, you know."

"About what?"

"The woman who came in. She really was there."

"I know."

Joseph's eyes widened. "You really do believe me?"

"I think everyone does, otherwise you'd be in prison right now."

"I suppose you're right." Joseph stared at his cutlery. "Awful, what happened. I'm not over it. I don't think I ever will be over it."

"You seem fine," Jordan noted.

Joseph looked at him. "I'm not. No, how can I be? The man was a good writer that I got to know. He died in my home, and most likely because I didn't stop whoever came in from administering that poison."

"You trusted the people that came and went in your house. A murder is not something you expect."

"It was a woman, of that much I'm certain."

"You've told me this."

"It wasn't Kim, if that's what you're here for."

"She's a woman, and I'm not ruling anybody out yet."

He peered at him. "Do you think she did it?"

"I can't tell you what I think."

"That means you do."

"It means everyone has a part in this, and I want to find out as much information as possible."

"I didn't do it."

Jordan and Joseph flinched, as if they had been interrupted right before a kiss. They turned to look at Kim, who was stood in the middle of the living room, holding two turkey Christmas dinners.

"Why don't you sit down and we can discuss this?" Jordan questioned.

"I didn't do it, but I think I know who did."

TWELVE

"Please, sit down. Let's discuss this informally."

Kim eyed Jordan as she hovered on the spot. She glanced at Joseph, and he encouragingly nodded. Kim walked across the floor, padding on the worn-out carpet, and placed the dinner plates, piled high with vegetables and turkey, in front of Jordan and Joseph.

"Let me get my own dinner, first."

"Of course."

Kim retreated, and once out of sight, Jordan turned to Joseph. Joseph spoke before Jordan could. "Hear her out."

"Do you know about it?"

"She hasn't spoken about it to me."

"What do you mean?"

But before Joseph could answer, Kim came back in the room, her apron off and her dinner in her hand. She sat in the middle of the table, between Jordan and Joseph. She faced a wall where there should have been a Christmas tree, but instead there was empty space.

"Dig in," Kim said. She pointed at the table. "Help yourself to mint sauce, cranberry, anything."

Joseph did just that, spooning mint sauce onto his roast potatoes. Jordan waited for him to finish, then did the same, picked up a fork, and speared a carrot. "This does look delicious."

"Thanks," Kim replied. "My mum taught me how to cook."

"She did it well," Joseph said, his mouth full.

"She did indeed."

After a slight pause, Kim spoke again. "You're here because of James."

"I am."

Jordan had learned to keep quiet, to let people speak when they wanted to speak. He had to put Kim at ease, to let her relax and know that

45

she could trust him. Joseph's cutlery clinked across his plate. He seemed to be thinking the same thing.

Kim drank from her glass of prosecco and stared at the wall. "He was a…well, he was a dangerous man."

"Dangerous?" Joseph asked. "Don't you think that's a little harsh?"

"Did you not see him, Joseph?" Kim questioned. "He couldn't keep his hands off the women. He was always trying to advance on us."

"He was?"

"Did he ever advance on you, Kim?" Jordan asked.

Kim sighed. "He tried. I learned to keep away from him. A polite hello here and there, and a discussion on what we were writing, but that was it. I wouldn't let myself be alone with him."

"That's interesting," Jordan said.

Kim looked at him. "Shouldn't you be writing this down?"

"I'm okay for now."

Kim glanced at Joseph. She was looking to him for reassurance. "He was also a drunk."

"He did like a drink," Joseph agreed.

"It got worse over time. And then a week or two before he died, he was kicked out of a pub I was in for embarrassing behaviour. He was throwing up and stumbling all over the place. Looked dazed and confused. He swore to the bouncers he had only had half a pint, and the barman said the same, but who knows what he'd been doing before that?"

They continued to eat, forks and knives scraping across plates. The BBC carried on with its Christmas schedule in the background. Jordan's gaze roved over the bare room. He wondered how Kim coped, having so little possessions.

"Did you see him outside of the writers' group often?"

"No," Kim eventually said. "He lived in New Inn, which is about ten minutes away from here. It doesn't seem far, but he stuck to his local and I hardly ever go out. I just happened to be in New Inn with a friend and he was there."

"What date was this?"

"Oh, I can't remember. But it was the first week of December."

"What was the name of the pub?"

"Lower New Inn."

"Was he alone?"

"I don't know."

"Did you see anyone leave with him?"

"I didn't." Kim shook her head. She seemed to be beginning to tire of the questions. Her tone had changed. "To be honest, I was ashamed. I'd been telling my friend all about the writers' group I was in and how prestigious it was. And then he throws up and gets thrown out of a bar, and I have to admit I know him and that he was a writer too."

"What was his writing like?"

"Oh, it was so-so." Kim looked at Joseph. "You can admit that too?"

Joseph looked a little awkward. "I don't really like to say writers in my group can't write. They're all there for a reason."

"Joseph's writing group is chosen personally by him. He nurtures talent that he believes are going to be the next writers. He's been criticised for his age ranges, because there's only one twenty-something. But he has a good eye. I'll be honest, though, I don't know what he saw in James Fairview."

"I'll admit, as the weeks went on, he seemed to struggle a bit. He got easily distracted."

"By what?" Jordan asked.

"Women. Alcohol. Discussions that didn't really contribute to anyone's work."

"Was he disruptive?"

"A little."

"And what did he publish?"

"He had the odd thing published," Kim said. "He was featured in a couple of anthologies. I don't think he ever published a novel."

"And have you?"

Kim looked embarrassed. "No. Well, I self-published, but I took that down on advice by Joseph."

"Why?"

"Self-published writers tend to get a bad reputation," Joseph replied. "That's my opinion at least."

"I've heard of self-published writers really taking off."

"Only in rare instances," Joseph said. "I want my writers to have a fair chance, and with only one book that shifted less than a hundred quantities, there was still chance for Kim. I'm not saying writers shouldn't self-publish. I think that's the future. But because it's so easy to do, there is a lot of bad stuff out there, and that's what publishers aren't so keen on."

Jordan shifted in his seat, spooned food into his mouth, and chewed. He swallowed and took a new direction. "Was James single?"

"Who knows?" Kim asked as Joseph laughed. "He said he had girls waiting for him on all ends, but I never saw him with anyone. Like I say, I wasn't close to the man. I sometimes wished he wasn't in the writers' group." Kim avoided Jordan's eye as she said this, and Jordan wondered if this was the whole truth, if maybe she would say more if Joseph weren't around.

"Okay. Did he have friends in the group?"

Kim sighed, tired of the questioning. "I thought you said this was supposed to be casual?"

"I'm sorry. It's just questions come to me as we talk, and I want them answered."

Kim put down her fork and reached for her drink. "Some of the girls spoke to him, yes."

"And did they get along?"

"I suppose some of them didn't avoid him like I did."

"Who did he really get along with?"

Kim picked up her fork and put turkey into her mouth. "Well, James seemed to befriend the good writers of the group."

"You are all good writers," Joseph interrupted.

"Fine. The writers with a bit more flair than others." Kim shrugged. "We had some writers stay for only a month or two, but they were very good and James seemed to just hook onto them. They were mainly women. The men he didn't care for as much. I tend to think he was praying he would go out with a woman that was a better writer than him, and hope for the best."

"The best being?"

"I don't know. How does that help?"

"Anything helps."

"Fine. The best being that maybe that writer would get a publishing contract and James would benefit from that."

"You said you know who killed him."

"Maybe that was a wrong choice of words."

Jordan waited a beat. "They're a very odd wrong choice of words."

Kim rolled her eyes. "James caused arguments."

"With who?"

"The writers he tended to latch onto."

"He was a womaniser and a sneak," Joseph said.

"Interesting," Jordan said. He turned to Joseph. "You mentioned Kim slept with him?"

There was silence. Kim looked at Joseph with shock. "You what?"

Joseph, instead of appearing uncomfortable, just smiled. "Just gossip. Nothing more."

"I *never* slept with him."

"Like I said, gossip."

Kim turned to Jordan with narrowed eyes. "He would cause a lot of arguments, usually in private but loud enough for the rest of us to hear."

"And who were these arguments with?"

"Well, Franchesca, Sally, Margaret. He was a key factor in writers leaving throughout the year."

"So he argued with everyone?"

"Mostly women."

"None of the men?"

"No, not that I can recall."

"So he had enemies."

"Enough enemies to want him dead," Kim muttered. "If you really want to find out who murdered James, then I'd start looking in Sally's direction."

"Why?"

"They were close. To what extent, I don't know. But they had arguments all the time, yet still seemed to be close. They were odd. Very cliquey."

Jordan pondered this information. "Where does Sally live?"

Kim looked at Joseph. He thought for a moment. "I'm pretty sure it's Chepstow."

"Other side of the M4," Kim added.

"I know," Jordan said, not impolitely. "This information has been great, Kim, and I must apologise for barging in on your Christmas."

"It's fine. You got a dinner out of it. Looks like you enjoyed it too."

Jordan realised his plate was almost empty. He had been picking away at his food throughout the conversation.

He smiled, then took out his mobile phone from his pocket. "There's just one more thing I need to ask you."

"You can do so."

Jordan found the photograph on his phone and turned it to Kim. "Who is this woman stood next to Joseph?"

Kim looked at the photo, her face expressionless. "That's Annabelle. She left a few months ago now. She wasn't with us long. I didn't really get to know her." Kim looked at Jordan. "Why's that?"

"I just wanted to know if she could have been involved."

"I doubt it. Came to the writers' group for a bit, left around about July time. She left because of James."

"And you can confirm that?"

"Well, no, not really. I just assumed that's why she left."

"Did you ever see the pair talk?"

"No."

"Joseph?"

Joseph looked at him, but this time it was different. He seemed pleasantly pleased, as if he had been waiting to hear this question the whole time. "No, I never saw them speak."

THIRTEEN

Jordan didn't leave Trevethin all that quickly. After food, he had hung around for only one more drink, one too many in his opinion, and then he had excused himself. He had imposed on Kim's Christmas for too long. Yet he had found out enough information to be going on.

To him, Kim wasn't a suspect. She had been there that day, and she had seen what happened, but Jordan knew a killer and Kim wasn't one. He'd be sure to tell Vanessa that, regardless of if it would be taken into account.

Jordan sat in his car, staring out at a foggy Christmas day in the Welsh valleys. He felt the bitter cold of frost seeping through his closed windows, attacking his car and freezing the exterior with each brush of Jack Frost's finger. He turned the key in the ignition, blasted the heat that wouldn't warm up until he drove, and then buckled up.

But still, he didn't move. He listened to the hum of the air being blown into the car. Cars drove past him, barely giving him a glance. He wondered what Kim and Joseph were now talking about in the house he had just left, so broken and frail and incredibly sparse.

His mother had joined the writers' group. Had she ever spoken to James? Not on a friendly basis, according to Kim. Yet that photograph in Jordan's pocket said something else. It said his mother, Annabelle, had hated the man. She was glaring into the back of his head. Was it a pure chance snapshot? Yes, that was possible. But Jordan couldn't shake the feeling. It was like his mother was trying to tell him one final thing: this man is evil.

From his discussion with Kim, Jordan had learned that James was trouble. He was a man that liked female attention, yet apparently never got it. Then, according to Kim, he was drunk and disorderly, though Jordan wondered if his behaviour was a sign of the poison he was unknowingly consuming.

50

Jordan wondered if he could find the bar. Would it be open on Christmas morning? He decided to take a chance.

He drove away from Trevethin, leaving Kim and Joseph behind for now. He dropped out of the valleys and made his way to New Inn, passing a petrol garage with a miserable-looking worker inside. He drove past Pontypool and New Inn's train station, which had once been a key part in the coal trade, and carried on through New Inn, passing houses that were rather spacious and good looking, all with twinkling Christmas lights in the front.

He speculated if he had passed James's house unknowingly. As he turned a corner and drove towards the end of New Inn, he began to wonder if he had gone too far. He had, after all, stuck to the main roads, as the Lower New Inn could have been further into the small communal area. But then, when he was considering turning around at the roundabout that led to Cwmbran, he spotted it.

It had recently been refurbished. The last time he had seen it had been a few years ago, and it had tired-looking window frames. Now, however, the building had been given a lick of paint and the windows had been changed out. The sign hanging above the pub was brand new, judging by the brass hanger it hung from, and the letters nailed to the wall were lit up.

The door was open, so Jordan knew the landlords had opened. He wondered, however, if the barman who had been there that night was working.

He parked his car on the curb, making sure he didn't take up any room for those that passed by. It wasn't a double yellow, and even if it was, he didn't fear parking attendants coming by, not today.

He locked his car and headed to the front door, imagining the scene when James was hurled out for throwing up and appearing drunk, both signs of the ethylene glycol poisoning he had consumed.

When Jordan walked into the bar, which smelled new but still had vintage appearing fixtures, he was surprised to see it was rather quiet. There were two people having Christmas lunch and one other person playing darts. Music played from a jukebox, a rock band that Jordan didn't recognise, being a fan of pop music. There were two people behind the bar, which went from one corner of the pub and linked around in an oval shape, into another seating area of the bar. One man was older, pouring a pint of Carling, and another was a young woman.

The young woman smiled at Jordan as he walked in. "Hello!"

Jordan, still taking in his surroundings, approached the bar. "Could I get a lemonade, please?"

"Of course."

The young woman went to find a glass, leaving Jordan where he was stood. A calendar hung on the wall, and fairy lights were tied alongside the ends of the back bar, lighting up the dull brown surface.

When the woman returned, Jordan leaned forwards. The woman appeared worried but leaned in all the same.

"I'm here to ask a few questions about a man that was in here a few weeks back. Is there anybody I can speak to?"

The woman's expression of worry changed to confusion. Jordan put her age at eighteen or nineteen. She glanced at the man that was now loading a glass washer. "That's the landlord over there. He could help you? Dad!" The man looked over. "This dude wants to speak to you."

The landlord approached, a polite expression on his face. "How can I help?"

He was just a little bit taller than Jordan, and much bulkier. Jordan thought he went to the gym, but he didn't quite have the muscles that graced the pages of fashion magazines. His hair was greying, and stubble grew over his chin and cheeks. He had a wedding ring on his finger.

"My name is Jordan Jenner. I'm a private investigator. I'm here to ask a few questions about a man called James Fairview, who was in this pub at the beginning of the month."

At the words *private investigator*, both of the people behind the bar stood up straight. The young woman looked a little afraid. Jordan was used to both expressions. The man regained his composure first. "Okay. Can this wait at all? It is Christmas Day, after all, and we have work to do."

Jordan eyed the pub. "It's fairly quiet. This won't take long."

"I can hold the fort for now, Dad."

Jordan threw the young girl a grateful look.

The father sighed. "Fine. But can we talk out back? Some of these locals like a gossip."

Whilst Jordan didn't think the people around had paid them any attention, he agreed and followed the man towards the back of the pub. They walked through a kitchen and out into a hallway, where coats were hung up and shoes left discarded. It dawned on Jordan that he was actually in their home now.

"What date are we looking at?"

"I'm not sure exactly. My source said it was just the first week of December."

"Did you want to see CCTV, or...?" The man was looking at him like he was alien.

"CCTV could help, but I was wondering if you knew anything about that night."

"What do you want to know?"

"Have you heard about James Fairview's murder?"

The man nodded. "Only briefly whilst it's been on the radio. More information on the writer's house and career, than this fellow."

"He came here before he died. He was drunk and disorderly."

"We get a lot of them in here."

Jordan agreed. He took out his phone and found a photo of James. "This is him."

There was a flash of recognition on his face. "Ah. He seemed quite drunk when I saw him. I remember the bouncers throwing him out because he was throwing up. It was odd, though, because the lad who was working here swore he was only served one half pint. The reaction was quite extreme." The man looked at Jordan. "He could have drunk elsewhere, though."

"Did he appear drunk when he came in?"

"Not that I can remember, no."

"And what was he acting like when he got thrown out?"

The man thought for a moment. "Uh, well, he kept saying he wasn't drunk. Said he had only had a pint. The bouncers didn't believe him, of course, because he was sick, but our barman said it was odd because he'd only had a half. He looked out of it, though. Maybe it *was* drugs. His eyes looked a little bloodshot and his skin appeared to be a different shade. He definitely wasn't right. It didn't click that the man we threw out was the man murdered."

"I suppose it wouldn't," Jordan replied. He took out a notebook and began to write down what the man said. The man seemed to remember how official this was and stood up a little straighter. A television murmured upstairs. "And what's your name, if you don't mind me asking?"

"Dylan."

"Dylan," Jordan repeated. "Okay, Dylan. Can you remember if James Fairview was alone?"

"He wasn't," Dylan replied. "He was with a blonde lady."

"A blonde lady?"

"That's right."

"Can you remember anything about her?"

"She was short but plump. Looked a bit older than him."

"If I showed you a photo, would you remember who it was?"

Dylan nodded. "Probably. I have to remember faces. Remember who's banned, that sort of thing."

Jordan appeared grateful. He scrolled through his images on his phone until he came across a photo of Franchesca. Dylan shook his head. Jordan tried a photo of Margaret, and Dylan nodded.

"That's her."

"That's her? You're sure?"

"Yes," Dylan said. "Do you want me to find you CCTV footage?"

"Have you got it?"

"We keep it all stored. We have to. It may take me a little while, but I can find it."

Jordan thought for a moment. "Listen, it's Christmas and you've got a pub to run, and I don't want you to waste any family time. It's not urgent, but if you could find this footage for me and let me know by New Year's, then we can go from there."

Dylan seemed to think this was a good deal. "That's fine. I appreciate that. Anything I can do to help, really."

"If I'm not available, then I will send police officers to come and collect the footage."

"This isn't going to be the scene of press speculation and police officers now, is it?"

"I assure you, once you've supplied the CCTV footage, you can have nothing to do with this case. You're not a suspect, Dylan. You're just an aid to me finding out James Fairview's murderer."

FOURTEEN

When Jordan returned home at six p.m. that evening, he felt elated. He was making steady progress on his case, the first since returning after his mother's death, and things seemed to be going well. Right now, he knew the people he had to speak to. He could wait, relax, and enjoy Christmas, if only for a little while.

But Jordan knew he didn't have the temperament, and that wasn't what he wanted to do. The CCTV footage kept him thinking: what would he get from it? How would it help him?

Jordan sighed. He was dressed in the clothes he had been wearing all day, and wanted nothing more than to get into informal clothes, lounge shorts and a loose T-shirt. Before that, he headed to a small unit in his hallway and bent down to open the door.

He rooted through the junk inside, such as old CDs and catalogues, and finally found a leather-bound photo book. He placed it on top of the unit and opened it. The spine creaked, and the plastic made a stiff noise as it was prised apart. He found a photograph of him with his friends from university, who were now off doing their own thing and hadn't bothered to keep in touch. He turned the page to an old photo of him with his brother, possibly before he moved away. Jordan couldn't remember.

Then Jordan came to the photo he had in mind. It was of him and his mother, a year before all of the truth came out about Terry. Judging by the sun and the clothes they were wearing, Jordan knew it was from a holiday. Jordan looked at his annoyed expression in the photo, a face that said he wanted to be anywhere else. He remembered his dad telling him off for not smiling, his mother dismissing it as late teenage angst. Yet Jordan remembered exactly what had happened before this photo: his mother hidden behind a wall at a restaurant, hastily talking to Terry, unaware her son was around the corner.

Jordan had always known when his mother was up to something. He could see it in the way she moved, the way she glanced at anything but the person in front of her. His mother would falsely smile, rush off, and spend too long out of the room.

His phone pinged with a message, and he took it out of his pocket. It was from Dylan.

I have the footage. What's your email?

Surprised, Jordan replied and then put his phone back.

He touched the image of his mother, as if he thought he could touch her. He wanted to ask her the simple question of what happened. He needed to know. Did she feel threatened? Had she known she was a target?

He brought his phone out again, only this time he texted his dad. *We need to talk. When are you free?*

Letting his dad know about the case was risky, yet he needed to. It was his right to know. And besides, maybe there was something he could do to help, though Jordan did not hold out much hope. He suspected his dad had lied plenty of times about how much he actually talked to Annabelle after they separated.

Jordan's phone made a different noise, and a notification told him there was an email from WeTransfer. The footage Dylan had managed to get him had been sent.

Jordan felt excited. He went into his living room and opened his laptop, and within minutes, he was downloading the footage by clicking on the link WeTransfer had created.

The video file was large and, once downloaded, was fifteen minutes long. He made himself a mug of coffee and sat down to survey the footage.

Because it was CCTV, there was no sound, but Jordan was getting the gist. The stamped time code on the footage told him it was coming up to nine p.m. James sat with his one drink, half empty. He looked happy. He was laughing with two men, but from their body language, Jordan thought they didn't know each other. They were talking but in a polite manner, big smile, a bit of distance between them, and alcohol in their hands.

Then, from the corner of the frame, Margaret appeared. She looked dazzling, even in this grainy CCTV footage. Her hair was tied up in a bun of her head. She wore a shawl over a dress that only just fitted and complemented her wide frame.

James said something to the men, before he walked away to a nearby table with Margaret, still in frame but only just. There were a lot of people around. It seemed like a busy night.

At eight minutes past nine, Margaret got up from the table and walked across the bar. The camera lingered on James, who stayed where he was sat, tapping the fingers of one hand to music Jordan couldn't hear. His other fingers wrapped around the glass of beer, like it had done when he had seen him dead.

The camera changed. This view was now of Margaret as she walked up the stairs and towards the toilets. Jordan sat forwards.

Margaret approached a woman with her back turned from the camera. She tapped her on the shoulder. The woman turned around. It was Kim.

Jordan paused the footage. Kim had lied to him. Kim had claimed that she didn't speak to James that night and had not seen the person he was with. But yet here was proof that Kim had seen Margaret. Had it really been that difficult to put two and two together? Besides, Kim hadn't even mentioned seeing Margaret. That seemed like a pretty big thing to miss out.

Jordan sipped his coffee and then pressed play again. The footage rolled, and the two moved aside for another woman to get to the toilet door. The two talked. It didn't look friendly. Kim had her eyes narrowed and her arms crossed. Margaret gestured wildly. A few moments later, with a roll of her eyes, Kim took something out of her pocket, looked behind Margaret, and then shook her hand.

The two women didn't say bye. They moved past each other. Kim heading down the stairs and Margaret going to the bathroom.

Jordan rewound and played the footage a number of times, but he could not see what Kim had taken out of her pocket. All he knew was that after the handshake, Kim's hand was empty.

Jordan tried not to let his mind run away. He had to stay rational. They could have exchanged anything, completely unrelated to what had happened to James.

He pressed play again and let the footage unfold. Margaret came out of the toilets at quarter past nine. She had been in there a while. Margaret glanced ever so briefly at the camera, as if she was looking straight at Jordan, and then continued on.

A few moments later, Margaret was back downstairs, the footage changing to the same angle of James at the table. She sat down with James and said something. James nodded and got up, moving out of frame. Margaret drank from her own gin and surveyed the pub around her.

Jordan almost expected something bad to happen. Something with enough evidence to tell him that yes, Margaret did it.

But at twenty-two minutes past, Margaret was getting up. She moved quickly, quicker than Jordan thought possible. The camera switched to an angle of the front door, to James. He had thrown up and was swaying, though he didn't look as drunk as Kim had made him out to be. Margaret hurried over to James, who was being escorted out of the pub by a bouncer.

They talked for a few seconds, but whatever Margaret said didn't change the bouncer's mind. The bouncer pointed for Margaret to leave, and she did. James stumbled along after, wiping his mouth but going quietly. It was outside when he began to shout.

He was pointing his finger at the bouncer, pointing inside towards the bar where the barman had only served him one drink. He didn't look drunk, but he didn't look sober. Jordan put it down to a reaction to the poison inside him.

The footage cut out just as James and Margaret were walking away from the pub. Jordan stared at his reflection in the black screen.

Kim knew something and she wasn't telling Jordan. After watching this, Kim had become a strong suspect.

FIFTEEN

Boxing day. The day that everyone either felt too tired to participate in much or were up at the crack of dawn for crazy sales. Jordan did not feel like doing anything, but not because he had drunk too much.

He had been up most of the night, watching the CCTV footage, trying to garner more information. He had replayed Margaret meeting with Kim over and over again until his eyes ached and he struggled to focus. He still didn't know what had been exchanged.

At five a.m., he had emailed Dylan again. He needed to speak to the barman. He could know something.

His father hadn't replied. Jordan had been fighting himself on whether or not to give him information regarding his dead wife. He had received an email at quarter past seven from someone wanting to hire him to investigate money laundering. He hadn't replied. He would not reply. This case was consuming him. He had no time for anything else.

Tired and aching, he got out of bed. But he stood in his room in his underwear, unaware of what to do with himself. The case had hit a brick wall. He had leads to follow, but he didn't know how to pursue them. Would Kim see him again? Did Joseph know Kim had exchanged something with Margaret?

He found his briefcase and brought out the paper that had the writers' group pictures and details. He found Margaret and her number. It was mid-afternoon. Jordan had slept in, and so Margaret should be awake.

Jordan dialled her number and listened to the ringing on the other end. It kept ringing. Margaret did not answer.

It was possible Kim had warned her that there was a private investigator involved. Oscar sauntered into the room, a bored expression on his flat face.

His phone buzzed, and it was a reply from Dylan. The barman would be in this afternoon for a night shift. He would be available to cover his shift whilst he was questioned. Jordan replied that he would be there at some point today. Giving a time would allow preparation, though he suspected Dylan knew nothing except for what happened that night. He had got himself caught up in a case that seemed unbelievable to him.

There was a knock at the door. Still in his underwear, Jordan groaned. He threw on the nearest clothes to him: an independent band's T-shirt and a pair of washed-out jeans. He hadn't brushed his teeth and his hair was in disarray, but at least he was dressed.

He walked to the door just as there was another knock. He opened it, not bothering to look through the peephole.

His father stood before him.

"You wanted to talk."

Two coffees in front of them and Jordan's mouth rinsed with mouthwash, Jordan was ready to talk to his father. Yet now he was here, Jordan didn't know what to say. His brain was fuddled, his eyes heavy. He had planned what to say last night whilst writing notes about the CCTV footage. Yet now it had gone in a puff of smoke.

"Good Christmas?"

"I missed having you around," Peter replied. "But that isn't why I'm here, is it?"

"We can make general chat, surely."

"Not when your text told me you needed to talk."

"You know it's about mum."

"Listen, I'm not sure if she was murdered," Peter began. "I think I was just clinging onto…"

"Dad. I think Mum is involved with the case I'm investigating."

Peter blinked. "The dead writer?"

"The dead writer."

Peter drank his coffee and looked out of the window, at a building that had an empty storage space level with Jordan's window. "So, she was murdered?"

"I don't know. It is too early to even think like that. But Mum, well, she was involved with these people somehow."

"How do you know?"

Jordan put down his own coffee and showed his dad the photo on his phone. It took him a little while to notice his ex-wife stood behind James and Kim, her eyes narrowed and burning into the back of the dead writer's head.

"They were together."

"Together?"

"Not together as in a relationship," Jordan quickly dismissed. "I just mean together there. Mum was part of the writers' group. She didn't stay long, according to the woman hugging James in the photo. She left in July."

"She died in September."

"Yeah."

"She told me she had someone coming over."

"Do you know who?"

"No. I did tell the police, but they told me there was no evidence that anybody had come into the house. Nothing was stolen. No sign of a struggle or a break-in. According to them, her heart just failed."

"Which could be perfectly true."

"It could be."

"But I'm beginning to think it might not be."

Peter sighed. "Why?"

"The writer was killed by poisoning. It looks like he had been given this poison a few times, but the dosage at the writers' group was high, and it killed him then and there. Why he was killed, I don't know yet. He may have been unpopular amongst the group, but you'd have to be a whole new level of unpopular to be murdered like that."

"Okay."

"His poisoning seemed to be done over time. There was evidence to show he had it in his system longer than just that night. All it took was another dose for him to die. Joseph tells me he went to make a drink and left them unattended, just as someone he couldn't make out came into the kitchen. He then tells me that the person in the kitchen disappeared and did not come and join the writers' group. To have access to Joseph's home tells me that they would have been at the house regularly."

"One of the writers."

"Yes."

"One of the writers that knew your mother."

"Yes."

"One of the writers that probably became good friends with your mother."

"Exactly."

"But that doesn't explain why she was killed."

"No, it doesn't," Jordan agreed. "But there's a connection. I'm sure of it. Dad, can you remember her saying who was coming over? Can you remember her talking about new friends?"

"No, Jordan, I can't. I didn't even know she joined a writers' group. After she left, she led a solitary life. I knew she wrote, but I didn't think she was taking it so seriously as to join a group."

"But she definitely told you she had someone coming over that evening of her death?"

"Yes."

Jordan made a note in his head: find out what time his mother died. "What time did she tell you this?"

"God, Jord…"

"Think."

Peter rubbed his eyes. "I don't know. About...uh, seven? Maybe a bit later. Wait. *Emmerdale* was on."

Jordan almost smiled. His dad had always been a big fan of *Emmerdale*. His religious watching of the soap had finally proven useful. "Seven it is, then."

"So her friend came around then. And then I found her the next day."

"How?"

"I went over and didn't get an answer. So I went around the back door and saw her lying there in the armchair."

"Like she was asleep."

"Like she was asleep."

"Okay."

"Is that what you wanted to tell me? That your mother could be involved in a murder?"

"She could be," Jordan said. "Don't go thinking she definitely was. It could just be a coincidence."

"A very big coincidence."

"Yeah." Jordan shifted in his seat. "James Fairview was an aggravating man. People left because of him. According to one of the writers, that is why Mum left. The image shows how much she despised him, if she is glaring into the back of his head."

"It could just be a perfect capture," Peter mused.

"A pretty good catch, if it was."

"She looked at me like that a few times near the end of our marriage."

Jordan felt a pang in his chest. "I'm sorry, Dad."

"Don't be. You've got nothing to be sorry for."

"If I had known how much stress you were both under..."

"It's nothing like that. Your mother didn't love me. She wanted her own life and she got it." Peter swallowed, composing himself. "She got it, and look where she ended up."

Tangled up in a murder case, that's where.

SIXTEEN

Jordan stood outside the Lower New Inn with a burning cigarette in his hand. He did not smoke, but he wanted to observe the pub. He was opposite it, leaning against a wall as the barman through the window went about his job. He was wiping down the bar, stopping every now and then to serve a drink. People came and went, some on their own and others chatting. He pictured the CCTV footage, and in his head, James and Margaret left. He spotted the camera that had been on them outside.

The cigarette he held was a decoy. It was something for him to do whilst he made mental notes. He tried to imagine what James and Margaret had done afterwards. James had lived not far from here, as this pub was his local. Margaret had probably gone home with him that night. Had she planned to kill him then?

Yet Jordan didn't know if Margaret was the killer. Kim had been involved and had left out some valuable information when questioned. The barman looked up, out of the window, his gaze falling on him. Jordan stared back, putting the cigarette to his lips. The young barman looked away.

His pitiful cover blown, Jordan stubbed out the cigarette and crossed the street. He pulled his long, draped black coat around him and entered the pub. There were considerably more people in here today. The necessities of family time yesterday were now gone. People were getting back to what they were comfortable with: their own time in a pub.

The barman looked at him as he came in. It was his job to clock people, to see who entered and who left. It was a good skill to have. Maybe one day he would be a detective.

Jordan walked to the bar and smiled. "Is Dylan about?"

He looked him up and down. He must have been late teens, probably nineteen, with pimples up his neck and a few on his chin. His hair was tangled and in need of cutting.

"What's the name?"

"PI Jordan Jenner."

His eyes widened. He had been briefed on his arrival. "I'll get him now."

The young man left, walking past an older man that shouted after him for another pint. He ignored him and disappeared out back. The man muttered about poor service, and Jordan avoided talking to him, in no desire to chat to a drunk about the supposed poor service of this place. The Lower New Inn had a ceiling that was made to look like an original feature, wooden beams seemingly supporting it in place. But judging by the fresh paint and the new slate tiles on the floor, Jordan's scepticism kicked in. The pub was warm, a nice place to have as a local.

A few moments later, the pair came out.

"You want to have a word with your barman, Dylan!" the old man hissed.

"Pipe down, Amos."

Amos seemed stunned. The barman uncomfortable. Dylan was unfazed.

"You go out back with this young man. I'll take over for a while. Take as long as you need."

Jordan nodded and walked past Amos, who looked him up and down, and went behind the bar.

Jordan stood in the hallway he had been in with Dylan. The young man pointed him into a small storage room that looked like Dylan's office. CCTV monitors hung against the wall.

"I'm Kyle," the barman said. "Dylan told me what you're here for, and I'm not one hundred percent sure how I'm going to help you yet."

"Don't worry about that right now. I'm just here to chat, ask a few questions. There are no right or wrong answers."

Kyle seemed placated by this. He visibly relaxed, his arms uncrossing. He pulled out a chair for Jordan to sit on and then perched on the end of the office table. Jordan saw a Liverpool FC calendar hung up on the wall behind him. On the table, there were Liverpool FC coasters. An old mug of tea sat on it. Jordan took out his phone and pressed record.

"You served James Fairview."

"I serve a lot of people," Kyle replied. Jordan said nothing, waiting for him to speak again. Keeping mute got people talking. "But yes, I served him the night he came in."

"What did he have?"

"Didn't you see that on the CCTV footage?" Kyle asked. Again, Jordan kept quiet. "He had a San Miguel, I believe. I don't know. I serve a lot of people."

Jordan nodded stiffly. "And who was he with?"

"A woman. Older woman…not sure what they were, you know, if they were together that way or not. They were just…together."

"And did you see him talk to anyone else?"

"How could I? I wasn't keeping tabs on the man. I forgot about him until he spewed everywhere and I had to clean it up after he had left."

A glass smashed out in the bar, and people chorused. Kyle looked at the door.

"That can wait."

He nodded. "Yeah."

"Did you serve the older woman?"

"No."

"But she had a drink."

"I didn't serve her," Kyle said. "But I did speak to her."

Jordan eyed the recording. "You did?"

"Yeah. She came up to me earlier that night. Said her friend only drank from one glass."

"You said you didn't know if they were just friends or not."

"Yes."

"But she said her friend?"

"I didn't take that literally." Kyle narrowed his eyes.

"Okay."

Kyle crossed his arms again. "She told me he only drank from one glass, and she gave it to me."

"She gave you a glass?"

"Yeah."

"It wasn't one from the bar?"

"No."

"But you served his drink in it?"

"Yes," Kyle said.

"Why?"

"Because we get fussy people in here, and you quickly learn to just do what they say, otherwise they argue at you. I'm not here to be shouted at. I'm here to earn some money and get the shift over as soon as possible." Kyle eyed the tape recorder. "Will Dylan hear that?"

"No. This is just for me."

"Okay." Kyle breathed. "He's pretty good, but yeah…"

"What glass was it?"

"It was a Guinness glass. She took it out from the bag she had. Told me to put it aside, and when he came up to order, he had to be served with that glass."

"How did you know who the guy was?" Jordan asked.

"She pointed him out. He was stood chatting at the door to a woman."

"A woman?"

"Yeah. Short-ish woman, black hair."

Kim immediately came to mind. "And how long was he chatting to this woman?"

"I don't know. Like I said, he was just another punter. I didn't keep tabs on him. I just put the glass on the back bar, told the people I was working with that the man by the door would order and wanted it in that glass, and then went to serve someone else. It just happened to be by chance that I served him when he came to the bar. I was free and my colleague wasn't."

"Did that glass move from where you put it?"

"No. It was where I left it." Kyle's eyebrow was arched. "Why?"

"Just a question."

Kyle didn't seem satisfied. "He was then throwing up. Stumbled a bit, but didn't seem all that drunk. It was odd. I thought he might have the flu, or something like that."

"And did he leave quietly?"

"No. He was shouting that he'd only had one and to ask the barman to prove it. The bouncer saw him as a disturbance so threw him out, along with the lady."

"Did you see them again?"

"The woman came back."

"That night?"

"No. The next morning."

Jordan looked Kyle in the eyes. "Why?"

"Said she wanted to collect his glass. I was working, so I gave it to her. It had been in the wash."

"What washers do you have?"

"Dishwashers. We don't wash by hand. We're not allowed to."

"Understand," Jordan said. "And she took the glass and left?"

"She did."

"How did she look the next morning?"

"Pissed off, but I guess you would be if you'd been thrown out and caused an embarrassing scene," Kyle said.

Jordan agreed. "Well, I think that is all I need to know."

"I hope I've helped."

"Yes, I think you have."

As Jordan left the pub, he saw a hooded figure stood at his car. The person was lifting up his windscreen wiper, a note in their hand.

"Oi!" Jordan bellowed.

The person jumped. The windscreen wiper jutted up in the air. Jordan began to advance on his car and the person, who quickly scarpered, running away from the pub and Jordan.

The person's trainers slapped the ground as they pounded away from him, but Jordan felt himself spurred on. He needed to know who was leaving those notes to him.

The person turned a corner and ran down a residential street. The person was a male, yet Jordan couldn't place in his mind which one of the writers it could be. A car beeped its horn as the man ran out into the road. The man panicked, pausing ever so slightly, enough time for Jordan to gain on him.

With arms outstretched, Jordan grabbed the man, and with strength he didn't know he had, he pushed the man onto the bonnet of the car. The engine underneath him ticked over, a heat rising up into Jordan's face. The horn continued to blare, but Jordan didn't even look at the driver of the vehicle.

The man he held was a young boy, probably in his early teens. He looked frozen, his eyes wide, freckles over his face. "Get off me, mate! Get off me!"

"What were you doing at my car?"

"I don't know!"

Jordan shook him, and the engine turned off.

"I don't know! Honestly! Some woman paid me fifty quid to leave a note on your car. I was just doing a job!"

"What's going on?" It was a man's voice. Jordan looked up to see the driver of the car had gotten out.

Jordan realised he was gripping a minor by the collar. He stood back, letting go of the youth. Before Jordan could ask any more questions, the youth ran, not bothering to look back, the note still clasped in his hands.

"Did he take something from you?"

Jordan blinked, wondering what had happened. "Yeah. Yeah, something like that."

The boy disappeared around the corner, fifty pounds richer and the note still in his hands, never to be read by the right recipient.

SEVENTEEN

"And what are the chances that the glass in question will still be out there as evidence?" Vanessa asked.

Jordan sat with Vanessa in her office. He had just played Kyle's interview for her. "That's what I thought. It's odd that Margaret handed a glass over and then came back the next morning to get it."

"It's possible it was laced with poison."

"Yes, it is."

"But like you say, Margaret took it back. That suggests to me she was cutting off any loose ends."

"Exactly."

"Do you think she did it?"

"It's too early to tell, but she's involved and a key suspect," Jordan replied. "Kim was involved too."

"Did you get that impression from her interview?"

"No. In fact, in her interview, I thought she was innocent. She seemed to just dislike the man, not hate him enough to kill him. But there is CCTV footage from that night in the pub, and Margaret and Kim exchange something. Kim told me they hadn't talked that night and that Kim hadn't realised Margaret was with James."

"I've been to the Lower New Inn," Vanessa said. "It's hard to miss anyone in there."

"Yeah, it's not the largest."

"So, are you going to question Kim again?"

"Yes."

"And what was on the CCTV footage?"

"Kim and Margaret met upstairs. They shook hands, and something was in Kim's hand and given to Margaret. I don't know what it was."

"Before or after Margaret had given the glass to the barman?"

"After." Jordan recalled James sitting at the table with his glass.

68

"Interesting," Vanessa mused. "And it was exchanged through a handshake?"

"Yes."

"The poison, maybe?"

"Speculation."

"Yes," Vanessa said. "Or money."

"Like the money she gave that bloke."

"You let him go?"

"He was just a kid." Jordan shrugged. "I have a job for you."

Vanessa grinned. "Okay. What is it?"

"Find out what time my mother died."

"Jordan…"

"It's relevant. I swear. Just find out what time my mother died, please."

Vanessa gave Jordan a look of pity. "Why don't you know it? Weren't you told?"

"I asked not to be told."

Vanessa sighed. "I'll find out for you."

"Thanks."

"Jordan, can I offer you advice?"

"Go ahead."

"Focus on this case."

"That's what I'm doing."

Vanessa pulled out a drawer from underneath her table and slid across a doctor's form to Jordan. At first, he was confused, wondering what Vanessa was trying to tell him. Then, Jordan saw Joseph's name.

"Ha."

"He wasn't lying."

Jordan could see that. The doctor's note from a surgery in Cardiff proved that Joseph did in fact have myopia.

* * *

Jordan hung up his phone after the fourth unsuccessful attempt at getting hold of Kim. It seemed she was avoiding his phone calls. Jordan decided that the best thing to do was travel to Kim's house and question her about the CCTV footage. The woman was up to something and had been avoiding the truth. Was it possible she had paid the youth to leave a note on his car? Was she following him, trying to warn him away? Jordan needed to find out.

He walked down Queen Street in Cardiff, past large shopping malls and retail premises that raked in the cash. HMV looked busy, which Jordan found comfort in. The street was full of people flitting between shops, talking to one another, and catching up before New Year's. Christmas lights still twinkled above them, and every now and then, Jordan caught melodies of overplayed Christmas songs coming from retail stores.

He needed to kill time, work out what he had seen and what he was going to say to Kim now. Christmas Day with her had seemed calm. She had seemed to open up and tell him everything she could possibly know. Now, he needed true answers. Walking busy Cardiff at the Christmas season should have infuriated him, but now he let himself get lost in the crowds and in the noise.

He got into St David's 2 shopping centre and stepped on the escalator. He came to the top floor by Starbucks. He ignored the urge to get a latte and continued towards the car park, smelling the aromas of the food court that drew people in.

He spotted someone reading *The Guardian* on one of the shopping mall benches. On the front page, Joseph was looking back at him. The headline was about how the author had been stripped of his Costa Coffee book win. Jordan thought that a little harsh: the man was innocent, after all. He was interested and made a note to find out more later, though he scarcely had time for newspapers.

He got in the lift, along with too many others, and rode to the sixth floor. He awkwardly made his way out, pushing through three women who wouldn't move, and paid his parking ticket. He got in his car and made his way to Trevethin.

An hour later, he was outside Kim's house. There were no lights on and the curtains were drawn, but that didn't mean there wasn't anyone inside. Jordan parked his car, walked to the house, and knocked twice on the door.

No answer.

He tried again and still nothing.

He bent down and peered through the letterbox.

The house was empty. No coats on the bannister. No table in the hallway. No shoes on the floor. Jordan tried the door handle, and to his surprise, it opened.

Jordan walked into the home and shut the door behind him. The hall was silent. There wasn't even the hum of heating. The house seemed barren, unwelcoming, and if it could speak, Jordan would expect it to shout at him to leave.

He went into the living room where the dinner table and the television had been, only to find all of that was gone.

In the kitchen, all the plates gone; the cupboard doors purposefully left open to show there was nothing inside.

Upstairs was much the same. There were no bathroom necessities, no beds, and no chargers for technology.

Kim had vacated the premises.

Jordan dialled Vanessa. She picked up on the third ring. "Kim has gone."

"What do you mean?"

"The house is empty. The door was left unlocked. Kim's disappeared."

"Shit," Vanessa said.

"Get someone on the tracking of her. Disappearing does not help her innocence. I need to find Margaret and ask her about that night and her relationship with James."

"Don't accept a drink from her."

"I won't." Jordan chuckled.

Not only had Kim disappeared, but so had Joseph. Had the pair gone together, or was Joseph now in his home? Then Jordan had a thought: was it possible that Kim had moved in with Joseph?

Jordan gave one last look at the empty bedroom, bathroom, and hallway, before heading back downstairs. The house was cold. There was no telling how soon Kim had vacated the house after their meeting on Christmas Day.

Jordan exited the house and was halfway off the premises when a man called. "Oi!"

He turned around, ready for an argument. The man was stood in the garden of the house next door, leaning against the fence. "Can I help you?"

He was tall and slim, with no hair. He wore glasses that looked like they were from the sixties, had a slim moustache, and his one hand was in his pocket. The other hand, holding the fence, had a wedding ring on his finger.

"I just came by to see if my friend was in. There was no answer."

"What were you doing inside, then?"

"She always left the door unlocked, so I thought she might be in. She wasn't, so I left."

"Your friend?"

"My friend."

"Your friend hasn't lived in that house for six months now."

Jordan thought he had misheard him. A car went roaring past, the exhaust blown, so he stepped forward. "Sorry?"

"Your friend? The woman who used to live in this house. Didn't see much of her, really. No husband, as far as I know. Kept to herself. Yeah, she moved out six months ago now, maybe seven."

"Oh."

"You fell out?"

"Excuse me?"

"Well, if you didn't know she had moved home, then she must have fallen out with you."

"Oh right. Yeah, you're right."

"Yeah," the man said. "I'm not sure where she went, but the internet these days can lead you to anybody."

"So she left six, seven months ago?"

"Been empty ever since."

Jordan looked at the house, in disbelief, as if Christmas Day had all just been imagination. "I see."

"Sorry I can't be much help."

"You've helped enough." Jordan turned, not wanting to talk to the man any longer. How had Kim left the house unnoticed? How had she gotten the keys for a house she hadn't actually lived in?

Jordan sat in his car and stared out the window, lost in thought. Someone he thought was innocent now seemed to be a culprit.

EIGHTEEN

Jordan pulled up outside the gates of Joseph's street. He drove slowly to the entrance and keyed in the code that had been relayed to him by the police officers the last time he had been here. With a satisfactory click, the gates began to swing open, and when it was safe to do so, Jordan drove in.

He cruised down the street that was full of expensive cars and came to a stop three houses away from Joseph's. He wondered if he was in there now and if Kim was with him too.

He got out of his car and shut the door as quietly as possible, aware that a slamming noise might alert the nosy rich neighbours. He walked across the street, checking that there were no cars heading towards him, and then stood outside Joseph's door. The last time he had been here, there had been a dead man lying at a table in the drawing room. Now, all that was left was a memory.

Jordan took a deep breath and rang the doorbell. For good measure, he knocked. He waited, and with a flip of his heart, he exhaled when the hallway light switched on. The door, with one pane of frosted glass, began to open. Stood on the other side was a woman who Jordan recognised as Margaret.

Jordan composed himself. "Hi."

"Can I help you?"

"I'm here to see Joseph."

"Who are you?"

"I'm..."

But before he could say any more, footsteps sounded behind Margaret and Joseph appeared behind her.

He was wearing glasses, and he smiled when he saw Jordan. "Jordan. You keep showing up wherever I am. Can I help you?"

"I..." Jordan was surprised to see him. If he was here, did that mean Kim was too?

"You know him?" Margaret questioned. She had a tight voice that seemed strained. She appeared older than her age. The photograph Jordan had of her didn't quite match up to the woman in front of him, yet he knew it was Margaret by the tatty going-white hair.

"This is Jordan Jenner," Joseph said, a slight air of shock to his words, as if he couldn't believe people would not know who he was. "Private investigator Jordan Jenner. He's investigating the death of James."

Jordan's gaze slid to Margaret to read her reaction, her expressions. There was nothing. A blank poker face except for a tongue that licked chapped lips.

"I see," Margaret said. "Would you like a tea, love?"

"I'm okay actually. I've come to see Joseph, so if I could just speak with him…"

"Can you make it quick, lovely, as we are organising our writers meeting?"

Jordan was shocked. "You are?"

"Why yes, of course. A death does not stop the pen," Margaret snapped. "Hurry up, now."

She turned and left Joseph stood at his door. He smiled at him, amused. "She's like that. As the vice chair of this group, she sure does think a lot of herself."

"Is she published?"

"Not quite," Joseph replied. "Though I believe she is close. Which is why she is vice chair. You don't have to be published to have a say here."

"Can we talk?"

"Here?"

"Not where I could be heard. You've got a big house. I assume you have room?"

"Yes," Joseph replied. "Come inside and follow me."

Jordan did as he was told. The door shut behind him, and Joseph guided him past the room where James had died and into a small office room where three bookshelves were full of well-read books and an old coffee mug sat on a glass table.

"This is where you write?"

"Yes, sometimes," Joseph replied. "Can I ask why you are here?"

"Well…"

"Is it about me losing my title at the Costa Book Prize?" Joseph questioned. "Because I can assure you, I'm not that bothered."

"Why would I be here about that?"

"Seems everyone is questioning me about this today. I've had phone calls coming through from reporters. I've had to unplug my phone."

"I see."

"It's okay, though. That award means nothing. I'm a better writer than awards."

"I'm sure you are," Jordan replied. Margaret walked past outside, but he was certain she had stopped just outside their door to listen. "I'm here to talk about Kim. Are you sure we have complete privacy?"

Before Joseph could reply, Margaret's footsteps started again, walking further away.

"Yes, I'm sure." Joseph grinned. "Kim. What about her?"

"I went to her house again."

"Right."

"It's empty."

"It's...what?"

"Empty, Joseph," Jordan replied. "Looks like no one has lived there for a while. Unless I was high, I'd say you were there just a few days ago."

"That's right."

"So, where has she gone? With all that furniture and all of her belongings?"

"I...I'm not sure," Joseph began. "She's definitely gone?"

"The house was empty."

"Wow."

"Had you been to that house before?"

"No."

"Had you been to a house she lived in before?"

"No, I never saw her in a personal setting," Joseph said. "Only when we went out to the odd writers' group party. That sort of thing. But I never saw where she lived, though I know she lived in Blaenavon. But then she moved, but where, I didn't know."

"Trevethin."

"Trevethin. So we thought."

"How did you end up at hers?"

"She told me she was free to house me whilst the media attention died down. Nobody else came to help, so I took her up on the offer."

"And when did you leave?"

"Two days ago?"

"Why?"

"Her mood got worse. She didn't seem to like having me around," Joseph said. "She kept getting annoyed because I wasn't finishing drinks she made me, or food, and so she thought I was wasting her resources and taking advantage. She told me that it was only supposed to be temporary, and that I should leave."

"What was supposed to be temporary?" Jordan asked.

"Me staying with her," Joseph replied. "Although now I wonder if there was something more there."

"Yes. Maybe that house was only temporary. Something for show?"

"Why would she put in all that effort?"

"I don't know. It seems odd. But odder things have happened. When you left, did she say she would be in touch?"

"I told her I was working on getting the writers' group back up and running. She said she would be waiting."

"Okay," Jordan said. "Right. So that was it?"

"That was it."

"What did you think of the house?"

"I thought it was a little bare, but I didn't suspect she didn't actually live there. Why would I? There was electricity, TV, heating..."

"Yes. I didn't suspect anything, either."

"I didn't go in any of the bedrooms," Joseph said. "Maybe they were empty."

"But you went upstairs?"

"Only for the bathroom."

Jordan was satisfied with this. He thought of Kim's house again, run-down and well lived-in, but not necessarily by the woman herself. "I suppose I will have to try and contact her myself."

"You can try."

"In the meantime, will you let me know if she gets in touch with you? At the moment, she seems to have disappeared off the face of the earth."

"Of course. I'll let you know if I hear anything."

Jordan stood up. A creak sounded behind the closed door, and he paused. "I wonder if Margaret will speak to me." His voice had raised just enough to let Margaret know he was aware that she had been listening, yet the door didn't open.

"You want to speak to Margaret?"

"She might know something leading up to James's death."

"I'm not sure she will, but we can see," Joseph said. He walked to the door and opened it. Margaret hovered a few feet away from the door, pretending she had been caught midwalk.

"All done?" she barked, peering into the room at Jordan.

"Actually, I'd like to speak to you," Jordan said.

Margaret's gaze darted from Joseph to Jordan. "Why me?"

"It is procedure," Jordan replied.

Margaret sighed. "Fine. In here alright?" She pointed towards the kitchen, the place Joseph had seen the figure.

"I'll be in the dining room if you need me," Joseph said.

The dining room where James had died.

NINETEEN

Jordan followed Margaret into Joseph's kitchen. The window looked out onto a secluded garden, with a pathway leading down to a gate. Trees grew around the house, and rose bushes hid the other neighbours. It had a sense of privacy. Jordan noted that on the night of James's murder, it would have been easy for someone to slip in unnoticed.

"Can I make you a drink, love?"

"No, I'm okay."

Margaret huffed and sat at the marble-topped kitchen table. Jordan took a seat opposite.

"I didn't think we'd meet so soon, but best to meet now rather than never, isn't it?"

"If you say so. I'm quite busy, so can we make this quick?"

Jordan was used to rude people, quick to leave his company. He didn't take it personally like he used to do. "It will take as long as I need."

"Right." Margaret huffed again. "So, is this about that James?"

"Who else would it be about?"

"I don't know."

"Yes, it's about James. How well did you know him?"

"Not that well."

"But well enough to drink with him in the Lower New Inn?"

Margaret visibly paled. She swallowed, her tough exterior denting. "I didn't dislike him as much as the others. We had a common ground, though we didn't get along."

"And what was that common ground?"

"It doesn't matter."

"In a murder investigation, I'd say it does."

Margaret glared at Jordan. "Fine. We didn't like the same people in the group. We bemoaned how the writing industry wasn't giving us our big breaks. We bonded on bitterness."

"And was James a bitter man?"

"He was more than just a bitter man. He was a narcissist. A cretin. A sleaze. He wanted all women's attention and snapped when he didn't get it."

"Were you woman attention?"

"How dare you."

Jordan took a different tact. "Just a friend?"

"Barely a friend," Margaret hissed. "I kept him on my side because he was an enemy. I wanted to keep an eye on what he was up to, what he was doing, that sort of thing."

"Such as?"

"The man seemed to get writing opportunities left, right, and centre, yet he always complained about writer's block. He kept coming to the group for inspiration, so he called it, but he never got it."

"Maybe he didn't really have writer's block."

"I don't know, love. Any writing exercises we did had him churning out complete crap."

Jordan nodded slowly. "And what opportunities was he getting?"

"Said he had commissions in place. Was on the cusp of something great. I don't know. He was always blabbing."

Jordan remembered Mark's words, remembering the possibility of James talking with publishers. "Was he on the cusp of something great before he died?"

"He was always saying to watch this space." Margaret's eyes rolled. "He made out there was always something around the corner. Nothing ever came of it."

"But specifically, before his death, was there anything?"

"Yes. He said he had something huge about to be announced. Wouldn't tell any of us what it was."

"So you don't know?"

"No."

Jordan let the silence draw out between them. Joseph dropped something in the room down the hall. "Tell me about that night."

"Which night?"

"In the pub?"

"I don't know what happened. He barely finished his first drink and then he was stumbling all over the place."

"You took a glass to the bar and told the barman it was for James?"

Margaret blinked. "I did."

"Why?"

"Because he liked to drink from the same glass."

"He had a different glass the night he died."

"When we went to public places, he wanted the same glass."

"Only public places?"

"Only public places."

"So, to know this, you must have gone to public places with him often?"

Margaret seemed to have been caught out. She swallowed again. "Yes. Like I say, we bonded over hatred. Nothing more."

"So there was a bond there?"

"Enough of one to spend time with him."

"The barman remarks that the two of you looked like an item."

"The barman is a gossip," Margaret dismissed. "Because any man and a woman at a pub would look like an item. It's not hard for someone to make assumptions."

"True," Jordan agreed. "Did you see anyone else that night?"

"Such as?"

"Anyone you knew?"

"No."

Jordan decided to leave Kim out of it for now. Margaret seemed to be bristling under the questions.

"Leading up to James's death, how was his health?"

Margaret thought for a moment, as if she was censoring what to say. "He always had periodically low moments. I thought he was depressed, or maybe even bipolar. He'd be king of the world, and then he'd crumble. Something would push him off the pin, and he'd be gone for a few days. He missed one or two meetings here, and it wasn't unusual for him to just…disappear." Margaret swallowed. "In the few weeks before his death, he was optimistic and kept saying about a big break he was about to get. But every now and then, he would be evasive, wouldn't answer questions that seemed too personal, and his sobriety became a problem."

"Do you know how he died?"

Margaret nodded. "We heard he was poisoned."

"Yes. It was a high dosage of the poison used in antifreeze. He had probably been consuming it for a few weeks."

Margaret remained evasive, though Jordan thought the news wasn't new to her. As far as Jordan knew, the police hadn't released this information, and the press hadn't leaked it.

"Could that have contributed to his behaviour leading up to his death?"

"Possibly. It could also have contributed to how he behaved that night when he was with you. It can make people disorientated."

"I see."

"Was James on his own at all that night?"

"Uh…I suppose. When I went to the bar or to the toilet."

When you met Kim. "Do you know if his glass was left unattended at any point?"

"I couldn't possibly."

"The barman said the glass was taken back home the next day. Seems odd for someone to come and collect that glass again, doesn't it?"

Margaret's eyes narrowed again. She puffed up, an animal ready to fight. "That was me, and you must know that."

"Tell me more."

"I came to collect the glass because it belonged to James. I stayed the night at his. I always took that glass home with me, because it was his. That isn't suspicious."

"I never said it was."

"Then why is it important?"

"Everything is important."

Margaret seemed to growl. She got off her seat and stood up. She was not much taller standing than sitting, so her attempt at imposing authority was not effective.

"I've had enough of this. You're leading nowhere. James is dead, and it's your job to find out who killed him."

"And that's exactly what I'm doing."

"I think you should leave."

"I haven't finished my…"

Margaret swiped her hand at a glass on the countertop. It slid across the marble and shattered on the ground. "Leave!"

Margaret glared at him, her nose flared, her breathing heavy. Her hands gripped the table, but they didn't shake. She seemed composed, despite the rage burning into him.

Joseph hurried out of his room and down the hallway as fast as he could. "What's going on in here?"

"This man is a joke. I've wasted enough time. Get him out of my sight."

Jordan stood up, keeping himself composed. "Well, cut short, but enough for now. I'll be back."

Joseph watched in awe as Jordan glided past Margaret and let himself out of the front door.

Margaret was hiding something. She knew more than she was letting on. What that was, Jordan would still need to find out.

TWENTY

When Jordan parked up outside his apartment that night, he was surprised to see a figure huddling in his doorway. The person, a man, was tall. He had a black coat wrapped around him, and he was hiding his face in his scarf, trying to ignore the bitter cold winds of New Year's. Jordan had a horrible feeling that Arthur had returned.

Jordan turned his car off and got out, then locked it behind him. He walked slowly to the door, his focus on the figure. This man could be anyone. He would need to be cautious.

He crunched over glass left behind from smashed bottles and cursed under his breath as a car beeped in the street on the other side of his building. The figure shifted, looking up at him.

Jordan relaxed. It was Lloyd Hutchings, the coroner he had talked to just a few days before.

"Lloyd. What are you doing outside my flat?"

"I…" Lloyd began, but he stopped. "Uh…"

Jordan cocked his head to the side. "Lloyd?"

"I just needed to come and ask you if you wanted to go out on a date."

"Sorry?"

"A date."

"At quarter to eight in the night?"

"Well, I've been here a little longer than that."

"You must be freezing."

"Every part of me is freezing, if I'm honest."

"You idiot," Jordan said. "Come on, come inside and get warm." Jordan walked to his door and reached to open it, but paused and turned back to Lloyd. "That's not an acceptance of a date, by the way."

"Just get me in somewhere warm."

They headed into the hallway and took a lift to the second floor. Lloyd was huffing as he went, trying to warm up, his hands rubbing together.

"I spoke to Vanessa." Lloyd said

"About what?"

"She thinks you might need a friend."

Jordan rolled his eyes. "So you came to ask me for a date instead of being a friend?"

"Hey, I don't want to be friend-zoned."

Jordan wished he had cleaned up. He wished he could be the type of man to appear to have everything together. He longed for a gorgeous apartment that was full of designer clothes, a great interior design completed by a top-rated professional, casual warmth that was achieved just by being content. Instead, there was darkness, shoes across the floor, and a chill in the air from a lack of heating.

"Sorry about…" Jordan began, but he didn't finish.

"Should see my place. It's a lot messier than this."

Jordan switched on the hallway light and hung his coat up on the rack on the wall. He pointed to the door at the end of the hall, opposite his bedroom. "Living room and kitchen is that way. Head in, and I can make us some soup or something."

"This is sounding like a date."

"Shut up!"

Lloyd headed down the hallway and began to open the door of the bedroom.

Jordan shrieked. "The other door!"

"Sorry!"

With embarrassment, Lloyd quickly closed the door and headed in to the living room. Jordan remembered he had left out two old coffee cups, and the coffee table was full of plates from days gone by and empty crisp packets. He hurried into the room and saw Lloyd sitting opposite the desk.

He looked from the table to him. "You're a monster."

"I'm not!"

"I'm joking. Remember? Mine's worse."

"I don't believe you, but thanks. Tea?"

"Two sugars."

"Gross."

Jordan busied himself making the tea. He let the kettle begin to boil, enjoying the rush of sound that filled his apartment. A quick look at his phone told him there was another email about the money-laundering case. He dismissed it again. He rooted in the cupboard and found two tins of tomato soup that had been there so long he forgot how long ago he had bought them. He emptied them into bowls and put one in the microwave.

"You microwave your soup?"

"Yeah…"

"Why?"

"Well, what else am I supposed to do?"

"The stove!" Lloyd exclaimed.

"No one has time for the stove." As the soup twirled in the microwave and the kettle boiled, Jordan stepped closer to the living room. "Lloyd, why are you here? Seriously?"

"For a date."

"Come on."

Lloyd sighed. "Fine. I'm here to warm up, that's one thing, but also because I worry about you."

This surprised Jordan. They'd only spoke a handful of times, and most of those times Lloyd had flirted with him and shrugged off each time he said no to a date. The man wasn't creepy; in fact, he wasn't even disrespectful. It was a game that had become a parody of itself. They both knew nothing could happen. Despite only talking a handful of times, Jordan felt like he knew Lloyd well enough. He understood his interests, and had only recently begun to understand his humour.

"Worried?"

"Yeah. You've been working too much."

"Too much?" Jordan scoffed. "Not really. There's a case that needs solving. Besides, if you know I'm working too much, that means you are too."

"But you don't spare any time. Vanessa was telling me you're out at all hours trying to interview suspects and piece together the murder. It's almost New Year's, hell, we've just had Christmas. You're supposed to be lazy."

"I hate them both." Jordan shrugged.

"No, you don't. Come on, Jordan. There are people around you wanting to get close, wanting to get to know you, but you're not letting anyone in."

Jordan almost laughed. "I've already told you, we're not dating."

Lloyd grinned, shaking his head. "That isn't what I'm getting at. I worry about you because your mum's death must have affected you badly, and you're at work too soon…"

"That's none of your business." The smile had gone from Jordan's lips.

Lloyd seemed to sense he might have gone too far. "I only say this because when my dad died, I took off a good amount of time."

"That's good for you. We all grieve differently."

"And are you still grieving?"

The kettle boiled. Jordan flinched. "Of course I'm still grieving."

"Vanessa is worried your perception is…warped."

Jordan laughed, yet the situation wasn't funny. "Tell me how?"

Lloyd shifted where he was sat. "Apparently, you asked her for your mother's time of death?"

Jordan turned to the kitchen again and took out two mugs. He dropped two teabags in them and poured in the water. "I did."

"Why?"

"It's none of your business."

"Well, I've got that information for you, if you really want it."

Jordan looked at Lloyd, his heart beating. "What time?"

"Seven eighteen," Lloyd replied. "In the evening."

Jordan glanced around for a notepad, a pen. He opened drawers until he found the small notepad he kept in the kitchen. He jotted the number down, fresh ink drying, reminding him of the time he shouldn't forget.

Jordan finished the teas, his attention lingering for just a moment on the time of his mother's death, and then he headed to the living room. He placed the teas down just as the first soup pinged in the microwave.

He got the bowl out by wrapping his hands with a tea towel and placed it in front of Lloyd. Forgetting about his own cold soup, he sat down, lifting the mug of tea to his lips.

After drinking, he sighed. "Thanks for letting me know."

"Why is that important?"

"I needed to know."

"But can't you see why people are worried? You're supposed to be investigating something else. You keep going back to your mother."

"It might be linked."

"Really?"

Disbelief was evident in Lloyd's voice. "Yes, really. It could be linked. That's why I'm investigating."

"Jordan, if you need any help with dealing with your mum, I can point you in the right direction…"

"I'm fine. If you've just come here at non-working hours to lecture me on my dead mother, then I'm afraid to say you're weirder than I thought."

Lloyd sighed. He shook his head. "I've just come to be a friend. You could do with one."

Jordan drank again. "Shouldn't you be out being a young lad? You must have friends? You should be getting a few pints, having a good time. You've got the world ahead of you."

"But I don't want to do that. And besides, you should be doing that too."

"I'm busy with more important things."

"What? And I'm not?"

Jordan sighed. "I'm sure you are. But I'm not interfering in your decisions so please leave mine out of it. It doesn't concern you."

Lloyd shook his head. "Vanessa said to me that you're a man that doesn't have many friends, and now I know why."

Jordan shook his head. How dare Lloyd appear at his flat and then insult him. He didn't like the direction this conversation was taking. "Why would Vanessa say that?"

"Like I said, I mentioned to her that I was worried about you. We got talking."

Jordan's anger felt warmer than the mug of tea in his hands. He glared at the surface of the liquid, as if it would set alight. "She's been gossiping about me?"

"Not gossiping," Lloyd quickly said. "She just mentioned that when people get close, you push them away."

"She's wrong. She doesn't know me as well as she thinks she does."

"Maybe there's a reason for that." Lloyd said. "We know you better than you think we do."

Jordan put down his mug harder than he intended, the tea sploshing out onto his white coffee table. "Please, can you leave?"

"Jordan…"

"Please, Lloyd. I'm tired and I don't want to talk right now."

Lloyd sighed. After a brief pause, he put his half-finished mug down and got up. "I didn't come here to offend you, and I'm not sure how conversation quite turned this way. But…"

"Just go."

Lloyd went to say something else, hovering where he stood, but then he left. He let himself out of the flat and Jordan counted ten seconds before locking the door behind him. As he turned back to his cold, messy, and small apartment, he realised what Lloyd had said held some truth. He had no friends.

TWENTY-ONE

Jordan couldn't sleep. He had been awake into the night, staring up at his ceiling. He got up and decided to go outside. Oscar followed him. Jordan didn't like Oscar being outside. His Persian breed meant he was worth money. But now it was the witching hour, and Jordan didn't mind Oscar being at his side. In fact, he liked the company and feeling as though he had a friend.

He knew Lloyd had a point. He cut himself off. He didn't mean to do it, but it was ingrained in him. He felt at a loss with people, never able to make strong connections. Lloyd's words had stung.

Oscar disappeared, probably finding somewhere private to go to the toilet. Oscar knew not to stray so far from him. It was a mutual understanding the pair had. The bitter cold of New Year chilled his skin. He shivered and wished for Oscar to come back.

When Oscar didn't return, Jordan started to feel apprehensive. "Oscar!"

He pictured the grey-and-white cat prancing back to him, keen to get back in the warmth. But there was nothing. Jordan walked away from his door, to the corner of an alleyway entrance where he had seen Oscar disappear. Inside the alleyway was old boxes, things left behind by previous souls. He shivered, not ultimately due to the cold, and stepped further into the alley.

He spotted Oscar behind one of these boxes, drinking from a china plate, which seemed out of place in this dingy abode. Jordan got closer and shone his torch light from his phone towards the cat. He was drinking a liquid that was blue.

As if with psychic intuition, Jordan snatched up Oscar and stepped away from the liquid. Oscar purred in his arms, licking his lips. Jordan stared at the liquid, thinking of only one thing.

Antifreeze.

Ethylene Glycol.

As if on cue, his phone buzzed. Oscar licked his lips and turned to the sound. Jordan saw the message on his screen. *Stay out of this. Next time, it will be you.*

Feeling sick and dizzy, Jordan rushed out of the alleyway, daring to look around him. He couldn't see another soul. There were no cars. Everything was still. But someone had watched him. Someone had waited. Someone had been there to send a message.

Jordan hurried back inside, trying to think of what to do. He put Oscar on the floor of the hallway and dialled an emergency vet's number. After being diverted by a prerecorded message, he was put through to somebody in a branch in Ystrad Mynach.

"Hi, it's my cat. He's just drank antifreeze!"

Questions came in a blur. Jordan explained it was recent, that there was time, that he prayed Oscar would be okay. He was told to get there as soon as possible. His car keys already in his pocket after leaving his flat, Jordan hurried back outside, carrying a bemused Oscar, and started his car.

He broke the speed limits. Oscar curled up on the chair next to him, seemingly unfazed to be inside a car that he had never been able to freely roam in before. Jordan took it as a sign that the poison was beginning to take hold of him.

"It's okay, Oscar. We'll be okay!"

Jordan found the surgery and parked his car over two spaces. He picked Oscar up. The cat seemed, to Jordan, to be deflating, and he hurried inside.

He didn't look at the waiting room, instead his attention was on the receptionist. "Please, it's my cat. I rang earlier. Jordan. Jordan Jenner. This is Oscar."

The receptionist was polite. Jordan hated that she didn't seem to have urgency to her. He was crying now, shaking, and Oscar was staring at the ceiling lights.

"Jordan?"

Jordan turned, expecting the worst. Instead, he saw Mark. "Uh…"

"What's going on?"

"Mark?" Jordan blinked away fresh tears. "Oh, it's Oscar."

"Is he okay?"

"Someone…" Jordan swallowed. "Drank antifreeze."

"Anti…" Mark paused. "Jordan?"

Jordan knew he understood. He nodded, about to answer when he noticed that behind Mark was the vet. Mark had been inside the veterinarian's room. He had a red Pomeranian on a lead. The vet saw Oscar and the distraught image of Jordan.

"Is this Oscar?"

"Yes."

Jordan hurried past Mark and his Pomeranian dog and put Oscar on the table. The vet spoke to Oscar, soothing the already placid cat. Jordan stroked Oscar, relishing his warmth, hoping that this wasn't going to be the end. Jordan explained how he found Oscar, how he had got him here, and how Oscar usually was.

The vet turned to his computer. Checks complete. D-Day. "Oscar has come just in time. You must have caught him just as he was starting to drink. We will need to monitor him and take more bloods over time. He may need treatment for any kidney damage which may arise. I will keep him in overnight, but there are no signs of vomiting or shakes, which are signs that it is too late. I will set up an IV line for the little man, and then we will administer the first course of oral medication."

"Is he going to be okay?"

"He's got a high chance of surviving, yes," the vet said. He was a handsome man, tall, broad-shouldered. Jordan only noticed once he realised Oscar had a chance of surviving. "I've seen pets poisoned by the same thing, and I've come to recognise when signs are bad. These signs are good. If the time frame is right…"

"They are. I got here straight away, as soon as I found him. I just…knew."

The vet nodded. "Then he will be okay. We'll keep him in tonight. Sorry to be spending New Year's this way, Oscar."

Oscar let out a yawn.

Jordan left the veterinarian's room, feeling dazed. Mark was still waiting for him. "Is everything okay?"

"The vet said he should be fine. IV treatment, blood tests, oral medication." Jordan exhaled. "I'm dreading the vet bills."

"Out of hours costs more," Mark said, aware he was in earshot of the receptionist.

"What happened to you?" Jordan said, indicating the dog.

"I thought she had broken something." Mark seemed embarrassed. "She woke me up whinging, and she was limping. I brought her here and she seemed fine."

"So she just wanted attention?"

"Expensive attention, yes."

Jordan shook his head. "Listen, Mark, I think they wanted to send a message to me."

"Who?"

"Whoever killed James."

"Why do you say that?"

Jordan showed the text on his phone.

Mark's eyes widened.

"They wanted to kill my cat. How sick is that?"

Mark brought his dog closer, as if to protect her further. "You don't know who that is?"

"The number is withheld," Jordan replied. "It's a do-not-reply number."

Mark looked again. "Do not reply."

"Yeah."

"Weird."

"Someone wants to make sure I stop looking for them."

"Then don't stop," Mark said. "Keep going. And don't let Oscar out of your sight."

* * *

It was New Year's Eve and the morning brought light rain. Jordan travelled to his dad's home in Newport after texting his brother out of formality. Peter had once lived in a grand house behind St Woolos hospital, just up from the city centre. Now, however, he had a one-bedroom flat that had mould growing on the walls.

"Do you have plans for tonight, Jord?"

"I don't," Jordan said. "I'm going to pick up Oscar later."

"Is he okay?"

"Looks like he is out of the woods, thankfully," Jordan said. "The vet is convinced the antifreeze he drank was watered down."

It had been a revelation given to Jordan before he left for his dad's.

"So, no plans other than that?"

"None."

They were sat in his living room, which was clean. A window was open, letting in cold air. The television played a football match recap, and his dad was watching it with mild interest.

"Why not?"

"I don't really feel like celebrating another day."

"When did you become miserable?"

"Well, you're not doing anything, are you?"

"No. But I'm an old man."

"Fifty-eight isn't old, Dad."

"Tell the other people that."

Jordan stared at the TV. He watched overpaid football players running, and when one fell and cried out, he rolled his eyes. "I don't know why you're interested in these things."

"I'm a man. That's what men do."

"Not all men."

His dad smirked. "No. Just the proper men."

"Careful. You almost sound like an outdated Brexiteer."

89

Peter looked at him. "Don't get me started on that debate, young man."

His father had voted leave whilst Jordan had voted remain. It was a common friendly debate between them. That is, when they actually had time to see one another.

"I read about your author in the paper today. It said he's worried about a missing writer."

Jordan cast around for the newspaper. "Where is it?"

"It's in the kitchen," Peter replied, his attention still on the football. "Haven't you heard about it?"

Jordan stood up and walked across the small living room towards the kitchen. "I guess Vanessa didn't think it was important to tell me."

Since his meeting with Lloyd, Jordan had ignored Vanessa. He had received two missed calls and three text messages, but none were returned. Vanessa just "wanted to chat." She didn't have anything new to offer on a case that was beginning to lose traction. As he walked to the kitchen, Jordan's phone buzzed. He ignored it, thinking that it was Vanessa, and found the paper.

A cheer went up from both the TV and his dad as Jordan saw Joseph on the front page. It was a snapshot of him driving into his private street. He was leaning out of a Range Rover, glasses on.

Jordan turned to the story page and saw the headline: *Another Writer Missing: Joseph Gordon Issues Statement.*

Jordan began to read.

Another writer from Joseph Gordon's writing group has suffered a questionable fate. Kim, a writer in her early forties, was last seen with Joseph near Christmas. The writer, who knew murdered James Fairview, reportedly disappeared from her local community four days go. When asked about the disappearance of another writer, Joseph quickly vanished into his house. Within an hour, he came out to give a statement.

Standing on the doorstep of his private home, Joseph invited a Daily Mail *journalist and a* Daily Mirror *journalist to hear what he had to say.*

"Kim was not a good friend of mine, but she was more like an acquaintance. I spent a few days with her after questioning regarding the James Fairview case, and we spent a few nights at her home in Trevethin. Recent developments in the case have been revealed to show that Kim never lived at the house we stayed in, and how she accessed that home is still unanswered. After being forced to leave, I returned home. Kim has not been in touch. As the days have passed, I fear that she may be in trouble. I am asking the police to start investigating this disappearance, as I want her safety to be taken seriously."

Jordan stopped reading. Kim had been declared a missing person, if only by Joseph Gordon. But that would be enough for the police force to spring into action. With press attention and social media speculation being relit, the pressure was on.

Jordan stared at the kitchen counter, lost in thought. His mother, dead. James Fairview, murdered. Now Kim was missing. This all centred on the writing group, but Jordan didn't know why.

He took out his phone, expecting to see a text from Vanessa and therefore be able to quickly start a message with her. Instead, there was a text from Sally, another writer from the group.

I hear you are investigating the murder of James, the text read. *Please contact me immediately as I believe I can give you some information.*

Jordan swiped right to open the message. He composed a reply. When are you free?

Within minutes, Sally had replied: *Tonight.*

Jordan was halfway through asking where, when another text came through. He swallowed.

Meet me in St David's car park on floor five. I will be in a red Nissan Juke.

"Jordan, what are you doing in there?" his dad called, making him jump.

"Just reading this paper," Jordan called back, his voice wavering.

If Sally had information, it could truly change the case. With Kim's disappearance, Jordan knew something was happening between the pages of these writers. There was a motive, yet Jordan did not know what that motive was.

He looked through his phonebook until he came across Kim's number. He pressed call. The call rang, but nobody answered.

If the phone was on, that could mean that Kim was still active. Where could she be hiding that evaded the eyes of the press and the police?

Jordan typed a text to Vanessa: *Read The Daily Mail and then get me research on Kim. We have to find her.*

TWENTY-TWO

Fireworks exploded in the dark sky, showering the stars in colours of red and green. Oscar, licking himself on the sofa, looked up. Jordan scratched the cat behind the ears, said a silent thank-you prayer to a god he didn't believe in, and left.

Jordan drove into the centre of Cardiff, where people walked the streets all dressed up, laughing, cheering, smiling, and excited that there was something new to celebrate.

"I'll make sure 2018 is my year," the man on his radio said. "I've got so many plans! I think I might give up chocolate. What will you…?"

Jordan turned the radio over to a CD of Lady Gaga. He didn't care what the radio host was going to give up. New Year's resolutions never lasted. He came to a stop at traffic lights next to Vue cinema. He looked to his right at the new BBC studios being built. They were imposing, despite not being finished. Inside was stone and cement. When he had been younger, he had sometimes thought about being a news presenter. Now, BBC News Wales was on his doorstep. But he had chosen his path, and with a degree in criminology, he didn't think his chances of broadcast journalism were quite for him.

Sat behind a Mercedes, he thought of his brushes with the press. He'd had his breakthrough when he solved the case of a semifamous Instagram personality, who had been killed in her apartment. For a while, the police had thought it was a crazed fan. There had been exchange between her and a person from Bristol. But that hadn't been true. Jordan discovered that her boyfriend had discovered the messages between her and the fan and lost his temper. It had been an accidental killing: a simple punch there and a fall down the stairs. But it had been enough for manslaughter. The press had celebrated him for discovering the truth, which he had done through neighbour interviews and close friends to the boyfriend. When asked how he had discovered the truth, he'd replied with: "I ask the right questions."

To him, that was all it was. He had to read the person he was sat with. Background information worked, but instead of following rigorous questions laid out and prepared, Jordan found that just conversing with a suspect ended up where he needed to be. Jordan didn't do it all alone; the police force helped.

Since solving the case of the Instagram personality, Jordan had solved other cases, albeit smaller ones, such as burglaries, crimes, the usual. The press followed him, asked him for quotes, and having an ex-boyfriend that was a journalist had ended up with his private information becoming public knowledge. But they soon realised he wasn't the most interesting of people. They wanted scandal, they wanted information, and they wanted a personality. Jordan didn't give them that.

He had developed a reputation in Cardiff and surrounding areas, but that was about it. After the death of his mother, there had been a brief write-up about his future as an investigator, but nobody seemed to care. Jordan had thought he would never return to work, but driving past the BBC and towards St. David's, Jordan found solace in other people's problems.

Now, he was about to meet Sally.

Jordan drove past the Motorpoint Arena, where revellers were stood, smoking. He drove up the spiral ramp into St. David's centre and found floor five. There were a number of cars parked there, but Jordan was looking for one. He drove past a burgundy Juke that was between two cars, but there was nobody inside. Rounding a corner and at the back of the car park, cut off from other cars, was the car he was looking for.

Sally was stood outside her car. Her hair looked freshly cut and styled, and she was smoking a cigarette. She was wearing an evening dress and jewellery, and her feet were wrapped in high heels. Jordan drove slowly, extending the wait before the pair met. He pulled up two spaces away from Sally, who eyed his car with distaste.

"I thought you might drive something nicer," Sally said as Jordan got out of his Golf.

"A nice car isn't my priority."

"Shame," Sally said. She was playing confident, but the way she looked left and right told Jordan she was nervous. "Get in the car."

"Hand over your keys, first."

"Excuse me?"

"You're illegally smoking in a car park. Either I take a photo of you now and get you fined, or you hand me your keys before I sit in the car with you."

Sally bit her lip and then rolled her eyes. She lobbed the keys across the car park, and Jordan only just managed to grab them.

"Get in. I haven't got long."

"You've got as long as I need you." Jordan walked around the side of the car and opened the passenger door. Sally shut her own and pressed a button, locking them in.

"I'm not going to hold you hostage," Sally replied. "Besides, you've got my keys. We're not going anywhere."

Jordan looked behind her, checking that there was nobody in the back ready to jump out at him. He didn't distrust Sally, but he wasn't wholly in favour of her, either.

"I'm recording this."

Sally just rolled her eyes. "Get on with it."

"Let's begin with your involvement in the writers' group."

Through the chain-linked bars in front of them, fireworks exploded out in the open. Jordan watched the colours shower down on the people beneath it, a glittering hope soon to be forgotten.

"I was there from the start..." Sally paused. "Pretty much the start, anyway. I might have missed just one meeting. I encountered Joseph when I was selling my novels at a fantasy convention in Somerset."

"You're already published?"

"Not traditionally," Sally replied. "That is, not published through a publishing house. I don't have an agent. Probably for the best, as I don't get on with them."

"So you self-publish?"

"Yes, I self-publish," Sally said. "It's a long slog, but I tried to get exposure as much as possible. I built a steady Twitter following, attended as many conventions as I could. Joseph happened to be a guest at the fantasy con I was attending. I had paid to sell my books there; he'd been paid to sell his. Funny, fickle world of books."

"And did he come to your stand?"

"I remember being surprised, because my stand was directly opposite the guests. I got a good trade that day because people were heading back and forth all day to get their meet-and-greet opportunities. I had made eye contact with Joseph a few times but only smiled or waved. Then, as I was packing up, he came over and showed interest in my books. He said he was setting up a writers' group."

"A good chance that you happened to be Welsh, then."

"Well, I live in Chepstow. But I travel to Cardiff once a month for that writing group of his. I knew of him, and when he told me this writers' group was different, that it only let in talent he could nurture and would probably have a better chance at publishing, well, I jumped at the opportunity."

Briefly, headlights from another car lit their interior. It drove past. Jordan noticed Sally had held her breath. She exhaled slowly.

"So the writers' group was quite exclusive, then?"

"Yes," Sally said. Then she realised she hadn't said enough. "Of course it was. I'd tried many writing groups before, and most of the people there couldn't distinguish the right way to spell *your*. It was ridiculous. How could they expect to improve on writing if they don't understand basic grammar?"

"Mm."

"I must admit, when I first turned up and saw the group there, I thought Joseph had lost his mind just a little bit."

"Why?"

"The people there didn't exactly look the part."

"Look the part?"

"Of a writer."

"Writers are supposed to look a certain way?"

Sally exhaled again, but this time out of frustration. "No. I don't know. They just didn't seem to wow me. But as we got talking, I noticed some of them knew their shit. I felt a little intimidated. That's unusual for me."

"When did you meet James Fairview?"

"That first meeting. Knew he was a dick instantly. I'm a good judge of character. I can tell you're a nervous wreck underneath this private investigating thing. You're a shy guy trying to be a dragon."

"This isn't about me, and we've only just met."

"I can tell within five seconds."

"Wow. A talent."

Sally rolled her eyes. "James made some comments towards the women. He said we were there for eye candy. Then he went on to say that women writers were only half as talented as men. The man was a dick. Joseph seemed to thrive off it, though."

"How do you mean?"

"He liked seeing us handle ourselves. He liked the tensions, the bitching, and the drama. The man is a drama queen, though he'd deny it."

"And what was your relationship like with Joseph?"

"Joseph was fine. He was supportive. Befriending. He helped when I needed it. He encouraged me a lot. I was there for a reason. I had strong potential to be published."

"What happened to your self-published works?"

Sally scratched the side of her head. "Well, Joseph asked me to take them down. He told me it was damaging to be self-published, and that to be taken seriously, I should work on writing something that will get me an agent and proper marketing. I listened to him. The man's a master."

"And your relationship with James?"

"Non-existent outside those walls."

Jordan thought that was odd. "Joseph prides himself on his relationship with his writers."

Sally laughed. "As if. I think he had a good relationship with Margaret." Sally paused. "He had a good relationship with some woman that joined for a bit, as well."

"What woman?"

"Oh, this dreary woman. Left her husband. Was finding herself again. She was trying too hard to be alternative and spiritual."

"What was her name?"

Jordan knew what was about to come out of Sally's mouth. "Her name was Annabelle."

Jordan swallowed. He stared straight ahead, hoping Sally would not read his expression. He let time pass. Two cars drove past, looking for somewhere to park. Sally was looking at her nails, as if she was bored.

"Why did you call this meeting?"

Sally's interest seemed piqued. Her eyes widened and she stared straight at Jordan. "Because I know who killed James Fairview."

TWENTY-THREE

Sally placed one hand on the wheel, her fingers wrapped around it. She nodded slowly. "Yeah. I know who killed him. I'm certain of it."

"Well, if you know, why have you been quiet?"

"Because I'm scared they'll kill me too."

Jordan watched Sally. The woman was avoiding eye contact now, as if she feared she had said too much. "They won't know you're talking."

"You can assure that?"

"Yes."

"Kim's disappeared. She spoke to you."

Jordan adjusted where he sat. "She talked to me, yeah. But just because she disappeared doesn't mean she's in trouble."

"Then where is she?"

"Well, to be missing usually means people don't know where they are."

"I'm telling you now, she is in trouble."

"Why would she be in trouble, Sally?"

"Because she talked." Sally blinked. "Isn't that obvious?"

Jordan shrugged. "Tell me how you know who killed James, when you weren't there that night."

Sally swallowed. "It's been leading up to that moment."

"Were you there that night, Sally?"

"What? No, of course I wasn't."

"Why?"

"I was...busy."

"Doing what?"

Sally let go of the wheel. "Just busy. Why does that matter?"

"Everything matters."

"Fine, I was just staying over a friend's house. That was it."

Jordan sensed this wasn't the complete truth. "Okay. So, how can you possibly know who administered that poison to James when you weren't there?"

Sally seemed to be trying to find the right words. "Tell me, who do you suspect killed James Fairview?"

"I can't tell you that," Jordan replied.

"Please. I've read up on you. You're apparently really good."

"Well, that's what the press say," Jordan said. "A few years ago now, mind."

"So, who do you think did it?"

"Tell me how you know."

"Okay, maybe I *don't* know. But I know a pretty good reason why this person is responsible."

"Who?"

"Margaret," Sally replied. "I think it was Margaret."

"Why?"

A car beeped its horn, making both of them jump. Sally breathed out, remembering where she was. She looked behind her, as if she expected to see Margaret in the responsible car.

"You have to keep this between us. I have a husband and two kids that can't find out about this, okay?"

"If this doesn't lead to anything vital, then it won't be found out."

"So there's a chance it could be?"

"I can't promise anything."

"Maybe I won't say."

Jordan sighed. "Sally, this could be very important."

A firework briefly lit up where they were parked. The lights reflected Sally's curious face. "I was sleeping with James Fairview."

The news stunned Jordan. It had been so unexpected. Jordan took a while to compose himself. "Yet you told me your relationship was non-existent."

"Well, I lied."

"Is this true?"

"Do you want me to prove it? I've got messages on my phone that prove we met and we were going out."

"I don't need to see them."

"I'm ashamed that I was seeing him. The man was a dick, yet he had a charm. I'm bored of my relationship, and he was there. So, we had a little thing going on."

Jordan thought of Margaret out with James in New Inn. Did James also have a relationship with Margaret? "Why does this impact his death?"

"When Margaret found out I was going out with James, she was jealous. And I mean, fucking livid jealous."

"What was her reaction?"

"She told me that to be dating another writer in the group was extremely unprofessional. She began manipulating Joseph and trying her best to exclude one of us. Group meetings would change so one of us couldn't come, for example. She also made it difficult for us by causing arguments, critiquing our work just for the sake of it. That sort of thing."

"When did you start sleeping with James?"

"Almost a year ago," Sally replied.

"Were you exclusive?"

"Oh, god no. It was just sex. It was excitement. I had a husband and James was a bachelor. I'm sure I wasn't his only woman. I never asked, either. I let him get on with it."

Jordan nodded. "Okay. So Margaret was jealous. Why would that prompt murder?"

"She hated that I had attention. She was jealous of me because I had a bit of a fan base, despite withdrawing my self-published works, and she didn't like that I was getting attention from this man. I don't think the other writers knew about us, but they still suspected something. I tried to keep our affair secret, for obvious reasons, but Margaret threatened that. They argued a few times. James tried telling her to mind her own business, that sort of thing."

"Do you know if the two ever spent time together?"

Sally shrugged. "If they did, I bet it was a miserable time."

"Anything else?" It was almost nine o'clock. He knew that the city below was alive with excitement.

"Well, yes," Sally said. "James had just signed a massive book deal. He was about to be a published author with an agent and a traditional publisher, and Margaret was furious that he told me and no one else."

Mark had been right. He had picked up on the discussions between James and a publisher. But now Jordan had been told there had been a deal struck. "And Margaret was jealous?"

"Of course she was jealous, but she had a good reason to be. I would have been furious too. I *was* furious."

"What was her reason?"

Sally looked at Jordan. "The manuscript belonged to Margaret. It was stolen work."

TWENTY-FOUR

Sally was long gone. She had exited her car after her accusation that James had stolen work and then promptly disappeared down into the shopping centre, where she was no doubt meeting friends for New Year's celebrations.

Jordan was tempted to follow her, to see whom she met up with, but something told him that would be futile. It seemed Sally didn't have friends in the writers' group anymore. Jordan knew where Joseph and Margaret were, and Kim was missing. James was dead. The other writing members didn't seem to be on his radar right now. He had wanted to question them about that night, but he thought it pointless.

Staring at the door Sally had disappeared through, Jordan wondered if Sally had told the whole truth. She struck him as a proud woman, someone who would dismiss her worries easily. Had her relationship with James ended badly?

Jordan drove home and sat in his car outside his apartment. Lloyd was not at his door tonight, but he wished he were. He needed to talk to someone about this, to tell a soul what had just been told to him by Sally. He had tried ringing Vanessa three times—either the officer was ignoring his calls like Jordan had been doing or she was busy celebrating New Year's.

Jordan sighed. He supposed people did deserve time out from everything. But this was a murder case that needed solving, and Sally's revelation distracted him from everything else.

Inside his apartment, Jordan ran himself a hot bath and sat in the tub as it filled up. His bathroom was probably the cleanest place inside his home. Large, thick towels hung up on the wall radiator. Matching floor mats were fluffy and dry on towel rails. The walls were tiled, too, with marble print. His bath was spacious, allowing him to lie down and properly stretch out. Oscar curled on the floor, soaking up the steaming vapour that filled the room.

He had the radio on and was listening to the latest updates on Brexit, but his mind was elsewhere. He was thinking of his mother.

Jordan had never known his mother to write. He had never thought of his mother as someone who would even consider taking a writing career seriously. Yet she must have been good to be headhunted and included in Joseph's prestigious writing group that celebrated new, fresh talent.

Jordan was aware of Literature Wales, and he wondered if Joseph had any partnership with them. He needed to find out more about how his mother had joined the group and why she had left. Was it simply because she found James Fairview uncomfortable?

Yet it seemed like many of the women in the group found James uncomfortable. Kim had distrusted him, Margaret had been envious of him, Sally had been fucking him. But none of them had been his friends. None of them supported him or had anything good to say about him.

Jordan wondered about the other writers, Franchesca, Andy, Sarah, and Graham. They had simply been bystanders in this. They weren't involved with the dramas between the writers, or the affairs, or even the hatred towards James. None of them had come up in conversation between what Jordan considered the main suspects of James's murder.

Yet simple association involved them, and to hear their opinions would be very worthwhile.

The bath half full, Jordan sat up and grabbed his phone, which was on a cabinet a few feet away. He dialled Joseph's number. After the fifth ring, Joseph picked up.

"Jordan? Why are you calling me?" Joseph sounded breathless. He could hear music in the background. He moved the phone away from his ear to find it was quarter to midnight. "Are you out? Has something happened?"

"Joseph, sorry to ring you so close to midnight, but I want to see the other writers. I want to speak to Franchesca, Andy, Sarah, and Graham."

"Can't you arrange that? I'm a little busy."

Jordan heard laughing on the other end, women cackling, music blaring loudly as a door opened. Was Joseph at a party in the city? "What are you doing?"

"Celebrating New Year's, like everyone else."

"Joseph, remember I've asked you this, please. I want to see them in a day or two."

"No rest for the wicked, hey?"

"Definitely not," Jordan replied. "I'll call to remind you tomorrow."

"Okay, fine," Joseph said. Then he hung up, not bothering to say goodbye, eager to get back to his New Year's party.

Jordan put his phone back down. He had only just got himself relaxed again in the water when it vibrated. He wanted to ignore it, but he couldn't switch off. What if it was Joseph confirming the meeting?

He sat up, looked, and almost dropped his phone. The message was from Kim.

TWENTY-FIVE

"She sent you a warning?" It was the morning of New Year's Day, and Vanessa was in her dressing gown at her kitchen table. Her house was in the middle of Cardiff Bay and had three bedrooms, though she only shared the house with her fiancé. Their kitchen had recently been refurbished. It glistened white and black and was modernised, overlooking a back garden that was very private.

Jordan could only dream that one day he'd get to this level of success.

There were empty wine glasses in the sink and empty wine bottles on the counter. Vanessa had enjoyed a house party last night and was now paying the price.

"Read it. It reads like a warning."

"If we talk, we'll be silenced. Stop asking questions, Jordan," Vanessa quoted.

"It came from Kim's mobile. I've been trying to ring it, but I've had no answer. Now this."

"What do you think it means?"

"I think you know what it means," Jordan replied. "The killer is still at large. Kim's run away from it."

Vanessa sighed, handing Jordan's phone back over. "We can't trust her as a credible source."

"What?"

"She could be saying this to add drama to your case," Vanessa said. "It's a common practice of people whose mundane lives are suddenly less mundane. She is probably enjoying this, which is why she's added tension by disappearing."

"You're saying she's attention-seeking?"

"Probably."

"But what if she isn't?"

Vanessa shrugged half-heartedly, squinting as she sat back. Jordan realised she was severely hungover. "Reply to her, try and see her, but don't pander to her."

Jordan picked up his phone, his clear head telling him that Vanessa didn't understand what was at stake. He got off the high bar stool he was sat on and walked away from the table, signalling he was ready to leave.

"I think I'll just find out myself. That's what I'm here to do."

"Jordan…"

"No, Vanessa, it seems as though interest has been lost in this murder case."

"We're busy with a lot of other things."

"And this isn't a priority?"

"His murder is a priority, yes," Vanessa said, just as a floorboard creaked overhead. "But Kim's attention-seeking is just a distraction."

Jordan dismissed this with a wave of his hand. "Kim has disappeared for a reason. She was inside a house she never actually lived in. Kim's on the run, and I want to find out why."

"Go ahead. That's your job."

Jordan rolled his eyes. "Thanks."

"The car was registered at that address, though, Jordan. She would have lived there at some point."

Jordan remembered what the neighbour had told him. The woman had kept to herself. If Kim had lived there, why had she left it empty for seven months?

He walked out of the kitchen and towards the front door. When he got into the hallway, he bumped into Jennifer, Vanessa's fiancé.

"Hey, Jordan. You're early. Good New Year's?"

"Yeah, it was fine," Jordan said, and then he spoke louder. "Happy New Year!"

Before Jennifer could engage Jordan in any more conversation, he opened the front door and left the house he would never be able to afford. He walked to his ageing car, got in, and put the key into the ignition.

He was in first gear, ready to pull off when Vanessa came out of her house. She looked around her, appearing worried the neighbours might see her in her dressing gown. She signalled for Jordan to wind down the window.

"Jordan, sorry, I'm just not in the right frame of mind today. I hate having to hide from this case, but I want to, just for a day. If you think that the text you got is significant, then follow it up. Try and track down Kim. I know the rest of us are having trouble trying to trace her."

"I think the text is a warning," Jordan said. "I think Kim wants to speak, but she's unable to. Something is happening in this group. Somebody wants something quiet."

Vanessa nodded, though she still didn't look convinced. "Take a break if you can. It's New Year's. Nobody will be working. Take some time out for yourself."

"I've done enough of that," Jordan replied. "I'll work as much as I need to."

Before Vanessa could reply, Jordan drove away, leaving her stood on the pavement in her dressing gown.

Jordan wasn't worried he had jeopardised his friendship and professional career arguing with Vanessa. The pair had come to blows countless times. It happened when working on a stressful case, especially one that garnered media attention. They never took it personally. That was rule number one of working together.

But this time, Jordan was getting annoyed with Vanessa a lot more than usual. The officer was painting an image of Jordan that he didn't like. He wasn't broken because of the death of his mother, and he wasn't clinging on to false hope.

There was something about this case that involved his mother, and Jordan needed to find out what that was.

To do that, he had to find Kim.

TWENTY-SIX

"You said you wanted to talk to the other writers? Well, you can. They're available this evening at my house, if you're free too."

It was Joseph. It was the middle of the afternoon, and Jordan could tell by his groggy voice that he had only just woken up. "What time?"

"From eight."

"Fine," Jordan replied. "Will everyone be in attendance?"

"Everyone you haven't spoken to, yes," Joseph answered. "Margaret might be here too."

"Margaret is spending a lot of time with you, isn't she?"

"Yes." Joseph yawned.

"It might be a good idea to talk to Margaret."

"You want to speak to her?"

"Yes. Something someone told me yesterday is important to discuss with her."

Joseph was silent for a moment. "That's fine." He yawned again. "She'll be here."

"Thanks, Joseph. Now pop a paracetamol and a Berocca and get yourself ready for this evening."

He laughed. "Okay."

He cut the call just as abruptly as he had yesterday. Jordan put his phone down and turned back to his computer. Being sat in his office was weird. It had been a while since he had come here. The surface of his desk was gathering dust and his monitor screen needed to be cleaned.

He worked alone, in a building that had rooms rented out to start-up and medium-sized businesses. It worked for him. The place was pretty private. You could go a whole nine-to-five day without seeing five people.

His eyes were aching and his head pounded. He had been looking at his screen for too long, reading up on Joseph Gordon. The man had it all. His literary career was envious to aspiring writers. He was a man that always got into the bestseller lists. His reviews on websites such as Amazon were mixed, but mostly he averaged four stars, except for three books in the past few years that had an average of three.

Joseph had been romantically linked to a few people, including Sally. Jordan thought this odd. The pair had been photographed together, but Jordan knew better than to assume this was enough evidence. The press liked to speculate.

Joseph had also appeared on national television. Images of him with Ellen DeGeneres were top of the results page when Jordan searched "Joseph Gordon Celebrity."

He looked at his notepad, where he had written a note to himself: find out who James's publisher was.

His phone buzzed and he answered. "Jordan speaking."

He always spoke briskly, in case it was a client.

"Jordan, it's your dad," Peter said.

"Hi, Dad."

"You answered quickly."

"Near the phone. What's up?"

"It's your mother's house. I think we need to put it up for sale."

Jordan sighed, swivelling his chair away from the images of Joseph with Stephen King. "Right…"

"So we have to move everything out. Her belongings. I think we should sell it furnished. Less hassle. But her belongings need to come with us."

"Dad…"

"I think as well it would do us both good to go into the house and see how she lived. It might let us link to her a bit better."

"You really want to do this?"

"I think we need to."

"Could you do it on your own?"

A door shut in the hallway, and then the automatic lights came on. Jordan looked at the door to his office as someone walked past, probably heading out for a cigarette.

Peter sighed. "I'd rather you were there, Jord. It would be quicker if we both do it. It will take a while."

"Is there no one else who could help you?"

"She was your mother, Jordan. Your brother is away. We're all she had left."

"She didn't talk to me for a year."

"She spoke to me."

"Occasionally." Jordan was being rude. But his dad needed to hear it. The woman they had known was not the woman who died. "But I'll help you. It might do us good."

Jordan realised now that going there would be a step in the right direction. If Annabelle was involved somehow in this case, then maybe going through her belongings was the best thing to do.

"Good," Peter said. "I'll be in touch. I know you're busy. I'll let you get on with it."

He said goodbye, feeling sorry for his dad who always struck him as lonely. He looked back at James's name on his notepad, wondering about what the man had been doing before his death. Jordan opened another tab, looking at a blog offering advice to aspiring writers on getting an agent.

To have a manuscript ready for publication meant James had been writing for a while. It meant he had spent time writing, drafting his work, and shaping it to a publishing standard. He had learned this from the blog and ones similar to it. James had gotten a deal that was pretty hard to come by. Jordan had been shocked to learn that many publishers published very few new authors in a year. He would hate to be a writer; it seemed so unfair.

But if James had got a publishing deal, it meant he didn't have writer's block like he had been telling people. According to Sally, it was stolen work. But Jordan wasn't ruling out the idea that James had been bluffing, letting the writers believe he was one to be underestimated.

He needed to find the manuscript, and he needed to find the publisher. Maybe then he could learn about what was happening and where his deal had come from.

The stolen manuscript was important. It gave the killer a motive. If Sally was correct, that manuscript had been Margaret's.

He wondered if Margaret would be there tonight. If she was, he doubted he would get answers. The woman was evasive and secretive. It was Jordan's job to find out just what she was hiding.

Jordan packed up and decided to go home.

TWENTY-SEVEN

Jordan rubbed his eyes, which ached and burned ferociously. His apartment came swimming back into focus. He had been scanning the internet to learn about the world of publishing, and it had been going in and staying at the front of his brain, heavy and blocked, no longer making sense. Oscar meowed as Jordan sighed.

James Fairview threw up no results. He had been in local papers, mainly because of some competition he had entered, but as a writer, his career hadn't really been flourishing. His Twitter account only had five hundred and twenty-eight followers, and he didn't have a Facebook fan page. How had a man so unknown been given a deal that could change his life?

The publishing industry seemed cold. There were thousands, maybe even millions of writers on the outside, all hoping for that dreamlike publishing deal. Writers that had a publishing deal were quick to say all wasn't as it seemed, but Jordan thought that was easy for them to say. Surely they had it all. He realised that the writing group were sharing the same common interest: to be just like Joseph Gordon. Writers seemed to be a congratulatory bunch, not allowing jealousy to get in their way. But when Jordan had found an anonymous writers' group that shared rants from anonymous writers, he could tell that there was an underlying dark side to the wholesome industry.

Jordan had written in his notepad "finances," multiples circles traced around this one word. Had James bought his way in?

The lead-up to his death must have had something to do with the publishing deal that had seemingly fallen into his lap. From what others had said, it seemed to have come so easily to a man that was struggling to string a sentence together.

Jordan stood up, wearing shorts and a T-shirt, and rubbed his eyes again. He didn't smoke, but he felt like he needed something to take the edge away, to relieve him and make him feel something. He went to the kitchen, found a bottle of Jack Daniels, and was considering pouring himself a triple glass when the phone rang.

He walked towards his mobile, thinking of the whisky that James had drunk, the drink that had killed him. It had been whisky on ice, murder on the rocks.

He answered the phone without seeing who was calling. "Hello?"

"Jordan! You answered," Lloyd's voice said. "Are you free?"

"Uh…" Typically, New Year's Day was supposed to be a day of relaxation, of no work, of that slump in productivity and doing anything.

"Come on, Jord. I'm nearby. I thought maybe we could get breakfast."

"It's almost the afternoon."

"And I just woke up." Lloyd laughed.

"Heavy night?"

Lloyd made a sound that was part snickering and part cough. "Could say that."

"Did you see the new year in with…someone?"

"Unfortunately not."

For some reason, Jordan found that hard to believe. Lloyd was always going out, and with his looks and charisma, Jordan knew from Vanessa that he rarely went home alone. "How soon can you be ready?"

"Why? Are you busy with something else?"

Jordan rolled his eyes. "I'm just focussed on other things."

"The Fairview case?"

"What else?"

"You're unhealthy."

"Says you, with your pickled kidneys."

Lloyd laughed again. "Meet me in 'spoons in about twenty minutes?"

Jordan looked out of the window, up the street in the direction of where Wetherspoon's was. "Fine."

They said goodbye, and Jordan went to get changed. He could do with food, a quick chat, and then it was back to work. He couldn't let himself slip off this case, when he was so sure a breakthrough was imminent.

He thought of his frustrations with Vanessa, and he wondered if he should be thinking the same towards Lloyd. Why should he be when it was Vanessa that was the one holding him back?

Jordan left his apartment, forgetting to turn off his laptop, and took a walk up his street. People here barely looked at him, and the street seemed emptier than usual. He thought it was because most shops were closed, with many people at home, nursing a hangover. 2018—the first year without his mother.

He hated New Year's. He always felt apprehensive, scared of what the year would bring, the idea that this could be his last, that the construct of time would date his existence. Everyone hoped for a new start, seeing another day as a new chapter on a blank page. To Jordan, that was true. He could leave behind everything that had happened last year and look forward to something new.

Though to him all he had to look forward to was a case that needed to be solved and then who knew what else. After his disagreement with Vanessa, he might need to find new clients.

He could go to London. There was always work in London.

He got to Wetherspoon's to find Lloyd waiting outside, smoking a cigarette. He looked effortlessly cool, wearing dark-blue skinny jeans, a long, tight fitted T-shirt, and a necklace. He didn't look like he had been out the night before, such was his fresh-faced appearance.

"You came."

"When I'm invited, I'll be here."

Lloyd stubbed out his cigarette, and they headed inside where old men regulars were downing their third pint, the New Year being yet another day to them.

They ordered at the bar, pointing vaguely to an empty table where they would sit for the barman to note on their order. When their drinks had been given to them, two lattes, they walked to their table.

"Have you ever used the app?" Lloyd asked.

"No." Jordan sat down opposite him. "I barely come here."

"Too good for 'spoons, are you?"

"It's not my first choice of place. I'd rather a meal that actually tastes nice."

"Then you're missing out on their breakfast."

Television screens were on every wall, displaying everything from the news to music channels. A separate music system was playing songs, so the TVs were on mute, which annoyed Jordan.

"When do you go back to work?" Jordan asked Lloyd.

"Let's not talk about work."

"Just a simple question."

"Fine. I go back next week. I like to have a week off in the new year to kind of just relax."

"Fair enough."

"And you?"

"I haven't taken time off."

"Jordan…"

"I'm freelance. I'm always working. I need to pay my bills. I don't have the benefits you have."

Lloyd sipped his coffee. "But still…Vanessa must be paying you enough."

"Enough, yeah, but not enough to be comfortable forever. I'm always thinking a few months down the line."

"Take on more clients. Plenty of work out there, I'd imagine."

"What sort of work do you imagine?"

"Money laundering, fraud, affairs. The list goes on."

"Yeah. I like to call them the filler cases."

The news broadcast switched to an image of Kim. It seemed the press were now wondering where the writer, linked to Joseph Gordon, had gone.

Lloyd glanced at the report, sighing. "You just can't escape work, can you?"

"She's been texting me."

"Kim?"

Jordan nodded, watching the image of Kim change to the image with his mother in the background. He wondered if Vanessa had issued the image. "She's telling me to stay back, to stop asking questions."

"But she's missing."

"Clearly."

"Do you think it's her that's texting?"

"I don't know. Whenever I ring, the phone goes straight to voicemail."

"So someone else could have her phone."

"It's possible."

Lloyd looked out of the window, tapping his fingers to the song that was playing over the speakers. "I wonder if her disappearance is related to James's death."

"It's almost certain that it is. I think Kim knew something and was probably going to talk. I told you that the house where I saw her over Christmas wasn't actually her house, didn't I?"

"I heard from Vanessa. Crazy. Do you know how she got in yet?"

"I don't. But Joseph was living with her and claims he didn't know it wasn't her house. To be fair, when I went in, I didn't suspect a thing."

"What did it look like?"

"She just looked poor."

Lloyd nodded that he understood. The breakfast came on blue flowered plates. They were the type of plates that always looked old-fashioned, like they belonged to a grandmother. Jordan admitted, however, that the food tasted good.

"So, how was your night?"

"Madness. Went out at ten, didn't get in until six."

"And you're awake now?"

Lloyd indicated himself. "Clearly. I'll sleep properly when I get in. I wish you had come out with me. We would have had fun."

"Where did you go?" Jordan asked, pretending not to notice Lloyd's hint at a relationship outside of work.

"Kings, Pulse, then Dirty Pop."

"I haven't been to Dirty Pop in forever."

Dirty Pop had been Jordan's best night out before work had consumed him. Every Saturday night, the nightclub played solely pop music, from the hot releases to those that were only known by the dedicated fans. Being a lover of pop music and knowing every release from Selena Gomez to Iggy Azalea, Jordan really did love it.

"That's what I mean. I was thinking of you all night."

"Surely that isn't true. I'm sure you had plenty of men after you that night. The gay bars like Pulse are always full at special occasions."

Jordan had been a fan of Pulse and Kings when he had been younger, accepting his own sexuality. Those clubs had been a haven to him.

"You know what those bars are like. A bit hit-or-miss. Sure, I had attention, but I wanted to dance the night away."

Jordan didn't ask about a New Year's kiss. With age, he'd realised things like that just didn't matter to him. He sometimes thought about spending special occasions with people, but he remembered his job, his own mindset of focussing on tasks at hand. He didn't suit a relationship with someone that just wouldn't understand how he worked.

Rita Ora's "Anywhere" came on, and Lloyd grinned. "This was fun last night."

"Good song."

"Yeah."

Lloyd was halfway through his food. Jordan was always a slow eater. "Why did you want to meet up?"

Lloyd swallowed. "I just like to keep in touch with you. You wouldn't exactly call a timeout, would you?"

"Well…"

"No, no excuses." Lloyd grinned. "You're always consumed in your job, and you alienate those that actually want to be friends with you."

"I consider you a friend."

"Friends go out for drinks, for food, for nights out. We haven't done that in ages."

"I've just been busy."

"And you're not yourself since…"

Jordan looked at Lloyd. "Since Mum died?"

"Not quite what I was going to say, but…"

"Yeah."

"I just want to make sure you're okay, that's all."

Jordan shook his head. "You, Vanessa, my dad. Why is everyone suddenly so worried about me?"

"I think sometimes you don't realise how much you're loved. You have humour that people like. You're kind. You're efficient and hard working. You give off this confident air that people like and feel safe with.

Lately, you've been closing yourself down, forgetting those that really want to spend time with you."

Jordan ate, though he felt his appetite disappearing. Lloyd's words, meant to be uplifting, were just annoying. "I know."

"I just want to spend time with a guy I like."

Jordan thought about his words, what he meant by what he said. At the end of the day, the man opposite him was a friend, one that had been let in and was now being shut out. Why was Jordan acting the way he did? Was he afraid? Did he fear getting too close would end up hurting him or ultimately disappointing him? He didn't really know. Yet what he did know was people had their own agendas, and sooner or later, they would grow, change their opinions, their thoughts, what they liked and didn't like. They met new people, ones that were more compatible for the life they were currently living, and those who had been there from the start were gone, changing, too, meeting their own people.

That hurt.

To get rid of that hurt, Jordan had developed a strong armour of defence. If he allowed himself distance, he'd be less likely to care when that person disappeared, fading away from his life, becoming just a memory.

"Well, I appreciate being called away from the case for a bit."

Lloyd allowed himself to smile. "I appreciate that you came."

TWENTY-EIGHT

"The last time I saw her, she was walking the street behind Joseph Gordon's home," a middle-aged woman walking a dog said to the microphone that was suspended in mid-air by an unseen hand. The BBC news ticker went sweeping by on the lower screen, but Jordan didn't pay it attention. "She looked drunk. She swayed a bit. She was carrying bags!"

"Did you approach the woman you believe was Kim?"

"Believe? I know it was her! Recognised her immediately when I saw her in the papers. She was visiting Joseph Gordon the day she disappeared."

The report cut to photographs of Kim, the reporter talking about how Kim had been brought up in an average household, always living in the same area of Torfaen. Jordan sighed, leaning back in his chair.

If the dog-walking woman was telling the truth, it meant Joseph Gordon had lied to him. It meant Joseph knew where Kim was or had at least seen her before she disappeared. The time to go to Joseph's was ticking closer, and Jordan knew he would have to leave soon. He had all his questions prepared for the writers he hadn't met yet, but also for Joseph and Margaret.

He thought back to the CCTV of Kim being spoken to by Margaret in the pub. He could picture Kim handing something over. Margaret leaving Kim behind, ignoring her the rest of the night, spending her night separate from her writing friend. He could see James, drinking from a glass that had been brought to the pub by Margaret and collected the next day.

He remembered what Lloyd had said, that James had been poisoned slowly, the killing substance residing in his system until it could not be handled anymore. He remembered how after one drink, James had seemed disoriented, mistaken for drunk.

If there was one thing that Jordan was sure of, it was that Margaret knew more than she was letting on. In fact, he was almost certain Margaret was responsible.

115

But there was no proof. And without proof, there was no conclusion.

Jordan got to his feet and headed to his car, thinking of where Kim could have disappeared. He hoped that the worst thought he had wasn't true. Kim knew something, and the likely explanation was she was hiding. But from who? Why?

Jordan was surprised at how quickly he arrived at Joseph's gated community. It was about fifteen minutes away from his own street, but traffic had been light, and he had been lucky with traffic lights. Instead of buzzing in through the intercom, he parallel parked on the nearby public street and got out, then pulled his coat around him. The air was mild, not quite as cold as winter could be, but there was a breeze that was chilly.

The residential street here looked cosy. Lights shimmered behind windows, and Jordan could hear a television coming from an upstairs part-opened window. The cars along here were at least from 2010, telling him that they had money, just not enough money to live in a gated community that brushed shoulders with authors.

Jordan walked away from the security barriers and around the corner of the street, trying to see if he could detect any weak spots. Joseph had said a woman had come into his home, as he always had his door unlocked. The more Jordan thought about it, the more that seemed implausible. Why hadn't she been spotted?

Jordan spotted a hedge that was next to the wall that looked like it had been kicked through. Approaching it, Jordan could see that past the thicket of branches, there was a small natural tunnel. He glanced around and found there was no one nearby, so he climbed through the hedge, ironically thinking of Alice in Wonderland.

He had to crouch to keep the branches from hitting him. The floor was earthy and bumpy with stone, and he moved slowly to avoid any injuries. The wall alongside him was replaced eventually with gates, towering above him. He could see the back gardens of the gated community houses. From his vantage point, hot tubs, sheds, and even a small second guest home could be seen. Each garden was immaculately trimmed, with cobblestoned walls separating each homeowner's land.

Eventually, he came to a turnstile. Jordan touched it and it moved. It was unlocked and opened directly onto Joseph Gordon's garden.

Jordan remembered what Joseph had said. The lady had entered through the back. But Jordan had assumed through the back meant the gate that led around the side of the house, which was accessed from the front. From this recently installed gate, Jordan could see the gate through which he thought the potential murderer had used. Looking at Joseph's Gregorian home, he noticed there were CCTV cameras on both corners of the house, facing front and back. They were prime position to film whoever came and went. Jordan remembered seeing the gate but hadn't thought of where it could lead.

Joseph had failed to mention that little gem of information.

Jordan thought back to the gate, where a security booth that was blacked out stood between either entrance. Was the CCTV feed available in there?

Jordan was hidden here in the shadows of shrubbery, but this was a directly accessed link into his home. A man like Joseph would surely know about this route, and if he didn't, he was truly under an invasion of privacy.

But the gate was intentional, not matching the iron fence on either side of it, which had been cut through by builders.

Joseph Gordon had put this gate here on purpose and probably knew about the back lane that was a serious security breach.

Jordan took out his phone, and forgetting about their tiff this morning, he rang Vanessa.

"Took your time," Vanessa answered. "Usually you break your silence before this. What have you found?"

Vanessa, she knew him well. "A secret entrance to the gated community but, more importantly, only to Joseph's home. Well hidden."

"But you found it."

"Of course."

"Tell me more."

"I parked and walked down the street, finding a hedge that went behind the wall. I noticed there was a bit of a break between the branches, and on further look, there was a little pathway between the bushes. So I climbed in, followed the path, making my back ache as I did so, and came across a recently installed gate that leads directly onto Joseph's home garden. I couldn't see it from the window in his house, the lawn slopes a bit."

"I don't think the force have noticed that. Good find."

"Thanks. It seems odd, though. Why would this be here?"

"Are you sure Joseph would have put it there?"

"Positive. It looks new. Not brand new, but new."

"Would you take me and Mark there?"

"Of course," Jordan said. "By the way, to give credit to Mark, he was first to mention there had been talk of a manuscript and publishers. He just didn't know there was a deal."

Vanessa grinned. "See? He's got the job for a reason. What are you doing now?"

"I'm going to watch the house for a little longer and then visit Joseph and the other writers."

"Keep in touch. Let me know when you're out."

"I will."

Vanessa hung up, and Jordan loitered in the shadows, watching Joseph's house. He felt tense standing here, knowing he was infringing on private property, and hiding in the shadows of the bushes around him. If someone spotted him, he would need to answer some awkward questions.

Joseph had kept this a secret from him. This gate had never been mentioned, yet it was a clear breach of privacy. Looking down the path Jordan had walked, he tried to imagine the killer that night, sneaking through the dark.

The kitchen was dark, and there was no light shining in any of the rooms upstairs or downstairs. The only light came from some LEDs that were decorating the garden. From the gate was a pathway, which led directly to the back door.

The killer had walked the path that night, gaining access to Joseph's home without being seen. Unwittingly, Joseph had led the killer straight to the door.

TWENTY-NINE

Jordan walked to the barriers that let in cars and to the blacked-out tollbooth-looking building in the middle. From the outside, all he could see was his own reflection, cars behind him cast in shadows and Christmas tree lights glistening from one of the windows of a house. He found the door, heavy-looking and closed, and knocked.

Movement could be heard from inside, and then the door opened, revealing a man wearing an overcoat. Behind him were rows of screens, CCTV cameras of the surrounding streets projecting images back to this individual. The inside was larger than Jordan thought it would be, enough room for two people.

"What?" the man asked, twisting his head to look behind him at the cameras.

Jordan had met these kind of men before. They were the type to take their job seriously, believing they had powers over others. "My name is Jordan Jenner. I'm a private investigator, currently investigating the murder of James Fairview."

"Got any ID?" the ageing man asked.

Jordan fished out his ID from his pocket. "I was just wondering if I could ask a quick question. Nothing formal. Right here, right now."

The man peered at the ID, then nodded, stepping back to let Jordan into the cramped room. The man took his seat at the monitors again, and Jordan acquired another seat.

"There's not much more that I can tell you. Not from what I've already told the police."

"You spoke to the police?"

"I was working the night it happened."

Jordan's eyes widened. "And did you see anything odd?"

"Not really, mate, no." Jordan cringed at the terminology used. He hated being called someone's mate. "Saw a couple of people that night, walking by. One person hanging around at one point, quite early in the night, but nothing unusual."

"No one sneaking in anywhere?"

"You can't sneak in in these parts," the man said. "I'm Henry, by the way."

"Henry, what is this area usually like?"

"Quiet."

"And that night?"

"Quiet."

"Where is the footage of that night now?"

"It'll be stored." He lifted his hands in the air, as if it floated above them. "Gets sent off to a hardware system. Easily achievable to get, though."

"So, can I request this?" Jordan asked.

Henry nodded. "I just need to fill out a form, say why you're requesting it, that sort of thing."

"It's to aid my investigation into the murder of James Fairview."

Henry exhaled. "Definitely murdered, then?"

"Yeah," Jordan said. "You say it was quiet, but people obviously dropped by that day and night. If you're here often, you must see regulars. Recognise anyone or see anyone new?"

Henry thought for a moment. "Usual people came by. They'll all be on CCTV."

Jordan picked up a notepad and pen that was next to Henry, and ignoring his incredulous look, he wrote down his number. "Give me a call when it's available, and I will come and pick it up. It's a big help to me."

"Yeah, I will." Henry nodded.

"Now, can you let me in, please? I have a meeting with Joseph Gordon."

Henry let Jordan into the estate after a show of locking up the booth where he monitored the videos and checking whether or not cars were approaching. He watched Jordan go the whole way down the street, making sure that he did in fact go to Joseph Gordon's home and didn't go snooping.

As Jordan walked, Henry's stare burning into him, he clocked where the CCTV cameras were positioned. The street was like Big Brother, a camera to cover every angle. He wondered if there were blind spots, if somehow the killer had got in undetected, yet he didn't think that would be the case. It was impossible to escape the all-seeing eyes of these lenses.

Jordan knocked on the door of Joseph's home, glancing up at Henry who kept watch. He had plans to snoop around the estate later, even though he would be on camera. Taking a stroll was not illegal, even in a gated community.

The door opened and Joseph stood before him, wearing jeans that were worn and baggy, a loose top, and smoking a cigar. There was music playing in one of the rooms, and Jordan could hear voices. It seemed like Joseph was entertaining.

"Happy New Year!" Joseph smiled. "Please, do come in."

Jordan did, wiping his feet on the mat as he did so. The door closed behind him, and once again, Jordan was in the grand home of an author that had got big. The voices seemed to be rushed and quieter now, all of them realising what the door closing meant.

"We're in the kitchen if you'd like to come in."

Jordan followed Joseph into the kitchen, as immaculate as ever. The writers he recognised only by photographs were all sat at the island table, glasses of wines in front of them, notebooks next to them opened to pages of scribbled notes. The music came from the top of the cupboard, a classical number that was neither too loud nor too quiet. Jordan felt like this was sophistication at its finest, and for the first time, he saw the same appeal that these writers did: it was a life that was opulent, a sense of entitlement and wealth.

"Jordan, please be introduced to my writers. Shame you haven't met them earlier. Great talents."

A man might have died within their ranks, but the people before Jordan did not look scarred. A male Jordan estimated to be in his late thirties, wearing a white shirt unbuttoned at the top to reveal hair on his chest, held out a muscular arm. Jordan took it, feeling the man's grip, looking into his brown eyes.

"Graham."

"Hi, Graham."

The woman next to him held out her bony wrist. Her hair was cropped short, her neck pockmarked with freckles. "I'm Franchesca."

Jordan shook her hand. "Nice to meet you."

A man who looked older than Joseph, wearing tweed and outdated glasses didn't bother to shake hands. Instead, he revealed a smile that was more gum than teeth.

"Andy," he introduced.

"Sarah." Sarah was the least enthusiastic out of the group. Her brown, lanky hair covered one eye, and Jordan thought she could either be early twenties to late forties. She was small and round and looked like she would fly away with a touch.

"Nice to meet you all."

"And of course I don't need to introduce you to Margaret."

Jordan followed Joseph's gaze to a pantry at the back of the kitchen. Margaret was inside, resting in the doorframe, looking at Jordan like he was holding a severed head.

"No, you don't need to reintroduce me with Margaret."

"I wish you'd just leave these people alone."

"When I find out who killed James, then I will."

Despite nothing changing, the atmosphere seemed tighter now. The music continued to play, but the smiles were wiped off everyone's faces, and Jordan couldn't have felt more out of place.

He looked at Joseph. "I think I'll have a drink please, but lay off the poison."

THIRTY

"Careful, you'd think you were blaming him!" Graham laughed.

Jordan took a seat opposite the writers, taking out his phone, a pen, and his own notepad. "Of course not. But one of you could be the culprit."

"What makes you so sure?"

Joseph headed away from the table, towards where the wines and spirits were kept. Jordan noticed that Sarah watched him go, following his every move. "Well, the man didn't drop dead of his own accord, did he? Do you mind if I record this?"

The writers shook their heads. Margaret walked past them, towards Joseph, glaring at Jordan as she did so.

"So that's why you have called us all here?" Franchesca asked. Her accent was a mix of French and British. "You think we killed that man?"

"Why do you call him that man?"

Franchesca shared a look with her fellow writers. "The man was a brute."

"He was more than a brute," Andy said, lifting his wine glass to his mouth. "He was a pig."

"He harassed the women," Franchesca said. "Including me. He belittled us all. He criticised the stories we wrote, and he made fun of our lives and our hopes for publication."

"He thought he was better than everyone," Graham said.

Jordan felt funny with the way Graham looked at him, his heart fluttering ever so slightly. He hoped it didn't show on his face. "Were any of you his friend?"

At that moment, Joseph returned, a glass of wine in his hand. Jordan took it and sipped, watching the writers exchange glances. Margaret sat across from Jordan, whilst Joseph sat next to him, placing his fingers together, watching the scenario in front of him.

"We weren't friends with him," Andy said. "He came to the group and was so up himself, the man didn't realise none of us liked him."

The group laughed at this, enjoying the joke. Jordan glanced at Joseph, whose face was impassive.

"James was a good writer, nonetheless," Margaret barked. "Which is why he belonged in this group."

"Was he really, Margaret?" Andy leaned forwards. "I seem to remember him being unable to write *anything*. He was always struggling to come up with something. In fact—" Andy turned away from Margaret's stony face to address Jordan. "—he told me he had loads of unfinished projects saved on his computer and printed out in drawers. He just could never finish anything. Something else always came along and *that* was *the one*."

The classical music changed on the radio. Joseph swayed slightly to the tune.

"Did you know he had a book deal?"

There was silence for a moment as everyone took in this information. Jordan knew that both Joseph and Margaret knew, but he wondered how widespread this information was.

"Yes, we knew," Franchesca finally said. "He bragged about it big time."

"Seemed odd," Graham said.

"Why?"

Graham leaned backwards in his chair, crossing his muscular arms. The man wasn't slim, and underneath his jumper, Jordan imagined him to be rotund, rather than ripped.

"Well, James hadn't written anything for months. That was very vocalised. Then, all of a sudden, he had this deal with Sphere, and we didn't know how that had happened," Graham said.

"Is it hard to get a book deal?"

Most of the writers laughed, except for Sarah and Margaret.

"It's very hard," Franchesca said. "The odds are slim."

"Though some people do it." Andy smiled widely at Joseph.

"That's right. Some people do. And there's no reason why you won't be able to, either."

Jordan allowed the writers to bathe in the glory of Joseph's words. Even now, he was encouraging them. He eyed the notepads on the table, where some people had written short extracts from a chapter and others had written plans.

"Do you have the notepad from James?"

"I don't."

Jordan chose Graham's notepad. "Do you mind?"

"No, have a look."

Graham had neat handwriting. He looked at the plot for a comedy novel that involved an ex-miner. Jordan flipped through the pages briefly, noting that other things had been written, such as character biographies and research into mining.

"Did James do all of this?"

"Barely," Franchesca said.

"He preferred to work at his own merit," Margaret said. "He did his own notes when he got back home."

"And you know this because?"

Margaret glared at Jordan. "Because he told me."

"I see." Jordan paused. "Does the Lower New Inn ring any bells to any of you?"

It was a conscious choice to issue it to the whole room, but it had the desired effect on Margaret, whose eyes widened and tough exterior fell. The pair had previously discussed it, but Jordan suspected Margaret would not want to admit it in front of her peers.

"Um..."

"Why do you ask that?" Margaret asked.

Jordan looked at her, feeling like the room was empty now. "Why do you think?"

"Joseph, this man has no idea what is going on."

"He's just doing his job."

"No, he's interfering in the death of a member."

"My job is to investigate how one of your members was murdered, Margaret. Now, do *you* know much about the Lower New Inn?"

Margaret looked like she wanted to leap across the table and wring Jordan's neck. He enjoyed her reaction, letting the accusation float in the room between them. He wanted Margaret to admit that they spent time together outside of the writing group to everybody else.

"I don't."

"Hm," Jordan said. "Margaret, I'm going to need you to tell the truth."

Margaret glanced at Joseph, then at the other writers. "I don't know."

"Well, I know for a fact that a week before James's death, you went out for drinks with him at the Lower New Inn. There, at that pub, you spent the evening with him, even escorting him home. Why was he kicked out?"

The other writers seemed shocked, Andy grinning to himself at this juicy revelation.

"He was drunk." Margaret was blushing, embarrassed that she had been caught out.

"I see. Why were you spending time with him?"

"We were just having a drink."

"A cosy evening, wouldn't you say?"

"Excuse me?"

"I'd just say you both looked pretty cosy."

"Oh my god, Margaret!" Graham gasped. "Were the two of you an item?"

Margaret flushed a brighter red, and the group collectively gasped, her reaction enough of an admission.

Jordan was pleased with himself. Now, the other writers would know what Margaret had been up to.

"It's not like that. You don't understand."

"I can't believe you were with him!" Franchesca looked disgusted.

"How long were you together?"

"Joseph…"

In the commotion, Jordan hadn't recognised Joseph's reaction. He looked annoyed, his eyes narrowed and his expression grim. He was looking at Margaret like he didn't know her.

"Joseph?" Jordan said.

But Joseph was deaf to the others, blind to them too. He could only see Margaret, and he was furious. "I think you need to leave."

Margaret stood up, but she stayed where she was. "Joseph, he's lying."

"There is CCTV evidence of you spending the evening with him in that pub. Enough evidence to even suggest you are more than friends."

"Suggest?" Margaret exclaimed. "That's all you have? Suggestions? He was a *friend*. That's all he was!"

"I said you should leave."

"I thought you said, Margaret, that James was not a friend of yours?"

Margaret shook her head. "No, none of you understand. There was a reason I was seeing James. A reason we were together…"

"Leave, Margaret." Joseph's tone was final.

The room seemed to pause as the atmosphere changed. The revelation that Margaret had been going out with James on a romantic level had been shocking. But Joseph's reaction was worse. Jordan studied the two people, the anger from one looking and the dismay of the other.

"This isn't over," Margaret hissed at Jordan. "You've got it wrong."

She stormed out of the kitchen and slammed the door behind her. The other writers all withdrew, their humour gone.

"Joseph…"

"Well, I'm sorry you had to see that." Joseph attempted a breezy personality, but his angry expression would not leave his face. "But I just found out my wife has been cheating on me."

THIRTY-ONE

"Why didn't anyone tell me Joseph was married to Margaret?"

Jordan sat in his car outside the private street where Joseph had quickly told his guests to leave. Jordan had been the last to leave, hoping to get more out of the author who had just discovered his wife had been seeing another man, but he had been met with one-word answers and a pointed look at the front door.

Vanessa breathed in on the other end of the phone. "Well, we didn't know ourselves."

"You're telling me there are no records? No hints in the media? This man lives a public life. How could we not know?"

Jordan was pissed off. Margaret being the wife of Joseph changed things. Jordan had a nagging doubt in his head, but he could not place it. Memories all blurred into one, and that annoyed Jordan even more. He felt like doors had been closed on them, but they had frosted glass, allowing him to see in, but only make out blurred shapes.

"I don't know. Joseph never mentioned a wife or a partner, and we asked him. He said he was single. The media never picked up on it. We didn't suspect anything, either."

"But now it makes sense that Margaret has access to that house."

"What are you saying?"

"Margaret can come and go. Joseph said so himself, though he told me that a lot of the writers can come and go as they please, as well as kitchen staff and cleaners."

"So then Margaret's access to the house is rather insignificant, don't you think?"

Jordan looked out of the window and spotted Graham in a 2014 BMW. Graham smiled as he made eye contact with Jordan, and once again, Jordan felt slightly odd. Jordan broke eye contact, wondering why the man was waiting, staring at him. Conscious of lip reading, Jordan covered his mouth as if yawning.

"Margaret is a suspect, just like everybody else. What I don't get is why she would want James dead, if she was having an affair with him. There's more to all of this than we know."

"It's your job to solve it."

"With your help, Vanessa." Jordan remembered that Vanessa was still annoyed with him, but he couldn't have her being unprofessional. Not now.

"I know. But we hired you to find out what you can to assist us. We have other cases on, and we're understaffed. I trust you, Jordan. You know I do."

Jordan glanced at Graham again, who this time raised a hand. "Listen, I've got to go. But I'll call you if anything else comes up. I need to think things through, piece a couple of things together."

"Of course."

Jordan hung up and got out of his car, then walked across the street to Graham, who wound down his window.

"How did you feel about that?" Graham smirked.

"Did you know those two were married?"

"No," Graham replied. "I'm serious. None of us did. Joseph lives in that house alone. We just thought Margaret wanted everything she could get from him, mentorship wise. She was his companion. He told her everything. But we never once saw them kiss or talk about their marriage."

"Really?"

Graham smirked again, and Jordan tried to remain focussed. "Yeah, really. Joseph has always been…aloof with his personal life. He never talked about a lover or friends. He was always about the writing."

"And how would you say he is as a mentor?"

Graham looked behind him, at the quiet street. "Look, I live five minutes away. Why don't you come back to mine and I can tell you what I know then?"

Jordan thought for a moment, wondering why Graham wanted him alone. Graham wasn't top of his suspect list, but he was involved somehow. Was it such a good idea?

"I don't know. Why not tell me now?"

"Because this is rather open, and I'd like to just relax. I'm pretty tired. Honestly, I'd like to help you solve the murder of James. The man was a pig, but he didn't deserve death."

Jordan checked his phone. It was late. But he knew if he went home now, he would be unable to sleep. "Fine. I'll follow you."

Eight minutes later, Jordan had parked up on the side street behind Graham's BMW, and the pair were walking into a small block of communal flats. Graham, probably in his early thirties, lived in a flat on the second floor. It had two bedrooms, a small bathroom, and a living room blended into a kitchen. It was rather clean inside, generic plasterboard white walls and beige carpets on the floor, unstained and still like new.

Graham seemed to sense what Jordan was thinking. "I come from Wales originally, but I worked in Liverpool for eight years. I came back to Wales last year, just over, and I've lived here since. I rent, but I want to eventually buy."

"What do you do for work?"

"I work as a car salesman," Graham said. "BMW, if you hadn't guessed by my car. I work in Newport. It's fine, but nothing fancy."

Jordan sensed Graham was thinking about something else. "What did you do in Liverpool?"

"I moved up there with my ex-husband." Jordan's eyes lost contact with Graham's. "It got pretty bad up there. His mother died and he changed. He was always angry, and it just didn't work."

"I'm…"

"Don't. You don't have to say you're sorry." Graham went to the kitchen and put on the kettle. He realised then that it needed topping up, so filled it with cold water and put it back on the platform, where it began to heat up. "I'm happy with this little place for now, but I'd like to get back into engineering, like I was doing up there. It would be nice to be able to actually afford a bigger place."

"I understand."

He did. His flat was rented, and he didn't see any way of getting a house of his own. His friends had all bought or were at least cohabiting with other people. Jordan sometimes felt as though he was behind the ranks.

"You local?"

"I live in Cardiff, yes," Jordan replied. "Anyway, this isn't about me."

Graham grinned. "Involved in your work, I see."

"A man's been murdered," Jordan said.

Graham's smile fell. "I know."

Jordan sat without being asked on a small faux-leather chair. Graham sat opposite him on a sofa. The TV's red standby light was on, but Graham didn't bother to spring the screen into action.

"Were you his friend?"

"A friend of James? Not really, no. He was a pig. I saw how he treated women, and the comments he made really pissed me off. But like I say, he didn't deserve death. No one does."

"Did you know he was murdered?"

"A man doesn't just drop dead like that. He was choking. It was so scary."

The kettle boiled, and Graham jumped as if he had been lost in the memory of the man's death at the writing table. Graham got to his feet and took out two mugs.

"I'll have a tea," Jordan said. "Not coffee."

"I only have tea, so that was what you were going to get."

Jordan smiled as Graham brought the teas over. He drank immediately, realising how thirsty he was. "What happened when Joseph went into the kitchen?"

"Well, I changed my order after he had gone in. I called Joseph, and Joseph comes back into the room to see what I want. I remember now being vaguely aware of noise in the kitchen. Just normal noises, you know? Just another person there, a clink on the glass that sort of thing. But I didn't think anything of it."

"Why?"

Graham thought for a moment. "Joseph's house was always a hub of activity. If there were no writers there, then there was usually a cleaner. I don't know if Joseph did it to everyone, but he offered me private mentoring, so I would go on an afternoon away from all the other writers and discuss my own work with him. He was very helpful. Like I say, seeing Joseph personally and in his home most of the time, you'd think I'd know if he was married, especially to Margaret. She was there a lot, but she never bothered us."

"Were you not sceptical as to why she was there?"

"No. The woman adored him. But she was always poring over notes. She was there to write, too, even when the other writers weren't. Joseph gave us all keys, access to the private estate and the street. I only used mine for my extra mentoring lessons. I felt cheeky coming and going. Margaret didn't, but now I wonder if that was because she was comfortable with the man."

"And Margaret, where does she live?"

"She lives in St Mellons," Graham replied instantly. "I know this because we went there for drinks before we went out last Christmas."

Jordan sipped his tea. "So they live separately?"

"Yeah, must do. I've heard of couples doing that. I guess everyone's different."

It wasn't implausible. Jordan knew of other couples that had been together for years but had not moved in with one another. Married couples, however, seemed strange. Yet living alone gave the pair plenty of time to see other people, as was the case with Margaret and James. Jordan wondered what excuses Margaret had made to Joseph when she had stayed in New Inn with James in the lead-up to his murder.

Jordan knew that Margaret was key in this. She had spent the most time with James, and so he hoped she knew more of what was happening in his life leading up to his death.

But what didn't make sense was why she and Sally were missing that night. James had been killed by a final dosage of poison inside Joseph's home. Which meant that either Joseph had administered the killer dose, or someone had come in from the outside with a perfect alibi.

"What are you thinking about?" Graham questioned. He had moved closer, ever so slightly. Jordan only now realised how small this living room was, and how close the chair was to the sofa. Their knees almost touched. Jordan could see the hairs on Graham's arms.

"I'm trying to work things out. You've been helpful."

Graham placed a hand on Jordan's knee. "If I can do anything, just let me know."

Jordan leaned in, and when his lips touched Graham, he was relieved that he hadn't been rejected. The kiss was good, smooth, and warm. They got closer, feeling warmth and companionship. As Graham raised his hand to Jordan's neck to pull him closer, their mugs of tea forgotten about, Jordan broke away.

"I…"

Graham sank back into the sofa. "It's fine."

Jordan stood up, shaking, considering the door and wishing he was out of this apartment. Coming back here had been a mistake. "Thanks. If you think you need to tell me anything else, then…" Jordan fished in his back pocket, relieved to find a business card. "Call my number. Anything that is relevant to the case."

Graham took the card, nodding politely. "I will. I'll have a think tomorrow. You don't mind anything?"

"Anything could help."

When Jordan left the apartment and was sat back in the comfort of his own car, he thought of what could have happened with Graham. It had been a few months since he had been with a man. The desire had disappeared after the death of his mother but even failed to burn before that. A night like this reminded him of the problems he'd had, of the way he let cases consume him, and the darkness that crept into his thoughts when he couldn't sleep.

Graham was a nice man. His reaction to the kiss had told him that. Temptation told him to go back, to submit to the man he had only just met. But that would be foolish.

A one-night stand was not the answer.

Taking out his phone, Jordan called Lloyd.

It was late, but he answered. "What's up?"

"I thought you might want to come over for a drink."

THIRTY-TWO

When Jordan woke up the next morning, the warmth of skin pressed next to him. Turning over, a topless Lloyd lay on his back, his eyes closed, breathing deeply.

Instead of being ashamed or even worried, Jordan turned over and laid his head on his chest, then wrapped an arm over him. Lloyd had shown up half an hour after the call. The pair had talked, had one drink, and then Jordan had allowed himself something he had been ignoring for months.

Stirring, Lloyd stretched. The blankets lifted ever so slightly, and Jordan realised Lloyd was naked.

"Morning," Lloyd's croaky voice said.

"Morning."

They laughed, neither of them looking at one another. Today, their relationship had reached a new point. There was no going back from this, yet there was no going forward either.

"I hope you're not thinking of that murder case," Lloyd said, wrapping his arm around Jordan's shoulders.

"Yeah, I was thinking I'd rather be putting that together than being here."

"Quite rude."

Jordan looked at Lloyd, who kissed him lightly on the lips.

"Quite rude indeed." Jordan smiled.

They could hear life outside on the street, since Jordan's window had been left slightly ajar from the night before.

Lloyd turned his head to the closed blinds. "What are you going to do today?"

"I need to get that interview with Margaret."

Lloyd shifted where he lay. "Instant turnoff."

Jordan grinned. "I'm sorry."

"You don't want to spend the day with me?"

Jordan moved away from Lloyd ever so slightly. "I just thought…"

"Calm, Jordan," Lloyd soothed. "I know."

Jordan felt relieved, if a little ashamed. Lloyd didn't need to be told that last night had been a one-off. Jordan had felt lonely, had felt a desire he had been suppressing, and Lloyd had been there. Of course, Lloyd had been hoping to get Jordan on a date ever since they had met. At least now the date had been skipped.

Lloyd went in the shower, walking past Jordan naked, and then the rushing water sounded in the room next door. Waking up today had been fun. Jordan missed companionship, someone to spend the time with. Friends were fine, but intimacy was on another level. And Oscar was, of course, a cat. Jordan hadn't been one to sleep around, and he didn't consider this to be something sordid. He knew Lloyd, knew that on some level they could work.

But Jordan wasn't ready.

Lloyd left after breakfast, saying he had something to do with his mother. The thought of Lloyd's parents made Jordan remember Peter and the emptying of his mother's house. Jordan said goodbye and kissed Lloyd lightly on the cheek, savouring Lloyd's cheeky smile, and then, once the door was closed, Jordan rang Peter.

"Do you want to go to Mum's today?"

Peter breathed in, seemingly afraid of the prospect of seeing the life of a woman he used to love. "Yes."

After showering and changing, Jordan quickly made some notes on the case. Why was it so important that Margaret was married to Joseph? There was a memory, rotting in his brain, but he could not call it.

"Be good, Oscar," Jordan called as he left his apartment.

Jordan waited outside for his dad. The air was cold, and it seemed colder because Jordan wasn't wearing a coat. As a bitter wind swept by and Jordan considered running in for his parka, his dad pulled up, not bothering to turn off the engine.

Jordan got in, and Peter drove off, towards where he knew Annabelle lived.

"Why today?"

Jordan shrugged. "I just thought it was something that needed to be done. I've been putting it off for too long."

"You and me both."

"You know where you're going?"

"Yes, Jordan."

BBC Radio 2 was on, and Jordan was relieved to find he had just missed Chris Evans's show. Many people liked him, but for some reason, Jordan couldn't stand the man.

"I heard from your brother last night."

Jordan looked out of the window. He thought of Ashley and the strong relationship they'd had when growing up.

"Did he have much to say?"

"Problems with Ben." His boyfriend. Ben worked in property, and when Jordan had met him, he had quickly had to leave the conversation. There was only so much of Ben's ego that Jordan could take.

"I see."

"I just told him to consider his options."

"You want him home."

"I thought I did, but he likes Australia."

"There are plenty of other men in Australia, I suppose."

"I'm not saying that," Peter began.

Jordan sometimes wondered how Peter felt that his only two sons were gay. Peter had always shown interest in their partners and whether or not they were dating anyone.

Peter turned up a side street in Caerleon. The houses here were petite and unique, the Roman layout of the street still evident even today. There was barely enough room for cars, which is why there were one-way streets, and as Peter parallel parked in a narrow alley, Jordan held his breath.

Annabelle's house was the first in a small community. All of the houses here had window ledges that were uneven, doors that you had to crouch to get into, and cobbled footpaths leading around to the small, back garden.

Peter fished in his pocket for a key, the golden metal glistening in the weak winter sunshine.

Jordan looked at the window by the door, which had a view into the living room. He swallowed. "Was that where…?"

Peter glanced at the top of the armchair that was visible. "Yes."

When the door opened, they were greeted with letters. Peter bent down to pick them up, and it was then that Jordan saw one in a familiar handwritten font.

"Dad, wait."

Peter did, crouched with a few letters in his hand. He moved aside as Jordan picked up the letter that was addressed simply to Annabelle. There was no stamp.

They walked into the hallway, which smelled of stale air freshener. Peter shut the door, looking around for a switch to light up the dim room. Jordan turned the letter over in his hand and opened the envelope. Inside was a single sheet of lined paper, a handwritten note on the page.

I know what happened. They're close to finding out. I could choose to spill it all, or I could choose to let them fail. Either way, you would come out the victim. Rot in Hell, bitch.

THIRTY-THREE

The letter lay open on the table in the kitchen. Jordan stared at it as he let the kettle boil. Peter stood out in the garden, once neat and well tended to, now overgrowing with dying flowers and bloated soil.

The font of the letter was the same as the writing on the letter the boy had tried to give him. Suspecting Kim, Jordan wondered if she had been here, writing to a woman who was dead? Jordan had tried ringing Kim's number immediately, but it had gone straight through to voicemail.

Being in Annabelle's house felt wrong. Remnants of her life were everywhere. Nobody had been in since her body had been removed, meaning there were mouldy cups left in the sink, a coffee-stained spoon stuck to the counter, a window open at the back of the house, letting in damp.

The kitchen was rather cosy, thick stone walls and hung-up trinkets, but it felt foreign to Jordan. This wasn't the mother he had known. The mother he had known had been tidy, neat, and annoyed when something was out of place.

As Jordan touched a damp tea towel hanging up on a drawer handle, he felt like his mother had shed her old skin and adopted a new life.

This house felt more carefree, more independent, and less strict. As Jordan walked through the hallway to the dining room, photo frames hung on the wall, all of Annabelle alone, stood somewhere with something behind her or next to her. His mother had gone to Amsterdam, Sweden, Paris. Who had taken the photos? Had she set her phone up on a timer, asked a stranger, travelled with Terry, or had she been living with someone?

Coming out of the dining room, Jordan found himself in the living room, a flight of stairs leading to bedrooms and bathroom to his left. He was faced with the chair his mother had been found in. There were magazines on the table next to it, a newspaper on the floor, and a house phone that was no longer used.

The chair she had sat in was plump, designed to look old yet without a thread missing. There was a rug on the floor, next to a real coal fire; all that was left inside were a few ashes. A window looked out onto the garden, and in the weak sun, Jordan's dad perched on the wall, his back turned and his shoulders hunched.

Jordan didn't sit down. He stood in the living room, feeling the life of the woman he no longer knew. Underneath the stairs was a cupboard, a key inside the lock. Jordan was about to look inside when the kitchen door clicked closed. Peter had come back in, after regaining composure after the letter.

"Jordan?"

"I'm in here."

Peter came in, a grim look on his face as he registered the chair. "Where do you want to start?"

Jordan knew that Peter didn't want to talk about the letter. The letter would go with him, to give to Vanessa who would add it to the other threats.

"Why not the kitchen? We can go from the back of the house to the front."

Peter agreed. They began in the kitchen, taking out black bin bags and organising what went where. Most of this stuff would end up in charity shops, but if there was something sentimental that Peter wanted, he put it in a green bin bag.

Peter found photographs and skimmed through them. "She really did live a different life when she was alone."

"Where is she there?"

"Looks like Spain. I can't be sure."

"Who did she go with?" Jordan asked, looking at a photo of his mother stood feet away from the camera on the beach.

"I don't know."

Jordan sensed sorrow in Peter's tone. The man was mourning the wife he had lost years before her death.

"Was she seeing anyone, Dad? Do you know?"

"She never told me if she was."

"But it's possible."

"I suppose. She never wanted to rekindle what we had. She lived a very private life once we split. These photos look like she's alone. There's no man."

"But who's taking them?"

"Could be anybody, couldn't it?"

Peter picked up another photo set, and this time, he looked confused. "Don't you know this man?"

His mother had been photographed with Joseph Gordon. The next photo showed his mother with Franchesca and Graham. "Can I take those?"

"Yes."

Peter watched as Jordan flicked through the photos. There were photographs of Annabelle sat at a table, notes spread out in front of her. There was a white wall behind her, which made it impossible to tell where she was. Annabelle was then photographed with Sally and Margaret. Margaret was barely smiling, whilst Sally looked thrilled. Annabelle looked impatient, as if she wanted to be somewhere else, her attention drawn over the camera, to someone behind it.

Then, as Jordan put one photo behind another, he came across one of Annabelle stood in Joseph's kitchen. She was caught in laughter, a genuine smile lighting up her face. Her arm was wrapped around James, who was holding a bottle of beer. Behind them was a birthday banner. With shaking hands, Jordan turned to the next photo to discover Annabelle stood in this very kitchen, smiling next to Kim. In the reflection of the dark kitchen window was James, holding up the camera.

"Mum was in the writing group. She was a friend of James."

THIRTY-FOUR

"Do you think Kim wrote this letter?"

It was late evening, and Jordan sat in Vanessa's office with Vanessa and Mark. The letter was on the table in front of them, crinkled at the edges from use.

"And it was at your mum's house?" Mark asked.

"Yes," Jordan said. "The letter was at my mum's house."

"Annabelle's," Mark stated.

"Yes."

"How long has she been dead?"

"Four months," Jordan replied, stung at the blunt tone in his words.

"And do we have any evidence she knew Kim?"

"Plenty."

"What sort of evidence?"

"Mark, there is plenty of evidence. Give it a rest," Vanessa interjected. "Jordan, are you feeling okay?"

"I just want to know where Kim is. Who knows when this letter was posted, but it's about us, isn't it? It's about the case we're working on."

The door opened, and Lloyd walked in, carrying a tray of one tea and three coffees. Vanessa's was black, and she took hers as soon as Lloyd set down the tray.

"What are you even doing here?" Mark asked. "This isn't your department."

"Forensics aren't in, so this letter will be coming with me, once you're finished ogling it. I can make sure it goes to the right people."

"Have you got the other letters?"

"Of course."

"Does the writing match?" Jordan asked.

Lloyd looked at the letter again. "I'd say so, but it could be extremely similar. There's ways for the forensic team to check if it's written by the same hand or a copycat. I couldn't tell you that."

138

"Kim is still a missing person. Mark, I think you need to visit her community and ask if anyone saw Kim snooping around."

"When?"

"Tomorrow. It's too late now."

Mark nodded, taking out his phone and typing the instruction in it.

Jordan rolled his eyes, exchanging an annoyed glance with Lloyd. "What's the address?"

Vanessa recited the address and then turned to Jordan. "You said you requested CCTV from the security guard at Joseph's. Have you managed to view it yet?"

"I haven't," Jordan replied. "I'll do that tonight."

"CCTV?" Mark questioned.

"Yes, CCTV. The private street has security cameras, believe it or not."

"Well, why didn't we get that?"

"We were told the footage would be sent to us, but it never was. Of course, we were pursuing it, but that's why Jordan is here."

"To do our job?"

"To help out where possible and ultimately solve the case."

"Right." Mark took his coffee. "I'm going to go and research the area. Let me know what happens with this letter."

Vanessa took the letter and handed it to Lloyd. "It's been contaminated, but see if George can find anything of significance. Check the writing to the other letters. We're still pursuing leads for Kim, but she keeps ending up a dead end."

"You mean she's disappeared?" Lloyd took the letter, reading it once more.

"We have no idea where she's gone. She was last spotted a week ago in a SPAR in Cwmbran. Her family are spaced all around the UK, and they haven't heard from her, either."

"It's highly possible she didn't post this letter," Jordan said.

Lloyd put the letter on the table beside him and perched on the edge. "How did your dad feel about going to Annabelle's house?"

Jordan had retold the story of discovering the letter earlier. Peter had refused to speak about it again once they had got to the cleaning. He had driven Jordan to the police station and said goodbye, pensive on the journey down.

"He realised just how much she had changed, I think. He remembered that the woman he married no longer existed, and not because of death. She changed after leaving him."

"The photographs of her in the writing group are an interesting development," Vanessa said. "Photographic evidence of her with James. Why has Joseph been keeping that from you?"

"I don't know. You'd think they'd tell me about it."

"Do you have the photos on you?"

Jordan nodded. From his pocket, he took out the sachet of photographs that he had taken from his mother's home. He passed them across the table, and Vanessa flicked through them.

Her face fell as she looked through them.

"Vanessa, what is it?"

"I've just realised. Remember I told you I was called to a disturbance once before at Joseph's home? I remember why. Your mother had been in a heated argument with two of the members."

Jordan felt like he had been drenched in ice. The conversation with Vanessa in December came back to him, sat in her van on the scene of the murder. Vanessa had told him about the time there had been a disturbance reported to neighbours involving the writing group.

Annabelle had been there.

"What was the disturbance?"

"An argument, between your mother, James, and Sally. There was alcohol, lots of smashed glasses. Joseph calmed them down when we arrived."

"Why had they been arguing?"

"Over work. Something they had been writing."

Jordan shook his head. "A manuscript?"

"They didn't say." Vanessa's forehead creased. "It was just a heated argument about their writing. But Jordan, there was something else. I didn't realise Annabelle was your mother, otherwise I would have put this together a long time ago."

"It's the last name. We didn't speak. You couldn't have known," Jordan said, feeling as though he was the only one in the room with Vanessa. Lloyd sat on the edge of the table, biting his lip, watching the exchange. "What is it?"

"Your mother. She told me she had been arguing with her boyfriend." Jordan knew what was about to come before Vanessa said it. "It's just clicked that her boyfriend was James Fairview."

THIRTY-FIVE

At home, Jordan flicked through the photos of his mother with the members of the writing group for the umpteenth time, trying to get information from anything, hoping it would make things clearer.

But instead of seeing the photos with her friends, he was remembering the photos of her on holiday in exotic locations, stood away from the camera with someone else taking them.

That had to have been James.

His mother had been dating James, yet Jordan knew James had also been having an affair with Sally. Sally, who had been in the argument with Annabelle and James the night Vanessa had been called to the disturbance.

Jordan couldn't believe it, but he knew it to be true. Why had this been kept from him? Did Joseph have a twisted game? Had he been waiting to see how long it took for Jordan to work it out?

Jordan cursed himself. Could he have worked it out sooner?

He felt like this was ironic. He had started work again to forget about his mother, to not dwell on the stranger that had died. Instead, she had consumed him.

Jordan's phone lit up with a text message from Ashley. He ignored it.

He wished he could go back to his mother's home, to investigate the links between her and James further. Surely his mother's phone was still in the house, with possible messages to James. When had the messages stopped? Had it been before her death, or had they stopped because of it?

Jordan stopped at a photo of his mother sat at a desk. It looked like an amateur candid author shot, as if she had taken it in the hopes of using it on the back of her novel. Who had taken it? There were no surfaces in the background to reflect the person behind the lens. Instead, Annabelle was in a cosy setting, a stone wall behind her, a desk with papers, a pen poised over a manuscript on the table. There was a full cup of coffee next to her.

The wall was not part of her home, yet it didn't look like a café. Intuition told him it was a home, maybe by the lighting or the closeness of the camera, the relaxed expression on his mother's face.

Had she lost weight? A little bit. She had always been slim, but Jordan remembered her face being rounder.

He touched the photo with his index finger. How had this happened to her? She hadn't deserved this. She'd been caught up in trouble, and it had cost her. But why?

Jordan made a note in his phone. What linked them was the affair with James, when James had also been linked to Sally and Margaret. That link meant there was motive. Joseph could be jealous, Kim could be jealous, Sally and Margaret could be jealous. But who would go far enough to kill, and to kill slowly and so brazenly?

With an aching head, Jordan got up and headed to his bedroom. He patted the bed and Oscar joined him. It was still relatively early in the evening, but with the winter sun already set, it felt like midnight. Hearing wind outside and a light rainfall, Jordan crumpled onto his bed fully dressed and fell asleep almost instantly.

When he woke up, he felt disorientated. There was knocking at his front door, but it could only be midnight, surely?

The clock on his wall said it was ten to eight in the morning. Feeling like he had only blinked, he got up, groggy and tired. Oscar stayed curled on the bed.

Upon opening the door, he found Peter, more awake than he should be at this time in the morning.

"Turn on the news."

Peter moved past his son and to the living room, where he could turn the news on himself. Yawning, Jordan followed his dad into the room.

BBC News was on, and there were scenes of a forensics tent erected in Belle Vue Park, which was in Newport, close to the hospital. Police tape had been set up, and the camera filmed police officers stood at the scene, keeping watch to ensure members of the public did not go in. The shot changed to the fences leading into the park, closed, with a police officer stood outside them. The frame of the camera zoomed out, revealing a reporter at the scene.

"The body of the woman was found in the early hours of this morning by a dog walker. They first spotted a dark mass lying on the floor and, upon further investigation, realised it was a body."

As if by psychic intuition, Jordan already knew what was about to be said.

"The body is said to belong to Kim Bennedict, who has been missing for over a week. Kim has links to recently murdered writer, James Fairview. The police have said that the incidents are not related."

"Not related?" Peter said.

Jordan didn't reply. He just shook his head. This was too much. Kim was dead. But her body had been left in the middle of the grass, for the first person to find.

"She's been dead longer," Jordan said. "I don't think she would have been left like that. Someone's toying with us."

Peter sunk onto the sofa. "Ghastly."

The footage changed back to the scene of the park. Jordan listened to the voice of a police officer from Gwent Police. "We are treating the case as suspicious, however, we don't have evidence yet that Kim's murder is related to the murder of her acquaintance, James Fairview. Kim has been missing for a while, and attempts to contact her have gone unnoticed. It is possible that this hasn't happened overnight, but we won't be able to tell until forensics has taken everything into consideration. We are agreeing to share jurisdiction with Cardiff Police."

The footage changed back to the reporter. "There have been no witnesses, and due to the nature of the body being found, it is uncertain if Kim came in to the park late last night. The gates usually close in an attempt to stop loiterers, but it is possible people can climb the gate. Kim was a writer in bestselling authors Joseph Gordon's writing group, and he has said he is devastated that his close friend has been killed. The victim was found with bruises on her neck, though there is no confirmation yet as to how she died. We'll bring you the latest when we get it."

The video cut back to the studio, where a passive-looking female reporter stood. Jordan muted the TV before she could speak, sitting down next to his father.

"You found that letter last night. Was it from her?"

Jordan rubbed his eyes. He couldn't make sense of what was happening. "I don't know."

Jordan's mind was elsewhere. Heading to his room, he found his phone. He had missed calls from Vanessa and Lloyd.

Jordan called Lloyd, but there was no answer. Upon dialling Vanessa's number, he also got no answer. He remembered Mark and dialled his number reluctantly, and after the fourth ring, Mark answered.

"Finally got out of bed?" Mark asked.

Jordan thought it was meant to be a joke, a way of bonding with the man he had got off the wrong foot with. Jordan wasn't in the mood. "Where is everyone? Any new updates?"

Mark sighed. "Kim's been murdered."

"Yes, I know."

"Vanessa thinks she was dumped there last night, on purpose, and probably not long before the walker came by. The walker isn't a suspect, by the way."

"Okay."

"We suspect Kim has been dead for a few days."

"And where is Kim now?"

"Her body has been moved for autopsy."

"Where is Vanessa?"

"She's on the scene."

"Get her to ring me when she returns to the office. I'm going to question Joseph."

"I'm not…"

Jordan hung up. He briefly thought that Mark had got the job because he was qualified, that he should treat him with a bit more respect, but right now, he wanted the man to know that Jordan had authority too.

You had to work together in this career, and he suspected Mark didn't understand that.

"Dad, I don't think we should go to Mum's today."

"But we need to. We need to clear things out."

"This has happened and I need to sort things out." Jordan looked at the news, the story now on something else. "Do you think I can meet you later?"

Peter nodded. "Of course."

After Peter left, Jordan showered and quickly changed, not bothering to tame his overgrowing hair. He left the house, got in his Golf, and drove to Joseph's home. The press were outside the gates and photographed Jordan as he drove in, being allowed in by the security in the box.

When Jordan parked outside Joseph's, the door opened, and Joseph walked out, his arms crossed and his face gaunt.

The man looked ill.

"I expected you to come."

THIRTY-SIX

Sat at the kitchen table, Joseph was already drinking alcohol. Jordan refused a drink, too tired to even consider something other than coffee.

"I'm not surprised she's dead, but it's awful."

"Why aren't you surprised?"

"Please, she's been missing. You don't just disappear like that. I feared the worst, hoped for the best, but we got the worst."

"When was the last time you heard from her, Joseph?"

Joseph looked Jordan dead in the eyes. "The day before she disappeared."

It was hard to tell if Joseph was lying or not. Either he was a great liar or he genuinely meant it.

Joseph drank his cider, looking out at the cloudy day through the window. "She was a lovely woman. Great writer, very kind. She helped us all, even me."

"Joseph, why did you stay with her when you were released after questioning?"

"I don't know what you mean."

"Instead of coming back here or staying with Margaret. Why Kim?"

Joseph shook his head. "I don't think you'd understand."

"I've investigated a lot of things and met lots of people. I'd understand anything."

Joseph almost grinned. "Coming out of that jail was going to be tough. I couldn't return here because I knew the press would be swarming, and I just wanted one night or so where I could disappear off the radar. Kim was my confidante. Whenever I had a problem with something personal, somehow I always told Kim. It was just a bond we had." He looked at Jordan. "Purely platonic, I assure you."

"And did Margaret know?"

"Of course she knew, and she understood. We've been married almost twelve years, and Margaret knows how I work and what I like. She

145

understood that Kim could help me, and she didn't mind. We had a good relationship like that."

Jordan noticed the past tense. Keeping this in mind, he asked his next question. "But Kim wasn't living in that house, was she?"

"I didn't know that."

"I see."

"Trust me, I didn't. I never went in the bedrooms. I didn't stay long enough to get comfortable there. I wouldn't allow it, and I felt like Kim wouldn't allow it either."

"Being close to Kim, did you ever visit her house?"

"Kim was private about her own life, so no. None of us did. She always said she lived out of Cardiff, and that was the extent of what we knew, but like I said before, I knew she previously lived in Blaenavon. If ever we met outside of this group, we'd go to someone else's home or somewhere in public."

"So Kim was a closed book."

"You could say that. We knew each other well, yet she was a stranger to me too."

"Do you know if Kim had enemies?"

"Other than James? No. I don't think she did. She was sweet and innocent."

Jordan remembered meeting Kim, how she had served him food, yet remained aloof, distant almost, lost in a different world. Had she been scared of someone?

"She trusted you."

Joseph looked at Jordan. "Yes, she did."

"Why?"

Joseph rolled his eyes. "We were close. That's all I can say, really. We understood one another, and she was there to help me. When she disappeared, well, I was pissed off. I thought she'd message me or tell me what was going on. I worried when I heard nothing from her."

"Nothing at all?"

"Nothing at all. She disappeared into thin air and I couldn't work out why."

"It does seem very sudden."

Joseph leaned back in his chair. "Do you think Kim murdered James?"

Jordan was thrown by the question. The thought hadn't even entered his mind. "Judging by the fact she was murdered, I don't think so."

"But they're not linked," Joseph said this with hope, as if he was clinging to it.

"There's no evidence to say that."

"But the reporter…"

"Reported on it incorrectly. At this time, there is no evidence that it is linked to the murder of James. Different methods of killing might suggest that, but it seems too coincidental to me. Don't you agree?"

Joseph swallowed, as if his mouth was dry. "I guess so. Oh, Jesus."

"What?"

"My writers, they're dropping like flies. It doesn't seem real."

"I appreciate that this is probably hard for you."

Joseph tapped his glass of cider. "I don't recommend drinking at this hour. But I need to. Ever since James, alcohol has been there."

Jordan nodded slowly, but he recognised the signs of an in-denial alcoholic. The regular meetups, the socialising over whisky and wine. The bottles in the cupboards and displayed in the wine rack. Joseph's muse was alcohol.

"Where is Margaret?"

"I don't know." Joseph breathed out. "I haven't seen her since…"

"Okay. You say you were married to her, and still are. Tell me more about that."

"What else is there to tell, young man? We met, we dated, we married a year later. When you know, you know. We lived together for two years in Port Talbot, but it didn't work out. Since then, we've lived separately. It works for us."

"And her affair, you knew nothing about it?"

"Clearly not. Don't you remember my reaction?"

"Of course I do."

"Well, then, don't ask silly questions," Joseph scolded. "I suppose it's almost to be expected, living separately. But I don't cheat. She has some explaining to do, and I'm not sure what will happen next. We've been together for too many years to throw it all away, but this has shocked me. The man was a pig, and she even said so herself. So I don't know why she cheated. Besides, I didn't think she was James's type."

"Why?"

"Come on. We're old compared to the rest of the group. Well, maybe not Andy. I didn't think James went for older women. Maybe he did it to spite me."

"It's possible, if the man was really that vindictive."

"He was more than vindictive, Jordan. He was sly. He was vicious. He wanted to undercut all of us. The only reason he was here was to try and get a good word in from me. I can't do that. Sure, I can recommend writers to my publishers, but if it was that easy, we'd all be writers."

The bubbles in the lively cider rose to the top. Rain had begun to fall on the winter streets of Cardiff. Briefly, Jordan thought about snow, wondering when they would get it or even if they would get it. It seemed strange to think about something so innocent when all around them there was disruption.

"Where is Kim?" Joseph's words sounded strangled, as if he didn't want to know but couldn't help asking.

"She's being looked at, to determine what killed her. Hopefully they'll find some DNA and bring her case to a close as soon as possible. I don't want it infringing on James's death if I can avoid it."

"Don't you ever feel like giving up?"

"Strange question."

Joseph gripped the glass in front of him. "I just mean it could be anyone. Don't you ever feel like giving up completely? Just...letting it go?"

"If I did that, I wouldn't be doing my job properly."

Jordan watched Joseph drink the cider, wondering what was going through the man's head.

"Well, if that's all..." Joseph made to stand, but Jordan didn't move. When Joseph looked at him, curiously, Jordan spoke.

"Why didn't you tell me my mum was in your writing group? And why didn't you tell me she was also one of James's lovers?"

Joseph deflated. "I wondered how long it would take you."

THIRTY-SEVEN

The rain was pouring heavily now, bouncing off the windowsill and soaking into Joseph's garden. Joseph had gone to the window, his back turned, looking out at the dreary sky. From where Jordan sat, the path was visible, leading to what he knew to be a small pathway that seriously breached security.

"Your mum was a great writer, and when she joined the group, she really hit it off with everyone. Straight away, I sensed there was something there between her and James. They bonded better than anyone else, and he seemed to genuinely like her, something that didn't seem the case with Sally. Of course, there was a lot of gossip, and when the pair started holidaying together, it was pretty evident what was going on."

"What were the reactions of the others?"

"Well, Sally seemed to berate Annabelle whenever she got the chance. Margaret suddenly started thinking Annabelle had an attitude. Kim didn't really say much. They spoke, but they weren't best friends. The rest of us enjoyed her company, loved her words. She was a better poet than a novelist, and I liked her because she was there to learn, not to compete. She didn't consider herself a writer. She got on with it and, one day, mentioned about having a completed manuscript that she was going to send off."

"Was this before James had his book deal?"

Joseph thought for a moment, then turned back to face Jordan. "Oh, before. Long before. We congratulated her, but then people seemed to turn against her. They called her an imposter, said she was a show-off, that sort of thing. It was cruel, but no matter how much I tried to stop it, I couldn't."

"You could have done better," Jordan stated.

Joseph walked back to the kitchen table. "I know that now."

"Vanessa told me there was a disturbance."

Joseph tilted his head back, seeming to wonder what Jordan knew. The drinking of alcohol, however, had made his tongue loose. "There was. Sally found out about Annabelle and James. We had suspected it, but there

149

was proof one night. James basically told Andy and Graham, knowing full well it would get back to the rest of us. He did that sort of thing. Stirred things up on purpose. He liked having women fighting over him. Sally was furious, and Margaret got involved, calling Annabelle a slut, telling her she was focussed too much on men and not the writing. Annabelle left shortly after, and two months after that, she was dead."

The words hung harshly in the air between them. There had been trouble, Annabelle had left, and then she was dead. It was so easy to say, to talk about how her fate played out. She had been so carefree after leaving Peter, and then someone had killed her.

Annabelle. James. Kim.

That's what kept repeating in Jordan's head.

Annabelle. James. Kim.

James was in the middle, flanked by two women who had been linked to him in some way. Kim on the CCTV giving Margaret something that Jordan couldn't see. James drinking from a glass supplied to the bartender by Margaret earlier that day.

Joseph, angry that his wife had been having an affair, only finding out about it the night Jordan had questioned the remaining members of the writing group.

Annabelle. James. Kim.

Sally, the woman who had supposedly had her manuscript stolen, according to Margaret, yet denying all knowledge of such a thing happening.

How had James managed to balance so many women? It was clear now that it had all been calculated. James had chosen the women in the group for a reason.

Jealousy mixed with hatred. That much was evident.

The question was, who hated him enough to kill?

"I think Annabelle loved him. But after the writing group, she cut us all off. I don't know what happened between the pair after that."

Jordan felt sad. The way everything had panned out for his mother. Had she wanted to fall in love so quickly? Had she been hurting? It seemed typical of his mother to be envied, to be argued at by opinionated personalities.

"Did she seem happy?"

It was a question that was only partly important to the wider investigation. Jordan was asking mainly for himself, for a peace of mind.

"Before everything kicked off, she was radiant." Joseph nodded. "When she left, I was gutted. She was a big talent, and I had been talking to her about helping her get published. My publishers were interested in what they had seen." Joseph paused. "Nobody else knew that, so be careful mentioning that around the other writers."

"What do you think the future is for your writing group, Joseph?"

Joseph crossed his arms and glanced to the left of the kitchen, staring at the wall, lost in thought. "I think the murder of three of our writers is scary. I think now, more than ever, the written word will unite us all."

THIRTY-EIGHT

Peter was already waiting outside Annabelle's home. He held her keys in his hand, but he hadn't gone in. Getting out of his Golf, Jordan pulled his coat tighter around him, trying to fight off the torturous claws of the cold.

"Why haven't you gone in? It's freezing!"

"I just…"

But Peter didn't need to say much more. Jordan understood. Going in alone felt like trespass. The windows seemed to squint down unwelcomingly at the men beneath.

"If houses could talk," Jordan said.

"You think it would solve everything?"

"It's possible."

They went into the house, feeling the chill in here too. The bills had stopped being paid, and so officially, the electric and gas should not be used. Peter switched on a light regardless. The day was too dim to work in the shadows.

"Any more news on the death of Kim?"

"I've asked CCTV to get a move on with sending me that footage from the night of James's murder, and now I've asked for everything from that date onwards. I want answers. Kim just disappeared. It seems very odd. I think she knew something."

Peter's eyes widened. "Like what?"

"I think she knew who the killer was. She probably wanted revenge but didn't want to go through with it. I think she panicked, and she was a liability."

It had been the only conclusion he had come to last night while lying in bed, messages from Lloyd ignored on his phone.

Annabelle. James. Kim.

Kim had met with Margaret the night James caused a disturbance in the Lower New Inn. Kim had denied this at first, and Jordan had not been able to question her about it again, which annoyed him. Margaret had faltered, leaving before he could get more out of her. The woman was MIA right now. Jordan had driven by her house this morning, only to see the curtains all drawn and the lights off. She was either inside secluding herself, or she had found a getaway.

Margaret had been having an affair with James, as had Sally and Annabelle. Jordan suspected Kim might have been involved somehow, too, but for different reasons. Had women scorned wanted revenge?

The truth was, he didn't know. There was the manuscript that had been given a deal. There was the argument between Annabelle and Sally and Margaret. There was the administration of the poison, slowly building up in his system. Was it one person or a group affair?

It hurt his head. He wanted answers, but now people weren't cooperating.

Peter stood at the stairs, his hands on the bannister, looking up into the dark hallway.

"I think we need to do the bedrooms first," Jordan said, his voice low. "We can deal with the living room last."

Peter nodded. It was where she had died. Disturbing it seemed like the final straw of erasing who Annabelle once was. Everything remained untouched, except for the removed glass of wine she had been drinking before her death.

They climbed the creaking stairs, the floorboards protesting underneath their feet. There were three rooms on this floor, as well as a small shower room. The main bathroom was downstairs, next to the kitchen. They hadn't been in there yet.

The first bedroom was the smallest, directly off the stairway. It was just big enough to be classed as a room, but judging by the window fitted into the original wall, Jordan suspected this had just been a cupboard originally. There was not a bed in here, just boxes and a chest of drawers. Peter sighed.

"Want me to do this room?"

Jordan knew he didn't want to find her bedroom. He nodded. Leaving Peter to the small room, Jordan walked past the second guest bedroom, the door slightly ajar, and went into his mother's room. It still had the smell of perfume, and near the window that overlooked the street sat a dressing table. Uncapped hairspray stood by the mirror, makeup brushes in a bag next to it. A hairdryer lay plugged in on the floor, the switch turned off at the wall.

The bed was neatly done, tucked in and untouched. Next to it was a nightstand with a lamp. The drawers were open, the contents spilling out onto the floor. It was the one disturbance in an otherwise tidy room.

Remembering the door that was ajar, Jordan began to suspect that the killer had been here. Walking back out, he went into the guest bedroom, and his suspicions were confirmed. The single bed was the only thing left untouched. Chest of drawers here had been completely ransacked, left on the floor with contents of clothes spilling out. The wardrobe doors were open, clothes on hangers hanging limply on the rail. It was impossible to tell if anything had been taken. Annabelle could have hidden anything here and Jordan would not have known about it.

He took out his phone and texted Vanessa, copying in Lloyd. He wondered if forensics had been here, or if they hadn't bothered, ruling her death natural. Within a minute, Lloyd had replied, confirming they hadn't.

Was it too late? Had evidence been contaminated? Or could this ransacked room lead to the killer?

Jordan stepped out of this guest bedroom and went back to his mother's room, feeling unsettled. The drawers had already been disturbed, but feeling a sense of responsibility, Jordan approached them and looked inside.

There was nothing unusual. A note pad, tablets, a rogue lipstick, and underwear. The wardrobe here hadn't been opened. Pulling his sleeves over his fingers, he opened the wardrobe, not sure what to expect.

His mother's clothes hung there, the smell of her skin and perfume drifting around him. He felt close to tears, remembering that the woman he had stopped talking to all those years ago had a life, had existed here. Had she ever thought of him?

The door in the hallway closed, and he knew Peter had probably cleaned out that small room. He walked to the doorway and spotted his dad about to enter the guest bedroom.

"I wouldn't."

"Why?"

"I think Mum had a burglar."

Now wasn't the time to voice his concern that the killer hadn't left the house immediately. Peter didn't need to know that his mother had lay dead downstairs whilst the killer went through her things, looking for god knew what.

"Impossible." Peter pushed open the guest bedroom and his mouth dropped open. "Oh."

"Don't touch anything. I'm going to tell forensics to come and have a look."

"Jordan, no. We can't cause a scene."

"I'll make sure it's understated."

Peter shook his head. "Who would do this?"

"Do you know what they might have taken? I had a look and I can't see anything of worth that's missing."

"Jewellery?"

Jordan hadn't even thought of that. In the guest bedroom, Jordan stood by as Peter went to the chest of drawers and looked inside.

He shook his head. "It's all still here."

Jordan saw for himself that her box was sat in the drawer.

"Maybe she was just messy," Peter said.

Jordan shrugged. He didn't know what to think, but it unsettled him to find upstairs so disturbed. "What did you take from the third room?"

"Not much. A few books, DVDs, CDs, even a few vinyl records. She didn't keep clothes in there, but there are a few bank statements and things like that, which I've put in a separate bag. I don't want her personal information going." Peter looked around the guest bedroom. "I took her laptop too."

"Laptop?"

"Yeah. It was in the corner of the room, underneath a stack of boxes."

"As in hidden?"

Peter looked confused. "Well, if I hadn't moved all the boxes to get to the stack, then yeah, maybe. I wouldn't have known it was there."

"Where is it now?"

"In the hallway."

Jordan went from the room and to the hallway. The laptop, charger on top, lay next to the black bags Peter had organised. "Dad, I'm going to take this with me."

"Why?"

"Mum was found with a laptop next to her when she died. It wasn't on, but they took it for examination. They didn't find anything on there, but I don't think they ever returned it. Even if they did, who would have hidden it under those boxes?"

"What are you saying?"

Jordan bent down and picked up the weighty laptop. It was a Toshiba model, scratches on the lid. "I'm saying this laptop might have the answers we're looking for."

THIRTY-NINE

George from forensics walked into the guest bedroom of Annabelle's home and winced. Despite working for a different district, Vanessa had called him in personally. "We didn't even think to come upstairs. There just seemed to be no point."

"Why would there be, when you thought her death was natural?"

Peter was downstairs making a coffee for them both.

"So you found the room just like this?"

"Haven't touched a thing, except for the door. The jewellery is still there. I don't know if she had any money savings, but I wouldn't be able to tell if that was gone."

"It just looks like someone emptied the drawers and were looking for one thing."

"All the drawers in the other bedrooms are the same."

"I see." George looked at Jordan. "How are you feeling? I imagine this can't be easy for you."

"Of course not, but I've seen worse."

"But not involving your family. Your mother, for god's sake."

"It's fine. I just want to find out what is going on."

"You think she's involved with the whole Fairview thing?"

Jordan sighed. "Definitely. But I'm not sure if James's killer is my mum's killer. I don't really know how that would work."

"I see."

"Dad said that Mum was expecting someone that night."

"And who do you think she was expecting?"

"Judging by the photographs of her on holiday and finding out about her relationship, I think she was expecting James."

"But you don't think James arrived?"

"No. Not until maybe after her death."

"Are there any records of James reporting the murder?"

"Dad found her, so he reported it. James never came forward. There's barely any photographic evidence of the two of them together, except for the writing group meetings, which she later left because she fell out with James. Now I'm wondering how he managed to get back in touch."

The stairs groaned, indicating Peter was coming back upstairs. He handed coffees to the two men and then glanced at the guest bedroom before heading back downstairs, presumably to get his own.

"What have you moved out of here?" George asked.

"Nothing. Only the third bedroom, which leads me on to something else I want to ask you about."

"Shoot."

"There was a laptop found next to my mother, closed, when she died. Correct?"

"Correct."

"Where is that laptop?"

"I believe we still have it. It's not evidence now, though. It's just no one wanted it returned."

"What did you find on that laptop?"

"God, I can't remember. I think my colleagues did the main job of searching through it. I can find out for certain, but I vaguely remember there being nothing incriminating."

"But can you remember?"

"I don't know, Jord." George sighed. "Maybe just search history about holidays, all of that sort of thing."

"No messages? No emails? No writing?"

"I don't know. Possibly. We weren't looking for that sort of stuff."

"But if her death was natural, why even look at her laptop?"

George nodded slowly. "I think we just did it as routine. Vanessa suggested it. Just wanted to see if she had been taking any medication ordered online, that sort of thing. She died quite unexpectedly, didn't she? I think as well..." George paused. "Well, Vanessa knew she was your mother. It didn't take long for it to click. I think she wanted to investigate it a little bit further, just in case it could bring you peace of mind."

Jordan felt a wave of affection for his friend.

"But now we know that you were all looking in the wrong place. It was ruled she had a heart attack. It was ruled as natural."

"Yes. But we didn't know to look for poisoning," George said. "We just thought years of medication might have complicated things."

"And that was that?"

"That was that."

"But how did you find out it was poison?"

"It made sense after you said," George replied, looking down at the floor of clothes. "Thinking it was complications because of medication was one thing. But it clicked when the murder was the same as James's. But she probably got administered the drug in small doses over time."

"Which is what happened to James."

"Yes."

"Which means James didn't kill my mother."

"Did you think he had?"

Jordan paused. His dad was opening drawers downstairs in the kitchen. "No. I don't think I did."

George looked Jordan directly in the eye. "Whoever killed your mother killed James. It's your job to find out who that was, and why."

Jordan drank a gulp of coffee, feeling the heat at the back of his throat. After swallowing, he listened to his dad walking up the stairs. "I know."

"So, what are you going to do?" Peter asked George, hovering in the hallway.

"I'll have to get a crime scene investigator in here. It's possible that the evidence has been contaminated. We don't know who's been here before, or if anyone came in afterwards, that sort of thing."

"But you can tell me who's been in here?" Peter asked.

"Yes, they can tell you that."

"That's all I need to know," Jordan said.

George drank the remainder of his coffee in one gulp. He put the cup out on the floor in the hallway, then excused himself and left the house.

"Shall we leave it for today?" Peter asked.

Jordan agreed. "I think we should do the living room after this."

Peter bit his lip. "You're right."

"I know it's going to be hard, but we have to do it eventually."

"It's just, that's it then, isn't it? We don't need to come back here."

"No, we don't."

Peter shook his head. "I just can't believe she's gone."

"I know, Dad."

FORTY

"Whoever moved the body was a man, or there were more than two people. There are no fingerprints, but there are bruises on the body that show she was tied up and dragged. There are tracks in the grass too. She was dragged there."

"She definitely wasn't killed in the park?"

"Definitely," Vanessa said. They were sat in her grand kitchen, Jennifer outside putting fresh oil and water in their cars. It was a dry evening, but cold. "We can tell that from many things. The body was stiff and cold, and the blood had already pooled in the lowest part of the body. Wherever she was killed, she was left there for some time."

"Did she have dirt on her?"

It felt so cruel to be talking so openly about Kim's murder, so brutal and cold. Vanessa shook her head. "Just some dirt on her clothes, not from the park. She was beginning to smell a bit. I think she was probably killed indoors and kept there for a while."

Jordan had a thought. "The house in Trevethin?"

"We've searched it. No sign of a struggle or a body. She just upped and left that place. Squatting, by the looks of things. We've tried finding her family, but there's no trace. Thought we found a sister, but she's denying all knowledge of knowing the woman."

"Poor girl," Jordan said. It seemed Kim lived a solitary life, with damage in her past. It made her death a whole lot worse.

Vanessa pushed the bottle of Hendrix gin towards Jordan. "Drink some more. Let loose."

"I don't want to have to get a taxi home. I'm fine with driving."

"Home? Don't be silly. We thought you'd stay the night." Jennifer swanned into the room, undoing her large puffa jacket. She helped herself to a glass of gin, adding Fever-Tree tonic water, and sat opposite Vanessa, next to Jordan. "Gossip on the street is that something happened between you and Lloyd?"

159

Eyes wide, Jordan looked at Vanessa. She grinned. "He can't keep his mouth shut."

"Fuck," Jordan said. "I can't believe he told you."

"He was so happy, Jord. You won't believe it. He's been trying to get you like that for ages."

"Since I started!"

"And now he's got it. But he's still interested. I asked." Vanessa smiled.

"Oh, don't start this, now. We're not going to become an item."

"You never know!"

"I think you'd make a cute couple." Jennifer laughed. "I've seen you both. You have a certain…I don't know, spark. Chemistry."

"Chemistry is the right word. You get each other. You're a little mysterious; he's a party boy. You complement each other well."

"He's a party boy, *exactly.*" Jordan couldn't help but smile too. "He's been around too much. I couldn't bear going out with him. I'd be paranoid he'd shagged every man we walked by."

"You think that highly of him?" Jennifer said. "If you think like that, you'll never have what you truly want. I'd say give him a shot. What's the worse that can happen?"

"Embarrassment," Jordan said. "I just don't think I'm ready for that added complication."

"You've said that ever since we've met. Remember Cory?"

Jordan did remember Cory. They had met during university, but hadn't really spoken much, then two years after graduation Jordan had bumped into him in a Bristol gay club. Cory, who had been studying with Jordan, had decided to pursue masters in Law. He was living, working, and studying in the English capital. They had hit a spark, Cory coming to terms with his sexuality. They'd had a few nights together, went on a couple of dates, but it never went anywhere.

"He wasn't interested."

"Oh, of course he was," Vanessa said. "But neither of you were brave enough to label it anything official."

"He was at a different place in his life."

"People make careers and studies work all the time." Vanessa glanced at Jennifer affectionately. They had met when Jennifer had been the victim of a mugging. She was studying a PGCE at the time, and now she taught English. "You just phased him out."

Jordan didn't wholly disagree. Cory had texted him, but Jordan's replies had been shorter and shorter every week. Finally, Cory valued his own self-worth and stopped texting. He went so far as to unfriend Jordan on Facebook, unfollow him on Twitter, and completely block him on Instagram. That was in the days when Jordan used social media. Now, his accounts were all locked down with a false username, and he barely logged in. He did this out of privacy. He didn't want clients to be able to use things against him, preferring to keep his online presence to a minimum. He also didn't feel the need to be friends with people online that he never saw. Online followers meant very little to him.

It made any hope of Cory trying to reach him again almost impossible. He sometimes wondered what the man was up to now, but he didn't care enough to find out. They had been young then. Now, they lived different lives.

Now, there was Lloyd.

"How long have you two been together?"

Vanessa smiled at Jennifer. "Well, about seven years."

"Yes. Eight?" Jennifer replied.

"Eight?"

"Isn't it?"

They all laughed.

"Something like that." Vanessa nodded. "Engaged for three."

"Not killed each other yet," Jennifer joked.

"If that happened, I'd promise not to put you down in prison," Jordan said.

"I'm glad you'd let me get off," Jennifer said. She looked at Vanessa. "Sleep tight tonight, babe."

Vanessa laughed. "Do you guys fancy a takeaway tonight?"

"I think that would be good."

"I'll order," Jennifer said, getting to her feet.

"How's working with Mark going?" Jordan asked.

Vanessa rolled her eyes. "He's fresh out of university, and I know that isn't a bad thing, but he's just really naïve. Thinks a month placement taught him everything he needed to know. Comes from a posh background in Surrey, always got what he wanted. He just doesn't have the right grip on reality, I don't think."

"Then why is he employed?"

"I don't get to choose who works with me. If I did, I'd have employed someone attractive."

"I heard that!" Jennifer called from the open-planned kitchen.

"He just seems a bit annoying."

"He's not completely useless, but he has a lot of learning to do."

Jennifer joined the table again and took their orders. Once she hung up, they were told the delivery of their Indian food would take up to an hour.

Hungry and very tipsy, Jordan was tempted to text Lloyd to see if he was free to join them at Vanessa's. But he thought better of it, and the three of them went to the living room, cosy and decorated elegantly with creams and shades of white, to watch TV.

Whilst they watched a film, Jordan thought about Margaret. He needed to go to her house, to get a chance to talk to her, to find out what the story was between her and James.

He was about to pick up his phone to possibly text Joseph to see if he had heard from his wife when a text came through from Sally.

We need to talk.

FORTY-ONE

The next morning, well fed and slightly hungover, Jordan arrived at the address Sally had texted him that night. He had wanted to meet her then, but she had said no.

He was now sat outside a rather-large detached house in Chepstow. His car parked on a pebble driveway, he looked up at the Victorian architecture and wondered what he was doing here.

The front door, sleek and black, opened. Sally stood there, a cigarette in her hand, looking like she was about to attend the Oscars. Her hair was tangled in a bun. She wore a dress that draped over her thin, bony body. Through hooded eyes, she stared at him, not offering him a warm smile.

Jordan got out of his ageing Golf, feeling embarrassed. His head ached more as he stood, and he was aware he was wearing last night's clothes—understated skinny jeans and an old band T-shirt from a gig he went to once.

"Thanks for coming," Sally said.

"Nice house."

He stepped into the hallway, which had chequered-tile flooring. The stairway had exposed wood, varnished just enough to look clean but still had a rustic feeling towards it. Sally shut the door with a thud and walked through the hallway and into the lounge. Jordan followed her in, and his mouth almost dropped open as he looked up at a high ceiling, a small chandelier hanging from it. The back window, rather large and crisscrossed into four panes, was tilted open, letting in the cold air from the back garden. Sally sat at a wooden table, and Jordan sat opposite her.

"So, you found out about Margaret and Joseph."

"Did you know?"

"No, I didn't know."

"Why did he keep that quiet?"

"I guess it never came up in conversation," Sally said. "But I think it is odd too. Why keep something like that secretive? It's weird, don't you think?"

"Yes."

"Yes." Sally dragged on her cigarette, letting the ash fall to the thin-carpeted floor. It struck Jordan as crass. "I called you here because I want to know if you've solved the case yet."

The question was so bluntly asked that Jordan had to think. He wondered if he had missed something, if maybe Sally had meant something else. But as she blinked those hooded eyes, he realised she wanted answers.

"No, I haven't." Then he added, "You'll know when I do."

"What's that supposed to mean?"

"That when I solve the case, the person responsible will be arrested."

Sally looked away from him, towards the wall, bumpy with years of mistreatment. "Have you come across your link to this whole thing?"

Jordan felt a jolt. "You knew."

It was a statement. Had they all been waiting to see if he'd find out? He felt like it was some sort of sick test.

"I realised after we met," Sally said. "I wondered if you knew but thought you would have asked me."

"How did you realise?"

Sally turned to him. "You look like her. I always thought she was so beautiful."

This surprised Jordan. "You did?"

Sally stood up. She stubbed out her cigarette into a saucer that was on the table, behind a dying plant in a small pot. She walked to a sturdy bookcase at the back of the room and bent down to open the cabinet at the bottom. She took out a leather-bound book and dropped it onto the table. Jordan watched the dust drift up into the air, caught floating like fairies in the weak winter sunshine.

With a creak, Sally opened the book to reveal a photo album. After a few sticky turns of the pages, Sally stopped at a photograph in the middle of the page. She turned it so Jordan could see.

It was a photograph taken by somebody else of Sally and his mother. The two women were sat outside, shadows of trees on them. It looked like a warm evening. They both looked happily at the lens, captured forever in a forgotten season.

"We were friends. Kind of. She was a talented woman. Very nice, but she never let me in."

"Where was this taken?"

With a flick of her wrist, Sally pointed to her garden. "She came over a week or two after the writing group. We met a bit more often then, and she fitted in well. My husband took the photo for us. He's not here right now. He hasn't been here since the whole thing happened."

"He's left you." Jordan remembered Sally in the car, convincing herself that she still had a family to return to.

"He'll be back." But Sally appeared doubtful and sad. "Annabelle was lovely, but she gave me the cold shoulder. I don't know why. I think I may have intimidated her. I've been told I can do that."

"God knows why."

Sally smirked, but she quickly stopped herself from looking too humoured. "Then I found out about the whole thing with James."

Sally sat in a different chair this time, pulling the photo album towards her again. She turned the page and pointed at a photograph of her and James. This one looked like it was in a pub somewhere. The close proximity of it told Jordan it was taken by one of them, though he couldn't tell who.

"You were going out with him, as was Annabelle and Margaret."

"I only found out about Margaret two nights ago. Graham told me." Sally looked at Jordan knowingly.

Jordan avoided her eyes. "What do you feel about that?"

"Angry."

"Angry?"

"Furious," Sally said. "How dare that…that monster string us all along? He didn't like any of us, did he? We were just toys to him."

"You had no idea he was seeing other women?"

"Look, it was just sex," Sally bluntly said. "But we met often. He spun me a spiel about getting in a relationship, but with my husband, I always said we could never work. We argued once or twice. He told me I wouldn't be doing this if I loved my husband. He was right, but he wasn't. I love my husband. But I wanted excitement. This idea that we have to stay with one man is outdated."

Sally reached for her cigarette packet and lit up another. She offered the packet to him, but he shook his head.

Putting them down, she dragged longingly on the freshly lit stick. She breathed out, smoke partially obscuring her face.

"But I never thought he was sleeping around with people I knew. I suspected he wouldn't keep it in his pants if I wasn't available. Some nights, he wouldn't text back or answer my calls, and I knew then. But Margaret? What was the man thinking?"

"Did he know about Joseph?"

"Probably. He had a way of finding things out." Sally closed the photo album. "He always tried to antagonise Joseph. Whilst at the same time sucking the man's cock to get a book deal."

"Which he got."

"He did. Do you know whose book that was yet?"

"It definitely wasn't yours?"

"No, it definitely wasn't. I never let him see my work. I think letting people glimpse your work early jinxes things."

Sally flicked ash onto the floor again, then puffed at the cigarette. The red inside the ash burnt brightly, hissing softly.

"Is it so impossible that he couldn't write the work himself?"

"He barely got words to paper. He was a big poser, and we all knew it. He was never going to be a writer. Then he gets a deal. It's bullshit."

"When you found out Annabelle had died, what did you feel?"

Sally looked away from him. "I felt…odd. We hadn't spoken since we argued that night at the writing meeting. I had found out about James going on holiday with her. It made me angry. Margaret got involved, and at the time, I didn't really get why. Now, obviously, I know she was angry that we were arguing over James when she probably found out for the first time he was cheating."

"Margaret was angry?"

"Yes. I didn't really get why," Sally said. "Now I do. I found out Annabelle had died, and I thought it was sad. The writing group the next week was sombre. James seemed different too. He was happier, bubblier, refused to even entertain her name. But whenever she was mentioned, his eyes dropped and he went silent. I think he was upset."

"You do?"

"Yeah."

"Do you know she was murdered?"

Sally bit her lip. She looked at Jordan and she was crying. "No, I didn't. But when Kim died, I began to rethink things through. Annabelle messaged me a week before it happened."

"She…she messaged you?"

Sally wiped her eyes with her free hand. The cigarette ash dropped without her doing anything. She quickly wiped the wooden table. "She told me she was scared."

"Scared? Scared of what?"

"She was scared of James."

FORTY-TWO

Sally had refused to say anything else. She excused herself, disappeared upstairs, and a door clicked closed. He hoped she wouldn't be long. He hadn't been asked to leave, so stayed seated at the table.

He got out his phone and told George he needed the laptop back as soon as possible. Within minutes, George replied saying Technology had got access, and nothing had been deleted. He could pick it up whenever he was ready.

When Sally came down again, Jordan was ready to leave. But she stood in the doorway, blocking his exit.

"They seemed to genuinely love each other. But James's reaction to her death was odd for a man that was in love. I don't know why."

"Sally. The night of James's murder, you didn't turn up to the writing group. Where were you?"

Sally shook her head. She seemed so flustered, considering the last time he had met her. It was if something had unhinged her, a realisation.

"I was...I was at Margaret's." Sally no longer held a cigarette, but Jordan could tell she missed having a distraction. She fiddled her hands one with the another, as if she didn't know how to use them or what to do with them.

"With who?"

"I was with Margaret. She was...worried."

"Why was she worried?"

Sally looked at the floor. She cleared her throat, playing for time. "Listen, I don't know what's happening anymore. But I wasn't there, and I didn't kill James."

"Did you leave the house at all?"

"I left at eight. Something like that."

James had been killed past ten o'clock.

"Where did you go?"

"Back home."

"Can anyone confirm that?"

"I…No. My husband wasn't in."

Jordan paused, watching Sally, seeing the sadness on her face at these words. "And why did you go to Margaret's that night, instead of going to the writing group? What time were they meeting?"

"They met at around half seven. I don't know. I guess I was rebelling. I told Margaret I was frustrated with some things. She told me she needed to be away from it too. So, that's what we did. We both stayed away. Kim was supposed to join us, but she never showed. I realise now it was because she was at the writing group instead."

"Why were the three of you considering skipping? As far as I'm aware, you almost always attended."

Sally moved away from the door and sat back at the table. "Have you never got sick of something? There was so much politics. The atmosphere there was getting, I don't know, toxic. I'm all for a bit of gossip, but it was draining. I wanted to just relax and forget about everything for a little bit."

"Did James have any factor in you not going?"

"What are you saying?"

"I'm simply asking if you didn't want to see him."

Sally bit her lip. She seemed to be thinking through an appropriate response. "We had…fallen out. He hadn't texted me in a while and had been ignoring me. And yeah, I suppose I didn't want to see him. It didn't help that a few weeks before he had given me a horrible voicemail message. He was pissed. And then I did one in return a week later."

"Do you still have the voicemail?"

"The police have the phone records."

"I'm not the police."

Sally viewed the table, locating her iPhone 5. She slid it across, telling him the number to dial and the passcode to log in. Jordan took it and put the phone to his ear.

He had to skip through two messages, one from Sally's mother and another from a friend. Then, he heard music thumping in the background.

"Sally. It's me. It's James." He had a Welsh twang to his accent, which Jordan suspected had been put on. "Yes. I've been out tonight. I just wanted to call to tell you that you're a fucking cunt." Jordan blinked. Sally, who could hear the message, recoiled. "You're a ball ache. Always calling me at your beck and call. Well, I've had e-fucking-nough of it. You won't leave Craig, and it pisses me off because the only reason you're with me is because you're unhappy. I can make you happy. I do make you happy. Fucking hell. Stop calling me. Stop texting me. Ignore me at the group. Before I tell everyone what you're really like." James hiccoughed. "I'll delete your number, block you. I don't care." The music stopped in the background, as if it had been cut at the power supply. "Ey, what you doing?"

A female voice came through the line, the words inaudible, replying something. He looked at Sally, who was looking at her nails.

The phone message cut off, but not before James coughed.

"Who's the woman?"

Sally looked up. "What woman?"

"The woman in the background?"

"I didn't hear a woman in the background."

But Jordan thought he knew. "You said this came a few weeks before his murder?"

Sally flinched at the word murder. "Yes."

"I think he was with Margaret."

Sally shrugged, a woman broken and no longer engaged with who James had been seeing alongside her. "I don't care."

Jordan handed Sally her phone back. She stared at the locked screen as if she hoped James would call or she could reach him again like she used to do.

"So, that's why you didn't go?"

"I couldn't bear to see him. My voicemail to him was worse. He never blocked my number."

"Why did you fall out?"

"When I found out about Annabelle."

"And Craig?"

Sally narrowed her eyes. "What about him?"

"Well, when did he leave you?"

"How dare you?"

"Sally, come on."

Sally's face crumpled as tears rolled down her cheeks. "He's moving his stuff out slowly. Says he's got a flat in Monmouth. He can never forgive me." Sally shook her head. "Now look at what I have to deal with. This fucking house that I can't afford."

"Because of James?"

"We'd been drifting before James. Hence why I did what I did. But now I'm scared. I'm scared of being alone. You might think I've got a very successful life, but I don't, Jordan. I'm a failure."

Jordan felt pity for the woman in front of him. There was so much he wanted to say, but he couldn't. She wouldn't listen to him.

"Why did the three of you plan to meet?"

Sally wiped the tears from her eyes. "It doesn't matter."

"I think it does."

Sally exhaled. "Kim. She was planning something stupid. Angry at the way James got away with so much, she wanted to get some revenge on him. Scare him a little bit."

"And you went along with it?"

"With Margaret too!" Sally growled.

Jordan nodded slowly. "How badly did James treat you all?"

Sally rolled her eyes. "The things he called Kim to her face. Called her beetroot, gammon, big fat chunk of beef. Quite funny, now you think about it. Funny as in, how very childish. But still, rude nonetheless."

"And you?"

"Complimented me, but always backhanded." Sally grimaced. "Nice hair today, he'd say, but would look better this way or that way or a different colour. Said I was too skinny once. Those sort of things."

"And Margaret?"

"Seemed to worship the ground she walked on when she was around. To me, he'd call her a fat milk maid."

"And the three of you were angry at him?"

"Seething. I'd found out he'd been cheating on me with Annabelle. Margaret was angry because, well, I guess now it was because she knew James had been sleeping with me at the same time as her, but I thought at the time she was just getting involved for the sake of it. Kim was pissed off at his treatment to her and to other women. The man was a pig."

Jordan nodded. "I've been told plenty of times."

"So, Kim was going to do something stupid. And she didn't show. And when I found out she'd gone to the writing group, and then that night he died, well…"

Jordan thought he knew what Sally was getting at, but he let the silence draw out between them.

Sally swallowed. "Kim knew too much. That's why she's been killed."

"How do you know?"

"Why else would she have disappeared so suddenly?"

"Do you think Kim killed James?"

Sally looked at him. "I think it's possible."

FORTY-THREE

At the door of Sally's home, Sally touched Jordan's arm, stopping him from leaving. Jordan looked at her, and recognised with a jolt that she was afraid.

"Kim's been murdered. James was murdered. I'm worried for my safety here."

"You think you're in trouble?"

"I think I could be."

Annabelle. James. Kim.

Sally?

"I'll get a car out here tonight to watch the place."

Sally let go of Jordan. She crossed her arms, seeming to shrink into herself, like an animal putting up defences. "Please."

"Keep the doors locked. Windows closed. Don't stay by a window. I'll be available to call if anything does scare you."

Sally managed a smile. "Thank you, Jordan."

They said their goodbyes, and Jordan drove away from Sally's home.

He needed to get his mother's laptop. She had messages to Sally, saying she was scared of James. What if there were messages to and from James?

Annabelle's relationship with James seemed stronger than the others. James had toyed with her just like everyone else. Jordan pictured him as a man with a problem, possibly addicted to sex, incapable of remaining faithful.

But he had travelled with his mother, something he hadn't done with the other women. Maybe she had intrigued him more, hooked him more than the others. She certainly had charm and charisma.

But why had he scared her? Had he turned on her, afraid of his own emotions? Or had he simply realised there were better women out there?

Maybe James was the type to have things burning intensely for weeks, maybe even months, and then get bored.

His thoughts drifted to Joseph. How much did he know?

That night, there had been plenty of information blurred over. Joseph hadn't seen the killer. He had left the room. When he had come back, he blamed his poor eyesight for not being able to see the woman leaving. But who was to say that the woman administered the poison? The autopsy had revealed a killer dosage. It must have been given to poor James that night.

Sally was not in attendance. But her whereabouts from eight in the evening were not verified by anyone other than herself. It was possible she had arrived.

Had Margaret stayed at home? Or had she ventured to the writing group, knowing she would not be told off for being late, seeing as her husband ran the group.

Something about what Joseph had said when they had first met was playing in his mind. But he cursed himself for being unable to remember. He made a mental note to go back through his audio interviews. There was something he was overlooking.

Jordan drove towards Margaret's home, hoping that she would be in, yet expecting to see the same drawn curtains, the lights all off.

As he got closer, he held his breath.

He was in luck. There was a parting in one of the upstairs curtains. Her home, red-brick and joined on to another, looked like a suburban paradise. The light in the chink of curtain told him that there was someone in, that the curtain had been moved and not replaced properly.

After parking a house away, Jordan got out and walked to her door. For some reason, he felt apprehensive.

He took a deep breath and knocked the door. Whilst waiting, he looked at the other houses. With red brick, they reminded him of houses built in the fifties. He imagined the neighbours to be housewives, their husbands out at work, happiness shared by all at their newfound wealth.

But of course, that view was outdated. The houses had two or three cars parked on their drive, most of them only a year or two old. It made Jordan realise that the homes were big enough for families, and that they probably all worked and paid their ways.

The estate wasn't as secluded as Annabelle's, with a long road leading to a dual carriageway just off from the end of the street.

The door didn't open. The curtain upstairs had closed.

There was definitely someone in.

Jordan knocked again, this time louder, one after the other, not stopping until his knuckles began to hurt.

But still, no one came to answer.

"You won't get much luck there."

Jordan turned to see an old woman walking up the street, carrying car keys in her wrinkled hands. "Sorry?"

"That home. She's ignoring everyone lately. Not sure why, though I suspect it has something to do with that dead woman found in Newport."

Jordan looked back at Margaret's house, then stepped down from her doorstep and onto the pathway. "This house does belong to Margaret?"

"I think that's her name, yes. She was part of that Joseph Gordon thing. She told me before. When I heard about the death of one of the writers, I asked her about it. She said she was devastated. Looked it, too, mind you. But since that other writer has shown up dead, I haven't seen her."

"But she's in?"

The old woman looked at the house. "Couldn't tell you, love. The curtains have been closed for a few days now. I've been meaning to tell the police."

"I can do that," Jordan said.

The woman's eyes lit up. "An officer, are you?"

"Something like that."

"Well. I'll leave you to it then!" And she hustled off, no doubt going to tell someone the gossip that Margaret had a police officer at the door.

Jordan turned back to her home and took a business card out of his pocket. Opening the letterbox, he crouched down.

"Margaret, I know you're in there," he called, looking through into the hallway where a lamp was on. The house was spotless, no letters building up on the floor or anything left behind in haste. "I've posted my business card through. We need to talk. Call me when you're brave enough."

Hoping those last words annoyed her, he shut the letter box with a snap and headed back to his car. Inside, he watched the house, letting time tick by, but there was no more movement from the curtains or any shadows by the windows. Margaret was playing him at his own game.

FORTY-FOUR

Jordan stopped at the offices of the police station and walked into reception to find Rachel again. This time, she didn't question who he was. Begrudgingly, she stood up and pressed a button under her desk, which allowed the barriers to open to let Jordan through.

He said thank you, and she curtly smiled, looking somewhat embarrassed.

Through the hallway, Jordan knocked on Vanessa's door, only for it to be opened by Mark. Jordan looked past him to Vanessa at her desk.

"Hi, Jordan," Mark said. "Can we help?"

"I've come to see Vanessa." Jordan walked past Mark. "Has Lloyd or George given you the laptop?"

"You'll have to check it out of evidence," Mark said, closing the door.

"I know what to do."

"Already done." Vanessa tightly smiled. She swivelled backwards in her chair and opened a drawer under her desk. She took out the large laptop and put it on her desk. "What do you think is on there?"

"Could be anything. I just want to see what her relationship was with James."

Vanessa nodded. "I understand. Let me know."

Jordan took a seat, the only available one, at the other end of the desk. Mark stepped forward. "I was sitting there."

"You're not now."

"Jordan," Vanessa said.

Mark looked from Vanessa to Jordan, slightly uncomfortable. "Um. Do you want to meet later?"

"Go and call the witness and let me know what they say," Vanessa replied.

Mark nodded, happy to have a task to do. He left the room and shut the door slowly.

"What witness?"

174

"Robbery in Canton," Vanessa dismissed. "You'll be happy to know security supplied the CCTV from that night."

Jordan exhaled. "About bloody time."

"Someone brought to my attention it hadn't come in, so we applied a little pressure. I think they were hoping it would expire and go away. Jobsworth."

"Or possibly something to hide."

Vanessa smirked. "Exactly what I thought."

"You keeping an eye on the security guard?"

"We are."

"Great."

Jordan placed a hand on the laptop as if he was worried it would disappear if he couldn't feel the hard evidence of its existence. He looked at the black exterior, wondering what could be on there, if it would give him answers.

"I'm waiting for it to come in on USB," Vanessa said, turning back to her computer. "Then I can email it to you. Probably at some point tonight."

"I appreciate it. But this will keep me busy for now."

"What are you hoping to find?"

"She knew James. My mum," Jordan said. "I just saw Sally. She told me Annabelle had told her before her death that she was afraid of James, but I don't know why. Maybe there is communication on here."

"Well, George got the tech guys to unlock it for you. He did well. There's nothing missing on there. They don't think it's been tampered with."

"Did you know Annabelle's house was broken into?"

"George said. He said you thought it might have been searched the same night she was…"

Jordan sank back into his chair. "Yeah. Obviously that wasn't looked at, because everyone thought her death was natural."

"George is going to look at the place tomorrow."

"I can't say there will be much hope of evidence."

"No, but it is worth a shot."

Jordan tapped the laptop. "I think they were looking for this."

"You do? Why?"

"Maybe it had something on there. Some sort of evidence. I don't know. It was hidden in the small bedroom. Dad found it tucked at the back of the room under a load of boxes. Why would you hide something like that?"

"Maybe she thought it was broken. She did have the other laptop."

"It's possible. But it seems uncharacteristic of my mum."

"You always say to trust your instincts. If you think it's worth looking at, go for it."

But having known Annabelle was romantically linked to James told Jordan there was more to her death. Who killed her? Was it the same killer of Kim and James?

"Has it struck you we're dealing with a serial killer?" Vanessa asked.

"We don't know the same person is responsible for all of their deaths."

"But they must be. It would be very unlikely if they're not."

"Do the killings look similar?"

"Well, James was poisoned, and there's a possibility Annabelle was too." Vanessa glanced at Jordan, hoping her words didn't affect him.

He nodded, to show her he didn't mind.

"Then there's Kim…"

"Butchered and strangled."

"Well, not butchered."

"She was dumped like rubbish."

"But she wasn't beaten. She was strangled, though."

"So different methods."

"A quicker way to kill her. It seems Annabelle's and James's deaths were quite thought out," Vanessa mused. "Premeditated."

Jordan pulled the laptop towards him. "Which is why I think this may have clues, help us to see what Annabelle was doing before her death."

"Are you sure you're going to be okay looking at that?"

Jordan sighed. "Of course. It will be weird, but the woman in here is a woman I didn't know. She's almost a stranger to me, which is why this case seems so odd. But I've got to find out what happened to her. For her. And Dad."

Vanessa smiled. "She'd be proud of you. I hope you know that."

Jordan thought otherwise. The woman had cut herself out of his life, just like he had done to her. Annabelle had hated her life with Peter, and Jordan reminded her of such a thing. She had cut everything away, shed her skin, and become someone new.

"I don't know about that."

"Did I ever tell you about Jennifer's dad?"

Jordan shook his head.

Vanessa got up and walked to a coffee machine she had on a table at the back of the room. She held up a mug for Jordan, who shook his head, and then she fitted the filtered coffee into the machine and set it to work.

Vanessa stood with her back to it, her arms crossed. "Jennifer loved him. They had a strong relationship. She was an only child, you see, so she was daddy's girl." Vanessa rolled her eyes at this, as if that sort of relationship annoyed her. Jordan thought of his brother, who was a bit of a mother's boy, until she cut him off too. "He was a banker, and he provided well for her. But then one day he became cold, she said. Came home late, drunk, sometimes went away for weekends. She remembers her mother becoming pale and tired, sick with worry. Turns out he'd been having an affair and left all of a sudden. He kissed her good night, and when she woke up, he was gone. Had packed up and moved out. Her mother was livid."

"Sounds dreadful."

The coffee poured into the mug, the machine hissing. Vanessa shrugged. "It was. She reached out to him, and even now, she still texts him. But he never replies. She can't accept that he's gone."

"He's dead?"

"Oh, no, not gone in that way." Vanessa took her mug out from underneath the machine and crouched down to a small fridge. She took out a blue-topped milk carton. "No, he lives in London. His wife is an executive of a financial company. He works at HSBC, I think. They seem to be doing all right. They have a new kid, a sister Jen has never met. She's shown me on Facebook."

"Why does he ignore her?"

"Maybe for the same reason your mother cut you out." Vanessa returned to her table, sitting down. "Memories he would rather forget. I've tried asking Jen what the relationship was like with her mother and her dad. She just remembers them being happy. But I think she knows now there were probably a lot of problems behind closed doors."

"What about her mum?"

Vanessa sighed. "She's getting ill. She's not been the same since he left. Rather broken. Never remarried. Don't think she's even dated since. Her mother likes to…well, play the victim. You can't talk to Jen about how problematic she can be, because she won't hear it. She's protective of her."

"Why did they split?"

"Unhappiness, I suppose." Vanessa drank some of her coffee. "I was a lucky one. My parents never split up. They're still together now."

"You know, you never really talk about them."

Vanessa smiled. "They're pretty standard. Retired, middle class bordering on upper. They live in a nice bungalow in Llandaff. Happy enough, I suppose. I see them as often as I can."

Jordan smiled. Vanessa, in her early thirties, really did seem to have things together, a beautiful home with the mortgage half paid off, a fiancée that she adored and adored her back, and a family support network.

Vanessa seemed to know what he was thinking. "Everything is going to be okay, Jordan. You have to believe that. Things will fall into place, and you'll work things out. It's difficult, and I'm half tempted to force you back into a break after this case is done. It's a lot to come back to."

Jordan stretched, signalling it was time to go. He needed answers, and sitting here talking was not going to bring him any. "I know. But don't go back to that again. I came back because I needed to. This case has given me more than I thought it would, but I'm fine to work."

"I know."

Jordan flashed a warm smile at Vanessa. "Make sure you keep Mark at bay."

Vanessa laughed. "Oh, I'm sure I will."

FORTY-FIVE

That evening, Jordan locked his apartment door, turned off the TV, switched off his phone, and plugged in his mother's laptop. He gave it half an hour to charge, pumping himself up to look through the contents on there. Oscar left him alone once he had been fed.

Going through his mother's private things would be weird. He'd find stuff he might not want to find.

He sat down on the sofa and brought the laptop closer to him, then pressed the ON button. With no log-in, the laptop sluggishly opened onto the home page until Windows 7 looked back at him.

He thought of his mother reading the horror stories of Windows 8 and then putting off the update that had made her laptop go so slow. He laughed.

He opened the Windows icon, finding all of the shortcuts that would lead him to where he needed to go. At the top, he double-clicked on the Google Chrome icon and waited for it to load.

After a few seconds, he was greeted with Google's homepage. Today, there was no celebration of someone's birthday, but the standard Google icon. He typed *Facebook* in the search bar and hoped that she would still be logged in.

She was.

There were sixty-eight notifications in the bell icon, and ten private messages. Annabelle had three friend requests. He looked at these first, hoping to recognise names, but he didn't. There was someone from Barcelona, another from the US, and someone from Surrey. Browsing their profiles, he managed to gather that they all had one thing in common: members of an online Facebook writing group.

He then clicked on the notifications. There were comments on a politic thread Annabelle had commented on. There were likes on an old status. And the rest were tributes posted on her wall. Jordan was tempted to read them, to indulge in the sympathy of these strangers, but he didn't want to.

Curiously, he clicked on the search bar, and was surprised to see that she had tried searching for him and Peter. They were her last searches. She hadn't been able to find them. Peter wasn't on Facebook, and he had a different name for security reasons.

Then he felt guilty, a terror that jumped at him like a tick. Had she been trying to find him to tell him something? Her number had been blocked on his phone, and she had probably deleted his. Facebook would have been her only option. Did she want to tell him a fear she had? If she had, why hadn't she gone to his apartment?

What if he had been reachable? Would all of this have been avoidable?

Jordan shook his head, breathing in as he clicked on the messages. Some were left by other writers, who only knew her online. They were dated the same month she had died. No one had tried contacting her privately since then. Clicking through them, he saw questions asking her about writing, a general conversation between her and a man living in Dartmouth, and a message from a neighbour asking her if she could put her bins out when she went away.

Scrolling down, Jordan was looking for one name. Eventually, he found it. *James Fairview: Writer.*

He clicked on his profile to discover that Annabelle had befriended him a month before joining the writing group. Had James told her about the group, possibly putting in a good word to Joseph?

He opened the messages between them, whilst keeping James's profile open, similar messages of condolences on his page, then trawled through the communication until he reached the top.

Conversation had started pretty innocently.

Great post in the writing group!

Thanks. I've seen you're working on a novel. Hope it's going well!

Then they didn't talk for a week.

James started the message again.

I am a member of Joseph Gordon's writing group. Would you like to join?

Oh, wow! Joseph Gordon! I have a book of his on my shelf. What writing group is this?

He chooses only a select few. Mentors them, with the hopes of getting us a publishing contract. I'd recommend it!

Annabelle responded with an emoji. Then, *I'd love to join. Thanks for thinking of me.*

A period of eight hours went by before James replied again. Jordan wondered what Annabelle might have done during this time. Maybe she had searched Joseph in an attempt to find out more information on the group and the writers involved.

I have a talent of being able to tell when a writer has potential. I've told Joseph. He's said you're welcome to join.

Two days went by, and Annabelle messaged again with her address and a time for James to pick her up. He replied with a thumbs-up icon. That night, he messaged her.

Hope you enjoyed the meeting tonight. Thanks for being so kind to me!

I got the impression they weren't so happy to see me. But I'll be back! It was a pleasure meeting Joseph.

Then she typed something else five minutes later. *I'm always here if you would like to talk.*

Annabelle then told James about a novel she was writing, boosted with confidence after the meetings and mentoring with Joseph. James encouraged her the whole way, but Jordan wondered if he was imagining the false way James replied. Gone were the innocent emojis, the friendly winks. Now, there were full stops, brisk sentences, as if James were busy elsewhere.

James asked if he could get a copy to read over and offered feedback. Annabelle replied, *Not yet. When it's finished.*

The messages went on like this for a while. There were more exchanges on where to meet, when the meeting was, whether or not Annabelle was enjoying it. Then James brought up Sally.

Ignore Sally. She's just jealous that there's another woman there that has better writing capabilities than she does. Your short story today was incredible! I know you don't know it, but the faces of the writers as you read out your work were outstanding. They were shocked. You really have a talent, and I'm glad I've spotted it!

Jordan wondered what had happened with Sally. Making a note of the date, he brought up Sally's profile, looking at a picture of her in a kitchen, a dog beside her. Upon clicking on the message icon, the last message Annabelle sent came up. *Sally, I need to tell you something. I'm afraid. I'm afraid of James.*

Jordan scrolled up to find Annabelle had tried reaching out to Sally before this. *Can we talk? And, I know you're angry. But I'm desperate to find something out.* Sally didn't respond to any of them.

Swallowing, Jordan scrolled up the messages and matched the date with the message from James. Sally had not communicated with Annabelle until two weeks after, where she complimented her on a poem.

Their conversation was stilted at first, small talk, and polite questions on how they had sparked an interest in writing. Then Sally became friendlier, inviting Annabelle for drinks. One of those invites led to the photo of Annabelle in Sally's garden. Had his mother finally felt included?

Then, there was the fallout.

Bitch. Sally's simple reply.

Annabelle replied diplomatically. *I had no idea James was seeing you, and I would never have gone away with him or even entertained the idea of him if I had known. What you must know is James contacted me first and invited me to the writing group, and I trusted him as a friend, which began to blossom into something else the more we met. He's a troubled man, and he found solace in me, and I guess he liked that. I'm hurt and devastated, and I am sure you are too. Please can we meet to put this behind us? I am going to cut all conversation with James.*

Jordan checked the date. The message was a month and a half before Annabelle's murder. Jordan hated that he knew what fate awaited her, whilst she had no idea. He flicked back to James's message and matched the date. They hadn't messaged online for a week before that. Jordan wondered if there had been trouble beforehand. He scrolled to earlier messages.

I'm a fool. Please can we talk?

When Annabelle did not reply, James messaged again. *Sally was nothing. I have a problem. You should know better than anyone, after everything I've told you. Please, Annabelle.*

And, finally, he messaged impatiently, *How dare you leave the group? After everything I've fucking done for you! You're just like everybody else. Using me, bitching about me. Sally isn't your friend. We're glad you're gone, you worthless whore.*

Jordan felt anger at his words and wanted to strangle the man. The disrespect he saw backed up claims made by Sally and Kim. James was a petulant man with anger problems. When things didn't go his way, he made a fool of himself.

The next messages with James started three weeks before Annabelle's murder. A chill crept through Jordan's bones.

Sorry if I scared you tonight.

Annabelle hadn't replied until an hour later. *I just didn't expect you to be outside. How long were you there?*

I was trying to knock the door, to build courage, but I couldn't do it. I know it looked wrong, but I was afraid of what I'd face if I got out of the car and knocked.

So James had been watching Annabelle's home. For how long? His rational mind told him that it could be something innocent. James really might have struggled with facing his problems. A man that causes so much tension probably never deals with the consequences. Why now? Why for her?

A few days later, Annabelle messaged again. *Don't you ever follow me again. I am going to call the police. I'm serious.*

Jordan wanted to stop reading. But he continued.

Annabelle, please. I've got myself into trouble. Can we meet?

Fine. I'm available tonight.

Upon checking the date, Jordan confirmed what he had thought. James had planned to meet Annabelle the night of her murder.

James Fairview had killed Annabelle.

FORTY-SIX

Jordan drank his second glass of wine, his mother's Facebook left open. Someone had messaged, a name he didn't recognise, but Jordan didn't look at it. No doubt someone was confused as to why she was online, probably hearing about her tragic demise. Oscar climbed into a discarded Amazon box. Jordan's eyes glazed over and his thoughts ran away with him.

James had met his mother that night. James had been the last man to see his mother alive. To Jordan, that was enough evidence.

And the bastard was no longer alive to pay the consequences.

He had run away from it in a final way.

Anger pulsated through Jordan now. He had seen the way James worked. Build the trust in a woman, hook her in, and then drop her. Annabelle had fallen for it, hopeful of a better life with a man she had common interests with. It had not been worth it.

Jordan wondered what James and Annabelle had talked about. What he told her that he hadn't told anyone else? Why had she believed him?

He poured himself a third glass, feeling tipsy. Oscar jumped up on the sofa next to him. His phone remained off, although he had considered turning it on to contact someone, anyone, that would hear him rant. But what was the point? His mother's death would not be justified. James Fairview had murdered and then been murdered himself. He'd got away with it.

But they had died the same way. That was the one glimmer of hope Jordan had that James hadn't killed his mum. Why would the killer use the same method if they were not the same person?

It was too confusing, too overwhelming. Jordan wished he could forget about it all.

He closed Facebook, fed up of seeing blue, and was about to shut down the laptop when he came across a folder pinned to the desktop. It was simply named Untitled.

Jordan double-clicked it and came across three documents. One labelled Plot, another labelled Characters, and finally a document called Novel Final. Annabelle hadn't named it yet, but she had finished it.

He double-clicked on the document titled Novel and waited for Word to power up. When it did, it displayed a formatted manuscript. A blank page looked at him. He scrolled through the first pages, the title of the novel, still called Novel, and underneath it Annabelle's name. His scrolling became faster now, and he read through almost three hundred pages of work until he finally got to the last chapter.

Annabelle had finished the work she had been writing. She had completed what she had told James about.

Then something fell into place.

The meeting with James, the contact he had made all of a sudden. Had Annabelle boasted about finishing her manuscript? Is that why James had gotten back in touch, after requesting to see her work before?

Now, with some determination, Jordan went back to her Facebook, again ignoring the new message sent to Annabelle's account, and scrolled through rows of tributes until her final statuses.

Feeling happy.

It seemed inconspicuous, but the comments underneath revealed all.

Do tell!

Finally finished my novel! Edited and everything. Time to submit and see if this old bird can become a proper author!

Likes flooded in on her comment, congratulations posted in the thread underneath. Annabelle had finished her novel, and James had found out about it.

James, who had been struggling with his own writing for months.

James, who all of a sudden had a book publishing deal.

Jordan's anger kept bubbling. But now he felt conflicted excitement, a realisation of what might have happened, of those final moments that led to his mother's death.

Annabelle had work that James wanted. He had stooped to a new low, and Annabelle would be his victim.

James had stolen Annabelle's manuscript.

Jordan reached for his phone and cursed as he knocked over his freshly poured wine. Cleaning up could wait. He rebooted his phone, impatiently tapping his foot as the screen loaded.

When it finally came back to life, he was halfway through typing his password when it rang.

Vanessa was calling.

"Vanessa! I'm glad you called, but…"

"Jordan. It's Sally. Something has happened."

Jordan gripped the phone as he listened, all the while remembering that he had forgotten to ensure a police officer kept watch of her home.

FORTY-SEVEN

When Jordan got to his car, he cursed as he saw he had only a quarter of a tank of petrol. With money tight, he begrudged getting petrol. He gave Lloyd a call. He prayed the man wouldn't be out dancing the night away, considering it was a weekday, and breathed a sigh of relief when he answered.

"Can you take me to Chepstow?"

"Why?"

"Sally. She's been attacked. It's my fault."

"I'll be there in five."

True to his word, Lloyd arrived in his Ford Fiesta, a year old, immaculate inside, and smelling fruity. Jordan got in and drew his seat belt, realising that the smell came from an air freshener hung up on the rear-view mirror.

"You'll have to tell me where Sally lives."

Jordan told him the postcode and waited as he typed it into his phone, which was held up to the screen by a phone cradle suctioned to the window. Lloyd drove off and kept to the speed limits. Impatiently, Jordan tapped his fingers on his thigh.

If anything bad had happened to Sally, it would be his fault. It would forever be on his conscience. How could he have been so stupid as to forget to get an officer at her home tonight?

Vanessa hadn't told him what had happened. She told him to get there as soon as possible, and then she had to go, no doubt to see someone or speak to a witness. Jordan had no idea who raised the alarm and about the details of the scene that was about to wait for them.

"Are you okay?"

Jordan looked at Lloyd, who was stealing glances at him. "I don't know. I saw Sally today. She told me she was scared of being alone there. I told her I'd get someone to watch the house and I fucking forgot."

"Well, that isn't your fault."

186

"It is."

Lloyd shrugged. "I mean, you didn't know an attack was actually going to happen. If we followed up on every paranoid mind, we wouldn't be able to focus on the real stuff."

Jordan looked out of the window as the trees seemed to sweep by on their drive out of Cardiff. Lloyd was going seventy miles per hour.

"You're right. I just got carried away with the whole laptop thing."

"So now you're saying it's my fault?"

"What? No! Of course not! I…" Jordan turned to Lloyd to find he was grinning. Humouring him, Jordan relaxed. "Fuck off."

"Hey, that's not nice now." Lloyd laughed. He placed a hand on Jordan's knee and tapped it twice. "It's going to be fine."

He removed his hand, but Jordan still felt the weight, the touch of warmth. He stared out of the window, trying to reassure himself that everything would be okay, that Sally was not another victim.

Annabelle. James. Kim.

Annabelle had died of poisoning. As had James. Had someone found out and wanted to kill him the same way, or was it possible their killer was the same person? A BMW came closer as Lloyd sped up to overtake.

"I think James killed my mum."

Lloyd's hands gripped the steering wheel. "Whoa. Why?"

"I found messages. She told Sally she was scared of him. They seemed to develop a relationship. Confided in each other, by the looks of things. And that manuscript James got published? I suspect it was my mum's."

"You do?"

"Which reminds me, I was about to place a call to the publisher before Vanessa told me the news." Jordan took out his phone and found the details of the publisher James had signed with. He had heard of them before, famous for publishing many bestsellers. The call rang through, and an automated message answered.

Jordan impatiently waited for it to stop before leaving a message. "Hi. My name is Jordan Jenner. I'm a private investigator, currently working on a case for South Wales Police, Cardiff. I'm calling about an author you signed, named James Fairview. Please get in touch."

Jordan left his number and hung up.

Lloyd looked at him. "What do you want from them?"

"The manuscript, so I can see if it's my mother's."

"You think it's possible?"

"Very," Jordan said. "They spoke about it, and James asked multiple times for her to send what she got over to him, but she always said no. Said she'd send it when it was finished. But they fell out, and when Annabelle said on Facebook that she had finished it, he contacted her again. They were due to meet the night she died. She told my dad she had a friend coming over."

"James."

"Very possible," Jordan said.

"Statistically, her killer would be someone she knew."

"Most cases are." Jordan rubbed his eyes, his head aching. "Sorry, it's a lot to take in."

"I bet. You would never have thought this murder was related to your mum."

"It's just fucking shit," Jordan said. "Really fucking shit. The woman wasn't horrible. She didn't deserve to be killed. And what for? For a stupid manuscript? Why kill and take the risk?"

"People do stupid things when they're desperate."

Lloyd followed the satnav's directions to Chepstow. The device told them they were only ten minutes away. Lloyd's speedy driving was getting them there faster than Jordan had anticipated.

"They wouldn't have even known that it would get published."

"But it might not have been James that killed her, Jordan. He might have stolen the manuscript, but you don't even know that for sure yet. It could all be rumours."

Anything was possible. There was so much he didn't know, and the key people with answers were dead. He wished he could ask them, to find out what really happened between them. James was his suspect, yet there was nothing he could do.

The rest of the journey passed in silence, except for Kiss, which Lloyd had tuned to a low setting so it wasn't invasive on their thoughts. They pulled up outside Sally's street, where two police cars and one police van were parked on the driveway.

With relief, Jordan saw Sally sat in the back of the police van, a blanket wrapped around her, talking to Vanessa. When he got out, she glared at him.

"You told me I'd be safe!"

Vanessa placed a reassuring hand on her wrist and said something that Jordan couldn't hear. Lloyd locked the car, and they walked onward, both of them flashing their ID cards at the nearest police officer, who nodded for them to go forwards.

Lloyd got in the van first. Jordan paused to appraise the house. It looked innocently homely, as if nothing had happened. Police officers were inside, scouring the place.

"What happened?"

"You fucking dick," Sally hissed.

"Come on," Vanessa said.

Jordan got in the van and sat across from Sally. He could see now that her face was bruised, a wound from a blow to the cheek. He winced.

She shook her head. "Where was my police cruiser keeping watch?"

"I forgot. I'm sorry, Sally."

"You...forgot." Sally breathed, her nostrils flaring. "I'm going to sue! I should sue!"

"We can talk about that later," Jordan said. "What happened?"

"I've already told the police." Sally nodded at Vanessa.

"I'm not police," Jordan said.

Sally rolled her eyes. "I heard a knock on the back door. I went to answer it, and then there was a smash. The living room window had been caved in. When I ran to see, someone in a balaclava came running towards me. I screamed, and they hit me around the face with a pipe. I think they hoped to knock me out, but I managed to deflect the main blow with my arms. I ran out into the back garden, screaming for help, and the person ran away."

"Just like that?"

"Just like that. I don't know what they were hoping to do, whether or not they were hoping to burgle the place. I just don't know."

"Do you know who it was?"

Sally looked at Jordan like he had sprouted another head. "I told you. They were wearing a balaclava."

"Right," Jordan said. He wondered if Sally was holding out on the truth but pictured the shock of the smashed glass, the pipe to the face. There hadn't been enough time to register a build of a person. "What were they wearing?"

"Leather. Black. Gloves," Sally said. "I don't know. They hit me with a pipe and I ran for my life. I wasn't in the mood to see if they were wearing the latest fashion."

"Who called the police?"

"My neighbour. They're inside being interviewed now. Witness and all of that."

Jordan got up and stood as high as he could in the van. "I'm going in."

Jordan stepped down from the van and walked over the pebbles, keeping his ID at hand in case anyone questioned him. But inside, he recognised the POs. They nodded briefly at him before turning back to a young male that was sat opposite them.

"Hi. Jordan Jenner," Jordan said to the brown-eyed youth. "Did you see what happened?"

"I saw the man running."

"It was a man?"

"I think so." The youth looked doubtful. "That's what I thought, anyway. Carrying a pipe. Sally was screaming outside. I made to chase after him, but it was too late."

"We've got this covered," one of the police officers said to him, indicating the brown-eyed boy. Jordan recognised the officer as someone from Abergavenny police. They hadn't kept in touch, and Jordan wondered if he had transferred to Chepstow.

Jordan considered arguing back, but it wasn't worth it. He nodded at the police officers, smiled at the youth, and then walked through the kitchen. The back door was open, leading out into the garden, and Jordan stepped out. He tried to imagine his mother sitting here in the postage-stamp-sized greenery, sitting in a deck chair next to Sally, the woman who had let her in on a perfect-appearing life.

The evening was cold, but that evening it had been the peak of summer. What had they spoken about? Would they have both been seeing James by that point? Two women bonding, unaware they were involved with the same man.

Jordan walked to the end of the house to find that the garden did not stretch much further. The grass was patchy and dead, the soil underneath bloated. He looked over the hedges at the tops of a neighbours' homes. This area looked very affluent. It was highly possible that Sally had been a victim of crime because of her status.

Yet it all seemed too coincidental. Jordan was dealing with a serial killer, and Sally could have been the next victim.

FORTY-EIGHT

January brought rain, so much so that Jordan wondered if there would be floods. He stood at his apartment window as the rain bounced off the tarmac, the cars driving slower than usual as their wiper blades dragged over the windscreens. Sally had assured him last night that things would be fine, that she would just go back in but only if someone kept watch of the house. This time, Jordan made sure someone stayed parked outside.

On the way back, driving home with Lloyd, he had been reassured it hadn't been his fault. Mistakes happened, and there was no need to get worked up about it. Luckily, Sally was fine, but her death could have been on his hands.

Jordan stood in his underwear and an old T-shirt, looking out at the street. He was waiting for a call from his dad. They were supposed to be going to Annabelle's. They would need to clean out the front room where she had died, but Jordan knew it would be hard for his dad to face.

As the rain poured down, Jordan thought of Margaret. Why was she ignoring him? Did she have something to hide, something connected to Kim's death? Or was she distraught at being caught out with her affair?

Jordan turned away from the window, where he had made awkward eye contact with someone in a Chinese shop, and picked up his phone. He called Margaret's number.

She didn't answer, which he didn't expect her to, but he left a message. "If you don't let me in, Margaret, I will personally order a search warrant for your house. You can't avoid me forever. It's Private Investigator Jordan Jenner, by the way."

He hung up, feeling oddly satisfied when his phone vibrated in his hand. He flinched, expecting to see Margaret's name, but it was a London number calling.

"Hello? If you're trying to sell me something about PPI, I'm not here for it..."

"Mr Jordan Jenner? Sorry, hi, no PPI. I'm Sandra Burke. I work at the publishing house. You rang about our client, James Fairview?"

Jordan blinked. For one, odd moment he couldn't remember what she was on about. "Yes, of course. Hi. Thanks for calling me back so quickly."

"No, that's fine. Can I ask what you need help with?"

"I need to see the manuscript James wrote."

"Can I ask why?"

"I'm investigating his murder, and I think he stole it."

There was a sharp intake of breath on the other end of the line. This was clearly shocking news to a woman who had probably nurtured plenty of writing talent during her career.

When she spoke again, her voice wavered ever so slightly. "Can I get your email address please, Mr Jenner? I can forward you over what he sent to us. We haven't gone through any edits yet. That was all still being negotiated."

"Can I ask how much this deal was worth?"

"We'd agreed a three-book deal, as he said this was a first in a series. We saw potential, and so we wanted to keep him on. We tend to do that, for a bit of safety. I can't disclose figures, it wouldn't be right of me."

"A six-figure deal?"

Sandra laughed. "Six figures for a debut author? Oh no, we don't do that. Email, please, Mr Jenner?"

"Then how much was it worth?" Jordan questioned, wondering if the rumours of a six-figure deal was spread by James.

"For authors, we sometimes offer an advance. Usually a small advance. Maybe five hundred pounds, sometimes a little more. Then the author pays out that advance through book sales. We never know how much will sell, so we don't offer six-figure deals to just anybody. Especially not a debut author."

"But James told people it was six-figures."

Sandra giggled once more. "Then he lied. Please, can I get your email?"

Jordan recited his email, and he listened to her type at her keyboard. "Did you ever meet James Fairview, Sandra?"

"No, unfortunately not. He seemed nice, though, when we communicated on the phone. Although once or twice, he didn't know what I was talking about when I mentioned a few things to change in the manuscript. I suppose it was because he had taken so long to write it. Writers do forget."

Or it was because he stole it and never bloody read it, Jordan wanted to say. Instead, he settled with "Of course."

"I've forwarded you the manuscript now, Mr Jenner. You should have it in your email soon," Sandra said. "Please, can you keep me posted? I know we're not going to publish it now, now that he's gone, but I'd like to know if he really did steal the work. I'll have to admit to my error, if that's the case."

"You wouldn't have been able to tell," Jordan said. "It's not your fault. But yes, I will keep you updated."

They said their goodbyes, and Jordan opened the app on his phone for the emails. He saw that Sandra had emailed him, the attachment being the manuscript. It wasn't called *Novel*, like Annabelle had named it. Now, the document was called *We See at Night*. Was it possible James really had written his own novel?

Opening it, the layout was the same as Annabelle's, only this time underneath the title was James's name, proudly italic and bolded, so no one could dispute it was anyone else's work.

After booting up Annabelle's laptop, Jordan compared the first chapter. With a chilling jolt, he discovered James's work was exactly the same.

He scrolled through the other chapters, and there were very little changes, if any. James seemed to have changed a punctuation mark here and there, and instead of numbering the chapters, he wrote them out. But the story, the characters, the dialogue all belonged to the hands of Annabelle.

Furious, Jordan sat back in his chair and called Vanessa's office. On the third ring, Mark answered.

"Mark here. How can I help?"

"Where's Vanessa?"

"She's out at the minute," Mark replied. "Can I ask who's calling?"

"No need. You already know."

"Jordan. I hear you forgot to get Sally a car. She almost died."

"She didn't almost die, and when you make a mistake, I'll be sure to remind you."

"I…"

Jordan hung up and called Vanessa's mobile instead. She answered straight away. "Jordan! Hi. I'm just getting a coffee. Had to get out of the office for a bit. I wished I didn't, though. I'm soaked. What's up?"

"It's the manuscript that James got a publishing deal for. It definitely isn't his. It's Annabelle's."

Vanessa said something to the person behind the counter at the coffee shop, and then she paid attention again. "Are you certain?"

"I asked the publisher to send me the manuscript. It matches what was on Annabelle's hidden laptop."

"Shit."

"That's right." Jordan scrolled through the manuscripts. There was no denying it. The work had first been Annabelle's, stolen by James.

"And he got a publishing contract?"

"It certainly wasn't six figures. They don't offer those sort of deals to debut authors. James was lying."

"So how much we talking?"

"An advance of maybe five hundred pounds."

"Well, well, well."

"Exactly."

Rain pattered as a background to Vanessa's voice now. He pictured her hurrying back to her car. "But why the death of James?"

"What do you mean?"

"He got a publishing deal, and then he was poisoned, the same way Annabelle died. Why?"

"I don't know," Jordan said. "I really don't know."

A ping, like that of a lift, sounded on the other end of the phone. A robotic voice repeated the floor Vanessa was parked on. "Listen, Jordan. I'm going to send you that CCTV from Joseph's street. I forgot to send it last night. Take a look through it and see if you find anything of interest. Send me that manuscript too. I want to look through it."

"How are we going to prove this, Vanessa?"

"It's easy to prove that the manuscript wasn't his. What's going to be harder to prove is why and whether or not he killed your mother for it."

FORTY-NINE

Peter cancelled. Jordan read the text message that explained he had to go into work to cover a shift and asked whether or not they could rearrange. Jordan politely replied, saying that was fine, but he knew his dad wasn't covering for anyone in work. It wasn't in his nature.

Choosing not to press his dad on the matter, Jordan decided to try to relax for the day. Still in his underwear, he cleaned up the house, made food, fed Oscar, and then sat down to play a game on his Xbox One, something he hadn't been able to do in a while. With thoughts of the murders running through his head, he hoped for a respite. He needed to recharge, but it was proving impossible.

As he drove through the streets of San Andreas on Grand Theft Auto, in what was supposed to be a Lamborghini, Jordan's phone vibrated on the table. He paused the game and found Margaret's name on the screen.

Jordan answered immediately. "Margaret."

"How dare you threaten me?" Margaret barked. "I don't appreciate being told that police are going to come storming through my house."

"I'm sorry, but you're someone I need to speak to, and you've been ignoring me."

"I have not. Can you blame me?" she contradicted. "Don't you understand that a woman needs to be left alone? I have nothing to contribute to this case. You need to find the murderer and leave me alone."

Jordan cleared his throat. "You were sleeping with the murdered, Margaret. I think you have some information that could really help."

Margaret's exasperation was audible on the other end. "You're interfering in things that don't concern you. There's nothing to go over."

"And why not? Did Kim strangle herself? How did my mother die? Did James kill her?"

"Your mother was a depressed woman who suffered with bipolar. I wouldn't be surprised if she did top herself."

Jordan paused. "And how do you know this?"

"I don't know. I'm just saying, not everything is as it appears. Honestly, you're looking for links where there are none. I'm sad he's gone, but he was a dick. There, that's my statement."

"Margaret, we need to meet. There are questions I need to ask you."

"No. I'm getting bored of all of this. I've had to lock myself away because you and the police are buzzing around."

"Margaret, did you know James's manuscript was stolen?"

"What?"

"The manuscript he got a publishing deal for. It wasn't his."

Margaret went silent as she thought this through. Then her voice came back, calculated in tone. "I'm not surprised. Didn't I tell you before that the man hadn't written anything in months? It's why we were all so surprised when he told us."

"After Annabelle's death," Jordan stated.

"After Annabelle's death, yes." Margaret sighed. "Jordan, look. There's nothing I can do or say to bring your mother back. If that's what you want to talk to me about, you're wasting your time, love."

Jordan thought for one moment that Margaret was about to hang up. "Margaret. What I said earlier still remains true. If you're not going to volunteer to let me into your home, then I will be there with a bunch of police officers to cause a scene."

"Ugh," Margaret breathed. He could hear her on the other end, breathing in and out, probably trying to sort things out in her own head. Finally, she spoke again. "Fine. Make it here by one p.m. If you're late, then I'm not seeing you."

She hung up. Checking the time, Jordan saw it was quarter to twelve. He got changed, then came back to turn his Xbox off. He sat down at the laptop and forwarded Sandra's email to Vanessa, the manuscript belonging to Annabelle attached.

He'd heard of plagiarism before. Mostly, the person responsible got sued. But never had he heard of someone killing for the work of someone else. It made him think about the mental state of James and what else he had been capable of. Had he been suppressing killing desires for years, finally to have it snap when Annabelle cut him off?

Jealousy. That was the only explanation Jordan had. The man was jealous of her ability to create a story. But was he jealous enough to kill?

Jordan drove out of Cardiff and stopped at a petrol station to fill up his tank. People talked around him as he stood in queue to pay.

"She was one of Joseph Gordon's writers, yeah," a middle-aged man was saying to a woman in front of him. "Apparently had a troubled life."

"Another case of a man killing a woman by the looks of things."

"Why'd you say that, love?"

"Her body dumped in a park after her death? Someone with strength would have had to move her." The young woman behind the till was pretending not to listen, but as her gaze darted from the woman to the man, she seemed desperate to impart her own opinion. The woman briefly turned back to the till to check the price before presenting her contactless card. "Poor woman. Remain sceptical by what else you read about her. They always tend to make out that it's the woman's fault."

"Had no family. Claimed on the dole. A history of thievery," the man said, clutching two packs of chewing gum, a full-fat Coke, and a sandwich. "She probably had a few enemies in her lifetime."

"Whatever happened, I hope the right person is found." The woman took her items and made to leave, clearly over the way the conversation was going. "Tragic story."

She left, and the man stepped forward, looking at the woman behind the counter. "Women, they'll make anything an issue."

The cashier took his items. "I personally think she had a point."

The man avoided her eyes the whole time. Jordan paid for his petrol, thinking about Kim, and then on a whim picked up a newspaper. It was *The Sun*, a paper he hated to entertain, but in a corner of the front page was a picture of Kim.

In his car, he drove out of the petrol station and parked on the side of the road, switched off his engine and opened the paper. The headline for Kim read: *Murdered Woman Claimed off the State and Dealt Drugs.*

The article wasn't much better. It described Kim as being poor, sponging off the taxpayer, and causing trouble. Supposedly, Kim had a criminal record. She had stolen from Tesco, Asda, and Argos, and had been caught trying to steal from a post office. She had served community service but had never gone to prison, the article mentioning not enough evidence and mental health issues. Jordan wondered how much of it was true but felt angry that her murder was being overshadowed by such bias.

Near the end of the article, the reporter wrote how Kim found solace and a new hope in bestselling author, Joseph Gordon. Truthfully, Kim had seemed to have her shit together when Jordan had met her, but he'd seen a side of her that had been completely fabricated.

Turning the page, Jordan roved over stories about Brexit and remainers causing a fuss. He was about to shut the paper and drive to Margaret when a small article in the corner caught his attention.

Woman's Heart Attack Case Reopened as Murder. He read the brief article: *Annabelle Skelton, a woman who had died alone due to a heart attack, has had her case re-opened as a murder investigation. Police believe Annabelle was murdered by a friend in her own home.*

The article made no mention of James Fairview or Joseph Gordon. Either the media didn't know her links to the current case, or they didn't think it relevant. Jordan looked at the road as cars drove by above the speed limit. If the press found out, there would be pandemonium. He had to solve this before they got wind of it.

FIFTY

"So, you are here to talk?" Margaret stood at her door, dressed in a flowery blouse and black trousers. She looked like she wanted to go out, to face the wet weather wearing summer gear.

Jordan stood on her doorstep, sheltered enough from the rain. "Of course."

Margaret walked away from the door and Jordan took this as his cue to enter. Her home looked outdated, with walls that had once been white, now appearing yellow. Her furniture looked like it was supposed to be antique, but Jordan had a feeling it was all mass-produced and cheap.

She shut the door, locked it with her key, and then pointed to the kitchen. "Go in there. I'll be in now. I'm just going to turn the radio off."

She pointed to a set of glass doors that led to the living room. Jordan opening them to discover classical music playing. He walked into the kitchen, which was small and had vinyl flooring. He sat at a little wooden table, again made to look older than it probably was.

Margaret came in carrying a tea. She put it down on the table opposite him. "Do you want a drink?"

"No, I'm okay, thanks."

Margaret raised an eyebrow. "The least you can do is have a drink when you've barged into my house." She bustled over to the kettle, flicking the switch. "Coffee or tea?"

Jordan sighed. "Tea will be fine."

He watched her make it. She lifted a mug out of the shelf above the kettle and then took a tea bag out of a pot. She poured the hot water in, stirred with a spoon delicately, and then added milk.

"Any sugar?"

"Just the one."

"Just the one," she said, playing mother hen.

She handed it to him, and he admitted to himself it looked good. But he wouldn't touch it. He waited for her to sit. "Lovely place."

"Is it? I can't afford to do it up. Been like this for years." She narrowed her eyes. "Can we get this over with as soon as possible?"

"It depends."

"On what?"

"On how much you want to cooperate."

Margaret drank some of her tea. She looked him in the eye. "Are you going to drink that?"

"I'm waiting for it to cool down."

Margaret placed her own mug down. "Fine. Ask away."

"Why did you keep it quiet that you were married to Joseph?"

Margaret's eyes widened. She seemed to be surprised by the first question. "It wasn't kept quiet, I can assure you of that. We don't believe in flaunting a relationship. We married, but we both agreed living separately was best. We tried living together and realised we couldn't share our space. I like living alone. We didn't feel the need to tell the writers we were married. If they couldn't tell, then that's their own problem."

"So you didn't tell anyone?"

"No one asked."

"But did anyone suspect?"

"You ask like it's a dirty thing," Margaret snapped. "It really didn't matter to us. No one cared, and we weren't bothered anyway. We hardly hid it."

"And have you seen Joseph since you stormed out of that meeting we had a few nights back?"

Margaret picked up her mug again but didn't drink. Joseph watched the steam rise over her, like a cheap illusion. "I've seen him twice."

"Where?"

"Here. And his place."

"When?"

"God," Margaret said. "I don't know. A week ago, the other night."

"The other night? Can you be more specific?"

"Yesterday? I can't remember."

"You can't remember yesterday?"

"Times go by in a bit of a blur." Margaret blushed. "It probably was yesterday, yes."

Jordan nodded slowly. He let the silence drag out, the only sound coming from the rain lashing at the window. "Were you aware that Sally was attacked last night?"

"So?"

"So, I'm just asking. Were you aware?"

"No, I wasn't."

Jordan touched his mug but didn't lift it. He noticed Margaret look at his fingers. "Yeah. Smashed glass, hit across the cheek with a pipe. Luckily, there was no serious damage."

"Did they catch who did it?"

"No," Jordan said. "But they're investigating."

"Good." Margaret drank from her mug. "What time did you see Joseph?"

"About eight."

"So you remember the time, but not the day?"

"I said about." Margaret glared at Jordan.

"I see," Jordan said. "What time did he leave?"

"About nine."

"He didn't stay long, then?"

"Let's just say we argued."

Jordan sat back. A gust of wind bristled past outside. "About what?"

"Usual couple things," Margaret dismissed. "You should ask him."

"I might do soon."

Margaret drained the rest of her mug and put it down, looking in to the empty contents. "He's upset with me because of James. He honestly didn't know about us."

"And can you blame him?"

"No. I was stupid. I don't know why I did it."

"Can you venture a guess?"

"What a stupid question."

Jordan just looked at her. He wanted her to feel uncomfortable, to venture something just to fill the gap. After a few moments, she did.

"I suppose it might have been because James had a certain charm. I'm an older woman. He was a younger man and, I don't know, he showed interest in me. I've not been looked at like that, like the way he looked at me for a long time."

Jordan kept his face passive, but he felt pity for the steely woman in front of him. He'd heard tales like this before, in both cases. Someone with low self-esteem feeling worthy again when someone else came along and showed them new attention, something they had lost with an existing partner.

"How hurt were you when he left you, Margaret?"

Margaret glanced away, suddenly interested in the decoration of her ageing kitchen. She took in the ceiling, where spirals had been pasted into the design. She traced them with her gaze.

"I was hurt, yeah. Of course I was. But I left him. When it came to light about Annabelle, I thought I could forgive him. Then I found out about Sally, and yeah, I was pissed."

"So you valued your own self-worth?"

Margaret looked at him. "That's right."

"Can you tell me why Kim was angry at him?"

"Excuse me?"

"Kim. I hear she was angry at James too."

"I don't know about that."

"Really? You seem to forget the CCTV of you and Kim from the Lower New Inn. The night you spent with James, at a pub, and he was thrown out." Jordan watched her shift in her seat. "I also have it from another source that you spent some time with Kim after you found out James had been cheating."

"Sally."

"Maybe."

"Fine. Look, Kim was unstable. She hated James because he insulted her all the time. It was quite sad. She wanted to get some revenge on the bloke, so I went along with it."

"What sort of revenge?"

"Just humiliate him in some way."

"So, on the night of his death, you were meant to meet Sally and Kim. Is that correct?"

Margaret blinked. "I met Sally."

"But not Kim?"

"No. You know why as well, so don't go making things up. Kim was at the writing group."

"She was. Yes. And you and Sally were panicked?"

"Panicked?"

Margaret had broken out into a sweat now, but she hadn't noticed. Her fingers tapped the porcelain mug she held between them. She seemed to be gripping tightly but was unaware of it.

"That's what Sally said. You feared Kim might have gotten a bit carried away."

"She wanted to humiliate him. She said she was going to blackmail him about something, but we don't know what it was," Margaret said. "Truthfully. Kim wouldn't tell us. She had come across something, and she wanted us all to find out that night. Sally wouldn't have any of it. Said it had been fun but had gone too far."

"And so Sally left yours and went home?"

"So she says."

Jordan nodded. "So she says. And what did you do?"

"I...stayed home."

"You...stayed home?" Jordan emphasised the pause.

Margaret, annoyed, kept to the story. "I stayed home."

She seemed more confident now, but Jordan sensed she was hiding something, keeping something quiet for her own protection. "Then he was murdered."

"That's correct."

"But Kim was in the study the whole time Joseph went out to make the drinks."

"So?"

"So, the poison was put into his drink when the drink was being made."

Margaret shrugged. "I was at the house, so I don't know."

"Margaret, can you tell me what you exchanged with Kim that night at the Lower New Inn?"

"I don't remember."

She had let go of the mug now and crossed her arms. Jordan remained expressionless, adopting a relaxed pose, as if he was talking with a best friend on something trivial.

"You must do."

"Can you remember what you did months ago?"

"Not everything. But I would remember exchanging something with a friend," Jordan said. "It looked pretty dodgy."

"Anything looks dodgy in a pub."

Jordan smirked. "Can you remember?"

"No."

She wouldn't play ball. Jordan decided to try a different tact. "Kim was angry, and she had evidence of something incriminating on James?"

"That's correct."

"What do you think that could be?"

Margaret exhaled. "Jordan, I don't know. Look, I'm no help to this. I've told you everything I know. We planned to humiliate James. And when I say humiliate, I mean get him drunk and make him piss himself or ridicule his work together. I don't mean poison him to death. Kim started to get a bit worked up, took it a bit too far, and went rogue. For all I know, she poisoned him."

Jordan shook his head, holding out his hands. "Then why is she dead?"

"You read the papers today? She had enemies."

Jordan almost laughed. Instead, he shifted in his seat, leaning forwards. "Can I use your bathroom?"

Margaret looked confused. "My bathroom?"

"Yes, please. I'm desperate."

"But you haven't drank any of your tea."

"I drank before I came." Jordan began to jig. "Bathroom?"

Margaret scoffed. "Upstairs, to the right."

FIFTY-ONE

Jordan climbed the stairs, leaving Margaret alone downstairs. He opened and closed the bathroom door, and then snuck into her bedroom, where the door was already open. The floorboard creaked and he held his breath, but Margaret had busied herself with something in the kitchen.

Margaret's bedroom was neatly cleaned with not much to offer. He wasn't sure what he was looking for, but he wanted to know how she lived. The curtains were drawn here, preventing anyone from the back of the house looking in. Twitching the curtain, he peered through the wet window out onto a cycle track behind Margaret's small garden.

Inside the drawer of Margaret's nightstand he found one book. It appeared to be a worn paperback, and Jordan wondered if she was reading it now. It was a romance novel, the cover depicting a toned man hugging a woman on the beach. After sliding the door shut, Jordan regarded the wardrobes and the chest of drawers. There was no point in looking through there. It was an invasion of her privacy.

He chuckled at this, quietly. His whole job was steeped in history of invading people's privacy.

He decided to leave the bedroom and crept tentatively across the landing to the bathroom. He opened the door slowly and crept inside, then closed it just in the latch, so it didn't make a noise. The bathroom was cramped with wooden panelling on the walls. There was a toilet, a shower cubicle, and a mirror cabinet hung up.

Jordan walked across the floor, which also had vinyl laid down and was peeling at the edges, and opened the cabinet door. Inside were two shelves, and they were piled high with things that Margaret had probably forgotten about. He took out medication, noticing Margaret had stacks of Ibuprofen.

There was also a tube of toothpaste, to quickly replace the one that was on the go at the minute. Jordan was about to move this out of the way when a noise came from downstairs.

He held his breath.

"Jordan!"

He jumped.

"What are you doing up there?"

"Sorry, uh…it's taking longer than I expected!"

Margaret made a sound of disgust and stomped away. Jordan cringed at what he said, disgusted at his own excuse, and then moved the toothpaste.

He reached for a perfume bottle that was at the back of the cupboard, facing away from him. He didn't think much of it but wanted to look at it to see what Margaret wore. The bottle was rather small in size, fitting in his palm. The substance inside was a pretty light-pink colour, a small metal chain around the top held on a metallic blue heart.

Turning the bottle over, his attention roved down from the pearl stopper to the name of the perfume. Naughty Alice. He smirked. The idea of Margaret wearing something so sexily named made him feel odd.

Then something inside him lurched. It was a perfume by Vivienne Westwood. A conversation with Joseph came back to him, and he let his hand holding the perfume bottle drop to his side.

Think, Jordan.

This didn't mean it was evidence. Vivienne Westwood was a world-renowned fashion designer. Jordan thought that a quick search would tell him this perfume was a bestseller.

Yet Joseph's words came back to haunt him.

"I was in the kitchen when I heard the back door open. I turned to the back door to see someone coming in. I was about to ask who it was when I was called from the other room. I left the drinks unattended and went to see who called me. When I went back to the kitchen, the woman was leaving. I know it was a woman, you see. I could see the blurred shape of a woman in shawls, and her hair was a light grey, and she was short. I could also tell by the perfume. I believe it was Vivienne Westwood. My wife used to wear it all the time. But Margaret and Sally look the same. They're roughly the same age, and they dress similar. It's been a joke running through our meets. I didn't think anything of it."

Jordan was shaking now, the perfume in the bottle jostling. He took a deep breath and put the perfume back where it was, but not before taking a photograph.

My wife used to wear it all the time.

The link to the murder case was right in front of him.

Joseph had let slip that his wife was Margaret. He also let slip when they first met that she always wore Westwood's perfume, and he smelled that as the blurred shape left.

But Jordan had never seen Joseph struggle with his sight. Did he actually know it was Margaret the whole time?

Jordan shook his head. "Fuck."

He flushed the toilet, opened the window briefly for good measure, and then calmly walked down the stairs. Margaret came out of the kitchen, a fresh cup of tea in her hand.

"You took bloody ages. If I had known you were going to do that, I would have said no."

"Sorry." Jordan smiled. "I'll have to apologise again. I used some perfume to freshen up in there, make it smell a bit nicer. Are you a big fan of Vivienne Westwood's stuff?"

Margaret squinted. "God no. Haven't worn that stuff in forever. Joseph bought it for me. Only wore it when he was around."

Jordan nodded, whilst all the time thinking she had just made a confession.

FIFTY-TWO

"Did you send that CCTV?"

Jordan drove to his house, thinking things through. He had his phone cradled in the holder on his dash and Vanessa on loudspeaker.

"Yeah, I've sent it. Don't you check your emails?"

"Not when I've been busy."

"Busy. Doing what?"

"I'll let you know soon, but I think this case is almost over."

"Jordan. What's happened?"

"It's Margaret."

Jordan swerved past a biker and then slowed down for traffic lights, cursing under his breath.

Vanessa breathed in. "Why?"

"Something Joseph told me when he first met. That the smell left behind by the woman was Vivienne Westwood. Margaret had it in her bathroom."

"But that could be a coincidence."

"Which is why I need the CCTV. But it makes sense, don't you think?"

"It's possible," Vanessa said, and Jordan could almost see her nodding. "Where are you now?"

"Driving home."

"You're on the phone and driving?"

"Relax, V, you're on speaker."

"Still! If it wasn't you, I'd be pulling you over."

Jordan laughed. "Why do you want to know where I am?"

"I'm about to finish, but I'll meet you at yours. I want to watch this footage with you."

"Hurry. I don't think I can wait much longer."

"I love it when you talk dirty to me."

Ten minutes later, Jordan arrived at his home and parked out back. Vanessa was already there in her own car that was newer than his. She got out when he did, having stayed inside in the warmth.

"You told me to rush and you were late."

"I was coming back from the Bay and there was traffic."

"Tell me everything you found out."

Jordan explained his conversation with Margaret. He told Vanessa how she seemed to be hiding something when he asked where she went after Sally left the night of James's murder. Vanessa nodded, taking it all in, working things out in her own head.

"There's certainly enough scope there to link her up to the final killing, yes," Vanessa said. "And she wouldn't tell you what she exchanged with Kim in the pub?"

"No, but I'm thinking it may have been money or the poison."

"Probably money. I think we would have seen the substance on the camera."

Jordan unlocked his door and they went inside. He turned on the lights and went straight to his laptop. Vanessa looked around the place, politely sitting across from him.

"It's small," Jordan said, signalling the place as his laptop booted up.

"I just think you can afford better."

"I'm too tight with money, and my freelancing can go to tits with no warning."

"I've already told you that wouldn't happen."

Jordan turned back to his laptop and typed in the password. "With budget cuts, I couldn't guarantee it."

Jordan opened his emails and found Vanessa's. He downloaded the CCTV attachment, impatiently watching as the bar sluggishly went by. Vanessa went to get them drinks and came back with lemonade for her and a Diet Coke for him.

He took it and gulped a much-needed drink. "You know me well."

"It's a school night, so no alcohol."

"That's fine. I'm bored of it."

Vanessa sipped at her drink and looked at the back of the laptop. "What about your mum?"

"What about her?"

"Well. Do you think the same person is responsible for that?"

"I couldn't tell you, if I'm honest," Jordan said. "There's something missing. Something I don't know. Margaret mentioned she was depressed, but she was probably being cruel. It wasn't suicide."

"It was definitely murder, Jord," Vanessa said.

Jordan saw there was only five minutes left on the download. He drank some of the Coke, wishing he could view the CCTV now.

"I think James is involved in that part of things somehow. What I don't get is what made Margaret do it."

"*If* she did it."

"Yes." Jordan nodded and lurched forwards when the blue bar disappeared. Without touching anything, the video player automatically launched on his Mac laptop. After a few seconds, the video appeared.

It was two hours long, and the first image was of a street at dusk. Jordan looked at Vanessa. "Why two hours?"

"It's the hours before and after his death," Vanessa explained. "Somewhere in that footage, James was killed."

"Does it include the back of the house?"

"I've sent you another video for that one. That took a little longer to get. The security guard said it infringed on Joseph's data, being from his house. We told him we were police officers and what we said goes."

Jordan laughed, remembering the stuffy jobsworth security man. "I bet that went well."

"He grumbled as he told me he would sort it, yes."

Jordan went back to his emails and tried to locate the second email Vanessa sent. When he couldn't see it, he went to junk and found it there. He was about to click on it when further down he noticed another email, one that had gone straight to his junk mail and hadn't been seen.

The sender was Kim.

Jordan clicked on the email to find that she hadn't written a title but simply typed in the body. He scanned the message, breathing deeply.

We have to meet, Jordan. I know something about Annabelle. There were letters. They explain everything. Meet me at this address. This is the last time I can tell you about this. I'm in trouble, and I need your help.

Jordan read her paragraph three more times. Vanessa was staring at him, reading his expression.

"Jordan?"

Jordan looked at Vanessa, guilt tearing through him like a tsunami. He felt sick, and for one horrible hot moment, he thought he was going to throw up. Kim had tried reaching out to him, but he'd never seen it. It was dated a week before her body was found. The whole time he had been trying to reach her, whilst thinking she had been writing threatening letters. But it hadn't been her.

Someone had been pretending, and someone was hunting her down.

"I could have stopped this."

FIFTY-THREE

A heavy rain had begun to fall again. Vanessa had now moved from her chair and sat next to Jordan, reading Kim's email. "This definitely her?"

"Don't you think it is?"

Vanessa read the email address, which was set up in Kim's name. "I'll get tech to see when the email became active."

"It must be her," Jordan said. "She was hiding. She wanted me to meet her, to help her."

Vanessa looked at Jordan. "If it was her."

"I don't know." Jordan shook his head. The guilt gripped him hard, a stone vice around his chest, squeezing the air out of him. "Margaret said Kim had blackmail for James. She had something that would do some damage."

"Maybe Kim knew who killed James?"

"It's possible, yes," Jordan said. "That's why was she killed."

Vanessa bit her lip. "Shit."

"I know."

"Download that CCTV. We have to see who went to Joseph's that night."

Jordan did as he was told, infuriatingly watching the download sleepily drag itself by. Finally, after five minutes, it was done, a little longer than the first.

The footage was of Joseph's back garden, cast in a setting winter sunlight. It looked like it had been raining earlier that day, and Jordan tried to remember what he had been doing the night before that. He imagined it had been what he was doing before he was called back in. Refreshing the news, keeping up to date with Vanessa, and trying his best not to think about his mum.

Vanessa pressed a key and sped up the footage. There was no audio, so they sat and watched tree branches quickly moving on the screen. They stopped when a shadow appeared, but it was just Joseph putting rubbish outside.

They forwarded further again, until Jordan glimpsed movement at the end of the garden. He stopped, and they watched the screen.

Nothing happened for the first few seconds, and Jordan began to doubt whether or not he had actually seen anything. He looked at the timestamp burnt on the screen. It was close to when James was killed. He glanced at Vanessa, who had her hand pressed to her lips.

Then, there was movement again at the bottom of the garden. Jordan's hunch had been right. The person had entered through the bushes where Joseph had put a new gate in. The concealed pathway that was a serious breach of security had been used.

The figure moved forwards slowly, as if stalking the house. Jordan leaned closer, so it would be better to see. But he knew they needed to walk forwards.

Night vision was on now, and the figure lumbered forwards. A nightlight came on, flooding the garden. The unknown person didn't flinch. In fact, it was as if they expected it.

The figure walked slowly up the garden. They were dressed in black, a hood over their face.

"Shit."

"Keep watching."

All of a sudden, the nightlight flicked off, and the green tinge of night vision came back. The figure walked quickly now to the back door, where they paused. Jordan couldn't see what was happening, but after a few seconds, the figure disappeared inside.

"Did the door open for them?"

"Maybe they were waiting for someone to leave the kitchen," Jordan said.

"You think they watched Joseph, hoping he would leave the drinks unattended?"

"It's possible, isn't it?"

"It is. But risky," Vanessa said. "It could have been futile."

"We know that it wasn't." Jordan rewound the footage. "Fuck, I wish I could see who it was."

"Keep going."

The rest of the footage played. After a minute and a half inside, the figure in the hood came slinking back out. They hurried away this time, down the garden path, and Jordan noticed something odd. He rewound and played it again, Vanessa watching him.

"The security light. It doesn't come back on as they move away down the garden."

Vanessa watched the replayed footage. "Jesus."

"Someone turned it off."

The figure disappeared at the end of the garden, out of the camera's range. Jordan stared at where they had gone, wondering if they had stayed to watch the house or simply fled from the scene.

Jordan fast-forwarded through the rest of the footage. After a few moments, a figure appeared outside again, this time from the house. Kim trod onto the patio, her arms crossed, and checked her surroundings. She seemed calm, considering that at this moment in time James had probably been killed. She inspected the bottom of the garden, then paused. She stepped forward and hunched forwards, as if she could see something that the camera couldn't. Jordan wondered if she had called out.

She walked out onto the grass and turned back to the house. Waving up at it, Jordan wondered if she was trying to signal to someone that there was something outside. But he realised she was trying to test the security light.

Kim turned to the place where the figure had disappeared and shook her head. She then walked back into the house with a speed that told Jordan she had been spooked.

"Kim saw," Vanessa gasped. "Kim knew who killed James."

Jordan replayed the footage of Kim appearing outside. It seemed Vanessa was right.

FIFTY-FOUR

Jordan went back to Kim's email. She had left an address, somewhere in Blaenavon.

"We should go," Jordan said.

Vanessa quickly searched the address. "It's on the outskirts of Blaenavon. Quite remote, by the looks of things, if Google maps are telling me the right thing." Vanessa considered Jordan. "It could be a trap."

"So you could come with me then."

Vanessa eyed her phone. "I think we should get a team there."

"Vanessa, come on. You hired me to find out what's happened, and this is part of it. Remember our titles? We're detectives. This is what we do."

Vanessa looked back at the computer. Jordan could tell she was remembering Kim, the way she looked down the garden path, seeing someone staring back at her in the bushes.

"If we go, then we have to tell the team where we are. Just in case."

"Fine by me," Jordan said.

Vanessa typed a message to someone on the force, copying Kim's address. A few moments later, someone replied.

"Who did you text?" Jordan asked.

"Mark."

"Mark?" Jordan blinked. "Seriously?"

"He's working tonight, so he'd be responsible for getting someone to us if something did go wrong."

"We're doomed."

Vanessa playfully hit Jordan. "Stop it!"

"We'll be fine. It's just a house. Take your baton and mace, if needs be."

Vanessa eyed him. "It's in the car."

They got themselves together, Jordan finding a coat to put on in a bid to combat the pouring rain outside. Vanessa had the address in her phone,

213

ready to go, and she unlocked her car by pressing a button on the key. Jordan got in the passenger side, and as Vanessa began to drive, the doors automatically locked.

Blaenavon was an hour or so away, but in this storm, Vanessa refused to go any faster. The wiper blades flashed furiously across the screen, back and forth.

"Hey, Siri. Call Jen."

Her phone lit up, and a few seconds later, Jennifer's name appeared on the screen.

After four rings, Jennifer answered. "They got you working late again?"

Jordan smirked. "I've whisked her away for a getaway."

"Jordan! Well, I had a suspicion the two of you were in love." Jennifer laughed. "But seriously, what's happening?"

"We've had a new lead, babe, on the murder of Kim," Vanessa said, pulling out into the faster lane to overtake a Micra that was driving slowly. "We're driving to Blaenavon."

"No one wants to go to Blaenavon," Jennifer sneered. "But okay, I understand. Is it safe?"

"It should be, yes," Jordan said.

"Where did the lead come from?"

Vanessa exchanged a glance with Jordan, one that said it was typical of Jennifer to be concerned. "Jordan found an email sent by Kim before she died. It went to his junk folder. She said she had information that she wanted to tell him before she was found. She sounded like she knew she was in trouble."

"Shit." Jennifer exhaled. "Poor doll."

"Hopefully, we can find out what's happened," Vanessa said. "We don't even know what the house will be like."

"Or if we can even get in."

Vanessa pointed at him. "Good point."

Jennifer laughed. "Okay. Well, I'll wait up for you. Text me when you're on the way back, okay? I want to know you're safe."

Vanessa promised she would, and after exchanging love for one another, the call was cut. Jordan felt warmth for their relationship. He thought about that type of relationship, the feeling of being cared for, of having something special.

"What are you smirking at?"

"Just Jennifer. She really does care."

"Well, you'd hope so, being engaged and all that," Vanessa said. "She wouldn't be honouring her vows if she didn't."

They drifted into a companionable silence, the only sound being the road underneath them, and the late-evening radio. They were driving through Newport, Vanessa glancing more and more at the satnav. Jordan watched the shadows cast by the streetlamps. He imagined what might lurk in them, the secrets that people hoped to keep in the dark. Branches from bare trees made claw-shaped shadows on the tarmac that Vanessa drove over, grasping at stone the same way the case grasped at him.

"I don't come up this way much," Vanessa said, as she indicated at a junction. "Crime hasn't really taken me this far."

"Strange for Newport."

Vanessa laughed. "Obviously, I've been to Newport. But this is all Gwent Police territory."

"Gwent Police..." Jordan paused and thought. "I wonder if Kim tried reaching them."

Vanessa's forehead creased. "You know, that could be possible."

"Do you know anyone there?"

"Yeah, I can find out if Kim ever got in touch with them," Vanessa said. "Though I doubt it. They know it's related to what we're investigating. I would have been informed."

"Did you see the press got wind of Mum's case being reopened as a murder?"

Vanessa sighed. "I did, but we're making sure they don't find out the connection. They don't need to know yet. It's possible there isn't any."

"Really?"

"Okay, very slim now. But still... We don't want them blowing everything out of proportion. The last thing we need is unwanted media attention."

Jordan agreed with that. "How did they even find out?"

"We get calls from the press regularly. Someone must have mentioned it. I'm not sure who."

Jordan looked at the road. "Mark?"

"I don't think so."

"Why do you defend him so much?"

Vanessa smirked. "I work with him, Jord. He's all right. He's got a lot of learning to do, yes, but he's got potential."

"Hitler had potential."

"Jordan."

"All I'm saying is he needs to start working with people and stop taking his role so fucking seriously."

"It's a serious job."

"So lighten up about it," Jordan said.

"I just think he gets a bit nervous..." Vanessa stopped speaking.

"Go on."

Vanessa glanced at him. "What?"

"You sounded like you didn't finish your sentence."

215

"He gets a bit nervous around you, I think."

Jordan laughed loudly. "Seriously? Why?"

Vanessa changed gear. "I don't know. He asks about you almost daily, wondering what you're up to. I believe he thinks your role is pretty cool. But I expect he tries to impress you when you come in, and it just ends up being a bit...silly."

"You're joking."

Vanessa shook her head. "I'm not. I think he has in his head that first meeting he had with you, and he hasn't been able to recover from it."

"Hilarious."

They were driving out of Pontypool now, and Blaenavon was only ten minutes away. Jordan started feeling apprehensive about what was waiting for them. Maybe this hadn't been such a good idea.

When they arrived at the remote house in Blaenavon, which they had found after coming off the main road and following a dubious off-road track, there was a light on in one of the windows upstairs. The house, dirty on the outside and looking like it was about to collapse in on itself, stood battered by the pouring rain. An old car was parked on the drive, and Jordan recognised it as the car Kim had picked Joseph up in when he had left the police station.

"This is the place."

Vanessa turned off the engine and cut the lights. Without the sound of the car, it seemed eerily quiet. The metallic pings of rain on the roof unnerved them. There were no streetlights, and the lane where Kim's house stood was in pitch darkness.

Vanessa sent a text to Jennifer and then another to Mark. She was letting them know where she was. "I attached my location to both, just in case."

They got out of the car, lifting their hoods to their heads. They walked across the ground, which went from stone to muddy earth, and then tried the front door.

"Locked."

Without saying anything, they both began to scour the outside of the house, using the torches on their mobile phones. After a few moments, Jordan discovered that there was a spare key hiding underneath the tyre of the car. He thanked Kim and then went back to the front door.

"Vanessa," he part whispered, part called.

She came trudging from the side. "You got in?"

"Yes." He unlocked the door and stepped inside.

A voice sounded upstairs.

FIFTY-FIVE

He stood in the living room in disbelief. It couldn't be. Vanessa pressed a finger to her lips and pointed up the stairs. The light was off in the stairwell, and Jordan's body was telling him not to go, but he knew he had to.

He didn't believe in ghosts, but the voice was too clear to be anyone else. Vanessa led the way, holding her mace at the ready. She looked up the stairs, and Jordan peered over her shoulder.

"I told him he wouldn't get away with it, and he threatened to kill me."

A light spilled out onto the landing from a bedroom with its door ajar. Jordan glanced at Vanessa, who had broken out into a sweat. She crept up the stairs and Jordan followed, trying to breathe as quietly as possible.

His heart, beating heavily, slowed as he got closer and the tininess of the sound became more apparent. Vanessa, easing ever so slightly, pressed the door and let it open gradually. She raised the mace, pointing forward. Jordan expected a hiss or a cry of pain.

But Vanessa dropped her arm and stood tall, looking in on the bedroom.

Jordan stepped next to her and gazed into the room, lit up by a bulb in an old lamp in the middle of the room. A television had been left on, and as Jordan and Vanessa entered, the voice they'd heard came from the set.

"So that's what I had to tell. I'm sorry I couldn't tell you in person."

Kim, sat in the same bedroom days before, looking tired and dirty, had tears on her cheeks. She got up and walked forward, reached behind the screen, and it went blank.

"A DVD."

A DVD player rooted back to the menu, making a whirring noise as it did so. Then Kim appeared on the screen again.

She was walking back to where she had sat, forever kept in a continuous loop. Vanessa sunk to her knees, and Jordan sat on the single.

217

Kim took a deep breath, avoiding the camera for a little bit, as if she felt uncomfortable. With an air of defiance, she looked at the camera, and she appeared afraid.

"I hope you get to see this before they do, Jordan," she said, and Jordan felt as though she could see him right now. "If you're having to see this, then obviously I haven't made it. I'm hiding out here, hoping they don't know where I am. But it won't take long. They know my links to this place."

Kim cast a gaze around the small bedroom, which appeared the same now. The bed behind her was ruffled, the blankets messy from where she had slept. Now, however, they were neatly done.

"Uh, yeah. I managed to film this and burn it to DVD, using the ancient computer that's in the dining room downstairs. I'm going to leave this playing upstairs, and I just hope it doesn't cut out or the electric on the meter doesn't go before you get here. You're not answering my emails, and I can't contact you by phone. I don't have it. Someone stole it from me."

Jordan remembered the phone calls he had got from Kim's number, with no voice on the other end. It was out there somewhere, being held by someone else. Was it still on? Jordan hadn't thought to get the number traced. He had always thought Kim had been the one who still had it. Since her death, the calls had been driven from his mind.

"She looks terrified, doesn't she?" Vanessa said.

Jordan felt a pang of guilt. He could have helped her.

"Firstly, apologies for not being honest with you about my home in Trevethin. I didn't technically break the law. It belonged to an aunt of mine many years ago, but she lost it because of debt. It never sold at auction, and I still had a key. By the time Joseph came, I had to convince him it was my home. I didn't want him knowing anything about me. I basically…well, I didn't trust him."

Kim turned around as if she heard a sound. She held her breath, and the only sound was the natural hiss a microphone on a camera picks up. Her paranoia reassured, she turned back to the camera.

"But I don't trust any of them. *Any* of them. They're all backstabbing people that only care for themselves. I'm talking about the writers, by the way. They're egotistical people. Some more than others. But I'm hoping you've worked out who the main suspects are."

"Do you think she knows who killed James?" Vanessa asked.

Jordan couldn't tell. Before he could answer, Kim spoke again.

"What happened to James, killed by whisky, such an innocent way to go, but his reaction was too much. I think they hoped it would look inconspicuous. And it was all because of that fucking manuscript."

Vanessa glanced at Jordan.

"Mum's manuscript," Jordan said to her.

"The whole group was furious, Jordan, when they discovered James had a manuscript. I told you before that James had serious writer's block. He wasn't putting it on. He was a poser in the writing community. Just liked telling people he was an artist, a writer, and a painter with words, all that bull. He was just trying to appear different. I think he romanticised the industry, and he wanted to buy his way in. That's what he hoped Joseph would do for him. Of course, that was never going to happen. But he lucked out with Annabelle."

Hearing Kim say her name sounded strange. Of course, the women knew each other, but he couldn't help feeling as though Kim knew Annabelle better than he did.

"I don't think Annabelle knew what he was up to. At least, I didn't think that was the case. But I discovered something, and it's important that you know about it too. Basically, the manuscript wasn't stolen. But I need to cover everything before I get to that bit."

Vanessa readjusted her position, realising that the DVD was going to be longer than expected.

"I know who killed James, and I know who is after me. I've had threatening letters. They're telling me to keep my mouth shut. I made the mistake of telling them I wouldn't, that when I saw you, I would explain everything. I know who is responsible, and by the end of this, I think you will too.

"Like I say, they don't know I'm here, but it won't take them long. Sally, Margaret, Joseph, Graham, they've all been here. James has too. He's dropped Sally off. It was the first time I realised something was going on. See, I own this house. Came into money and I bought it. It was cheap, mainly because of where it is. But I had to leave and appear to be living elsewhere after James's death. I knew one of them had murdered him when he had that reaction to the poison. I just couldn't tell who."

Kim began to cry, tears falling down her cheek. Jordan wondered if she was mourning James's unjustifiable death, or whether the pressure of everything had finally got to her. She held up a hand in a signal of apology as she wiped the tears with the other.

"Margaret wanted revenge for James, and so did Sally. Sally had been cheated on with Annabelle, and Margaret refused to say why she was angry too. I don't know, but I suspect maybe James had wrangled her into this affair he had going."

Jordan wanted to tell her that she was right. He wanted to let her know that Joseph had revealed the marriage when he found out about Margaret's affair.

"I decided to go along with it, too, because the man was cruel. Insulted me many times, and I just wanted him to be knocked down a peg or two. At first, it was really innocent. We laughed about ridiculing his work in front of the group or spilling a drink over him by accident. That sort of thing. But then it got a bit...well, twisted, I suppose. There was mention of a finished manuscript going around, and it had been submitted to a few publishers, who were beginning to fight over it. Apparently, it was so good it just *had* to be published, but no deal or offer had been made."

Kim stopped speaking. She glanced over the camera, then back at the lens. "Sorry. If I hear something, I have to stop. They could come at any time." Kim peered over the camera, then seemed reassured. "Joseph found out the manuscript was written by Annabelle, and I remember he was furious. She hadn't told us about this thing. She had showed her talent, but by the time it was written and finished, she had left. I don't know if you know, but Joseph's books hadn't been selling all that well, and, uh, he didn't take it nicely that one of his recruits suddenly had something a lot better than he did."

Joseph. He had supposedly helped many of his writers with mentorship. Jordan wondered what had happened in the private mentorships, particularly any he had with his mother.

Kim brushed a loose strand of hair away from her face. Jordan noticed it looked dirty, and he wondered if she had been showering or if the truth had been consuming her.

"I overheard him and James talking one evening after a meeting. They were in the kitchen, and James was saying that Annabelle had told him about the manuscript, but he hadn't been informed it was finished. By this point, James wasn't talking to her, though he let Joseph know he hoped they'd get back in touch, and Joseph really encouraged it.

"But it wasn't just Joseph who was jealous. I know Sally was, and I know Margaret was. Hell, even I was, but I felt more congratulatory to the woman. She had left us and *still* made it. Though the talk kept coming back to us that it was all hype, that no deal had been struck, and Joseph wrote it off as an event of nothing. Especially when Margaret talked about her disdain for the whole thing."

Kim shook her head. "Anyway, during this time, James was getting weird. He kept avoiding conversations about Annabelle, and when I asked if they had spoken recently, as innocently as possible, he bit my head off. I began to suspect something was up. So I reached out to Annabelle, and she accepted and invited me over."

Vanessa looked at Jordan again. Jordan shrugged. He hadn't found any correspondence online between Kim and Annabelle.

"When I was over, this was about...what, three of four days before her death, I found out everything I could about the manuscript. She said she had written a novel that would be her legacy. Her goal was to get one novel published, and that was what she had done. Though she remained coy on whether or not there had been any deal made. I got annoyed, internally, because I just wanted information. Anyway, when she went to the bathroom, or maybe it was to make us drinks, I can't remember, I had a snoop, and I found some letters."

Kim reached behind her now and took out a small stack of papers, which she smoothed as she put them onto her lap. Jordan expected it to be the manuscript.

"These letters…I didn't believe them at first. I read over them after I took them home with me. I don't think Annabelle knew they were missing, and if she did, well…" Kim let the rest of the sentence hang in the air. Annabelle had died a few days later. "If you check under the bed, you'll be able to see what I have here."

Jordan, sat on the bed, peering down. He almost expected to see the wad of paper at his feet, as if Kim's ghostly hands had pushed them out. Vanessa paused the DVD.

He got to his knees, peered under the bed and found them in the middle of the floor. Jordan reached and pulled them towards him. He sat on his knees and turned the papers over.

He instantly recognised his mother's handwriting. It had never changed. Shuffling the paper, he saw her handwriting was mixed with someone else's.

Dearest Annabelle, read one. *James*, read another.

Every paper was the same, a two-way conversation between two people.

Annabelle had been writing to James before she died.

FIFTY-SIX

James,

I think this may be our final communication. Ever since that day you got in touch with me on social media—at first I was wary of you—you've been a great friend, a wonderful man, and a huge support to me. When your first letter came through after we stopped talking, I couldn't hide my happiness. Lucky, I'm the only one in my house!

I will miss you, and I hope you will miss me. But you must know that this has been a desire of mine since I was a teenager. I don't want to grow old or frail or get a disease and lose all sense of who I am. I know you're afraid, and I'm afraid too. I'm afraid of you, I'm afraid of what will happen to me afterwards, and I'm afraid of what might be the consequences.

But please, can you know that there will be none? I've done my research. The poison will be untraceable. I'll add it to my wine. And if ever it does get traced and you are accused for my murder or even for manslaughter, then I give you full permission to use all of our correspondence by letter to plead your innocence. I have purposefully stashed copies of these letters so they can be easily found. They are in my living room, underneath my coffee table, stored in a hatbox that I bought from our trip to Barcelona. Quite a lovely ode to us, don't you think?

This is terrifying. I write this with shaking hands, so I truly am sorry if you find this hard to decipher.

We have the day set. It's a special day to me, and I want to go on that day in particular. It was my mother's birthday. She always said she never wanted to end up like she did. James, it was awful. She had a brain tumour, and it completely took her away from me. She would have hated it, and my only solace is that she was so far gone she wouldn't have known about her last few weeks on this cruel, callous earth. That was what cemented my decision to not go the same way. I'm too afraid to do it alone, and you've been there for me. We've confided in each other. You know my deepest darkest secrets, and you know me intimately, and you're the only person I can trust to do this right.

You see, I went to the doctor's recently. They told me I had nothing to worry about. But I fear that as I age, something will creep up on me. At the first signs of that, I want to end it. But why wait for signs?

Besides, have you ever felt like something feels right? This is it. I may be healthy— for now!—but I just feel like this is the right time. My manuscript is completed. It's printed out and it sits in the guest bedroom upstairs. I want you to ensure it gets published, like I told you. I want to leave a legacy, and this will be it. Finally, my name on a bestselling book! It will just be a shame I won't live to see that. I could go on a little longer, but the truth is I'm tired, and I think this adds to the intrigue, don't you?

If you reply to this letter, then don't be offended if I don't respond. I hope you go through with what we have planned. The things you need are in the house. If you don't turn up, I will assume you have thought better of our plans. And if you have, know that I will forgive you. I will leave my door unlocked, if you don't turn up as planned. At the very least, you could discover my body.

I love you, and I always will love you.

You have a talent, and I know you will get through this.

All my love, Annabelle.

Dearest Annabelle,

What you have asked of me is terrifying me too. I am unsure if I can go through with it, and I really hope this letter gets to you before that dreaded day. I hope you can reconsider. You say yourself that you're healthy, that there is nothing wrong, and so why would you want to die? It makes me angry. You have so much more to give.

I've heard about this manuscript. Have you signed a deal yet? It's important that you tell me, so I can look over what you've agreed to. If you truly want this to be a legacy, the deal has to be right. I will support you. I always will. But I can't support this assisted suicide.

You say you are afraid to do it alone, but at the end of the letter, you still tell me that I should at the very least discover your body? Think of the consequences that will have on me? On my well-being? Do you think that is fair?

Annabelle. Please. We've been through a lot. You know how I feel about you, and you were my saviour. So I hope I can save you. Don't let your fear of dying get to you. You can't control everything.

I'm still not sure if I will come to your home like we planned. I didn't think you were serious. I know I agreed, but now the reality is setting in, the idea of it is horrible. I can't help you with this. I refuse to. It will truly ruin me. What if people find out?

I can't afford to go to prison. I know I will get in trouble for this. This is too much for one person to handle. I seriously urge you to reconsider. This isn't right. You're not well.

After everything we've been through and after everything we have talked about, it just seems like a slap in the face. I really am disappointed in you. You have kids to think about, an ex-husband who still loves you, and you have a talent that could really enrich the world. One book isn't enough.

Do you not realise how lucky you are, by the way? To have people fighting over your work? That's almost unheard of. What you've done is incredible. It seems so ungrateful to top yourself and throw it all away.

I'm not going to communicate with you again. I suppose we'll have to see what happens on your mother's birthday. I don't know if I will be there. I really hope that you don't go through with this if I'm not to arrive to help you.

Whatever happens, we'll make sure your manuscript gets published. I just hope it's under my terms, and not yours.

James.

FIFTY-SEVEN

Kim's DVD was on pause. Jordan read through the letters again. They all started so innocently by Annabelle. She had written to him because of a "social media detox," and James had written back. As communication went on, Annabelle spoke of a plan. The letters after that referenced a plan already formed.

"They must have met during this writing," Vanessa said. She had gone pale.

Jordan had to agree with her. Annabelle and James had rekindled their bond, and as part of that, Annabelle had asked for help with her suicide. The poison in the wine had been their plan.

"Do you think James turned up?"

Jordan remembered the upstairs, everything being torn apart and thrown out of the drawers. He looked back at the letter. *I have purposefully stashed these letters so they can be easily found. They are in my living room, underneath my coffee table, stored in a hatbox that I bought from our trip to Barcelona.*

Jordan hadn't seen a hatbox, and he knew now that Kim had taken it. Had Annabelle noticed?

"I don't think he did," Jordan said. "I think he must have turned up after, looking for the manuscript and the boxes of letters. I think he got the manuscript. At least, we know he got the manuscript, but he panicked when he couldn't find the hatbox."

"Because Kim had taken it."

"Yes. With all the evidence she needed to blackmail him, to humiliate him. She had evidence that he had helped with Annabelle's death. He would have been terrified."

"Do you think Kim really wanted to blackmail him?" Vanessa asked. "Do you think she was going to threaten him?"

Jordan looked back at the screen, where Kim was frozen. "Turn it back on."

Vanessa lifted the remote and pressed play.

"I'll let you read them. But they tell you everything you need to know about *that* death. Annabelle killed herself, and the plan was for James to help her. James never turned up. I know he didn't, because after Annabelle's death, he was distraught. He missed a meeting, and I heard from Sally that he was really struggling with the news. Anyway, when he came back, he was the happiest man we'd ever seen. He seemed in his element, but he always remained mute on Annabelle. If her name was mentioned, he'd tense up. He'd look away. I think he was scared of where those letters might have been."

Kim sighed. "Those letters you were getting, Jordan, they were from me. That kid took my fifty pound just like that. He didn't care what it was for. He wanted my money. I thought...hoped I could scare you away from this case, but you didn't give up."

Kim viewed the letters at the same time as Jordan. She brushed a finger over the one on top. Looking back up, she was crying again.

"That was the final correspondence between them. I don't think he helped her with the death, either. I think she added the poison and let it kill her. James received the letter with her instructions. It was something else to add to what I knew had really happened."

Jordan was crying now, the reality of what had happened to Annabelle sinking in. She had done it on purpose, a selfish act to help with the intrigue and mystery of what would be her only book.

Only her plan hadn't worked.

"When James came back, happier than ever, he said it was because the creative juices were flowing. Annabelle's death had hit us all hard in different ways. Joseph found out what happened to the manuscript and who it belonged to. The publishers stayed away from it. They weren't going to publish it because it didn't seem right," Kim explained. "A few months go by, and then James tells us one night he's got a book deal. Well, our faces were all pictures. None of us could believe it. And when I met with Sally and Margaret afterwards, they were both furious. We got talking, and I don't know how it happened, but I heard myself saying we should poison him."

Jordan's heart thudded heavily. Vanessa gasped. *Kim* had poisoned James?

"We had been drinking. And knowing what I knew, I thought it would be a well-deserved thing to happen to him. I said it as a bit of a joke, if I'm honest. Of course I wasn't going to poison him. Sally and Margaret laughed, too, but they kept asking questions. How would they do it? When would be a good time? I was suspicious, but I never thought it would happen.

"But on our next meets, outside of the writing group, they kept saying the idea was good. They didn't want to kill. I asked them that. They just wanted to make him throw up or seriously ill. I wanted none of it, so I left. I stopped meeting them."

Kim was crying now. Jordan felt her pain. She had planted the seed in the minds of two women that were scorned. Revenge had never been handed to someone so willingly.

"I tried warning James. I told him to be wary of the two women and he laughed me off. I said they were unhappy, that they were planning to seriously endanger him, and he told me I was mental." Kim looked angry now, furiously wiping her tears. "So I told him what I knew, and his face went white, and he got angry, and he was shaking all over. I told him he wouldn't get away with it, and he threatened to kill me.

"And then, it happened," Kim stated. "That night. He was dead." Kim shook her head. "It was a month or so after I stopped meeting with Sally and Margaret. I don't know what they planned or what they did after. On the night, they called me and said they wanted to meet. They didn't feel like going to the writing group. But I went. I didn't want to meet them. Now I know why they didn't want to turn up. They wanted an alibi."

Jordan paused the footage again. He looked at Vanessa. "But Sally said she was leaving Margaret's early. She knew Kim wasn't coming and wanted to go home."

"Where did she go?"

"She told me she went home after that."

"And Margaret?"

"Left at her house, but could easily have gone to the writing group for the murder."

"Is there anyone to testify to their whereabouts?"

Jordan shook his head. "Both in empty homes."

Vanessa swore. "The CCTV footage is all we have. We know someone turned up."

"But we don't know who," Jordan said.

Vanessa lifted the remote and looked at Jordan. He nodded for her to press play.

"I looked outside when he died. I could see someone watching us from the bottom of the garden. It was a female. I knew then that they had done something stupid. But I couldn't see who it was. It was too dark."

Jordan shook his head ever so slightly. Kim hadn't seen the killer. She didn't know who it was.

"And now I know that the same person is after me. I know too much. They want me out of the picture. Whoever it was killed James because of what he did to them and because he was about to become hugely successful. It was jealousy and revenge and anger. But I don't know who hated him enough to do that."

Kim swallowed. She had stopped crying now, and her face was red.

"But what I do know, is that they were angry enough to kill me. If you've found this place and this video, then they succeeded." Kim's head dropped. She seemed to be sobbing silently, the reality of what she had got herself into tearing at her. She faced upwards. "So that's what I had to tell. I'm sorry I couldn't tell you in person."

Then she stood up and walked to the camera once more.

Vanessa switched the DVD off and went to the player. She ejected it, took the DVD out of the draw, and put it in the plastic case on the top of the player. She switched off the TV and turned to Jordan.

"What are you thinking?"

It was a lot to take in. So much had been revealed, yet there was still so much left unanswered. Who had been responsible for killing James, and how had they done it? The footage of Kim exchanging something with Margaret came back to him. Had she supplied the poison? Or had it been something else, something innocent?

Jordan got to his feet, the letters between Annabelle and James in his hands.

"I think it's time we found out who killed James Fairview."

FIFTY-EIGHT

The next day, Jordan was up bright and early. He had an idea that he needed to execute, but he had to do it without alerting anyone else.

"I've got a plan, Oscar," Jordan explained. "And it's going to work."

He knew that to catch the killer, he needed evidence, and so in an ode to the detectives of history, he tracked his suspects the old-fashioned way.

Vanessa, dressed inconspicuously, had been assigned by him to follow Margaret for the day. Jordan was following Sally. He knew Vanessa would be able to track closely, Vanessa barely having any contact with Margaret. Sally would be harder.

Jordan spent the morning parked outside Sally's home. He'd had no updates from Vanessa, and he had a worried feeling of nagging paranoia that something might have gone wrong.

At 11:28 a.m., there was sign of movement from Sally's home. Jordan slouched down in his seat so he wouldn't be seen. Sally walked out of the door and towards the Range Rover parked on the drive. She got in, and after a few moments, the car started and the reverse lights came on. Jordan slumped again, worried she would see him as she came out and checked both ways to ensure it was safe to reverse.

When she was on the road, she drove straight past him, giving no indication that she had seen him or even registered the car. After five seconds, Jordan did a three-point turn and followed.

He let three cars go between him and Sally on the drive from Chepstow. She went into a Morrison's car park, and he drove in after her and a red Toyota. She parked as close to the entrance as she could, but Jordan decided to park further away, where the spaces were sparse.

He watched the Range Rover, seeing the driver's door open and close. He craned to the left as Sally locked the car and walked into the shop. Going inside would be risky. She might easily see him.

But Jordan had trained in stealth during his career. He could do this.

Jordan got out of his car, found a trolley from one of the bays, and pushed it into the store. Inside, the store was larger than he thought, airy and light. It looked like a brand-new supermarket.

There were lots of bodies around him, some carrying baskets, others empty-handed. He stopped at the plants by the entrance, took the largest one, and put it in the trolley. It was large enough to cover his face as he pushed it, yet sparse enough to see through. Sometimes you had to do what you had to do.

He decided to go aisle by aisle, until finally he spotted Sally looking at the fishmonger's deli. Jordan hovered behind her, pretending to be interested in nuts that were for sale. Sally, with a trolley that had fruit and veg in it, seemed to be in her own world. As the buzz went on around them, she remained oblivious to the people walking by. To Jordan, it felt like they were the only two in the store.

Sally left the deli without a fish, probably deciding it wasn't for her. She went down the frozen food section. He walked in that direction but decided to stay directly across from it. This time, he was looking at tins of food.

Sally took out fish fingers from the freezer and looked up. Jordan, hidden behind his plant, hoped she wouldn't be able to tell it was him. But she wasn't observing him. She was saying hello to someone else, a woman who must have been a friend.

"Yes, Craig is working away," Sally said.

"Do tell him I said hello!" the woman responded.

When she left, Sally's façade faded away. She looked upset, as if her feelings of abandonment were firing up again.

As Sally went down the next aisle, Jordan decided to take a risk. He wanted Sally to see him now. He wanted information.

He walked past her aisle and into the next, looking at the selection of crisps and dips on offer, thinking about a movie night he was never going to host. He felt his phone vibrate and glanced down to discover it was Vanessa. She had seen Margaret outside, talking to a neighbour, but then she went back inside. Jordan quickly took a photo of himself hidden behind his planted tree. Vanessa replied with a laughter emoji.

A few moments later, Sally rounded the corner, looking to the right. Jordan, hidden behind his plant, walked forwards. He angled his trolley to go directly into hers.

It clashed, and Sally exclaimed. "Watch it!"

Jordan poked his head out from behind the plant. "I'm sorry!"

Sally's eyes widened, and then they narrowed. "What are you doing here?"

Jordan stepped to the side, so he could see her fully. "I'm just doing some shopping."

"In Chepstow?" Sally scoffed.

"Yes."

"And all you've bought is a plant?"

"Yes," Jordan said. "So far."

Sally didn't believe him. "Right."

"Nice to see you here."

"Is it?"

"How have you been?"

Up close, Jordan could see the bruise on her cheek. It didn't look like it had healed that much, and Jordan realised that was probably why Sally had looked down most of the time. She was embarrassed.

"People are gossiping," Sally said. "They know it was me that was attacked."

"And you care?"

"Of course I care. They're already speculating that my husband has left me. Now this bruise. They think it's all an elaborate ruse to hide domestic abuse."

Jordan raised an eyebrow. People really did like to make their own stories up. He glanced into Sally's trolley at the three bottles of wine inside. "Big night tonight?"

"What?" Sally looked at the trolley. "Oh, those. No, not really. Well, we're meeting tonight. The writing group. We've been asked to raise a glass to Kim."

"Did you do that for James?"

"Of course not."

"Are you going?"

Sally raised her chin. "Yes, I'm going. Is that any of your business?"

"No, I'm just curious."

Sally gave him a look that many people gave him: the look of suspicion. Jordan was used to it, doing the job he did, especially when it came from suspects.

Sally tightened her grip on the trolley. "Well. I guess I better get on with it. I've got a few things to do before I go tonight."

Jordan stepped aside, pushing his trolley with him. He let Sally walk by before speaking again.

"Oh, by the way, Sally. Do you know if Margaret will be there?"

Sally narrowed her eyes again. "I...I suppose she will be, yes. Being Joseph's wife and all."

Jordan nodded. He let Sally turn and walk away, and without looking back, he pushed his trolley out of the aisle. Halfway down, he left his trolley on the shop floor and walked to the exit, feeling as daring as he had so far this year.

FIFTY-NINE

"Writing meeting tonight," Jordan said in the car to Vanessa. He had called her as soon as he left the store. "Sally told me."

"You *spoke* to her?"

"I wanted to find out the next meeting."

"Well, good job," Vanessa said. "I've had a boring day. Margaret has done nothing."

"Are the curtains open now?"

"Yes. Why?"

"No reason. Just wanted confirmation that she was ignoring me."

"Yes. How did you manage to get to see her?"

"I told her I'd call the police and get a warrant."

"Nice one," Vanessa said. "Did you buy the plant?"

Jordan laughed. "No, I don't think it matched my apartment."

"Shame. I texted Jennifer to get the same one. It matches mine."

Jordan started the car, the engine ticking over. He said goodbye to Vanessa and then left Morrison's. Sally had told him the information he needed.

As he drove, he thought about his plan to discover the killer. Whoever it was had made a grave error with one thing, and he hoped it would be their downfall. He kept his eyes on the road, music playing from his phone on the stereo, and headed back home to Cardiff.

Was there a guarantee that everyone would be in attendance? What if Sally alerted them? What if she was the culprit and suspected a setup? Jordan thought twice about bumping into her, but it was a risk he had to take. Knowing that there would be a meeting tonight was valuable.

Jordan thought of the private streets, the CCTV cameras covering every inch of the grounds. He thought about the security box and being unable to drive straight outside to Joseph's door.

Yet he had another way in. Another error made.

232

Nearing Cardiff now, Jordan took the route to the police station, driving past a blue plaque in Llandaff that was dedicated to Roald Dahl. Further along the road, he drove past the BBC Broadcasting House, and he wondered if they had wind of Annabelle's murder being linked to the writing group, to James Fairview. Soon, they would be out in full force, trying to get the best coverage.

He had been surprised by how much the media had missed what was going on. Kim's murder was still being talked about, but so far the media had failed to link up her murder to James, instead only speculating on her death. Jordan had struggled to come up with Kim's link to the murder of James, but he had known more than the press. He had suspected she knew something that the murderer did not like. It was a classic trick by someone who had killed. If they had a problem, they dealt with it the only way they knew how. It was a final way to keep things quiet.

Yet it was never quiet. Somewhere along the line they always tripped up.

Jordan arrived at the police station, found a space in a visitor car park, and walked in. Rachel wasn't working tonight; instead a handsome man was. Jordan managed a brave smile, and the man barely acknowledged him. Jordan, now with a pass, buzzed his way into the main body of the building.

He walked through the hallway as Mark walked towards him. Jordan wasn't ready for this today but managed a smile.

"Hi, Mark."

"So, you're safe then?"

Jordan looked at his own body. "Clearly."

"Vanessa didn't text me."

"We found out a lot of things. She probably got a bit overwhelmed."

"I see."

"But you didn't call a search party, so I'm guessing you weren't that bothered."

Mark looked away. "Yeah, I knew Vanessa could handle herself."

Jordan remembered what Vanessa had told him about Mark. Could it really be that the man admired him? He wasn't someone to be looked up to, not when he just did his job, and not when he was so broken personally too. If these people only knew the type of life their so-called heroes lived, they would be a lot happier.

"Mark, Vanessa told me that you're doing really well here."

Mark looked at Jordan, failing to hide his amazement. "She did?"

"Yeah. She did say you need to learn a bit more and change your attitude, but she says you have serious potential," Jordan said. "There's clearly a reason why you're here."

Mark stood up tall, the words seeming to inflate with his ego. "Of course there is. I studied and worked hard to get where I am."

"But you're no Vanessa," Jordan said, mustering an edge to his tone. "That takes serious experience."

Mark swallowed. "I understand."

Jordan smirked. "Is Vanessa about?"

Mark shook his head. "I think she's still out. I don't think she's working today, either."

"No, but she's tracking a suspect of mine, and I wondered if she might have popped in for any reason," Jordan said. "No worries."

He made to go, but Mark stopped him.

"Do you know who killed James, then?"

Jordan remained impassive. "Possibly."

Leaving Mark behind, Jordan followed the corridors to the coroner's office, where Lloyd was sat. Jordan knocked the glass door, knowing full well Lloyd could see him but knocking out of politeness.

Lloyd beckoned him in. "I hear yesterday was eventful."

Jordan shut the door and took a free seat across from Lloyd's desk. Lloyd's computer wasn't open with anything useful. Instead, he was doing a quiz online.

He saw Jordan looking and managed a wry smile. "Just needed to find out what Hogwarts house I'm in."

Jordan nodded his agreement. "I understand. I'm a Hufflepuff. Yeah, yesterday was certainly something to go on. I think I know who's responsible, but I've got a plan to find out for certain."

"Tell me."

Jordan smiled. "No, I think you can find out after I do."

"Don't want to jinx anything?"

"Something like that," Jordan said.

"And your mum?"

Jordan knew Lloyd was asking what had really happened. What was done was done. There was no going back. What mattered now was that the truth had been found out.

"Assisted suicide."

Lloyd's eyes widened. "What?"

"We found letters," Jordan said. "Well, *Kim* found letters. Annabelle and James had been communicating, and Annabelle had asked him to help her with her suicide. She said she wanted to go before she got ill, when the time felt right, and James agreed. But I don't think he went through with it." Jordan sighed. "I think my mum was alone when she died."

"But upstairs…" Lloyd said.

"That's right. I think James went by that night, hoping he wasn't too late, but he was. He found her," Jordan explained. "He'd had instructions to take the letters that proved what their arrangement was, in case it ever got found out and he got into trouble, and also to take the manuscript that she wanted published. She wanted to leave a legacy. She wanted it to be a bestseller by an author that had died tragically. Some sort of art, in her head, probably." Jordan looked at Lloyd. "The stolen manuscript, the one James got a deal for under his own name, well, that was Annabelle's. He left it a few months for the hype to die down and must have found himself a publisher who hadn't realised this was the well sought-after manuscript."

Lloyd turned away from his computer. "I just can't believe it."

"It's odd, yes," Jordan said. "What it looks like is Kim knew the manuscript wasn't his, and she planned to blackmail him with the letters she had. I think she wanted him to rethink his decisions and to be fearful that he was about to be exposed. But at the same time, there were women scorned by him, and writers jealous that all of a sudden this mentally blocked writer now had a three-book deal in the multi-figure sums."

"So there was motive all round."

"Jealousy and revenge," Jordan said. "I think Kim managed to see the murderer that night, but she couldn't tell who it was. The murderer saw her, saw that they had been seen, and wanted Kim dead too."

"And they succeeded."

"They succeeded."

"Shit."

"Kim said in the tape she left behind for us that she had suggested, whilst drunk, to Margaret and Sally that they poison James, but as a joke, something to make him ill. I don't think Kim meant it, and by the sounds of it, Sally and Margaret got carried away."

"So…they're your suspects?"

Jordan thought for a moment. "Oh, they're all suspects. But it's always been them. They were the only two unaccounted for that night."

SIXTY

As Jordan left the police station, Lloyd telling him to be careful for the night ahead, Jordan's phone rang. He answered to find it was his dad.

"Are you free today, Jordan, for your mum's home?"

Jordan checked his watch. It was late afternoon. The writing group was this evening. He would be pushed for time, but going to Annabelle's home might be worth a final visit.

"Sure, Dad. I'm just leaving the police station now. Want me to pick you up?"

"Sounds good to me," Peter said, sounding anything but happy.

Jordan picked up Peter, and then they drove in mostly silence to Annabelle's home. The weight of what Peter wanted to do today had hit him, and Jordan's apprehension for the night ahead was mounting.

Outside Annabelle's, Jordan looked at the innocent-looking home with a difference. Suddenly, the truth of what had really happened that night was in front of him. Annabelle had formed a plan, one that she was determined to go through with. It made Jordan realise that he truly had never known her, even when they had lived in the same home, shared the same rooms, lived similar lives.

Jordan wanted to tell his dad. He deserved to know.

Inside the home, which was now looking bare except for the furniture, Jordan led the way into the living room, where the death had happened.

This time, Jordan didn't glance over the chair where Annabelle had been found. This time, he stared at it, imagining Annabelle's final moments. He imagined the wine being made, the poison being added. He imagined Annabelle sitting in the chair, a newspaper on her lap, as if she was settling in for a normal night, knowing full well that she was not going to see the morning.

He imagined the conflicting feelings she must have felt. Terrified of dying alone, yet terrified of a disease taking hold of her. She must have been

236

checking the time to see if James would arrive. When had she realised he wouldn't be coming? Had she been tempted to contact him?

"Jordan?"

Jordan looked at his dad, who was staring at him. "Hm?"

"I said, where do you want to start?"

"Oh, sorry," Jordan said. "Well—" His gaze darted underneath the coffee table, where the letters would have once sat in the hatbox, only Kim had stolen them. "I don't mind."

Peter walked away from the armchair, going to the cabinet at the bottom of the room, next to the TV stand. "Should look through this. She's got some ornaments here that we bought together. Some that I bought for her."

Annabelle had kept memories, however small, and Jordan thought it might have been for comfort. She hadn't completely forgotten them. How could she? Jordan was beginning to think it had been her plan to cut her relationship with her sons. They didn't need to know about her desire for suicide. It had been her way of trying to protect them.

"Dad, sit down." Jordan regarded the sofa, across from the armchair, but Peter stared with horror at the single chair. "Not there. On the sofa."

Peter glanced at his son, obviously wondering what was going on. He sat on the sofa, the furthest seat away from the armchair.

Jordan remained on his feet.

"What?"

Jordan cleared his throat. "I found something out yesterday. About Annabelle and…and about what happened."

Peter shook his head. "I don't want to hear it if it's just speculation. She was murdered, and that's that."

"Dad, listen," Jordan snapped. "I know this is hard for you, but wouldn't you rather know the truth? It's my job to discover what happens to people, and I think I've found us a bit of solace. You're going to be angry, but you're going to see why it happened. It will offer you some…closure."

Peter was already crying. Jordan wished he could reach across and hug his father, but it was hard to do.

Jordan perched on the end of the coffee table, across from his dad. "Annabelle's death wasn't murder. It was suicide."

"Excuse me?"

"Suicide, Dad. Assisted suicide."

Peter went white. "I…"

"Don't say anything," Jordan said. "It'll be easier if you just listen. Annabelle was seeing James Fairview, the writer who was killed. They were an item. They told each other things, mainly about their mental health and other things that I can only begin to speculate about. What I get from it is that they clicked. Annabelle fell in love, and I think he did too."

"Oh, god…" Peter moaned.

"Dad, I know it's not easy to hear, but you have to," Jordan said. "She wrote to James in letters. It came after they had fallen out. She told him she had a finished manuscript that she wanted published, and publishers were fighting over it. Well, she wanted it published in her own terms. She told James she always wanted to die on her own terms. She didn't want to get ill like…"

"Her mother." Peter sighed.

"Yes," Jordan said. "How much do you already know?"

"She never talked about suicide," Peter said. "But she told me she wanted to end her life if she ever did get ill." Peter blinked. "Was she ill?"

"I don't know. Kim, the woman who was murdered, found these letters, and yesterday at her home where she had been hiding before she died, she left a DVD for me and Vanessa to see. In that tape, she told us about the letters and I've read them, and Mum mentioned going to the doctor's, but she was in perfect health."

"So why did she do it?"

"She was scared of dying," Jordan said. "She writes in the letters that she thought the time was right. She wanted a book to be published by an author who had died. It was part of her plan. A sick plan, but one that she thought she deserved."

"She was wrong." Peter was crying hard now, tears pouring down his face. He had flushed red. "She left me in the shit. She…devastated me. She left you behind and your brother."

"I know, Dad." Jordan adopted a calming tone, hoping to reassure his dad. "But she didn't consider the implications. She thought selfishly, if I'm honest."

Jordan felt a chill, and for one odd moment, he expected to see his mum stood between them, watching the exchange, realising what she had caused. He imagined her ghost listening, regretting her choices. If she could see Peter now, she would have felt dreadful, Jordan was sure of it.

"Dad, she asked James to help her. He agreed, but on the night, he didn't turn up to assist her. She died alone."

Peter let out a wail at this. Confirmation that his wife had died in fear, letting the poison take control of her life was difficult to hear. Now, Jordan reached out and gripped his dad's arm. But his dad pulled him into a hug.

"Shh," Jordan soothed. "Shh."

When Peter calmed down ever so slightly, Jordan broke away. Peter was furiously wiping his tears. "Sorry."

"Don't be sorry," Jordan said. "James did turn up. I think he hoped to stop her. But it was too late. She had left him instructions. Take the manuscript to get published, under her name, and also to take the letters. The mess upstairs was because James realised the letters had gone. He knew someone had dirt on him."

"Who?"

"Kim," Jordan said. "She had information that he didn't like. Months later, when James had let Annabelle's death settle in and the hype over her book disappear, he went to a different publisher and got a deal, knowing he would."

"Under Annabelle's name?"

"No, Dad. He took it and hoped to pass it off as his own. But Kim knew and wanted to expose him. James didn't like that. But there were writers in the group who didn't like James having a deal. Annabelle was forgotten about. But, Dad, we won't forget. We'll justify what has happened to her, I promise you. I just thought…well, I just thought you should know what really happened."

Peter looked at Jordan through his tears. He held out his hand, and Jordan took it. This intimacy between him and his father was hard. They had never had a relationship like it.

"Thank you, Jordan. Honestly." Peter gripped his hand tighter. "I'm glad I know, but I find it hard to accept."

"I have the letters, Dad, if you want to read them."

Peter hesitated for a moment but eventually nodded. "I think that would help."

Jordan let go of his dad and allowed him to calm down. He turned his back on him, deciding to look at the ornaments in the cabinet, playing a guessing game on which ones were a present from his dad. He spotted a small statue of a dog next to a red postbox. The dog had a bandana around its neck, the British flag on the front. Jordan remembered the trip to London they had as a family, a few years before Ashley moved abroad. It had been a rare occasion when they had all got along. Now, Jordan wondered if maybe Annabelle had temporarily cut Terry out of her life, pursuing an optimism that was short lived. He remembered being on a pod on the London Eye, his mother putting her arms around her two sons as they watched the sights of London beneath them.

"If James was murdered, does that mean now you know who did it?" Peter asked.

Jordan looked at his dad's reflection in the glass. He was looking at his son for answers. He turned around. "I think I know who did it. I'm going to find out tonight."

SIXTY-ONE

Jordan drove slowly towards Joseph Gordon's home that evening. Stuck at traffic lights, Jordan watched the people of Cardiff walk by, wrapped up warm. He thought about their lives, wondering what they did, picturing who they went home to. He thought of fate, trying to even begin to comprehend why this life had been handed to him.

He and his dad hadn't made much progress on Annabelle's home. His dad had been too consumed by the letters, and so Jordan had driven Peter home and left the letters with him, asking him to be careful because they were evidence.

Now, nearing eight p.m., Jordan found himself outside the gated community where Joseph lived. Instead of parking on the public street and trying his luck, he drove straight past, remaining inconspicuous.

He found himself on the side street running horizontal to Joseph's. He parallel parked in the street and waited inside the car. He felt nervous, anticipation of what the night entailed pounding down on him.

He looked around him and spotted Vanessa's black Mercedes. She had cut the engine and the lights, and because of the streetlamps being turned off, she was cast in shadow. But Jordan knew her car, and knew she was nearby.

He got out his phone and texted her. They were not going to interact.

If Vanessa was here, it meant other officers were here, too, all awaiting the signal.

Jordan got out of his car and locked it. He took out his phone and walked casually across the road, then stopped on the pavement. He looked up and checked that there was no one around, not daring to even glance at Vanessa, and then he slunk through the bushes onto the pathway that he had discovered weeks before.

He crouched down, walking as quickly as possible, until he got to the gate that gave way to Joseph's garden. He peered at Joseph's house.

The lights were on in the kitchen, and Jordan began to imagine the night of the murder. Had the killer looked up at a scene similar to this? Had their heart been beating heavily, so fast it was as if they had run a marathon? Jordan felt his own heart thudding and wondered what he was going to do.

He couldn't be seen walking up the garden, and this time, glancing at the security light, he didn't think it would conveniently be cut off for him. He imagined the killer being flooded in light, panicking that they had been seen.

But the conveniently timed cut-off of the light told Jordan there was a possibility of an accomplice.

Someone inside had assisted with the murder.

Jordan walked to the gate, still unlocked, and pushed it. He imagined just the slightest movement would trigger the security light. But there was nothing, only darkness and warm glows coming from the rows of houses.

Jordan checked his phone was on silent and then walked up the garden, keeping to the edge. He made his way slowly, pausing in the cold breeze and remaining in the shadows. He couldn't see anyone inside, but there could be someone watching him in one of the blacked-out rooms upstairs.

Finally, the ground underneath him became stone. He was now walking around the corner of the house. Still in shadows, Jordan pulled the coat up over his head. He could never be too certain that he wasn't being watched.

He thought of the scene inside. He pictured the writers gathered, talking about their work but also reminiscing on their past members, finally talking about Kim. He briefly thought of Graham, who had asked for a change in his drink, causing the drinks to go unattended. He thought of Joseph, being unable to see the killer leave.

Jordan pictured the kitchen. Big enough for space, but not big enough to be so far away one was indistinguishable.

Now he was at the front of the house, the street appearing so innocent, the neighbours unaware a murderer was nearby. He clocked the CCTV cameras, no doubt picking up his frame, and lumbered up to the door, not wanting to have security raise the alarm.

He knocked, once, twice, three times.

He waited, his hood still up, his back against the billowing wind.

The door opened. Joseph, holding a bottle of Budweiser, and wearing a pair of glasses, stood there.

At first, he seemed confused, and then as Jordan removed his hood, he smiled. "Jordan. Hi! What are you doing here?"

Jordan smiled back. "I just had a few more questions." Checking the time on his wristwatch, Jordan looked worried. "Oh, is it too late?"

Joseph checked his own watch, considering what to say. Jordan prayed for politeness. "No, not at all." But now Joseph's polite smile seemed strained, as if he suspected something. "Actually, the writers are here. We're having a little...memorial."

Jordan pretended to be surprised. "Oh!"

"But it's fine. No, they'll be glad to see you."

Joseph stepped aside, and Jordan walked in. He thought of security and hoped that if they had been suspicious of him, that now they would know he was a guest, a potential new writer in the folds of Joseph's mentorship.

Jordan could hear music coming from the kitchen, but the voices were coming from the dining room. It was the room where James had been found, and Jordan thought it possible that it was the room where Annabelle and Sally had argued.

Joseph walked in and Jordan followed. All of the writers were gathered around the table. It was as if it hadn't been the scene of James's death. There were half-finished glasses mingled with empty bottles and stacked plastic cups, telling Jordan that the party had been in swing long enough for the writers to at least get tipsy. Jordan could smell cigar smoke again, and the light only came from the tripod lamp in the corner of the room, just like it had done on the night of James's death. Jordan briefly looked at the books in the bookcase, still undisturbed and gathering dust.

Sally was in full conversation with Graham, clutching a glass of wine. Graham seemed surprised to see Jordan, managing a smile but avoiding his eyes. Margaret, her back turned, noticed the other writers looking and turned around to see her husband with the detective. The atmosphere in the room changed, as it always did whenever Jordan entered a room.

"We have another guest," Joseph said.

"Get him a drink!" Franchesca called.

Jordan shook his head. "I'm fine, but thank you."

Propped up on the bookcase was a photograph of Kim, candles lit around her. No one was paying the display any attention, but Jordan couldn't help staring at her. She stared out at the crowd before her, as if watching her killer.

"So, what brings you here, Jordan?" Andy asked. His cheeks were flushed, and he smiled.

"Honestly, forget about me," Jordan said. "Carry on with your night. I just wanted to speak to Joseph."

It was hard to tell in the dim lights in the room, but Jordan thought Joseph seemed to pale ever so slightly. "Me?"

"Yeah. Let's sit."

"Shall we go to the kitchen?"

"No, it's fine. We can sit here." Jordan pulled out a chair at the top of the table.

Joseph, glancing at the other writers who were watching, offered a reassuring smile. "Carry on. This won't take a minute. Then we can get the cake."

Cake, at a memorial. Jordan almost laughed.

The other writers reluctantly began chatting again, but Jordan could tell now it was subdued.

He let Joseph sit next to him, head of the table, looking down at his protégés.

Joseph tilted his glass towards Jordan. "Are you sure you don't want a drink?"

"No, no, I'm fine."

Joseph nodded, drinking slowly from his own glass, attention over on the writers. The music managed to drift into their room through the doorway leading directly into the lit kitchen. It wasn't loud enough to cover conversations, and Jordan listened the whole time.

"Weather has gone a bit shit, hasn't it?" Joseph conversed.

But Jordan didn't answer. He listened to Graham telling Sally about his desires to get a new job and kick-start a career, his passions not entirely in a career in writing or authorship. Franchesca leaned across the table to talk to Andy. Margaret was watching the writing group, but she was not saying a word.

"It was a tough decision, calling everyone here tonight. I knew it would be fun, but I thought it might be too soon," Joseph said, his voice low and his gaze flickering to Jordan, as if trying to read the expression of the man next to him. "But it felt like the right thing to do."

Jordan didn't entertain Joseph's musings. Sally laughed, Margaret laughed afterwards. Andy said something to her, but Jordan didn't catch the words. Franchesca glanced towards them, and Graham was pretending to listen but staring at the floor.

"You say you wanted to talk, but you're not talking." Joseph half laughed. "Everything okay?"

Jordan remained mute, looking at the grooves in the table. His focus drifted to where James had lain slumped, his hands wrapped around the glass that had killed him.

Joseph lifted his drink to his lips, uncomfortable now, the sheen of sweat on his forehead giving him away.

Joseph swallowed. "We mentioned James tonight. We miss him too. Greatly. We miss them both. They were big characters in our group. And it just feels odd to only have us here. Our numbers have dwindled, and it's noticeable. I sometimes think I see James…"

"Save it," Jordan finally said. "I know what happened. I know you killed James Fairview."

SIXTY-TWO

The man's face before him stared dumbfounded. It was as though Jordan had lifted his drink and threw it all over him. The writers around them talked, drank, laughed as if they didn't have a care in the world. Jordan stared directly at Joseph, watching him, reading the expression on the author's face.

Joseph let out a loud bark, a mixture of laughter and something else. The writers quietened, looking at him. "Excuse me?"

Joseph looked old in this lighting, as if the world was catching up with him. Sleepless nights and consumption of alcohol had given him a blotchy complexion. He had dark circles underneath hooded eyes that had at first seemed kind, but now only seemed to be plotting.

"It's fine. You can tell me now. I must admit you kept it cool, but you slipped up. I found out."

"I don't know what you're talking about," Joseph said, and he lifted a steady hand to drink from his glass. He glanced at the writers, who were listening. "I wanted you involved in this case. You think I...? Preposterous."

"I have police officers waiting outside. We can do this the right way, to save the embarrassment, or you can continue to deny it."

"What's going on?" Margaret asked.

Jordan looked at her. "I think you already know."

Her colour drained, and she scooted back in her chair to make a move. But Joseph held a hand, signalling her to stop, and she did, as if he had an unbeatable power.

"Jordan. I appreciate this has been a hard case for you. But you've got it all wrong."

"What's going on?" Sally asked.

"I haven't got it wrong."

"You have. My poor boy, you have."

"Jordan, what's happening?" Sally spoke again.

"Will you shut up?" Joseph ordered.

"Excu—"

"Shut up," Joseph said again, a tone of finality. He looked at Jordan now, angry. "I won't have you coming here, ruining our night, accusing me of something I didn't do."

"Oh, you didn't do it alone. I know that." Jordan looked at Margaret. "You helped."

Franchesca, sitting next to Margaret, moved away, towards Andy.

"Joseph," Margaret said. It was the first time that she looked afraid. Her steely exterior had been damaged.

"It's fine," Joseph dismissed. "He's got it wrong."

Jordan sat back in his chair and took out his mobile phone from his pocket.

Joseph watched him, trying to work things out.

"I was getting texts from Kim. I thought she was alive, threatening me, telling me to stay away from this case to let secrets die. I thought she was responsible at first, the way you were telling me about her hatred towards James. But then things linked my mother's death to what happened to James, and then of course, Kim died. That really changed what I was thinking."

Margaret looked at Joseph again.

"Jordan, what's going on?" Sally repeated.

"Do we need to leave?" Graham asked.

"I'd rather you all stay," Jordan said. "I won't let these two hurt you like they did the others, but I'd advise you to stop drinking what they've supplied. You might find there is something deadly in it."

The writers eyed their beverages, and Graham put his cup down on the table and wiped his mouth.

"I thought you were supposed to be a good detective," Joseph scoffed. "Did that change when Annabelle died?"

"Oh, I thought you were innocent. Trust me, Joseph, your acting skills are impeccable with the dodgy eyesight, the hero that nurtured fresh talent, your whole sprightly personality. Why would you kill one of your own? It made no sense. But you slipped up."

"I won't hear this." Joseph stood up.

"Sit back down, or I will signal the police officers surrounding this house to come in and arrest you," Jordan said.

The smell of cigar smoke came drifting towards Jordan, and he noticed for the first time that Graham had been smoking one. It burnt brightly, held aloft, forgotten about now that something else had grasped Graham's attention.

Joseph looked doubtful, and Jordan wondered if he believed him. After a few moments, Joseph sat but angled his chair away from Jordan.

"You told me, when we first met, that your wife wore Vivienne Westwood, and that's how you recognised the perfume the killer left behind," Jordan said.

"That's right," Joseph said.

"A very popular perfume, wouldn't you say, Margaret?"

"I…"

"Oh, I know you've got it," Jordan said. "I saw it in your bathroom."

Margaret's eyes narrowed. "That proves nothing."

"No, it doesn't," Jordan said. He looked at the female writers. "Do either of you own Vivienne Westwood?"

"I used to," Franchesca said, whilst Sally remained silent.

"There we go," Jordan nodded. "Proves that it's a popular choice for perfume. But you said your *wife*, Joseph, and that wouldn't have clicked if you hadn't told us that you had just found out your wife had been cheating."

Graham gasped. Sally was shaking her head.

Joseph glared at Jordan, not saying a word but breathing deeply.

"That got me thinking. I had heard about a manuscript, something that James had managed to get published. You were all confused, and I sensed resentment. The writer you all hated had made it, and the rest of you hadn't. Hell, it was going to be more popular than any of your books, Joseph. Or so you thought. Correct?"

Joseph refused to say a word. He lifted his glass, but his hand was shaking now, and he didn't drink.

"Then, of course, you were all angry with James. He had insulted you all at one point or another. James, who was fucking Sally, Annabelle, and Margaret."

"How dare you?" Margaret hissed.

"What? It's true. You all found out he had been playing around. Joseph, you despised the man."

"You're wrong."

"I'm not," Jordan replied. "Jealousy and anger, plenty of motive, and Sally, I did wonder if it was you that had murdered him. You see, Kim left a DVD. Killing her may have been silencing her, but it was too late."

"I didn't kill Kim," Sally gasped.

"No, I know you didn't." Jordan smiled at her. "She said on the tape that they were after me. She told me about your meeting. Kim, Sally, and Margaret. She mentioned the schemes to hurt James, and that one night you all joked and laughed about poisoning him. But she didn't know then that she had given you the idea, Margaret. Did she?"

Margaret turned to her husband. "Come on. Are we going to let him do this?"

"Like I say, feel free to run, but you'll come face-to-face with the police outside."

Joseph held out a hand, and Margaret took it. It was his way of telling her to stay, that he had a plan, that nothing would happen to them.

Jordan had seen it all before.

"You killed Kim because she knew who had poisoned James. Unfortunately for you, Margaret, she had seen you that night."

"No."

"Yes. You were at the bottom of the garden on that pathway that I entered through today. Well hidden, Joseph, but now I know why it was there. Tell me, how long had you been plotting this scheme?"

Joseph laughed. "You're ridiculous. You said yourself it was because I was angry that he was sleeping with my wife. I found out when you were here. Your logic is redundant."

The writers looked at Jordan for answers.

Jordan smirked. "Sure. But like *I* said, you had discovered the manuscript. Jealousy gripped you, and you were angry he had managed to pull this off. You must have suspected it wasn't his work, coming so soon after Annabelle's death, and the hype around her manuscript, which was never published. Come on, Joseph. Isn't it clear to you yet? It wasn't your idea. It was poor old Kim's, who never meant for it to happen. But it did. It got into Margaret's head, who at this point had learned of his infidelity. A woman scorned. She wanted revenge, and it worked out well with what you were feeling. You couldn't let her do it alone, so you helped her. You helped the woman you loved commit two acts of murder.

"There's CCTV footage. Don't you remember that camera outside your house? Now, security was reluctant in handing it over. It made me wonder how much you paid them, but that's all speculation, of course."

"How dare you?"

"Speculation." Jordan held up his hands, one of which still held his phone. "But we finally got it, and the security light you have on outside conveniently cut out when the killer left. With Sally and Margaret not here, you hoped the killer would get away with it. Sally, did you wonder why Margaret was still befriending you, even though she had been cheated on too? It was because you had to be an accomplice, even though you didn't know it. Margaret purposefully cut that meeting short that night. She couldn't help but go through with it."

Joseph was shaking his head, and Margaret was clenching her fists.

"Margaret came to the writing group that night, and Joseph saw the light go on. You offered the writers drinks, playing perfect host, and then you went to see her. Of course, by now you knew what the plan was. You knew she wanted to kill, and you didn't mind helping. I don't know where you got the poison from, but I suspect you had it at hand, waiting for

Margaret to come. It's unfortunate that a writer you had mentored had finally got a big break, and you couldn't handle it, Joseph. But of course, I understand. Any other writer and you may have been different. But this was James. He didn't deserve such success, did he?

"Graham, your call to Joseph came at the right time. No doubt Joseph was wondering how he could get away with this, but this was the perfect excuse. He could leave the drinks unattended, enough time for the killer to deposit the poison. Margaret had enough time to put the poison in and slink away unnoticed. As far as you were all aware, she was never here."

"Liar."

"I'm not," Jordan repeated. "You see, you didn't intend for James to have *that* reaction. You hoped he would just drop dead, a tragic heart attack, just like it was thought with my mother. I suspect you knew she had died by poison, and I suspect it quite possible that Kim had told you about the letters. Hence how you were aware that Kim knew so much about this whole thing. It was why she had to die."

"He's lying," Margaret said to the group. But no one acknowledged her.

"But Margaret had been poisoning James slowly in the weeks leading up to his death. Take the Lower New Inn as an example. Margaret was with James that night, and she found a way to deposit the poison into James's drink. I think she got a thrill from it. What she didn't know was that the poison was building up in his system. That night he was kicked out for being embarrassingly drunk, but he'd only had one drink. And on the night of his death, pushed for time and frightened, she gave too much, and so he had a reaction to it. There was no denying he had been murdered, and so suddenly you had a murder case on your hands. The intention was always to kill, but it was never to be caught for it."

"Liar," Margaret said.

Jordan shook his head. "It's all there. CCTV, motives, letters, and a DVD. Kim knew, and so she had to go. She saw it all, and you hoped to manipulate her, Joseph, by staying with her over Christmas. But it didn't work, and she fled, and you were angry. But don't forget the messages I got. It was never from her, because her phone had been taken from her when you left her home, Joseph."

"Kim was a nut job. She ran away with a conspiracy and she believed it. She was mental," Joseph said.

Jordan looked at his phone. "If that's the case, lets ring this number."

And before anyone could do anything, Jordan called Kim. After a second, the phone began to ring in the room. All eyes turned to Margaret, who reached in her pocket and took out Kim's phone.

Before Jordan knew what was happening, Margaret had launched herself over the table towards him. Glasses and drinks flew, and claws came at him, like a tiger hunting a gazelle. Jordan, in his chair, swayed back, just as Margaret launched on him. They fell to the floor together, a foot connecting with the table and making an almighty crash.

With Margaret's hands around his neck, Jordan realised she was going to kill him too.

SIXTY-THREE

There were shouts all around him, the phone still buzzing, and vodka dripping onto his face from the table. But Margaret was heavy, and she had his arms pinned. Her nails dug into his neck, and Jordan thrashed but couldn't push her off him. He was stuck between the bookcase and the upturned table, and he was losing air.

Margaret screamed out, obscenities leaving her mouth. There was another bang, more shouts, and then Margaret was being wrestled off him. Jordan lay on the floor. He'd had a blow to the chest and was winded. His view was of shoes around him, but he couldn't get up. As he turned over, he discovered Joseph advancing on him.

Joseph raised a fist, ready to deliver a blow to Jordan, but then Joseph convulsed. A Taser had been fired at his back, and Joseph fell to his knees, his eyes rolling, and his mouth open as he shouted.

Jordan got to his knees and looked at the room. The writers had fled, except for Sally, who was shouting at Margaret as she was being arrested.

"You evil cow! You witch! I should never have let you manipulate me! I'm so stupid! You cow!"

Sally was trying to hit Margaret, but Mark was holding her back, saying something to her, trying to calm the situation.

Joseph lay on his front, his arms pinned behind him as an officer Jordan didn't recognise handcuffed the author.

Vanessa stood in the middle of the room, scanning until she found Jordan. She gasped, and he waved a hand to tell her he was okay, but he knew his neck was red and he couldn't breathe properly from the kick to his chest.

Vanessa was next to him now, her hand on his shoulders. "You did it, Jordan. We got them."

The scene around them died down. Joseph, weak, was being dragged away. Margaret was screaming outside, and Vanessa opened the curtains, looking at the scene outside. Flashing lights illuminating the walls inside.

Through the window, a police van was visible. Joseph's neighbours had come to see what the commotion was.

"Jordan," Sally said, walking over to him, avoiding the upturned table and the spilled drinks. The other writers stood in the doorway of the kitchen. Franchesca ran to the front door, her phone in her hand, no doubt filming the whole thing. Jordan saluted her. If she needed money, now was the time.

"How long have you known?" Sally asked.

"Not long. But that doesn't matter now." Jordan rubbed his neck and looked at Vanessa. "Is it bad?"

"Just grazes," Vanessa said. "She had a tight hold on you by the looks of it."

"It's so lucky you were outside," Graham said, standing behind Sally.

"Can you believe it?" Sally asked him.

"I can't."

Jordan was ready to get up, but he swayed as arms wrapped around him. He smelled Sally's perfume, and for one bizarre moment, he thought of Margaret, of Vivienne Westwood, and of the thread that had let this spiral out of control. She was crying, sobbing into his shoulder.

Hands patted Jordan's other shoulder. He glanced up to see the writers gathered around him, looks of admiration and shock on their faces.

"Thank you for discovering the truth," Sally said.

"It's my job."

"Will we get checked for poison?" Andy contemplated his half finished drink.

"You will, but I don't think you were on the hit list."

Sally broke away, wiping her eyes. Graham smiled at him, and Jordan managed a smile back. Andy looked at the house.

"Shame that this will go elsewhere now," he said.

"I guess our writing meets are over," Graham replied.

Jordan got to his feet, his head feeling light. He remembered when he'd first come in here, surrounded by the same writers, only there had been one more, and she hadn't been a photograph.

He turned to where the photo had been, but it was no longer there. In the fight, it had fallen onto the floor. Jordan walked over and picked it up. Kim had a smile on her face in the photo, her eyes hiding a past that Jordan could only begin to understand.

The tragic demise of Kim had been horrible. But she had saved him and provided the information he needed. Pulling the thread that Jordan had discovered, Kim had exposed enough of the truth for the two people being escorted away outside to go to prison, to be sentenced for what they had done.

"Do you all have your own transportation home?" Vanessa asked the writers.

"We've been drinking," Andy said.

"Although I feel like I've sobered up now," Franchesca said, stood in the door, her phone in her hand. "Am I allowed to send this to the press?"

"You tweeted it before we could stop you," Vanessa replied.

Jordan grinned at her. "Bad girl."

"That's me."

Just then, Mark came back into the room. He looked flushed, and Jordan was reminded of the first time they met, in this very room, when Mark had questioned what Jordan was doing here.

"Mark?"

Mark blinked. "Yes?"

"Congrats on arresting Margaret," Jordan said.

Mark couldn't hide his elation. "Thank you."

Outside on the street, officers told neighbours that everything was fine and to go back inside. Mark helped arrange transport for the other writers, who had been planning to stay at Joseph's that night.

"What's going to happen now?" Sally asked Vanessa, huddled against the wind.

"They'll be going to prison. They'll have a chance to plead not guilty, but we're going to enforce on them that there's no point."

"I hope they don't get away with it."

"They won't."

Sally looked at Jordan. "I remember Kim saying about the poison, but I promise you we never planned to do it. I had no idea Margaret had got carried away with it. We were just three girls with a hatred for a man, but Kim certainly didn't want to kill and neither did I."

"If I didn't know that, you'd be in the back of the van, too," Jordan replied.

Sally laughed. She looked up at Joseph's house and then down at the photograph of Kim she had taken from inside. "What has my life become, hm? This is so tragic."

Jordan offered her a smile and silently wished for her life to get better.

An officer approached then. He appeared to be nearing his fifties, his hair thinning on top of his head. "Mr Jenner. We've discovered a scene of a crime downstairs in the basement. There's blood."

"What crime?"

The officer looked wary, as if the crime had affected him more than he could admit. "We think it's where Kim was kept when she disappeared."

Jordan remembered that Kim had last been seen at Joseph's door, an unconfirmed sighting being taken with a pinch of salt and not being followed. That decision had cost Kim her life.

Jordan looked at the home, the dark sky above casting it in sinister shadows. It was a house that had seen bloodshed and murder, that had kept a lot of secrets.

Jordan thought of Kim and whispered a prayer. For a man that wasn't religious, he felt like it was needed now.

SIXTY-FOUR

By the next day, the press had found what had happened. They were still yet to link up Annabelle's death, but it was only a matter of time. Joseph and Margaret had been put into remand immediately, and they had a trial pending. Vanessa had interviewed them both, and they had said they would plead guilty.

Jordan, now at home, was locked in. The press had discovered he was responsible in finding out the truth, and they wanted quotes. With his curtains drawn, Jordan speculated on what the street was like outside. He pictured news crews and photographers stood in the bitter winter cold, all hoping for a quote for tonight's broadcast.

He wouldn't give it to them. He wouldn't even tell Oscar.

Jordan planned to stay inside, to let the hype die down and speculation grow until someone else from the police force spoke out, denying rumours and putting things to rest.

He found himself refreshing the social media of South Wales Police, hoping they would say something, but still no announcement came. With a high-profile client being arrested for murder, it was attracting attention from all over. This wasn't just Wales's problem. This was national.

Jordan's phone had been ringing all day. He had ignored every call. His brother, Ashley, had rung three times, and Jordan wondered if the news had reached Australia.

When his phone buzzed again, Jordan looked at it out of habit. And instead of an unknown number, he saw it was his dad.

He picked up the phone. "Hi, Dad."

"What the hell happened? I can't believe it. One of the writers there said you were attacked."

Jordan remembered Franchesca's footage, and he wondered if she was cashing in on the story now. He didn't blame her for doing so. "Yes, I was attacked."

Peter exhaled. "Jordan. My god. Are you crazy?"

"I had to make sure the right people went down."

"Yes. Two people? Did you know it was two?"

"It clicked," Jordan simply said.

"Are the press outside?"

Jordan, wearing lounge shorts and a T-shirt, went to his window. He tweaked the curtain to look down on the street. Straight away, flashes were directed at him and people shouted.

"Oh, yeah. They're out there." He got a glimpse of television cameras and reporters and knew he couldn't go out there. They would bombard him.

"Shame."

"Why?"

"I wanted to go to Annabelle's grave."

Jordan sighed. It would be nice to see where his mother rested. He had never been, but he knew his dad had been plenty of times.

"I see."

"Can I pick you up? We can go together."

Jordan considered it. Being cooped up inside, away from the world, was starting to grate on him. He needed air and to feel like he wasn't trapped. "Okay. But come the back way. I can find a way out, then."

Oscar, his fluffy fur beginning to get long, meowed. Jordan fussed over him by finding a grooming brush and running it through his fur. Oscar purred, all the while trying to bite the brush. He thought about Oscar's poisoning, wondering who had been responsible for such a thing. He knew now that it would have been either Joseph or Margaret, but some things would never get answered.

Jordan got changed, and half an hour later, his dad texted to say he was outside. Jordan left, dressed as casually as possible, and pulled the hood up over his head as he passed the entrance to the apartments. He heard the shouting get louder as the reporters looking through the glass recognised him, and when he left through the back exit, he prayed there would be no press.

Arthur approached him, wearing a trench coat that reminded Jordan of Sherlock Holmes. He smiled as if there had been no problems between the pair.

"Jordan. You cracked it! Fantastic! Tell me, what did Kim's murder scene look like? I heard she had been tortured."

Jordan had been asked to visit Kim's scene of death, but he had refused, out of respect to the woman. Yet he had heard that Kim had been there a few days and he shuddered to think what could have happened.

He saw his dad and hurried to the car, walking past Arthur without a word. He didn't want to see Arthur. His dad drove them away, and Jordan breathed a sigh of relief.

Annabelle was buried in St Woolos cemetery. It was the main graveyard of Newport, a mile away from the church. They entered through a stone archway, and Peter led the way to his mother's final resting place.

Jordan hated that he had never been here, and despite meaning to visit after her death, he had always stopped himself from going. It had been too hard to do. He had always considered himself to be a hypocrite. After a year of not talking to the woman, he felt as though going to her grave was wrong, like he was just being nosy or going for the sake of it.

Only now, it felt right. He felt as though he had helped her and that they had made amends, even though he knew that was impossible, that it was too late for a truce.

They walked off the pathway, past gravestones that were missing names and other stones that were bare. Jordan pitied the bones underneath the ground, wondering where their family links had gone.

Peter pointed out the grave for Jordan. It was black and looked brand new. Jordan remembered that it was only a few months old, and he felt a pang in his chest. There were fresh flowers laid down, and when Jordan looked at Peter, he shook his head.

"Maybe someone came to remember her after the press wrote about her murder."

It was possible. Jordan got to one knee and read her description: *A woman who was strong willed and always got what she wanted.* He smirked, remembering the times she had always been the boss of the house.

"I did it, Mum," Jordan whispered.

"She would have been proud of you," Peter said. "I know she would have."

Jordan shrugged. "I know she didn't like the career choice."

"But she knew it was what you wanted," Peter replied. "You're doing good for the world, and she would love that."

"Especially now."

Jordan got up, and he saw that Peter was smiling. "Especially now."

They stood side by side, looking at Annabelle's grave. Both men were lost in their own memories of the woman they had known. Jordan's memories soon turned to Kim, to the answers she had. He decided he would make sure she got a gravestone, her family still being untraceable. He also thought of a funeral. He wanted to remember the woman even if no one else would.

"What is going to happen with her manuscript?" Peter asked.

"You read the letters?"

"Yes."

Jordan shrugged. "I don't know. We've got a copy. The publishers wanted it published, and so did she."

"What do you think the chances are of getting it published ourselves?"

Jordan liked the idea. "I'm sure we can arrange that."

"I think we should."

Jordan made a note in his phone to contact the publisher who had agreed to publish the novel under James's name. He hoped they would still want the novel, once the circumstances were explained to them.

A light rain had fallen now. There was a breeze, and Jordan crossed his arms, shivering. He hoped his dad didn't want to stay here too much longer. He couldn't shake the feeling that soon the press would find him. He was not in the mood for PR right now.

"Oh."

Jordan looked at his dad, to see that he had turned around and was now looking behind him. Jordan turned too. He had to blink twice to make sure he was seeing the right thing.

Ashley Jenner, Jordan's brother, stood before them. He was holding flowers, and he sheepishly smiled at them. "Hi, bro."

Peter looked at Jordan. "Did you...?"

"No."

Ashley stepped forwards, the cellophane around the flowers crinkling. "I came to pay my respects. Hey, Dad."

Peter stepped aside, ashen faced as if Ashley was a ghost.

"Why are you here?"

"For Mum."

Jordan shook his head. The text messages, the missed calls. Ashley had been trying to get hold of Jordan more often than was necessary. To come to Wales, from Australia, months after his mother had died didn't add up.

"What are you *really* doing here?"

Ashley bent down and placed the flowers at his mother's grave. He touched the stone, tracing his fingers over her name. "I'm in trouble. I need your help."

ABOUT THE AUTHOR

J.S. Strange is a writer from south Wales, United Kingdom. He lives near Cardiff, where Murder on the Rocks is set. He lives with his boyfriend, James, and two black cats, Miley and Dolly. Whilst not writing, Jack works for a television channel as an editor.

Other work by J.S. Strange

Winter Smith: London's Burning – Available on Amazon.
Winter Smith: The Secrets of France – Available on Amazon

Acknowledgements

What a journey it has been to write this murder mystery novel. After writing two zombie novels in 2016 and 2017, I hit a wall and wanted to try something different. Being an avid reader of crimes and thrillers, I set out to write a gritty crime novel and ended up with something different, but something I was proud of.

It's incredibly important to me to write a novel featuring a gay male detective. Jordan Jenner started off as a female before re-plotting and re-thinking got me to him. I wanted to create a character that was investigating murder, working with the police to do so, and just so happened to be gay.

Murder on the Rocks was shortlisted for Penguin Random House's Write Now Live scheme in 2018. With this story, I got to travel to Liverpool and attend a workshop run by Penguin. From applications of 1,700, Jordan Jenner was narrowed down to the top 150. At Liverpool, an editor from Penguin gave me advice and went through the manuscript. It was incredibly invaluable. Penguin decided not to take me further, but I was ecstatic to be in the top 150.

Since then, I've been on a crazy ride of trying to get publishers. In total, seven publishers requested the full manuscript. Rejection after rejection came through, with one being incredibly nasty, until finally Panther took a punt. To the small team at Panther Publishing, a new independent publishing house set up in Wales where I'm from, I thank you. Finally, Jordan found a home. I'm excited to continue our Panther journey together.

I'd like to thank my partner, James. Even though you interrupt me without meaning to do so by popping in to the writing room with the cats, you've supported where this book has been going and what it could become.

Mum, Dad, Becky, Emma—always there to keep me going even when I feel like giving up, especially after that horrible rejection came through.

Christine Fletcher and Jason Bradley, my editors, you have both been fantastic. I really appreciate your help, and every bit of support you have given me. Kelly Kenrick, you have been so helpful, and C.L. Raven, you are always my favourite.

Rhianedd Sion, without you we wouldn't have a book cover. Your photographs were amazing, especially the ones of me that I used for Instagram. I hope you love the cover just as much as I do!

And to you, the reader, I really hope you've enjoyed the first Jordan Jenner novel, and enjoyed it as much as I enjoyed writing it.

Winter Smith: London's Burning – J.S. Strange

Winter Smith is a 17-year-old socialite with a troublesome past. She's forced to live a life under scrutiny from the press, and judgement from her successful parents. With friends that are enemies, and more socialising parties on the horizon, Winter feels as though she will never be able to change her life. But all that changes when London falls victim to the apocalypse. Escaping a party that her parents have thrown, Winter Smith teams up with a group of survivors. Government are promising safety in France - but survivors must get to the Thames. As Winter tries to escape, she learns that not everybody is to be trusted, and not everything is as it seems. Betrayal, gore, drama and fear mix together to create a story of survival for London's hottest starlet. This is no Hollywood story. This is an emotional rollercoaster of a ride. London's Burning is the first in a zombie apocalypse series, written by J.S. Strange.

Available on Amazon.

Winter Smith: The Secrets of France – J.S. Strange

A new world order, a city under control, and a new breed of zombie known as The Martyrs living alongside humans. France isn't safe. It never has been. After fleeing from London, seventeen-year-old Winter Smith and her surviving friends learn that to survive in Paris means trusting those they don't know. An anti-government, known as The Union, are forming to take on V, a woman who has gained control of the world and has created the dead to establish a new world order. But surviving in Paris is hard, as those who don't conform to V's new rules are quickly wiped out. This not-so-typical zombie novel is the second instalment of the Winter Smith series. An action packed young adult horror that will keep you guessing, and wondering what could possibly happen next.

Printed in Great Britain
by Amazon